The Darling Girls

EMMA BURSTALL

HEAD OF ZEUS

First published in the UK in eBook in 2013.
This paperback edition published in 2014 by Head of Zeus Ltd.

9 7 5 3 1 2 4 6 8

A CIP catalogue record for this book is available from
the British Library.

eBook ISBN 9781781857854
Paperback ISBN 9781781857861

For my Godchildren,
Hugo Ellis, Helen Peacock and Miranda Smith

PROLOGUE

Vienna. December 1938

'Hurry up,' hisses the woman.

'But I don't want to go.'

The woman grabs her small son by the hand and pulls him out of the front door and down the steps to the waiting car. His boots crunch on the snow and once or twice he nearly slips.

It's very early, much earlier than his normal wake-up time. A cold grey light has only just started to creep over the rooftops and through the spaces between buildings.

He's clutching the small leather suitcase which contains the things his mother says he will need: pyjamas, change of clothes, warm sweaters. He's allowed to take his teddy but not his violin. 'We can buy a new one in England,' she tells him.

The boy doesn't know anything much about England except that there's a king with a crown, a tall clock called Big Ben and it rains every day.

His mother bundles him and his bag into the taxi first, then hops in beside. She's wearing her big fur wrap which takes up half the back seat and smells of mothballs.

'Wait for me!'

A little girl comes skidding down the steps after them, fumbling with the buttons of her red coat. She's followed by a young woman with a white shawl thrown over her nightclothes.

'Come back,' the young woman says. 'You'll catch your death of cold.'

The boy's mother starts to close the taxi door.

'Wait,' says the boy, not understanding. He can see his breath coming like wisps of smoke from the cigarettes that his father used to smoke. 'We can't go without Anna.'

He leans over, trying to keep the door open.

The little girl has begun coughing, an awful ratcheting sound. She's doubled over now coughing her insides out, or that's what it seems like. The young woman in the nightclothes puts her hands on Anna's shoulders.

'We have to go,' says the boy's mother, slamming the door shut. He's still scrambling to get out and his arms jar painfully.

'What about Anna?' he cries as the car pulls away.

The truth hits him: she isn't coming; he's going to that country called England without her. His heart's beating very fast and if he could open the window and jump out, he would. He wishes Father were here; he wouldn't allow this to happen.

The small boy kneels up and stares out of the back window until the car rounds the corner. He can't see very well because he's crying so much. The last thing he remembers is watching the little girl tearing down the street after them, her arms outstretched, her mouth wide, red coat flapping.

'I'll come back for you,' he's shouting, but he doesn't know if she can understand.

'Sit down' says his mother, yanking at the sleeve of his coat. 'Stop talking about Anna.' He does as he's told.

An empty blackness settles in the centre of his chest and after that, he says nothing at all.

FIRST MOVEMENT

CHAPTER ONE

London. Wednesday December 9th, 2009

It didn't seem possible that it was him lying in the pale wooden coffin in front of her. How could it be? It was only, what, two weeks ago that they'd been in bed, their hot sticky bodies entwined, their galloping hearts drowning out Liszt's second Hungarian Rhapsody on the CD player.

He'd been so *alive*. His poor broken heart. She brushed the thought away, preferring to dwell for a moment longer on the happiness.

Afterwards he'd kissed her nose, her forehead, and told her she was beautiful. Cat squeezed her eyes together, trying not to remember that she'd never again go to his beautiful flat where he'd make love to her, playing her as he would one of his beloved instruments.

Was it really all over? Forever was too painful to contemplate. She took a crumpled paper tissue from her jacket pocket and blew her nose. She must focus on the here and now and try to get through the ceremony without drawing attention to herself.

She was standing at the back of the chapel; she'd deliberately arrived late so she could slip in without anyone noticing. It hadn't been easy; there were two police officers at the main entrance to the crematorium making sure no one tried to gate-crash.

She sniffed. Hardly likely. He was a conductor not a bleeding pop star. Cat had removed her nose ring, brushed her hair and bought a posh black suit and court shoes from Primark to look the part. She'd told the police she was family and they'd let her in.

She listened. It wasn't right to use piped music. Leo would expect a string quartet at least, preferably an entire orchestra. But someone had insisted on a quiet cremation and Cat was hardly in a position to argue, was she?

She looked down at the order of service – Leo's own recording of Mozart's Requiem. Well, he'd approve of that. She remembered watching that film with him one evening about the composer – 'Amadeus,' curled up on his comfy cream sofa. He wanted to educate her about music, he said.

She'd yawned a couple of times – it was a long movie – and he'd got really irritated. 'Pay attention. You might learn something.' He'd made her feel like a naughty kid but she hadn't minded. Just to be with him for a few hours, to have him all to herself, was enough.

The music faded and the priest came forward to speak. There was only one bunch of simple white lilies on the coffin but Cat could smell them from here. She wanted to cry so badly and hated herself for it; Cat Mason didn't do crying.

She hardly heard Father Stephen's welcome address; she was too busy trying to calm down. Then suddenly she was desperate to see Victoria. Standing on tiptoe, she craned her neck hoping to spot the woman with her two children in the front row, but she was disappointed. Cat was only short and there were too many people.

She wanted to know if Maddy were there, too, and her kid, Phoebe. It was obvious Victoria would be in place of honour at the front but Cat wasn't sure if Maddy would be invited.

There was a glamorous blonde two rows in front but she was very tall and Cat knew Maddy wasn't. She longed to see both her rivals' faces – longed and dreaded at the same time.

Father Stephen announced that Leo's and Victoria's children, Ralph and Salome, were going to speak and Cat felt her stomach lurch. She watched, mesmerised, as a tall thin boy and much smaller girl walked over to the lectern. She'd never seen them in the flesh but the boy, she knew, was seventeen and the girl, just eight. It was her birthday a month ago; Leo had mentioned it.

You could tell that Ralph, dressed in a dark suit and thin black tie, was trying hard to appear confident, but the hunched shoulders and hesitant walk gave away the truth. Salome, on the other hand, in a green and black checked dress and patent shoes, looked totally together. Her fair hair was tied in two fat neat plaits and she stood up straight and smoothed her skirt as she came to a halt beside her brother.

Ralph began to read the first verses of Psalm 21, The Lord is My Shepherd. He opened his mouth and out came a hoarse croak. Cat held her breath, wondering if he'd break down. She sensed the congregation squirm and felt a stab of sympathy; he'd lost his dad, after all. But to her relief he cleared his throat and his voice started to come through loud and clear.

It was surprisingly deep for a boy and sort of rich, like Christmas pudding. Tracy might have said posh, but Cat knew he hadn't really had a posh upbringing. He'd been to state schools, just like her.

She took the opportunity while he was reading to examine his face. She'd once begged Leo to show her pictures of his son and he'd produced one from his wallet, but it wasn't the same as seeing the boy for real. She wanted to study the features:

the nose, eyes, mouth, jaw-line, expressions, to check for her lover's imprint.

Leo was so lined, with deep crevasses on his brow, round the eyes and running down either side of his mouth, that it had been hard to imagine what he'd been like when he was young. But she could tell Ralph had his father's genes. He had the same strong features: deep set eyes, lean smart face. His nose was smaller, though, and he was fairer than Leo, who was very dark, almost black, apart from the grey at his temples.

Ralph finished reading the first part of the Psalm and stepped aside to make way for Salome. Cat found she was less interested in the little girl and moved a couple of paces to her left so that she was standing in the aisle.

Now she could spot the back of what she took to be Victoria, with two empty seats beside her. She had big broad shoulders and wild wavy hair piled high and held up with clips.

Cat was surprised; there was quite a bit of silver. She'd tried to imagine Victoria so often and had built up a mental picture of this beautiful sophisticated older woman. But from the back she looked rather old and frumpy.

Salome finished reading and she and Ralph returned to their seats. They sang a hymn, Be Thou my vision, O Lord of my heart, but Cat just mouthed the words; she couldn't trust herself not to break down.

The rest of the service passed in a blur. The Priest gave a long eulogy all about Leo's achievements, his awards, his crucial contribution to music, his assured place in history, blah blah blah.

He spoke of Victoria, 'Leo's long-term partner, the mother of his children and his most loyal and loving friend.' Cat's ears pricked. That was an interesting way to describe her. But there was no mention of the mistress, Maddy, or the child. And no reference to Cat because, of course, they didn't even know she existed.

She wanted to scream: 'It was me he loved. We were soul-mates.' That would give all those stuck-up, star-fucker so-called friends something to gossip about. But she wouldn't spoil the dignity of the occasion; she loved Leo too much for that.

Tears started to trickle down her cheeks as the exit music started – Bach's Cantata No 156, 'Ich steh mit einem Fuss im Grabe ('I stand with one Foot in the Grave'). It was so beautiful and sad that she could have stayed listening to it forever. But she had to leave.

She slipped out of the building while everyone was still seated and stood for a moment on the stone steps, looking out across the flat green grass and grey headstones towards the horizon.

It was cold and windy, the kind of chill wind that gets right into your bones. The sun was shining weakly but seemed to give out no heat and Cat's thin suit wasn't nearly warm enough.

She shivered. So this was it, then. This was how it all wound up: a few words, a quick prayer or two, a bit of music and off to the flames. She certainly didn't believe in an afterlife or anything like that. The end was the end.

Leo was seventy-eight but she'd never expected him to die; he was too brilliant, too big – not in height, of course, but his personality, his presence, was massive. You'd walk into a room and spot him immediately; he radiated power and energy. Men like that didn't die, surely?

What was she going to do without him? She felt so alone. A sob that had been stuck in her throat all through the service burst out and she tried to turn it into a cough, but it made her choke. She couldn't go home like this.

She looked round and spotted a tree with a big thick trunk to her right, running as fast as she could in her heels – she never normally wore heels – and hiding behind it. She could hear people coming out of the chapel, the shrill sound of children's voices, doors being banged, cars starting up.

A small boy in a grey duffel coat sprinted past her crying, 'Catch me!' She tried not to make a noise but he must have heard because he turned, took one look at her scowling face, shouted 'Mummy!' and raced back in the direction he'd come from.

Cat slid to the ground and rested her back against the hard knobbly bark, burying her head in her arms. Her tears soaked right through to the skin and she didn't care that the grass was cold and damp.

She was interrupted by a voice close by, which made her jump.

'Are you all right?' Someone touched her lightly on the shoulder.

Cat looked up and saw, through her tears, a middle-aged woman. She had big kind grey eyes that were rimmed with red, and hair that was thick and wiry with a few silvery streaks of grey. It was tied up but messy wiggly strands fell around her face. She was wearing silver dangly earrings and a black jacket.

Cat gave a start of recognition: Victoria. This was Leo's 'long-term partner', the woman he'd been with for twenty years. She stood up quickly and nodded, her eyes fixed firmly on the ground, aware of being closely observed.

'Fine,' she mumbled, wiping away the tears with her sleeve. This was weird, freaky. She was way out of her comfort zone. She started to push past Victoria, who stopped her.

'You're Cat, aren't you?'

Cat's heart missed a beat.

'It's all right,' Victoria said, sounding weary. 'I know all about you. Leo told me. He told me everything.'

Cat's head started to thump and she could feel the blood pounding in her temples. She was thinking fast.

'Did he?' She gave a tight little smile, not wanting to give anything away.

'I'm sorry you're upset.' Victoria's voice was so gentle that she sounded like a mother comforting her child.

Cat felt her defences weaken. She didn't want to look at the other woman but couldn't stop herself; it was obvious that Victoria was taking the mickey but Cat needed to check. Her eyes, though, were big pools of sugary compassion. Cat couldn't handle this; it was worse than being mocked or screamed at.

'I'm going,' she said, intending to push past Victoria who still stood in the way. Cat realised for the first time how tall the other woman was. She must be getting on for six feet – and broad with it.

Cat stared at her defiantly, experiencing a surge of new-found energy. If Victoria wanted a slanging match or fisticuffs, so be it. Cat might be shorter but she was tough; she'd give as good as she got.

'Excuse me,' she said, straightening her shoulders.

Victoria didn't seem to hear or even sense Cat's hostility.

'He was a great man,' the older woman said quietly, seeming to stare at something in the distance. 'We're going to miss him so much.'

She paused while Cat, fists clenched, wondered what was coming next.

'Would you like to come to the reception? I know he was fond of you. It's right that you should—'

Cat felt her face go hot. 'Fond? He wasn't fond of me, he loved me.'

Victoria shook her head and there were tears in her eyes. 'Did he tell you that? Poor girl. That wasn't fair, he shouldn't have said that.'

There was a gust of cold wind that whipped up Cat's thin sleeves and down the back of her neck and she hugged her arms around her. She was trying to think of the best swear words to pick from her sizeable repertoire when a quite different voice made her jump again. Her nerves were smashed.

'It was a beautiful ceremony.'

She spun round and saw a small slender woman with shoulder-length, very blonde hair and big gold earrings. She was wearing a lot of eyeshadow and her face was a slightly unnatural shade of beige. Cat thought she was beautiful, though, in a slightly scary way. Like those women behind makeup counters at department stores.

She sensed Victoria stiffen.

'What are you doing here?' There was real venom in her voice.

Jesus, Cat thought. If she wasn't so shocked she'd probably laugh.

'I just wanted to say how sorry I am because we've both lost someone very special to us,' said Maddy, Leo's other woman.

Victoria stood up straight – she really was very tall – and raised her chin. 'Don't patronise me.' She seemed to have forgotten all about Cat now. 'You meant nothing to him, don't you realise? He only carried on seeing you because he felt guilty and was determined to fulfil his obligations as a father.'

Cat watched Maddy's face. There was a flicker of something behind her eyes – pain? Anger?

'I shouldn't have interrupted,' she said quietly. 'I just wanted to say sorry, that's all, because I know how you and the children must be suffering.'

Victoria's shoulders drooped. 'It's different with her.' She nodded in Cat's direction. 'She's young and didn't know any better. But you knew exactly what you were getting into. You knew he was a married man with children.'

Maddy shook her head. 'Not married.'

Victoria's eyes narrowed dangerously. 'We didn't need a piece of paper to prove our feelings.'

Maddy suddenly turned to Cat, who felt herself shrink in the spotlight. 'What do you mean, it was different with *her*?'

Victoria paused before throwing back her head and laughing out loud. She had big rectangular teeth, very white.

'You mean you didn't know about this one?' The wiggly strands of hair that had escaped from their clips shook and her silver earrings tinkled. 'Oh dear me, you weren't the only mistress, you know.'

Maddy's eyes widened and she took a step back as if she'd been struck. It crossed Cat's mind that it would be a very good idea to make a run for it now, but somehow she couldn't move. Her limbs felt weighted to the ground.

She glanced towards the exit and noticed that almost all the cars had left now and the crematorium was practically empty. She couldn't feel her fingers or toes, they were so cold.

Maddy – the blonde woman – spoke again, this time very quietly.

'He called me his darling girl.'

Cat stopped looking into the distance and stared. Maddy's face had turned a strange blotchy red. Gone was the immaculate businesswoman and suddenly she looked pitiful, in her expensive plum-coloured velvet jacket and crisp white shirt, like a little girl in her mum's clothes.

Goose bumps were running up and down Cat's arms and she could scarcely believe what she'd just heard.

'But that's what he called me.' Her voice sounded far away and seemed to belong to someone else.

She looked desperately at Victoria, the older woman, hoping for some sort of reassurance but none came.

Victoria's big soft grey eyes swept from one woman to the other. 'And me.'

The three women stood for a moment in silence. Cat felt as if a great weight were descending on her, crushing her lungs and ribs together so that she could scarcely breathe.

My darling girl? But this had been Leo's special name for her. He'd sent her a postcard only recently with those very words written on the back in his strong artistic hand. She'd treasured that card and kept it under her pillow.

She was vaguely aware of Maddy turning and stumbling back across the grass and of Victoria following. Cat didn't want to go after them but she didn't seem to have a choice. She felt numb and needed someone to tell her what to do.

There was a little group, still, outside the entrance. Cat registered Victoria's kids, Ralph and Salome, and started to walk as fast as she could towards the exit, cursing her bloody shoes with their stupid heels.

'Wait!'

She turned and saw Victoria speed-walking towards her, taking big strides with her long legs. At one point she nearly tripped. There was something slightly clumsy about her, Cat decided, as if she wasn't quite in control of her limbs. She hesitated; should she run? She was frozen to the spot.

'Will you be all right?' Victoria's grey eyes were full of sympathy. The woman must be crazy.

Cat swallowed, keeping her eyes firmly on the ground. 'Yes... I don't know.'

The next thing she knew, she was running, running towards the exit and up the long winding street leading from the crematorium. She didn't stop or look back until she reached the bus stop and was able to slip into a seat right at the back of the vehicle beside the window. No one looked at her and no one knew who she was. Which was exactly what she wanted.

CHAPTER TWO

It took ages to get home. Leafy Mortlake was miles from Bethnal Green in every sense. As far as Cat was concerned, it could be on a different planet.

She didn't really mind about the time, though, as it gave her thinking space. She felt as if she'd been tossing this way and that, her insides churning like dirty water in a washing machine. She needed to sort things out in her head.

Leo was gone, burned to ashes already. And Victoria knew about her. This put things in a completely different perspective. And Cat had met Maddy, who obviously didn't have a clue about her.

And he called them all, 'my darling girl.'

What did it mean?

Cat bit her lip. Victoria and Maddy were living in cloud cuckoo land if they thought they mattered to him as much as she did. It was just a soppy term of endearment, like 'honey' or 'babe.'

But she'd imagined all along that it was something personal, reserved for her alone. She frowned, huddling down in her seat and chewing the back of her hand, a habit that she'd never quite grown out of.

She got off the bus and caught the tube at Hammersmith, scarcely noticing anyone or anything around her. Once or twice she might have bumped into someone but she didn't pause or apologise. If they cursed her, she didn't hear.

The District Line would take her all the way to Bow Road and she counted about nineteen stops. If you allowed roughly two to three minutes per stop, that'd be at least forty minutes. The train rattled along and she resumed her thoughts.

Leo. She could still picture so clearly the first time they met. It was a Monday morning in mid-December. A year ago, nearly. Felt more like a century. She was tidying the books on one of the tables at the front of the shop, restacking the old ones and putting out newcomers in the 'recommended reads' section.

She looked up when a car door banged and watched through the window as a man stepped out of a black cab, paid the driver and strode through the glass doors towards her. She'd never seen anyone quite like him before. He was extraordinary, dressed in a long black coat that was unbuttoned and flapping and reached almost to his ankles.

On his head he wore a black, wide-brimmed hat and he was carrying a cane with a silver handle. He looked as if he'd been teleported to Islington from a previous century, or stepped off the set of a costume drama.

Cat wanted to giggle and glanced at the pay counter to see if Rachel or Gervaise were there but they weren't. They must have been out back. She half wondered if she were dreaming.

The stranger swept in. 'I'm looking for a book for my daughter, who is seven,' he said, his voice low and commanding. He wasn't especially tall – five feet ten, maybe – but he was strong and upright and his presence seemed to fill the entire room. Cat was intrigued. He had to be someone famous or important, but who was he? Had he been on X-Factor?

'Of course,' she said, hurrying out from behind the table. 'What sort of things does she like: magic, fantasy, adventure, or is she more into girly things like ponies?'

'I don't know what she is into,' he said grandly. 'Certainly

17

not ponies or hamsters. I would like to buy her a book that will spark her imagination, that will set her young mind racing.' He rested his cane against the book table and raised both hands in the air to emphasise the point.

Cat thought for a moment. 'There's so much to choose from. What sort of reading age is she? Does she read a lot?' She was frightened of making the wrong suggestion.

'Did you read a lot when you were a little girl?'

Odd question.

'Yes. All the time. I adored books. I couldn't get enough of them. My mother was always taking me to the library to choose new ones.'

'I thought so,' said the man, who looked at her intently, an amused smile playing on his lips.

Cat was suddenly conscious of her unbrushed hair, nose ring, baggy T-shirt and jeans stuffed into fake brown Ugg boots; she must look a right mess. She reached up and tucked a strand of hair behind an ear. He didn't seem to notice because he was too busy studying her expression. She felt herself redden.

'Tell me what you liked when you were seven years old,' he went on, sounding gentler now. 'I'm sure my daughter will enjoy that, too.'

Cat took him to the children's section and together they spent at least half an hour looking through all the books that she'd loved: Ballet Shoes; the What Katy Did series; Arthur Ransome; The Moomintrolls.

She took the books off the shelves one by one and he scanned the jackets while she explained exactly what they were about and why she liked them. Every now and then he'd ask questions and she found herself telling him bits about her childhood, more than she normally told anyone except Tracy. She even told him that she still kept her favourite children's books on a shelf beside her bed and that she liked writing herself, silly stuff like poems and short stories. It was just a hobby, really.

He listened intently, nodding sometimes, his head on one side, making encouraging noises. 'Really? Ah! That's fascinating.' He used words like 'enigmatic' and 'innocuous' that she'd read but never heard anyone say before.

It crossed her mind once or twice that he might be teasing, but she only had to look at his face to know that he wasn't. His whole focus was on her and he made her feel like the most interesting girl in the world.

It seemed to be getting warmer and he removed his big black hat and long black coat, which he folded up and put on a small wooden child's chair in the corner. He was wearing a camel-coloured waistcoat underneath with the gold buttons done up, and a clean white shirt.

He rolled up his sleeves and Cat noticed the strong forearms and wrists, the expensive gold watch, his slim, straight fingers and neat nails. His skin was a creamy brown colour with smooth dark hairs and she badly wanted to know what he did for a living, but was too shy to ask.

It seemed as if something weird were happening but she thought she might have been imagining it. When their arms brushed against each other she jumped, like she'd touched an electric fence.

'I can tell that you have an enquiring mind,' he said seriously. She had no idea of his age but guessed he must be old because his face was craggy and careworn. She imagined that every line told a story she wanted to hear. She was conscious of an extraordinary energy. That and his dancing brown eyes.

In the end he chose The Secret Garden by Frances Hodgson Burnett, the What Katy Did series, two Arthur Ransomes and all of the Little House books by Laura Ingalls Wilder. He wanted two copies of each which seemed odd, but she didn't ask why.

'May I take you for a drink sometime so that we can continue our most interesting discussion?' he said in his precise English, holding her gaze as he paid the bill. He was polite and formal to a fault, but there was a little smile at the corner of his mouth.

Cat's heart pitter-pattered. He was so well-spoken, clever, handsome and elegant – and he wanted to go for a drink with *her*!

She said yes immediately, only wishing that her hands weren't trembling so as she wrote out her phone number. She decided not to tell the others in the shop what had happened, especially not Gervaise.

She arrived at her stop and the spell was broken. She climbed the dingy staircase leading to the exit, thinking hard. She couldn't get the fact that he called them all by the same pet name out of her head. It hurt and she was confused. She needed time to sift through her feelings and weigh it all up.

She was surprised to discover that it was dark outside now and she'd forgotten how cold it was. She hadn't eaten since breakfast but she wasn't hungry; in fact she'd hardly been able to eat since he'd died.

Wiggling through the back streets, she stopped a few yards down outside Mr Yum Yum's Tasty Kebabs. A strong smell of spicy kebab meat mixed with fried onions and chips made her wrinkle her nose. Out of the corner of her eye she spotted the small, dark, wiry figure of Mr Yum Yum himself – otherwise known as Ali – grinning and waving at her through the shop window like a friendly goblin.

She supposed they were mates in a way because she'd lived above the shop for nearly five years. During that time she'd seen quite a few businesses come and go, but old Ali seemed to be on to a winning formula.

Normally she'd stick her head round the entrance to say hello, but she was no way in the mood today. Pretending not to notice him, she carried on rummaging in her bag until she found her keys, then she let herself in through the black door to the right of the shop.

The narrow, lino-covered hallway was very dark and the smell of kebabs and chips followed her in. Cat slapped a button on her left and a dim light went on overhead, illuminating a steep flight of steps in front of her.

On the bare first floor landing she opened the door to the flat, which was just as they'd left it: books and magazines spread across the oval wooden table in the middle of the room; knickers, socks, bras and a T-shirt draped over the radiator against the right-hand wall, and the blue-and-white IKEA checked curtains that she and Tracy had chosen half-closed.

Cat flung her suit and shirt on her bedroom floor and pulled on the clothes that were on her bed: jeans, grey woolly socks, white T-shirt, grey hoodie. Then she took a cleansing wipe out of a plastic packet on her chest of drawers and scrubbed off her make-up.

She never normally wore much, just a bit of black kohl under her eyes, but she'd nipped to the chemist in her lunch-hour yesterday and bought the cheapest foundation she could find, along with blue eye-shadow, blusher and mascara. She'd felt the occasion demanded it.

She turned on the purple fairy lights round the full-length mirror propped against the wall and stared at herself as she wiped the unfamiliar colours off her face. She was very pale underneath with dark circles under her eyes that wouldn't come off even with rubbing. Her features seemed to be sliding downwards as if they might eventually drop off.

It was hardly surprising, given what she'd been through. The only time she'd ever felt so upset was when her father – well. She didn't want to remember that.

She couldn't go back to how she was before she met Leo: turning up at the bookshop every day, scribbling away in quiet moments only to have her work rejected left, right and centre. Visiting Mum, coming home and getting pissed most nights, falling into bed, back to work the next day ready for the whole thing to begin again. Like her pet mouse Roddy on his squeaky wheel.

She'd been trying not to think too much, to expect nothing and just get on with it, but there had been a massive empty hole in the centre of her which she'd imagined would be there always.

Then Leo came into her life and suddenly everything was different. When he was with her each hour, every moment seemed to have real meaning. She seemed to see the world afresh in technicolour 3D.

And there was his music, his beautiful music. She'd never listened to classical until he began to educate her and he loved her music, too: Cold Play, Lily Allen, even Amy Winehouse. She swallowed, feeling the hard lump reforming in her throat.

She fell asleep, curled up uncomfortably on the pale blue sofa in the sitting room and didn't wake until Tracy came through the door at six-thirty, smelling of sickly sweet dry cleaning fluid. By which time it was pitch black outside and condensation had started to form on the inside of the windows because the radiators didn't work too well.

***

Victoria's radiators, on the other hand, were in perfect working order, owing to the fact that she'd had the whole lot replaced recently when she finally got her new boiler.

Leo had handed over a big wodge of cash quite out of the blue. She hadn't asked and he hadn't told her it was coming; he'd just produced it one Sunday afternoon wrapped in silver tissue and tied with a big red bow. The following morning she'd ordered their spanking new Megaflow heating system.

She was thrilled with it, so much so, in fact, that she'd been known to invite friends to come and admire it, marvelling at how quiet and efficient it was compared with the old one.

'Mu-um,' Salome would tease, 'they don't want to know. It's just a boring old boiler.'

'It's your mother's pride and joy,' Leo would reply, twinkling. 'I'm surprised she didn't put it in the middle of the drawing room with an ornament on top.'

Victoria smiled briefly at the memory. He'd been a great one for grand gestures, loving to surprise her. Well, there'd be no more surprises now. Her mind clouded over again.

She was sitting in the old brown leather armchair in her bedroom, warming her hands and knees on the radiator beneath the window. A couple of buttons on the back of the chair were missing – picked off by one of the children or their friends when they were younger, no doubt. But it was still her favourite place to think.

It was dark outside but she hadn't wanted to draw the curtains, preferring not to be closed in. One or two people passing the house looked up, drawn by the soft light coming from the bedside lamp behind her, but they quickly averted their eyes when they spotted her and walked on by.

She was wearing her comforting tartan brushed cotton pyjamas and thick fleecy white dressing gown, having taken off her funeral clothes the minute she'd got home; she wouldn't be going anywhere tonight. She glanced briefly at her slippers, the big pink fluffy ones that Salome had given her last Christmas. She'd always disliked them, though she'd never dream of saying, because she thought they made her size eight feet look even bigger. As if that mattered now.

She wondered vaguely what time it was and thought Salome ought to be getting ready for bed but she hadn't the energy to stir. She was so tired, more tired than she'd ever been before.

She missed Leo so much: the familiar sound of his key in the lock, the leap of her heart, his footsteps on the stairs, the brush of his lips against hers, his deep resonating voice. 'Here I am,' he'd say as he entered the room, as if he'd only been gone an hour or two. 'How is my darling girl?'

Then he'd scoop her up in his arms, crushing her head against his heart, and she'd know that everything would be all right.

He was often absent – working, of course. Vienna, Berlin, New York, Sydney, unless he happened to be doing a stint at the Royal Opera House in Covent Garden. And even then he'd sometimes stay in his rented flat near the Royal Albert Hall, because he needed to be up early for rehearsals and didn't want to disturb her.

She'd always suspected when he wasn't with her that one of his lady-friends might be keeping him company; he hated being alone. She'd minded a great deal at first, of course, until she'd made a conscious decision to stop asking questions. She guessed that others must speculate behind her back and probably thought her a fool, but she knew the truth.

At least when Leo was home she had his undivided love and attention, unlike some women she knew whose husbands were emotionally absent even when they were living under the same roof.

When Leo returned from a trip, he'd be up to speed with her job and family life in no time. She'd fill him in on everything that had been happening, all the little details and worries that they couldn't easily discuss on the phone. He'd listen intently, his head on one side, making pertinent comments, helping her to consider her problems from a different angle. She valued his opinion more than anyone else's in the world.

Then he'd drive to the local shops to buy special food that he knew she loved: fresh fish; organic vegetables; the ingredients for a sticky pudding – one of her vices – and make a delicious meal. He was an excellent cook, saying he found it relaxing. She'd put candles on the table, open a bottle of their favourite wine and they'd laugh a lot. He was a great raconteur, delighting her with tales of his performances, the things that had gone wrong as well as right.

Later, when the children were asleep, they'd make love in their king-size bed. Then he'd lay his head on her breast and she'd stroke his hair and he'd sigh deeply, saying how much he'd missed her. It would be just as if they'd never been apart.

The other women were just silly, misguided creatures who'd thrown themselves at him because he was famous. This was her story and she was sticking to it. That wretched Maddy, who'd turned up uninvited to the funeral. And Cat.

Victoria shivered, remembering Cat's thin little body and pinched face. She looked so small, cold and frail, as if she might blow away in the wind. She realised that she felt strangely protective towards this little slip of a thing, who was clearly besotted with Leo and who wasn't much older than Ralph.

At least she'd managed to protect her precious children from all that.

She knew that despite everything Leo adored her, they were soul-mates. And now he was gone. She felt her being, her essence disintegrating, her thought processes jumbling. It was scary, giddy-making, like being on top of a tall building and looking down. There didn't seem to be anything to hold on to.

Oh Leo, Leo, how could you do this to me?

'Mum?'

She turned and saw her son, Ralph, silhouetted in the doorway and managed a smile. He was so handsome and tall – much bigger than his father. He must have inherited her height gene.

'What are you doing?' he asked.

'Thinking.'

He padded into the room and sat on the end of her bed. He'd changed out of his suit and was wearing jeans and a dark green sweatshirt and his feet were bare. She moved her chair slightly so that she was no longer facing away from him.

'Can I get you anything?'

She shook her head.

Ralph leaned over, resting his elbows on his knees. He was staring at the pale blue carpet and she couldn't see his face, only his thick brown hair.

'You're going to have to pull yourself together. You can't spend the rest of your life moping.'

She flinched, feeling naked and vulnerable. Something or someone would only need to brush against her skin to draw blood. He was angry with her of course. In fact she could scarcely remember a time when he wasn't. But couldn't he set that aside and be gentle with her for one day at least?

'I've just got back from the funeral, Ralph,' she said, aware that her voice was quivering. 'It's going to take time. You can't expect me to bounce back immediately.'

Ralph ran a hand through his hair and looked at her, holding her gaze for a moment. He reminded her so much of

Leo: the dark, deep-set eyes, the intense expression. Yet they were very different characters, father and son.

'Of course not, but you've got Salome to think about. And your work – and me. Life has to go on.'

She nodded miserably before glancing away.

Ralph rose and stretched. 'I'm going out.'

Victoria stared at him. 'What?' She didn't mean to sound sharp but he never ceased to amaze her, that boy.

'Why not?'

She looked out of the window again at the black sky above the rooftops. 'I thought you might want to be with us tonight, to keep us company.'

'Nah.' She heard him walk towards the door. 'I need to get out, you know? It's claustrophobic here. It's doing my head in.'

He paused. 'You should go and see Salome. It's way past her bedtime.'

Victoria started, as if registering the name for the first time. Beloved Salome. The little girl hadn't even had supper and needed her mother. She must be strong, as Ralph said, for both her children's sakes. They were her priority and she loved them completely. Grief seemed to have turned her to ice.

'I'll make some pasta,' she said, thawing. 'Would you like some before you go?'

'I'm not hungry.'

'But you haven't eaten for hours.'

'I'll pick something up later.'

She blinked a few times, waiting until he'd left the room. She heard him collect his keys from the hall table, put on his coat and shoes and bang the front door shut. Then she got up, drew the curtains, shutting out the cold night, and walked slowly downstairs in her big pink slippers to attend to her daughter.

CHAPTER THREE

Thursday December 10th

'I've brought you a cuppa.'

Tracy plonked a mug on Cat's bedside table and sat down beside her.

'How are you feeling?' she asked.

Cat swallowed. Her mouth felt dry and sandpapery and she'd bet her breath stank. Her head was fuzzy as well: one too many glasses of vino last night. Of course she hadn't been tired after falling asleep on the sofa like that and she and Trace had stayed up for hours, drinking cheap red and smoking.

She propped herself up on her elbow and took a sip of the tea, which was hot and sweet; two sugars, just how she liked it.

'Rough,' she said, flopping back. 'What time is it?'

Tracy looked at her watch: 'Seven-forty. I need to leave in a minute. You'd better get your skates on.'

Tracy's yellow hair was still wet from the shower and she smelled of soap and shampoo. She was wearing a thick red sweater and jeans. She didn't need to dress up for the dry cleaners. No point.

'You mustn't skive,' she said, 'You'll lose your job.'

'I won't.'

But really Cat wasn't at all sure that she could face getting up, let alone spending a whole day at work. She took another sip of tea. 'I'll just finish this – thanks.'

Tracy suddenly stood up and yanked the duvet off the bed, leaving Cat shivering in her pyjamas.

'Don't!' she yelled, trying to drag the covers back, but Tracy was holding on tight.

'Get your arse out of there, Cat Mason. You might be grieving but I'm not letting you go to the bloody dogs. You can go to work like everyone else.'

Reluctantly Cat rose, pulled off her pyjamas and started to get dressed in the clothes that she'd worn last night while Tracy stood, arms folded, watching. Her round face, normally smiley and approachable, looked stern and school-mistressy. Right now she was being a pain but Cat was grateful really. She didn't know how she'd cope without her. If it weren't for Tracy she might go to bed and never get up, just fade quietly away until there was nothing left.

She waited until Cat was fully dressed and had washed her face and brushed her teeth. Cat was aware of her hovering at the door while she was in the bathroom, keeping a beady eye on her.

When she emerged, Tracy shook her head. 'The hair's shocking. You'll have to do something about The Weasel.'

Cat felt the back of her head. It was true. There was a huge tangle, like a giant dreadlock. It was big enough to hide a bird - or a mouse - in there.

Tracy had christened it 'The Weasel' some time ago, and it did seem to have a life of its own. She reckoned Cat must do a lot of tossing and turning in bed and it would take ages to tease out.

'I can't,' said Cat. 'No time.' She went back in the bathroom, found a hair tie and pulled her unbrushed hair up into a ponytail.

Tracy frowned. 'Hmm. You'll have to get a conditioning hair mask or something.'

As if.

'Where's your bag?' she asked, 'your Oyster card, your money?'

Cat looked around and saw her bag by the door where she'd left it last night.

'I have to go.' Tracy pulled on her black coat. It was true; she'd be late. 'You will leave on time, won't you?' She gave Cat another of her strict looks.

'I swear.'

Tracy pulled the door behind her, leaving Cat alone in the middle of the room. She felt scared suddenly and almost ran after her friend but managed to stop herself. She couldn't expect Trace to hold her hand twenty-four-seven; it wouldn't be fair.

Instead, she put on her black Doctor Marten boots with the orange laces, her green parka, and was about to pull on the furry hood when her mobile rang, making her start. She didn't recognise the number and considered ignoring it but curiosity got the better of her.

'Cat?'

She thought she recognised the voice but couldn't be sure.

'It's Victoria Bruck.'

She sounded nervous, almost as nervous as Cat, whose heart started thumping.

She stood frozen to the spot while Victoria stammered out her reasons for calling. Cat could tell she was trying to sound in command but she was making a bad job of it.

'I wanted to check you were all right,' Victoria was saying.

Cat didn't reply.

'I'd like to help you,' she stumbled on, 'give you something.

I don't know what Leo has left me yet,' she added hastily. 'I mean, I haven't even seen the will.'

Still, Cat said nothing.

'But you're young. I don't suppose you've got much—'

'How did you get my number?' Cat knew she sounded harsh but the woman couldn't be serious, surely?

'Leo's phone,' came the reply.

It made sense.

'Why are you doing this?'

There was a pause. 'It's difficult. I suppose, well, the truth is I'm angry with Leo for getting involved with you. It would be different if you were older. I'd like to try to make amends in some way.'

Cat nearly blurted that she didn't need Victoria's help or sympathy. She could look after herself. She'd been doing it since she was fifteen years old, after all. But she didn't. Victoria sounded kind and genuine and Cat was furious with herself for wanting to cry again.

'I have to go to work,' she said in a small voice. 'I'll be late.'

'Of course.'

'I hope you're OK.' Where did that come from? 'You and the kids I mean.'

'It's so hard.'

Cat could hear sniffing and felt like joining in but clutched the phone tightly instead. 'I'll call you back another time.' She was desperate to escape.

After hanging up, she stood stock still for a few moments mulling over what had happened. It was the strangest thing, extraordinary. She'd never have expected to hear from Victoria. Not in a million years. After all they were rivals, weren't they? If you could be rivals over a dead person. They were supposed to hate each other.

Victoria said she wanted to make amends. She seemed to feel sorry for Cat in spite of everything. So how come Cat was left with a peculiar sense that it was the older woman who needed *her* help – and not the other way around?

*** *** ***

It was still icy cold when Cat finally left the flat and she could see her breath. Quite a few shops were open already but there was no sign of Ali; he didn't usually appear till eleven-ish. She felt disconnected from what was going on around her, as if she were floating in her own personal bubble of confusion and misery; no one could know what she was going through or what she was feeling.

She climbed on the bus and stared out of the window. It was moving very slowly in the traffic and her eye was caught by a brightly dressed black woman walking very fast alongside her. She was clutching a dark brown briefcase, which looked out of place with her orange scarf and purple headdress. Cat wondered where she was going and what Victoria would be doing with herself now.

She gave herself a mental shake. Forget her. She didn't have enough space in her life to worry about someone else. Despite what she'd said, she wouldn't be returning the call.

The black woman rounded the corner and Leo crept back into her consciousness making her eyes prickle. She realised that she mustn't have thought about him for, what, three minutes? That had to be a record since he'd died. She didn't know if this was a good or bad thing. She just knew it was so.

As she approached the bookshop she was pleased to see the familiar figure of Gervaise unlocking the door top and bottom. He turned and looked at her apprehensively.

'How did yesterday go?' he asked, straightening up.

'I got through it.'

Cat had waited several months before she'd told Gervaise anything about Leo. Predictably enough, he'd said he was far too old. Rachel, the boss, was still in the dark because she'd just scoff. She didn't seem that keen on men, full stop.

Gervaise frowned. 'You look awful.'

'Thanks for the compliment.' Cat pushed past him into the shop and started to take off her coat.

'Rachel's going to be late,' he called after her. 'I'll make us a coffee. Put the kettle on, will you?'

She hung her coat on a peg in the storeroom and went into the tiny kitchen to fill the kettle. When she came out, Gervaise was behind the till taking a call on his mobile and seemingly deep in conversation.

There were no customers yet so she strolled around the shop floor looking at what needed to be done. They'd worked hard on the Christmas displays in the front and side windows. She'd also written a list of personal stocking-filler recommendations and presents for all the different members of the family, which they'd printed out and pinned to an easel by the door. She read all her recommendations from cover to cover; it was no hardship. She didn't need any excuse to get stuck into a book.

She found herself drawn, as usual, to the children's section, her favourite part of the shop because it reminded her so much of Leo. You'd think it would make her miserable now that he'd gone but it didn't. She liked to imagine that something of him was captured there for all time, like the negative image on a strip of film.

Gervaise, who was still on the phone, gestured that he was nearly done and she shivered, wishing that she'd worn an extra jumper. It was freezing in here and Rachel was so stingy about heating.

The shop was owned by an old guy who used to live in the flat above with his mum until she died. He moved after that and didn't come in very often. Business wasn't great. Rachel said it was important to keep costs down or they'd all lose their jobs but you could take things too far. Sometimes Cat's fingers were so cold she could scarcely open the till.

Gervaise put down the phone and did a thumbs up. 'Guess what? An audition.'

His eyes were shining and there was a wide grin on his face.

Gervaise was an out-of-work actor from Donegal. He had quite a lot of auditions but never seemed to land any parts.

'When?' she asked.

'Next week.'

'What for?'

'Napoleon in a re-make of a classic film about the battle of Waterloo. It'd be a fantastic break.'

Cat smiled, she couldn't help herself. 'But Gervaise, Napoleon was tiny. He was famous for it. You're six feet three!'

He shuffled uncomfortably.

'Don't you think they'll be looking for someone, er, a bit shorter?'

Gervaise shrugged. 'If all the others are tall it won't show. Besides, I'm an actor. I can make myself *seem* small.'

He lowered his long gangly legs and leaned forwards, taking a few mincing steps around the shop. 'With the right costume and make-up you'd never guess my height.'

Cat laughed. 'I've never heard of a six foot three inch Napoleon with an Irish accent.'

Gervaise stood up straight and scratched his head. His bushy black hair had a touch of the pudding bowl about it; it was a seriously bad cut. 'There's no harm in trying.'

She felt guilty. 'Of course not. I'll test you on your lines if you like.'

'Would you?' He brightened. 'You're a darling.'

That word – darling. Leo. Her face darkened.

'Do you want to talk?' Gervaise asked gently, noticing.

She shook her head.

'Let me take you out for a drink tonight? I'll do my best to cheer you up. Look – chicken legs!'

He bent his legs and did a silly knock-kneed movement. Normally, his skinny pins made her laugh.

She turned away, feeling her eyes prick again. 'Not today Gervaise.'

* * *

After dropping Salome at school, Victoria drew the curtains and went back to bed. She'd cancelled all her clients; she might feel up to seeing one or two next week.

The conversation with Cat had unsettled her but it hadn't banished that feeling that she wanted to do something for her. She supposed that she felt it was her duty, in a way, as Leo's wife-in-all-but-name. And more than that, she felt sorry for the girl.

Cat had sounded prickly and defensive which was hardly surprising, but the fact that she'd asked after Victoria and the children was strangely touching. If she didn't call back soon Victoria would try again.

She drifted off to sleep once more and when she woke it was almost two o'clock. She was tempted to roll over and close her eyes again until it was time to collect her daughter, but there was a dull nagging sensation in her gut and she knew it wouldn't go away until she took action.

After heaving herself out of bed, she put on her dressing gown and big pink slippers. She could hear music coming from Ralph's bedroom across the landing even though the door was shut. So he hadn't gone to school, then.

She frowned, thinking it wasn't good; he had A-levels in a few months and it was important to get back to some degree of normality as quickly as possible. But she supposed his teachers would understand about the funeral yesterday and she hadn't the energy to argue with him. Everything she said to him these days seemed to end in a row.

She walked slowly down the landing towards the large room at the back of the house and opened the door. Her stomach lurched and she had to pause for a moment and take a few deep breaths.

The room still smelled of Leo – that tangy citrus smell that was partly his aftershave, partly just the scent of his skin. This was his study, his own personal space, and no one was allowed in here. The children had complained it wasn't fair that they should have the small bedrooms when he was rarely at home but he'd ignored them. Victoria hadn't been in here once since he'd died.

It was fairly dark inside because the room was north-facing and the white Venetian blind across the window overlooking the garden at the back was half closed. Victoria turned on the overhead light and looked around.

Everything was exactly as he'd left it. The left-hand wall was lined from floor to ceiling with shelves containing hundreds of music scores all neatly lined up in alphabetical order, biographies of every famous composer you could think of, the odd novel – though he wasn't a great novel reader – musical dictionaries and other reference books.

His elegant upright Steinway piano was in front of the window next to a grey filing cabinet, and around it hung a number of framed black-and-white photographs of him.

Mostly he was conducting and you couldn't see much of his face, just the breadth of his shoulders, his raised baton, the orchestra's heads and the bows of their violins. He wasn't making extravagant gestures, though. He was a very careful conductor. He was renowned for his neat, elegant, precise little movements. He always said a good conductor shouldn't scream and shout or work up too much of a sweat. That wasn't his style.

To the right of one such photograph hung a close-up portrait of him that made her heart hurt. Often, in life, he looked intense and serious, but here the photographer had caught him unawares. He was slightly in profile and you could see the strong neck, the precise line of his jaw, the handsome nose with just the hint of a curve, and the straight teeth.

His dark hair, greying at the temples, was cut short above the ears and slightly longer on top. She supposed that he must have dyed it but it had never bothered her. He seemed so much younger than his years and grey wouldn't have suited him.

It was a distinguished haircut that told you he cared about his appearance, that his image mattered to him. Well obviously it did, he was a performer. And he was physically fit right to the end, though he never did any exercise and ate exactly what he liked. It had always amazed and irritated her slightly that he managed to stay so slim and flexible while she gained weight with alarming ease. She supposed the cakes and puddings didn't help.

He was smiling widely at something or someone and seemed amused and delighted. It was how he looked when he saw her again after a long break. His whole being seemed to be refined into that one smile.

She turned away quickly, unable to bear it any longer.

She was tempted to leave the room but steeled herself, knowing what had to be done. She walked over to his desk against the right-hand wall, above which there were more rows of shelves with hundreds and hundreds – maybe thousands – of classical CD's. No jazz or pop; he couldn't bear it. The desk itself was a large oak pedestal with big brass handles and she swallowed, almost scared to look.

There was a score – Wagner's Tristan and Isolde. She remembered that he'd been going to perform it at the Theatre des Champs-Elysees in Paris. They'd talked about her going over for a weekend to join him but she wasn't sure that she could make it because of Salome.

She sighed, thinking about the numerous occasions when she'd said she couldn't come because it seemed just too difficult. She wished, now, that she'd been to every single one of his performances. Salome could have joined her, a mother and daughter thing. So what if she'd had to miss a few days of school?

There was a notepad lying open on the desk, one of his red leather-bound ones. He always insisted on expensive stationery. He'd jotted down a few things in his bold artistic handwriting and she could picture him sitting there, his eyes closed, listening to one of his CD's, beating out the time with his hand, stopping every now and again to scribble something down about this or that conductor's particular interpretation.

She found herself swaying slightly and steadied herself on the back of the chair. She'd have to do better than this. Tentatively, she opened a drawer on the right hand side and pulled out his small black address book. She knew he kept it there as a backup, for numbers that he hadn't yet transferred to his iPhone.

That he owned an iPhone at all was unusual. Most conductors his age wouldn't have anything to do with modern technology. They were more likely to have a small diary, an old mobile phone and a secretary or agent to run their lives. But Leo was different; he loved gadgets and made a point of keeping up with technological developments. He was better with computers and digital cameras and so forth than she was.

Giving herself a mental shake, she flicked quickly to the letter P before scanning down the page until she found what she was looking for: Pearson Chapman Solicitors. Leo had used Robert Pearson for years; he'd have the will.

She sat down at the desk, picked up the phone and dialled the number, relieved to be put through immediately.

'Victoria!' said Robert Pearson. It was a little informal, given that they'd never met, but she supposed he might have difficulty calling her Ms Royce. People often did. Sometimes she called herself Mrs Bruck just to avoid awkwardness.

'I'm so sorry,' Robert went on. 'Dreadful business. The funeral was yesterday, I gather?'

Victoria didn't think she could cope with a lengthy preamble and decided to get straight to the point.

'I'm calling about the will,' she said. 'Leo told me that you handled all his legal matters. I would have rung sooner but I wasn't feeling up to it; it's been such a shock.'

There was a pause and she braced herself for more words of condolence.

'I'm afraid he didn't leave a will, Victoria,' Robert said. 'I talked to him about it countless times and he always said he'd get round to it next week, next month. I'm sorry. I know this makes things difficult.'

Victoria frowned, not understanding. 'But he told me he'd made a will leaving everything to me and the children. It's what he wanted.'

She heard Robert clear his throat. 'There is no will.' He spoke very slowly and precisely, as if to emphasise his point and fix it in her consciousness. He needed to because her thoughts were sliding all over the place.

'The best thing would be to make an appointment with my secretary,' he went on. 'Come in and we'll talk it all through.'

Victoria could feel the blood pulsing in her temples. She thought of the wodges of cash that Leo had given her down the years: £500 for Ralph's school trip, £12,000 for a new kitchen, £200 for a winter coat. And money for the Megaflow, of course. They'd never shared an account; she didn't even know how much he was worth. But he'd looked after her. And he'd promised that if anything happened to him, she and the children would be all right.

The house. Thank God she didn't need to worry about that. He'd bought it for her outright. She also had a little cash left to her by her mother and grandmother. But still, without his regular handouts how would she cope?

There was a mistake. She'd go through all his drawers and get Ralph to help. There'd be a will somewhere. She almost laughed at her own foolishness. Of course it would be OK.

'Are you still there?' Robert's voice pulled her back.

Another thought crossed her mind and her insides tilted.

'His wife! What about his wife?'

'Excuse me one moment.' She could hear Robert saying something in the background but couldn't make out the words.

'I do apologise.' He returned to the conversation. 'Can you repeat what you just said? You mentioned something about a *wife*?'

Victoria's heart was fluttering and she could feel sweat under her arms.

'He had a wife in Austria,' she explained. She was gabbling. 'They met when he was very young but it was a disaster. He left her after just eighteen months. They never divorced because they were Roman Catholics. It's why we couldn't marry.'

Robert sounded very steady, very legal; he must be used to difficult situations and highly-strung clients.

'Leo never mentioned this to me. Look, in a nutshell the situation is this: as he left no will his estate will be governed by intestacy rules as set out in the Administration of Estates Act 1925. Under these rules, because you weren't married his wife is entitled to what is known as the 'statutory legacy', which is at present £250,000, and the rest of the estate will be divided between the wife, in trust for the rest of her life, and the children. But we can discuss this when we meet.'

Victoria could take in only snatches of what he was saying. She couldn't seem to find a toe or a hand-hold.

'And me?' she asked breathlessly.

'I'm afraid, if Leo's wife is still alive, it's unlikely you'll be entitled to anything.'

She closed her eyes, hoping the giddiness would pass.

'However,' he went on, 'you might be eligible to apply to the courts for provision under the Inheritance (Provision for Family and Dependants) Act 1975 as you lived together as a couple within the same household.'

The *what?* It was a nightmare. She'd wake up soon.

'But the courts would be looking for you to demonstrate that you were financially maintained by the deceased immediately before his death.' He paused. 'You have two children, is that right?'

'Yes, two.' She knew that.

The image of a small featureless girl, Maddy's daughter, Phoebe, swam in front of her. Victoria had never met the child but she was only a year younger than Salome, she knew. She almost cried out but managed to stop herself.

'Because where intestacy is concerned,' Robert said carefully, 'all children are entitled to the estate. Maternity and legitimacy aren't relevant.'

'I see,' said Victoria, though she didn't.

She realised that she had no idea what or whom he spent the rest of his fortune on. Maddy? The wife? His mother? She clenched her teeth. She'd bet he'd spent a fortune on that blonde. And the child went to private school, too.

She managed to make an appointment with the secretary and write the date and time on a scrap of paper. When at last she put the phone down, she sat with her head in her hands.

All she could see was trouble and strife, pain and possibly even scandal ahead. Most of all she couldn't bear to think of scandal, for Leo's sake, for his memory.

And now she wouldn't be able to do anything for that young girl, Cat.

This was more of a mess than she could ever have imagined, but where did it leave him? She wished she could look into his mind and ask what on earth he'd been thinking of. She glanced back at the picture of him smiling on the wall. He was so handsome, so funny and sensitive, a genius. And he'd chosen *her*.

Whatever lay ahead, nothing would poison her love for him. Of that she was absolutely certain.

CHAPTER FOUR

Same day

Maddy glanced at her watch: 3.15 p.m. Jess would be doing the school run. What day was it? Thursday. Of course. They'd be having a quick snack then off to ballet lessons.

She smiled fleetingly at the thought of Phoebe in her white tutu and pink ballet shoes, her round, still babyish tummy sticking out of her leotard. Her daughter wasn't a natural dancer and was unlikely to be the next Darcy Bussell, but she was so cute and bright; sharp as a tack. Maddy had great plans for her.

She bit the end of her pen and stared at her computer screen. She was creating a draft running order for the annual Best of the Classics Awards to be held at the Royal Albert Hall in May. The job had been put out to tender and she'd fought hard to win the contract.

The live events business was becoming increasingly competitive. Gone were the halcyon days of the Eighties and Nineties when companies would splash out vast sums of money on corporate theatre. Now, spends were being squeezed and some of her biggest clients had melted away.

Landing the Best of the Classics had been a massive coup and she'd had to use all her charm to get it. As Production Director the success – or otherwise – of the event was totally her responsibility, and she was under a lot of pressure to stay within budget whilst delivering an experience no one would forget.

She scanned down the page on her screen and tapped in the name of Hungarian gypsy violinist Roby Lakatos, who was to make an appearance.

Her mind started wandering. It was Leo who'd introduced her to 'The Devil's Fiddler'; he was a huge fan. Leo had an eclectic taste in music and wasn't predictable by any means. When they were together he'd often put on Hungarian folk music or steamy jazz. In fact he usually preferred not to listen to the old masters because he said that's what he did all day at work.

She found herself logging on to YouTube and closed her eyes while listening to Lakatos play. Picturing his fingers flying along the neck of the instrument, goose bumps ran up and down her spine.

She put her forefingers in the corners of her eyes and pressed quite hard. No one at work, apart from her boss, Blake, knew about her relationship with Leo or where she'd been yesterday, and that's how she wanted it to stay.

She was aware, of course, that her colleagues must gossip behind her back but it didn't bother her. Leo had never lied to her; he'd said right from the start that he wouldn't leave Victoria or the children, yet Maddy had chosen to remain with him; there was no question of her having been duped.

'I'm a bad catch my darling girl,' he'd sometimes sigh, touching her ever so lightly on the cheek with his hand. 'You deserve better.'

She didn't like the fact that he was living at least part of the time with someone else but it wasn't as if Victoria didn't know about her. She'd accepted the situation. Leo said he loved her and didn't want to hurt her or the children, but that they hadn't been 'in love' for a very long time.

In a way, Maddy respected him for his loyalty to his other family. But there was another reason why she hadn't tried to force him to choose: she'd sensed almost from the very beginning that beneath the veneer lay something deeply troubled, a sadness at the centre of him that he'd never speak of.

She'd seen that lost expression. He thought she hadn't but she had. Try as she might, she'd not been able to coax out of him what lay at the heart of it, but she understood that he *needed* her.

Besides, she was a strong, independent woman. She'd had to be. She swallowed, thinking of her bitter, disapproving mother and weak father. There was no doubt that Verity, her younger sister, had been the favoured one in that family and Maddy couldn't wait to leave home.

She'd found herself a job and a flat straight from university and climbed her way up, never asking her parents for anything. Everything she had she'd earned herself and she was proud of her achievements. She hadn't particularly wanted a marriage certificate and Leo didn't have to look after her financially; she'd learned to look out for herself.

She recalled their last conversation less than two weeks ago and only hours before his death. He'd been talking about buying a ski chalet in the mountains somewhere. They adored skiing.

'It will be a bolt-hole for just the three of us,' he'd said on the phone. She could tell that he was smiling at his own turn of phrase.

She'd laughed and said, 'how nice!' But of course it would never happen. He was full of ideas, always thinking up things to try to please her. But he couldn't bear to be away from his beloved work for more than a few days and they'd hardly use the place.

He was in Cardiff when he rang, conducting at the Wales Millennium Centre. It was appropriate that it should have been there that he'd had his heart attack, halfway through a rousing performance of Berg's Wozzeck. She'd seen him perform the powerful psychodrama before; he was obsessed with it.

The music stopped and she logged off YouTube, needing to get on with her work. But it was so hard to concentrate; she'd never experienced real grief before and hadn't realised how debilitating it was. She took a sip of water and closed her eyes again.

Leo had received fabulous reviews for Wozzeck and Maddy had read them all. Critics had said things like 'intense, brutal and uncompromising'. She couldn't help thinking that this is how he would have wanted to go: in a blaze of glory, performing one of his favourite operas, surrounded by his adoring public, quickly, dramatically and, she imagined, painlessly.

Apparently they'd tried desperately to revive him but couldn't get his poor heart beating again. He'd died instantly, they said. This was some comfort.

But she wished so much that she'd been there, watching him perform, and that she could have rushed to his side when he collapsed. She would have gone in the ambulance with him. He would have wanted her there on his final journey.

And now she'd never see him again and Phoebe was without a father. Maddy didn't believe her daughter understood that Daddy was gone forever, it was too difficult a concept. Perhaps it was better that way.

She opened her eyes and looked out of the window of her office on Frith Street, Soho, staring for a moment at the blank grey sky above the rooftops. It was already getting dark and the Christmas lights would soon come on. It was extraordinary that anyone could be feeling festive now.

Victoria had been so big and grand in her grief yesterday, so proprietary. She clearly had no idea how much Maddy and Leo loved one another. Anger and frustration seemed to spring from nowhere and bubble inside her. No one would ever know now. Victoria would receive all the condolence cards and sympathy. It was her name and those of her children that would appear in newspaper articles and biographies in years to come, while Maddy and Phoebe might never have existed. That hurt.

She glanced back at her computer screen and tried to focus but there was an uncomfortable pulling in her guts that she couldn't ignore. Victoria's attitude to Maddy outside the crematorium. She'd been furious, spitting venom, hardly the behaviour of someone who'd accepted Leo's other relationship. It didn't square with the way he'd described things.

And that scrawny girl in the cheap suit. Victoria said she and Leo were involved. It had shocked Maddy to the core, ripping her already frayed nerves, and she'd felt like throwing up. She didn't know how she'd managed to stumble to her car.

On the way home, however, she'd given herself a stiff talking to. Victoria was in a highly emotional state and had lashed out, saying the most hurtful thing she could think of. The girl looked lost and wretched, with her scraggy hair and blue eyeshadow. She was barely more than a teenager and wasn't his type at all – far too waif-like, almost dirty.

There again, what was his type? Maddy and Victoria weren't exactly similar. And the waif had said that he called her 'my darling girl.' It wasn't the sort of thing you made up. A nasty thought wormed its way into Maddy's head, making her feel sick again. Maybe it was true. Maybe he *was* sleeping with her. But he wouldn't do that to Maddy. He told her everything.

She put her head in her hands and pressed her temples with her palms, hoping to drive the bad thoughts out.

The phone rang. A welcome diversion.

'There's a Mr Ralph Bruck wants to speak to you. He won't say what it's about.'

Maddy's heart fluttered. Ralph? Leo's son? She wasn't strong enough for a confrontation but knew immediately that she wouldn't turn him away.

She took a deep breath, pulled down her white blouse and straightened up, aware that her hands were trembling. This wasn't like her. She was Ms Cool and Confident. She had a reputation for it.

She wondered if Victoria were behind this. If so she must be desperate, involving her own son and getting him to do her dirty work. If there were any nastiness, Maddy could always hang up. She didn't need to sit here and take it from a teenage boy. She cleared her throat and assumed her most efficient voice.

'Put him through.'

* * *

'I realise this must seem very strange but I wanted to talk to you.'

He sounded tentative and nervous rather than aggressive. Maddy was relieved and felt her body relax a little.

'What do you want to talk about?' Her voice came out thin and a bit quavery. Pull yourself together, girl, stay on top.

'You and Dad – and your daughter.'

'What about my daughter?' People could say what they liked about her but not Phoebe.

There was a pause and a sniffle and her heart sank. She couldn't deal with her own grief, let alone someone else's.

'It's just so weird, this whole thing,' he said. 'I mean, Dad's gone. You. Me having a half-sister and not knowing her...'

Maddy hesistated. He'd lost his father and must be so cut up, but she was suspicious. She didn't want to walk into some sort of Victoria-laid trap.

'Does your mother know you're calling?'

'No.'

'OK.' She breathed in and out slowly. 'Next question. How did you get my number?'

'I heard Mum mention the name of your company once to a friend. She didn't think I was listening. I looked the number up.'

It sounded plausible but Maddy was still wary. Suppose Victoria was lurking in the background, sharpening her claws?

'I can't see what purpose talking with me would serve. It would just make you more upset.'

She felt no antagonism towards the boy. Leo had always spoken of him fondly. She and Leo had been together so long – over eight years – that she felt she almost knew Ralph anyway. She'd day-dreamed about getting to know him and Salome properly one day and going out together as a 'family.'

'Please,' he said.

She wanted to say yes to this young man who had Leo's genes, who reminded her so much of him and who was also Phoebe's half-brother. But she was afraid. There again, what harm could he possibly do her, this lad of, what, seventeen?

'I can't speak on the phone,' she said, suddenly decisive. 'I'll meet you tomorrow. Come to reception and ask them to buzz me. One o'clock?'

She hung up and stared again out of the window at the

49

bright red, white and yellow lights above the bar across the road. This was a bizarre development but there again, everything felt strange and different. Even the fillings in her teeth seemed to be on edge.

She got up, slipping on the jacket on the back of her chair and picked up her coat from a peg by the door. It was no use, she couldn't get anything done today; she'd tell her colleagues that she felt unwell, which in a way was true.

Blake would understand. In fact he'd urged her to take as much time off as she needed. They'd known each other years, she and Blake. She'd worked for him ever since he'd set up his company – Blake Smith Event Management. They were friends as well as colleagues. Rock solid, thank God. She'd trust Blake with her life.

***

Maddy owned a pretty, four storey mid-terraced Victorian house in Brook Green with roses in summer round the freshly painted, dove-grey front door and a window box on the front sill. It was no more than a ten minute walk from Hammersmith tube station and there were regular buses running up the road to Kensington High Street.

She'd lived there for three years and it had cost an arm and a leg, but it was the perfect size for her, Phoebe and the nanny, Jess, and she loved it. It was tall and thin – the rooms weren't especially big – and she'd had a loft conversion eighteen months ago. She'd also revamped the basement which had been pretty dingy.

She'd put in a bigger window at the end facing the street and French doors on the garden side, which made the place much brighter. Phoebe used it as a playroom and there was a

TV in there as well. Maddy had needed to borrow a lot of money from the bank to get the work done but at the time, business was booming and she was confident that she could meet the repayments.

Shame the job wasn't going quite so well now.

She took off her high heels and went straight upstairs to change. Phoebe and Jess weren't home yet but it wouldn't be long.

Her bedroom at the front of the house was her sanctuary, her chill-out zone, with pale cream-coloured walls and a white ceiling and woodwork. The carpet was white and fluffy and there were two big picture windows overlooking the narrow street.

Her bed, though, was the best thing there, the biggest she could find and the most comfortable in the world. She and Leo had loved it so much. She sat on the end and hung her head, wondering if she could ever be happy again.

Phoebe used to be so excited when she'd wake up on a Saturday or Sunday morning and rush into their bedroom to find her father. She'd squeal with delight before jumping in for a cuddle. Often he'd read her stories that he'd bought her in his clipped English accent. They were half way through the Little House books by Laura Ingalls Wilder when he died.

On lovely lazy mornings like these they wouldn't get up till eleven or even later. Then they'd wander round the corner to the little coffee shop that served the best croissants, hot chocolate and cappuccinos. She'd tell him all about school and he'd talk about little things that had happened to him – about the oboist who was in love with the lead violinist and couldn't stop making moon-eyes at her, or the moment when they thought that Violetta was going to fall off the stage during rehearsals.

Phoebe loved these tales; she'd roar with laughter, tug Leo's arm and say: 'Tell me more, Daddy. I want to hear more.'

Maddy reached up to grab a cushion from the top of the bed and hugged it to her chest. Everything seemed to remind her of Leo, everywhere she looked he'd left an imprint. Even the cushions, because the covers were made in Thailand and they'd stopped off there for a rare break on their way back from Australia.

He'd been working at the Sydney Opera House and she'd gone over to join him. It was before Phoebe was born and she remembered spending hours exploring the City alone while he was rehearsing.

At the end, though, he'd taken a whole glorious four days off when they'd travelled to the tropical rainforests of Queensland and gone scuba diving off the Great Barrier Reef. They'd never been diving before and he was the one who'd insisted. He loved pushing himself to the limit physically and was incredibly fit for a man his age.

They'd play tennis, too, at weekends and somehow he always managed to win. 'Technique, darling, technique,' he'd joke. After a match, they'd try out a new restaurant for lunch and sometimes supper, too. Neither of them cared much for cooking.

Thank God she had photos of him, though she wished now that she'd taken many more. Would she one day forget what he really looked like? Would his features blur and the memory of his touch fade?

Her eyes fluttered open in panic and she looked at the ring he'd given her when Phoebe was born, twisting it round and round the third finger on her right hand. It was white gold with a sapphire in the middle.

Phoebe's birthstone. Something solid and tangible. They'd

wanted a baby so much but it had taken Maddy a while to conceive. Finally Leo had offered to pay for tests, but before they'd even had their first appointment with the doctor – bingo! Nature had stepped in. They were both so happy.

She was reassured to find she could still picture his face when he came to visit her in hospital. He hadn't wanted to be at the birth, he was old-fashioned like that. Maddy knew that it was little more than a year since his other daughter, Salome, had been born. Yet he'd looked so delighted, so awe-struck, when Phoebe came along that it could have been his very first child.

She'd passed the baby over to him, wrapped in her little white blanket with the yellow ribbon round the edge, and he'd gazed at her with such pure, uncomplicated love.

'My little princess,' he'd said. Then he'd looked at Maddy: 'My clever, darling girl.'

She swallowed. That phrase. The thin, scruffy-looking girl. She clenched the muscles in her jaw, trying to block out the image, preferring to dwell on the good times.

Leo had explained that Salome had been an accident, a one-off; 'These things happen,' he'd said, shrugging his shoulders and assuming that boyish expression that was both infuriating and irresistible. 'I'm sorry.'

Maddy had considered throwing him out but decided in the end that it didn't matter; that was the other shadowy life he led. This life with her was the real one.

Phoebe's high-pitched voice in the hall brought her crashing back to the present.

'Is Mummy home?' She always shouted when she was excited.

Maddy rose stiffly, catching her reflection in the mirror of her rosewood dressing table, and a thin, gaunt face stared back. So this is what bereavement did to you; she hardly recognised herself.

Her mind flitted to Ralph. She'd be intrigued to know what he had to say, this man-boy. She couldn't help wondering what Leo would think to see the two of them together. Would he be pleased – or angry?

Strange that she couldn't decide. But then lots of things about Leo had been mysterious. It was one of the reasons why she'd loved him so much.

CHAPTER FIVE

The lift had broken down again, which meant Cat had to plod up four flights of dingy stairs to her mother's flat at the top of the apartment block. She was carrying two heavy shopping bags in either hand and needed to stop every so often to catch her breath.

Her mother was parked, as usual, in front of the TV and looked up briefly when Cat walked in but didn't speak.

The square room, that doubled up as a sitting and dining room, was suffocatingly hot. There was too much furniture, too many pictures hung on the walls and the heavy floral curtains seemed to want to swallow you up. Cat felt like turning round and walking right out again.

'I've brought you some shopping,' she said wearily, plonking the bags on the floor. Her hair and face were wet from the rain and she could feel water dribbling down the back of her neck. 'I got Jammy Dodgers. Your favourite.'

Her mother continued to stare at the screen.

Cat sighed before walking down the corridor to the bathroom, poking her nose in the bedroom as she passed. The bed was unmade and there were clothes all over the floor. No change there, then.

She took off her coat, draping it across the shower rail over the bath so that it wouldn't make a mess. Then she went into the kitchen and started unloading the shopping: milk, ham, marmalade, tea, ready-meals that you could stick in the microwave.

The kitchen looked suspiciously tidy, the surfaces crumb-free. She checked the silver bin under the sink, which was empty. There was an unopened loaf of bread in the fridge, some untouched cheese, six eggs – the ones she'd brought last time – a packet of tomatoes.

'Have you eaten anything today?' she called through to her mother.

No reply.

She stuck her head round the door. 'I said have you eaten anything today?'

Cat's mother glanced up from the TV, a look of confusion on her face. 'What? Sorry, love. I had scrambled eggs for breakfast. And soup for lunch.'

Cat frowned. She didn't believe a word of it.

'I've got you Shepherd's Pie,' she said, turning back to the shopping. 'With beans and broccoli.' She found the kitchen knife and started to chop the vegetables.

Her mother reduced the sound on the TV and Cat's ears pricked as she became aware of the older woman hovering by the door.

'Shepherd's Pie? I don't think I could manage anything now. I had such a big lunch.'

Cat put the knife down and took a deep breath. 'Please let's not go through this again, Mum. You need to eat. You'll get sick.'

'Can I have just a little, then?' It could have been a whiny child speaking.

Cat glanced at her mother, who was staring at the ground wringing her veiny hands. Her thin hunched shoulders were like folded bird's wings. She'd been so beautiful once. So full of life. Who was this poor little creature standing there in a faded dressing gown and worn-out slippers?

'You need to pull yourself together,' Cat said. 'You're not the only woman in the world who's lost her husband, you know.'

Her mother started snivelling. Tears dribbled down her cheeks and on to her chin, but she didn't do anything about it.

'I'm such a burden to you.'

Cat took a few steps forwards and put her arms around her mother, hugging her close. 'I'm sorry,' she whispered, stroking her thin soft hair. 'I've had a bad day, that's all. Of course you're not a burden, you're my mum.'

'No, you're absolutely right, Catherine. I've got to pull myself together. It's going to be different from now on. I'm going to stop being so down in the dumps.'

Something flashed through Cat's mind – the memory of what might have been her mother's voice back then, a pair of comforting arms. Yes, she seemed to remember that they'd been comforting once.

She shook the image away. She hadn't been a child and her mother hadn't been a mother for a very long time.

She finished the vegetables, plopped them into boiling water in a pan on the stove and laid the table. When the meal was ready, the older woman followed her into the other room.

'Is it man trouble?' she asked. Her mind seemed to jump about a lot these days.

Cat grimaced. What would *she* know about Leo? How would she understand? She thought she was the only woman who'd ever loved and been abandoned. Yet Leo was ten times the man Cat's father had been.

It took a while to persuade her mother to eat. Sitting opposite her at the little table in the corner of the sitting room, Cat watched her push food around her plate.

'And the broccoli,' she coaxed, 'and the meat,' until at last the plate was empty.

When it was time to go, a look of fear crossed her mother's face. 'Won't you stay for a cup of tea?'

Cat shook her head. She had to be tough otherwise she'd never get away. She'd end up putrefying in this place. The local council would turn up one day when neighbours complained about the smell and find the pair of them decomposing quietly in a corner.

'I'll pop in again tomorrow,' she promised. 'You should have a bath and wash your hair. Get some fresh air in the morning.'

'Bye, love,' said her mother, fake-brightly. 'Now you have a lovely time, won't you?'

A lovely time? Cat managed a weak smile.

She started the ten minute walk back to her flat at a march. Her pulse was racing and she felt like whacking something or somebody. Her father, that's who she wanted to thump. How dare he do that to them – to her? He couldn't have loved either of them. Everything had been all right until then.

She was practically running now, desperate to get as far away as possible. She checked behind and around her, relieved that no one was there. It was dark and raining slightly still and she stopped at a lamp post and punched the metal several times until the pain in her knuckles made her feel better.

'Loser,' she muttered under her breath. 'Coward.' But she didn't really mean it.

On rounding the corner into Roman Road, she was relieved to see the familiar bright lights of Mr Yum Yum's takeaway. Ali spotted her at her door getting her keys out and waved happily over the top of his till. There were three or four people queuing at the counter. Brisk business; he'd like that.

Right now, though, what she needed was a beer, a smoke,

her pet mice and Tracy. She'd lend an ear, she was lovely like that.

* * *

They propped themselves up against the pillows on Cat's bed, cigarettes in one hand, bottles of beer in the other, the ashtray between them. The curtains didn't quite close and a chink of light from the streetlamp outside pierced through the gap, illuminating a thin strip in the middle of the room. It didn't feel lonely, not with the two of them. Anyway, people were talking noisily outside Ali's shop.

Tracy took a drag of her cigarette. 'So what are you going to do?' she asked, pursing her lips and puffing out perfect smoke rings. It was one of her party tricks, along with lighting a match with her toes. She had to be really drunk to do that, though.

Cat stubbed out her half-finished cigarette and started making rabbit shadow patterns on the wall with her hands.

Tracy prodded her with a foot. 'I'm talking to you.'

'What?' Cat put her hands down.

'You heard.'

'Just carry on as usual, I s'pose.'

'That's not an option.'

Cat took a swig of beer and pulled a face.

'Look at you,' Tracy sighed, 'you're so miserable. You need to make changes. You should send off more of your short stories for a start. Just because you've had a couple of rejections doesn't mean anything. Everyone gets rejections and you're really good.'

She was in her white pyjamas with the pink hearts on and had a garish purple towel on her head, having just washed her hair. Her round face was covered in a white cleansing mask with holes for the eyes. She lit another cigarette, squinted and the mask cracked round her mouth, making a network of tiny criss-crosses.

Cat couldn't help laughing. 'When are you going to take that thing off your face?'

'Stop avoiding the subject.'

Tracy brightened. 'I know, let's go on holiday. Just for a week or ten days. It would do you the power of good.'

'What with? I'm broke.'

Roddy, one of Cat's two pet white mice, started going round and round on a squeaky wheel in the corner of the cage, making the kind of noise that jangles your fillings. Tracy took the damp towel off her head and threw it at the animal, who fell silent.

'What about the money that man gave you?'

"That man." Cat pretended she hadn't heard. Tracy couldn't stand Leo. She and Cat had known each other since toddler group and there was nothing – well almost nothing – they wouldn't tell each other. But when Leo came on the scene Tracy had gone all funny, insisting he was bad news and Cat would only get hurt.

She shuddered, thinking how close they'd come to falling out. Yet Tracy had been so lovely to her since he died. In fact she was the one who'd found out first, bursting white-faced through the door of their flat and brandishing a newspaper. They'd sat and read the whole article side by side on the sofa.

'World-famous conductor dies', the headline said. Cat could still remember the feeling of shock, like someone had dropped a nuclear bomb and they were waiting for the planet to combust.

Tracy had stayed with her all day, hugging her and making cups of tea. There was never a hint of malice or 'I told you so'. However much she disapproved of him, she knew Cat was heartbroken.

'You're not listening to me again.' Tracy put her empty beer can on the bedside table. 'Surely you haven't spent it all?'

'Spent what?' Cat had been miles away.

'The money he gave you. You have, haven't you? It's all gone isn't it?'

Cat shrugged. 'I bought him a new hat to replace the one that fell in the river. And a few theatre tickets. And dinner out once or twice. It goes quickly.'

'You should have let him pay. That money was for *you*.'

Cat curled up her legs and wrapped her arms around them, chewing the back of her hand in that way she had.

'I know, but he always paid for everything. I wanted to treat him occasionally.' She tried to sniff back her tears. 'I'll never see him in that hat again.'

'Oh Cat.' Tracy placed the ashtray on the floor, bum-shuffled over and put her arm around her friend. 'It'll get easier.'

Cat wiped her nose on her sleeve.

'He must have left a will,' Tracy pressed. 'Did he ever say anything about it?'

Cat hadn't yet told Tracy about the conversation with Victoria, mainly because she hadn't decided what she thought, but it came out now.

Tracy stared at her. 'She *phoned*? How come you haven't told me?'

'It was really odd. She said she wanted to give me something, to make amends.'

'That's it!' said Tracy, clapping her hands. 'We'll go on holiday with the money. It's just what you need. Leo would have wanted it.'

'But I don't even know how much she's thinking of, or even if I want anything from her. Anyway, I was in a hurry to get to work and hung up.'

'You'll have to call back.'

Cat frowned. She really didn't care about Leo's money, that was never an attraction. But she supposed she would miss the cash he'd given her. He'd been paying her rent for the past year. She hadn't asked, he'd insisted. And every time she saw him he forced another wad of dosh into her hand: £100 for a dress; £300 'for a proper winter coat,' he'd said, pulling crisp £20 notes out of his wallet and looking disapprovingly at her parka.

She'd felt like a plonker in the red wool and cashmere thing that he'd insisted she buy from Liberty, but she'd worn it a couple of times to the opera with him.

He'd also given her £3,000 for a wall-mounted, Bang and Olufsen CD player. She'd never had so much money in her hand as she walked to the shop to buy it and it had become her pride and joy, the most expensive thing she owned.

It would be wonderful to get right away, she thought, even just for a few days. She was sure she could sort something out with her mother, ask the neighbours to keep an eye on her. And Tracy was right, Leo would hate to see her so sad.

'I s'pose I could,' she said doubtfully.

Tracy's eyes glittered in the half-light. 'Do it.'

***

Friday December 11th

The following morning, before leaving the house, Maddy picked up a pile of letters which had landed on the mat and stuffed them in her black leather briefcase. Then she checked herself in the white-framed oval mirror on the wall to her left and rubbed her lips together to smudge her signature pink lipstick.

Her black Mercedes smelled of polish; it had only recently been valeted. She'd decided to drive rather than take the train as she had an out-of-town meeting later on.

She settled down in the leather seat, opened her briefcase and took out the bank statement she'd just received. Her overdraft had gone up and she frowned, trying to remember what she'd bought.

She'd popped over to see Leo in Munich last month, having persuaded him to go ski-ing for a couple of days between rehearsals. They'd stayed in a gorgeous hotel and she'd insisted that it was her treat, but she'd used Visa.

She scanned the outgoings column and clocked several hefty purchases from the same designer clothes shop; she wasn't exactly thrifty. Then there was the new furniture, curtains, carpet and so on for Phoebe's bedroom which they'd had completely re-done.

She vaguely remembered handing over a large cheque to the decorator just after Leo died. She had an inkling that it was more than they agreed but she'd been in no mood to argue, just wanting to be rid of him.

She shoved the statement back in its envelope and started the car. She'd have to have an economy drive soon but not now; she was grieving. She hoped there wouldn't be much traffic on the roads as it was still early, just after 6 a.m.

The office in Soho was sandwiched between an Italian cafe on one side and a nightclub on the other. It had once been a terraced house, probably built in the late seventeenth century and added to. By the time Blake bought it, it had become a patisserie.

It still looked a bit like a quirky little shop, despite the modern display window and glass door. The company name was written in bold trendy letters above the window and the

woodwork was painted faded lilac. Blake's wife had chosen it
– she said it looked 'shabby-chic.'

Inside the walls were grubby white and the stripped, painted
floorboards had been professionally scuffed. There were several
distressed brown leather chairs in the reception area and a
modern glass and wood staircase led up to the first floor, where
most of the employees worked in an open-plan arrangement.

Jules, the receptionist, wasn't in yet, but Blake's coat was
hanging on the coat rack in the office entrance. Maddy bypassed
the Christmas tree near the door, tastefully decorated with
white lights and glass baubles, and picked out some letters with
her name on from another pile. Then she walked up to her
office on the second floor, noticing that Blake's door was shut,
and logged on.

There was the usual mound of emails and she spotted a new
one from Louise, Head of PR at Smooth as Silk. She clicked to
open and started to read: 'Hope you have a good Christmas...
off on hols shortly...'

She scanned down further and her heart fluttered. 'I'm sorry
to say...'

Maddy took a deep breath. It was true. They'd given the
contract to someone else. How could they? She'd known Louise
for years and had worked so hard on the pitch.

She read the rest. Money was tight and the other company's
quote came in cheaper, it was as simple as that. But Maddy had
budgeted so carefully; she didn't know how she could have
given them what they wanted if she'd cut any more. As it was,
she was worried they wouldn't have been satisfied with the end
result.

She wondered how she was going to break the news to
Blake. He was a bit down and she'd given him to believe that
this one was in the bag. She scrolled down a few more emails

and found an upbeat one from the alcopops Tequila Tease people who liked her pitch and said they'd be getting back shortly.

OK, she thought. Give him the bad news first, then follow it up quick with the good stuff. She decided to nip out and get him a macchiato to cheer him up.

She was putting her coat back on when he stuck his head round the door. He looked pasty-faced and needed a holiday. He was far too conscientious and it didn't benefit the company in the long run. You just got burn-out.

'How are you feeling?' he asked vaguely, his eyes darting this way and that. He was wearing his usual uniform of jeans, brown brogues, brightly coloured shirt and a round-necked sweater with the sleeves pushed up to his elbows. 'Mind if I sit down?'

He pulled up a chair and started to prattle on about his wife and kids and how the little one had agreed to eat one Brussels sprout on Christmas Day. Maddy laughed politely. Why was he telling her this?

She'd better come out with the email because it was making her jumpy. 'I've got some good news – and some bad.'

His left eye twitched.

'Which do you want first?' She laughed, trying to make light of it.

His face was creased with worry. He needed a chill pill.

'It's not that bad,' she reassured. 'Smooth as Silk have turned us down—'

'Oh God.' He put his head in his hands.

'But I've had a great email from Tequila Tease. They love—'

He groaned and she thought she'd never seen him this depressed. Maybe he'd had a row with the wife. He didn't need to take it out on her.

'Can I get you a coffee or something?' she asked brightly, but he didn't seem to hear.

'The thing is,' he said, fiddling with his watch, 'I've been looking at it every which way and juggled the sums and I can't see what else I can do. I know it's a terrible time for you.'

She didn't like his tone, which unnerved her. He really was in a black mood. She noticed quite a lot of silvery strands in his fox-red hair.

'What are you talking about, Blake?'

'I'm going to have to make cuts.'

'What are you saying?' She didn't understand.

He licked his lips. 'I need to cut your hours. I'll be speaking to the others, too. I'm sorry, Maddy. We've been friends a long time.'

Maddy paused while she absorbed the words. He'd caught her completely off balance.

'What sort of cut are we talking about?'

He ran a hand through his hair and there were beads of sweat on his forehead and upper lip. 'I need to ask you to go down to three days a week for the time being.'

She gasped. 'But I can't—'

He looked straight at her with his greeny brown eyes. 'There's no choice.'

She stared at her pale pink manicured fingernails, noticing a tiny chip in one corner. She was thinking of the mortgage repayments and the loan for the building work, as well as Phoebe's school fees, the nanny, the after-school activities.

'I can't do it,' she said quietly.

'It's not as bad as you think,' he replied, sitting more upright. 'What I'm suggesting is this – you do three days here and the rest is on commission. You get the deals, we pay for the results.'

She tapped her pen on the edge of her desk. 'But you know

how much work it takes even to get to the pitch stage. And then if they say no—'

'There's no other way,' he interrupted. 'If I could think of something else believe me I'd have told you. You can always do freelance work to top up your salary.'

'You'd let me work for the competition – really?'

'It's not what I want, of course, but needs must. You're great at what you do. You won't be out of pocket. Hopefully it'll only be for a few months while we get back on our feet.' He lowered his eyes. 'I know I'm asking a lot.'

Maddy shrugged. 'I can get freelance I'm sure, no problem. But it's a shock. I didn't think things were that bad.'

He pulled a face. 'Trust me, it's that bad.'

She thought of her colleagues – Jed, Steph, Lola and Ben in particular – and frowned. They had families, too. Well, three of them. It was only a small company and they'd got to know each other pretty well.

'How will the others take it, do you think?' She wondered who would be the first to try to bail out. Trouble is, they were all effectively trapped. No one was recruiting at the moment.

Blake took a deep breath. 'I don't know. Like I said, there's no choice.'

He shook his head. 'I feel so bad. We go back a long way. And so soon after the funeral...'

She straightened up and managed a smile. 'Don't worry, I'll be OK. You know me. Tough as nails.'

He gave a pale smile in return. 'Thanks, Maddy, you're a star. I know you'll be fine.'

CHAPTER SIX

Same day

Her insides were jumping around like squirrels as she walked downstairs to meet Leo's son. He was standing beside the Christmas tree, tall and lanky, his shoulders hunched, hands stuffed into the pocket of a grey hoodie, the crutch of his jeans drooping somewhere around his knees.

'Ralph?'

He glanced up and nodded. He was pale and seemed underdressed for December and his big brown eyes, surrounded by thick black lashes, were too big for his face.

Maddy felt a flicker of – what? Maternal sympathy. The lad was seventeen but he was half boy still, unsure of himself. She found herself thinking that if he straightened up and squared his shoulders he'd be very handsome. As it was, he looked like any other disaffected teen.

She was aware of Jules, the receptionist, examining them both, trying to work out the relationship. Well, she'd have to keep on guessing.

'Do you eat pizza?' Maddy finished buttoning her camel coat, realising that she had no idea what teenage boys liked to eat. They were an alien species.

She turned to Jules. 'I'll be back in an hour.' At least he'd know how long he'd got.

They walked slowly up Frith Street without talking and

turned right into Old Compton Street. The Italian cafe was fuller than usual but they managed to find a table for two at the back.

It was a small cramped place with low ceilings, dark wood cladding and cheesy oil paintings of famous buildings in Rome, Florence and Venice. The staff were foreign and very loud and you could watch them preparing the pizzas behind a counter and shoving them in a giant oven.

Maddy passed the menu to Ralph who scanned down the page before looking up and flashing her a wide amused grin. 'What do you recommend?'

She was taken aback. Suddenly he looked older, more confident and in control. She reached up and fiddled with the hair tie at the back of her head.

'I usually have a salad but I'm told the Sicilian pizza's good.'

'I'll go for that, then.'

Maddy ordered. He wanted a Peroni beer, she had fizzy water. She took a sip and looked at him. 'So what do you want to see me about?'

He took a swig straight from the bottle and frowned. He was jiggling his leg under the table which was making her nervous, too.

'I wanted to meet you, to find out what sort of person you are.'

His voice was surprisingly deep and for the first time she noticed something oddly chameleon-like about his accent, as if he hadn't yet settled on who he really was.

'I know you and your daughter were very important to my father and I wanted to see for myself, to find out why. To get some answers.'

Maddy squirmed, thinking she didn't want to have to

account for herself and should have put him off. Especially after the dreadful news she'd just received from Blake.

'Did Leo talk to you about me?' she asked, shifting the focus. 'You make it sound as if he did.'

Ralph shook his head. 'I tried to ask but he totally evaded the subject. I wish he'd told the truth. It would have been so much easier.'

'Easier? I don't understand.' Maddy took another sip of water. A few months down the line and she would have felt stronger and better able to field his questions.

Ralph was still looking down and she noticed his fine cheekbones, the pronounced line of his jaw and the full sensitive mouth. He really was very like his father, only bigger, taller and slightly fairer. She felt a stab of loss that nearly took her breath away.

He cleared his throat, unaware, it seemed, that she was studying him; she couldn't help it.

'You see all through my childhood, for as long as I can remember, anyway, I was aware of this other person in my father's life. My mother pretended she didn't mind, that everything was all right, but I knew perfectly well it wasn't. Children aren't stupid.'

Maddy cast around for something suitable to say and found herself fiddling with the Sapphire ring on her right hand that Leo had given her. Ralph was grieving too, she mustn't forget that.

'Your father loved you very much,' she said quietly.

He didn't seem to hear. 'I couldn't stand the secrecy.' His hands were resting on the table and she was aware of his long, sensitive fingers, the boney knuckles slightly too big for his hands. 'We all knew what he was up to. Why couldn't he just be honest and come out and say it?'

She felt her pulse slow a little. He didn't seem to be here for a fight. 'Maybe he was trying to protect you from things he felt you weren't old enough to understand,' she said carefully. 'Maybe he thought if he told you about us, you'd think he didn't love you. Or your mother,' she added with a cough.

Ralph glared at her suddenly. 'My mother's a fool.'

Maddy's eyes widened. 'What do you mean?'

'I mean that almost all her life – all the time that she was with Leo – she lived a lie. And the worst thing was that she tried to make us live it, too. She made out we were this perfect, happy little nuclear family and we were so lucky to have this amazing fucking conductor for a father, even though he was hardly ever there.'

Maddy started breaking her bread into dozens of little crumbs, which she rolled between her fingers before dropping them on the red and white checked tablecloth.

'She practically worshipped the ground he trod on,' Ralph continued. 'She wouldn't hear a word said against him. And all the time he had another life with you – another child, for God's sake. She was so naive, so blinkered.' He pushed his chair back angrily.

'Our family was totally dysfunctional. He hardly ever made it to my sports days, parents' evenings, things like that. He wasn't a normal father in any way, shape or form, but my mother made this huge pretence that he was. Sometimes I think I hate her.'

It was taking Maddy time to digest what he was saying. This wasn't what she'd expected. She realised that she'd never considered what Victoria might or might not have said to her children about Leo's other life.

She was relieved when the food arrived as it gave her a moment to think. She picked up her knife and fork while

Ralph removed a slice of pizza from his plate and ate it with his fingers.

She was surprised to find herself feeling almost sorry for Victoria. She might have been naive, stupid even, as Ralph said, but she wasn't, as far as Maddy knew, a bad woman.

'Have you tried talking to your mum about this?' she asked at last.

Ralph rolled his eyes. 'She won't listen, she says I don't understand. Her line is that every relationship's different. She claims they were blissfully happy together. And she's a relationship counsellor – hilarious isn't it?' He gave a gloomy laugh.

Maddy bit her lip. It was hard to hear about this other side of Leo's life and she found herself wondering what Phoebe would make of her father in years to come. Soon, no doubt, the questions would come. She brushed the thought away quickly.

'It's true,' she said gently. 'Every relationship *is* different. Maybe your parents were happy in their own way.'

She knew it was bland and clichéd and what's more, she didn't believe it. But it was the best she could do.

Ralph turned red. 'Don't bullshit me.'

Maddy put a hand up, a sign of truce. 'I'm sorry. I didn't mean...'

His expression softened and he leaned across the table so that their faces were quite close.

'I'd love to meet your daughter – my sister,' he said urgently. 'How would you feel about that?'

Maddy flinched. There was something touching about his shy intensity and he was trying so hard to be strong and seem in control. But she had Phoebe to think of.

'I don't think so. She adored her father and she doesn't know anything about you or Salome. She's only seven.'

His shoulders drooped. His pizza was virtually untouched and she wanted to tell him to eat up; weren't growing boys always hungry? But she wasn't his mother.

'Will you think about it at least? You needn't tell her who I am. I'd just like to meet her.'

He looked up and caught Maddy's gaze. The whites of his eyes were very bright and clear and the dark brown irises were glassy reflections.

She glanced away quickly. 'I'm not sure that's a good idea.'

She felt a sudden rush of sadness. Phoebe was an only child and would never have a brother or sister. She'd fantasised about her meeting her half-siblings one day.

'It would help me,' Ralph said.

'Why should I help you?'

'Because I'm Leo's son.'

It was true, and the poor boy was so mixed up. She motioned to the waiter to bring the bill.

'All right,' she said briskly, picking up her bag from under her chair and putting on her coat.

She hoped that Ralph couldn't hear the way her heart, for some strange reason, had started hammering in her chest because it seemed, to her, to be loud enough to wake the dead.

***

Monday December 14th

It had been a difficult weekend. Salome had been crying a lot, wanting constant reassurance, and she and Victoria had spent all one morning baking cakes and making puddings in an effort to cheer themselves up.

It was something they'd always enjoyed doing together and now the house was filled with fairy cakes, flapjacks, desserts for the freezer and gooey chocolate brownies, but even that couldn't lift their mood.

They'd also been on a couple of long walks on Wimbledon Common and in Richmond Park. Wrapped in warm clothes they'd trudged, hand in hand, around ponds, through woods and up hills.

They'd watched dogs chasing into the murky water after sticks, emerging dripping wet and triumphant, observed groups of deer lurking in the bushes and stopped to tempt hungry squirrels out of trees to feed them bits of bread, which they'd brought with them in a plastic bag.

'Are you lonely without Daddy?' Salome kept asking, needing to be convinced that her remaining parent wasn't about to disappear, too.

'How could I be lonely when I've got you?' Victoria said, hugging her daughter tightly. 'Everything's going to be all right. You'll see.'

In truth, though, she didn't know if she would be all right. Every minute, every hour seemed bleak and meaningless and her thoughts were all over the place. It was easiest to try to focus on the practical things – putting on the washing, planning the supper, Salome's violin practice. She was a good little musician unlike Ralph, who'd also played the violin like his father when he was young but had no interest now.

Ralph had been particularly moody and uncooperative, coming in late and rising even later. Victoria was relieved, come Monday, when he'd got himself dressed and off to school as she'd been bracing herself for a big row. He'd missed over a week of lessons since Leo died and it really was time for him to knuckle down.

And now she was on her own in the house again. She glanced at the dark blue chequebook in her hand and opened it. His name was printed under the box in the bottom right hand corner: MR LEOPOLD SEBASTIAN BRUCK.

She'd always liked the Sebastian and had considered it as a name for Ralph, but Leo had been keen on Ralph after the composer, Vaughan Williams, whom he knew a little and admired greatly. So Ralph he had become.

She took a bite of last night's leftover treacle pudding and closed her eyes, relishing the sticky sweetness on her tongue. She oughtn't really to eat cakes or puddings at all; she was fat enough already. Leo had favoured sophisticated desserts like crème brulee and tiramisu but for her, nothing could beat a comforting stodgy sponge or spotted dick.

She took another mouthful, sighed and opened her laptop, which was sitting on the old pine kitchen table. She often chose to work here because she had a good view of the back garden which, though smallish, was quite secluded. This was thanks to the bamboo hedge that she'd planted all round the edge some years ago.

Friends had warned that it would require constant attention or the bamboo would take over, but she didn't mind the frequent clipping and pruning. She'd watch the tops of the bamboo stems swaying gently in the breeze and find it soothing.

After Googling the name and branch of his bank she dialled the number, feeling her heart pitter-patter when a strange voice answered.

'My husband has just died and I need to speak to someone,' she heard herself say, fiddling with a coil of hair that had escaped from its clip, twisting it round and round her finger.

'I'm very sorry to hear that. Could you spell your name for me?' said the stranger calmly. 'I'll put you through to our

Estates Department.'

Estates Department? Victoria found herself marvelling that there were people especially trained to deal with such matters. But of course there were; folk died all the time. It wasn't easy to get the information she needed, however, because the woman at the other end seemed hung up on the fact that she and Leo weren't married.

'You'll need to come in and notify us of the death,' the woman said. 'We'll need to see a death certificate.'

Victoria had that. Thankfully they'd made no fuss when she'd turned up, distraught, at the hospital and she'd been allowed to register the death and later arrange the funeral. Though of course Elsa, Leo's mother, had had her own strong views about the service.

Victoria shivered, remembering the nightmare journey that she'd taken alone by cab all the way to Cardiff. She didn't know how she'd remained sane. Her friend Debs had insisted that she wasn't to drive. She'd offered to take Victoria herself but she needed Debs to look after the children.

'I'm sorry but I won't be able to give the information to you,' said the woman from the bank, interrupting her thoughts. 'I can give it to your son as next of kin.'

'But he's at school,' Victoria stammered. 'And he's so cut up. I don't want to have to put him through that.'

'It must be very difficult for you,' the woman said smoothly.

Her saccharine kindness was beginning to grate on Victoria's nerves. She decided to push for the sympathy vote: 'I don't know how I'm going to manage. I mean, I work, but Leo was always the main breadwinner.'

'You'll have to obtain probate,' said the woman patiently. 'You don't have a joint account – money that you can access now?'

'No.' Victoria realised how strange this was going to sound. 'Leo always gave me cash for the house and the children, that sort of thing. We were married in all but name. We lived together for over twenty years, you see.' She hated having to explain her relationship, it was humiliating.

'I'm sorry but we really can't give you any information at this stage,' the woman repeated.

'Look...' Victoria was trying hard to suppress her frustration, which wouldn't get her anywhere. 'I'm not trying to take any money out. I know I can't. I just want to be told how much is in there so I can make some plans – for the children's sake. Surely you can do that for me?'

The woman hesitated. The figures must be tantalisingly close, at her fingertips. Victoria was willing her to take pity.

'Well...I'm not meant to but I don't suppose there's any harm. Just don't tell anyone I told you.'

'I promise.'

There was another pause and Victoria drummed her fingers lightly on the kitchen table.

'Did he have any other outside accounts?' the woman said finally.

Victoria glanced at the grey building society book beside her that she'd found in his desk, too, but it wasn't a lot of use. There was hardly anything in it: the princely sum of £25.02 to be precise. He clearly hadn't used the account for years.

'I don't think so. I've been through his drawers. I think he kept just about everything in his current account. He wasn't much good with money, you see.'

The woman coughed. Victoria waited.

'There doesn't seem to be much in here. I can see that there were some sizeable deposits last month but they were drawn out.'

A lump lodged itself in the bottom of Victoria's throat. 'What's the balance?' *Spit it out!*

'One hundred and ninety-five pounds and three pence,' the woman replied at last.

Victoria froze. There must be some mistake. 'Can you repeat that?'

The woman did as she was asked.

'Are you sure?' Victoria's stomach was rolling. 'Does he have other accounts with you that I don't know about?'

'Not with us. Do you have a good solicitor?' The woman's voice was kindly but impersonal. Of course she was detached. She was used to dealing with awkward, faceless customers.

Victoria said she had.

'I should talk to him,' the woman added, abandoning her efficient edge. 'Good luck.'

Victoria hung up and stared out of the window at the slate grey sky and wispy clouds. A tiny bird landed on the edge of the bird bath on the paved area beneath the back window, and flapped its wings.

She couldn't understand what she'd just heard. It made no sense. Leo must have earned a fortune. He always had cash in his wallet and was able to pay for things. Where had it gone?

The reality of her situation began to sink in. She'd known, if there were no will, that she'd have a battle on her hands, but at the back of her mind she'd been convinced she'd get the money that Leo had promised her in the end.

How was she going to cope? She could up her hours at work and cut back on non-essentials, but her circumstances were going to be very different. No more holidays with the children, fewer clothes, school trips, after-school clubs for Salome. And how much was Ralph's university going to cost?

She hadn't even bothered to check, having assumed that Leo would pay.

She realised she was shaking. Maybe he had offshore accounts and secret hiding places. She knew nothing, really, about money. She supposed that Leo's solicitor would be able to find out eventually but it might take months. And there was always the possibility that Leo really did have nothing, that he'd spent it all. And now she couldn't even help that poor little child-woman, Cat. It felt like a double betrayal.

She rose unsteadily from her chair and stood for several minutes frozen to the spot, unable even to cry. She hadn't finished the treacle pudding but she didn't want it now. The phone started ringing but she ignored it.

He'd left no will and he didn't have any money anyway.

What else hadn't he told her?

CHAPTER SEVEN

Same day

The shop was usually pretty empty on Mondays and Cat had sneaked a notebook and pen out of her bag and was bent over some writing she'd just started, scribbling feverishly.

'What are you up to?'

She felt a prickle of irritation. Gervaise had sneaked up behind and was peering over her shoulder: 'What's that about?'

'None of your business.' She put a hand over the page and he took a step back, wounded.

'Sorry,' she said. He was far too thin-skinned. 'It's just one of my silly stories.' She closed the notebook and put it away quickly.

'I bet it's not silly,' he said. 'I'd love to read it. I'd be really interested.'

She made a face. 'Nah. It's just something I like doing, y'know? It's not much good.'

It crossed her mind for the first time that day that he seemed different.

'What have you done to your hair?' she asked, keen to deflect attention.

He patted his head. 'Cut it myself last night. It was getting a bit long. Do you like it?' He did a girly twirl to show her the back and sides.

She didn't know what to say as his bushy black mop

seemed to be perched on top of his skull like a tea-cosy. The fact that he'd completely shaved off his sideburns didn't help.

'I think you need a decent barber.'

'You can talk.' Gervaise grabbed her ponytail and pulled. The Weasel, lurking just beneath the surface, was worse than ever. 'Bob Marley eat your heart out,' he joked. 'What do you keep in there? Ferrets?'

'Shut up!' Cat elbowed him in the ribs. 'Any news on the Napoleon part?'

'Didn't get it.'

'I'm sorry.'

He was wearing a long droopy knitted sweater with orange and navy stripes. It looked like something his granny had made him when he was a boy, which had stretched year by year and now reached almost to his knees.

'Anything else on the horizon?' she asked hopefully.

'I'm up for a part in a new play by this really hip writer. The audition's next week.'

'Great!' It was important to keep his spirits up. 'What's the role?'

He rubbed his stubbly chin. 'I'll play this American lad who goes to a British university and gets heavily involved in student politics.'

Cat raised her eyebrows. 'So you have to do an American accent?' She hadn't been overly impressed with his accent skills to date.

'Jewish-American to be exact. I'd be playing a New York Jew from a really religious family.'

Cat scratched her head. 'Tricky.'

He yawned and stretched his long skinny arms. 'Not really. I just need a bit of practice. Thought I'd go to Blockbusters after work and get some movies.'

'I'll watch them with you if you like.' She regretted it the instant she'd spoken but he needed encouragement.

'Would you?' He smiled widely.

Rachel appeared from the back of the shop. She was a big woman in her mid-thirties with thin, straight, shoulder-length gingery hair. She was wearing her usual uniform of faded blue jeans, trainers, T-shirt and black cardigan. She had a pasty face and the widest backside Cat had ever seen.

'Do you want to have lunch now?' she asked Gervaise. 'Cat, you go next. I'll have mine at three.'

She was always keen to sort the lunch rota.

Cat picked up a book she'd been meaning to read, one of the new arrivals. 'It's OK, you go first. I'm not hungry.'

Gervaise's eyes narrowed and he looked at her strangely. 'Are you all right? You're very pale.'

As a matter of fact she was feeling pretty rough. Must be nerves.

The other two wandered off and she chewed on a fingernail. Having made the arrangement she was going to have to go through with it. Victoria was rich, with all that money Leo would have left her. She could afford to part with a few hundred so Cat and Tracy could go on holiday. Anyway, she was the one who'd raised the subject of money in the first place.

A holiday. Cat pictured blue skies and warm sea. Maybe even a palm tree or two. She hadn't been on a beach holiday for years, not since she and Mum and Dad...

She gave herself a mental shake. No good dwelling on that. Things were bad enough without dragging Dad into it.

* * *

She left work promptly and got off at Wimbledon Station, trudging slowly up the hill clutching her A to Z. It was a good long walk but she was glad to have some fresh air and was in no hurry.

It was cold and dark but she was panting by the time she reached the edge of the village. It looked very inviting with lights on in shop windows and people sitting in restaurants and cafes, talking and smiling. You could tell there was lots of money around; you only had to clock the names of the clothes boutiques she passed.

She turned left down the south side of the Common and left again into Victoria's street which was wide and tree-lined, with great big houses on either side. Nothing at all like Bethnal Green.

When she reached Victoria's place she stopped and stared. It was a 1930's detached building with a pointy roof and black Tudor-style beams. There was a short gravel drive and a yellowy light shining in the porch illuminated the dark green front door.

It wasn't the grandest house in the street but it looked comfortable and expensive. An elegant silver birch swayed in the front garden and the curtains in the windows were drawn. It spoke to Cat of respectability; dependable middle-class values. Something chewed at her insides. Envy? She didn't think so. She couldn't imagine herself anywhere but the East End.

No, she wasn't jealous. But the house made her feel small, that was it. Insignificant. If it was a symbol of Leo's and Victoria's relationship it seemed frighteningly sturdy.

Something fluttered in her chest: the memory of Leo's touch. The way she'd caught him gazing at her when he thought she wasn't looking. The way he'd whispered in her ear when they made love: 'You're so beautiful'. His interest in her soppy writing. He was always encouraging her to send her stuff out to magazines and literary agents, like her really believed in her, really cared. She hadn't imagined it.

She straightened her shoulders and walked boldly up towards the front door, glancing left and right, before nearly tripping over a small pink wellie boot in the porch. The other one, plus three larger green pairs, were tucked away neatly in the corner.

She almost lost her nerve and turned tail, thinking this was madness. She had nothing to do with this family establishment in this grand street. She was an intruder, an outsider.

She'd told herself that it would be better to speak in person, as Victoria had suggested, but maybe she'd been kidding herself. Perhaps it was just an excuse to see where she and the children lived, to get a sense of this other life that Leo had led, tread the path he'd trodden and smell the different air he'd smelled.

Of course it was his dissimilarity, his talent and amazing knowledge of the world that she'd first been attracted to but somehow, when she'd been in his presence, the divide hadn't seemed so great. But now he was no longer here, she sensed his other life spreading out, seeping into the tiny gaps that she'd once hidden in, like paint dripping on canvas. Soon all trace of her would be gone.

She squeezed her eyes shut and pressed the bell quickly before she could change her mind.

* * *

It didn't take long for Victoria to come to the door. Her eyes widened when she saw Cat as if she'd forgotten all about the arrangement, but she let her in without a murmur.

Cat started to babble something about only staying for a moment but Victoria shushed her.

'I'm glad you're here,' she said reassuringly, leading the younger woman by the arm. 'Sit down. I'll be with you in a second.'

While Victoria was gone, Cat had time to check out her surroundings. She was in a wide square room at the front of the house. The first thing she noticed was how warm and comfortable it felt with a welcoming whiff of baking in the air. The second was that it wasn't as richly furnished as she'd imagined, nothing like Leo's apartment.

There was a small friendly fire burning in the grate, but one of the yellow sofas had a stain and the antique coffee table was slightly scuffed.

She perched on the edge of a sofa, nervously chewing the back of her hand, and glanced at the large photo in a silver frame on the side table next to her. It must have been taken at Salome's christening because she was a tiny baby in a long white lace gown in her mother's arms. Leo stood proudly alongside Victoria, his hand resting on the shoulder of Ralph in front, a small boy in a smart shirt and tie with a short back and sides.

They were smiling broadly in the sunshine, the perfect nuclear unit. Cat swallowed. They didn't look like a broken unhappy family but the picture must have been taken a while ago, nearly eight years. A lot can happen in eight years.

Victoria reappeared and sat down in the armchair facing Cat. She was wearing a brown jumper, a black calf-length skirt and a ridiculous pair of large, fluffy pink slippers. Cat couldn't help staring at them and Victoria, noticing, gave an embarrassed cough.

'Salome gave them to me for Christmas. They're awful aren't they?'

She grinned sheepishly catching Cat's eye, who smiled back.

Victoria's corkscrew curls were piled on top of her head and held up with a tortoiseshell clip. She had no dangly earrings today and her face was free of makeup. She looked tired, Cat thought, with dark circles under her eyes and heavy lines around her mouth.

Cat took a deep breath and started to explain about Tracy and the holiday. She was aware that she was stumbling, saying 'I mean' a lot, and 'you know.' She sounded inarticulate and stupid.

Victoria soon interrupted. 'I'm sorry,' she said slowly. 'There's no money. I found out this morning.' She stared at her hands in her lap, picking at the edge of a fingernail.

Cat's eyes narrowed. Was the woman lying? Backtracking? Had asking her here been a sick plot to humiliate her? But she looked as if she were telling the truth. Cat would hear her out for a few moments at least.

She listened while Victoria explained about the will and the empty bank account. 'I should have called to tell you only I was pretty shocked, as you can imagine. Then I decided it would be better to speak to you in person anyway.'

Cat felt the hairs on the back of her neck prickle. It seemed incomprehensible that Leo would leave his family in this situation.

'But how will you manage?' she said at last, having forgotten all about the holiday. 'You and the children, I mean?'

The other woman sighed. 'It's going to be hard. I'll have to cut back and try to work more hours and we're going to have to adapt to a different lifestyle. But we'll survive. We must.'

Cat frowned, feeling a little dazed. It was going to take time to reassess. Ever since she'd known Leo, she'd thought about Victoria in a certain way and imagined her living this comfortable, secure existence, enjoying all the material things that Leo gave her. Now it seemed her thinking was faulty. It was going to take a while to re-programme.

'How about you?' she heard Victoria say. 'As you know I had hoped—'

Cat shrugged. 'I'll manage. Always have.'

Victoria hesitated for a moment, working her mouth in a funny way. 'How did you meet him? I'd like to know.'

This was getting into dangerous territory. But maybe the older woman deserved to hear if she really wanted to. She must be desperate for answers.

Cat explained about Leo's arrival at the bookshop and how he'd asked for her number. She spoke tentatively, pausing often to gauge the response and expecting Victoria to snap, but she didn't.

She described how Leo had called the day after that first meeting and they'd met in the American bar at the Savoy, London. She'd never been anywhere like that before. He'd told her that she had to wear something smart, so she'd raced to Top Shop and bought a black mini dress and ballet pumps. She'd taken out the nose ring, too, and washed and brushed her hair.

He talked about his music, his dazzling life travelling the world as a conductor, the places he'd visited and the people he'd met. Later he invited her to an opera in Berlin.

'I said I'd never been to one and he was horrified,' Cat said, smiling at the memory. 'He paid for my ticket and accommodation. In different rooms, different hotels,' she added quickly.

She glanced at Victoria again and noticed her left eye twitch. 'So when did you start sleeping together?'

Cat took a deep breath. 'About three months after he'd

come to the bookshop. He was back in London and invited me to a rock concert.'

Victoria started. 'A rock concert? But he hated pop music.'

Cat looked at her strangely. 'He loved Lily Allen as well as bands like the Eagles, The Stones, Green Day, Cold Play especially.'

'Not with me he didn't.'

The two women exchanged glances.

'Go on,' Victoria said bravely.

'Later we went for a drink,' Cat resumed. 'I remember I was tired and rested my head on his shoulder. He said he should put me in a taxi but I didn't move. Then he said: "Or you could come back to my flat?"'

Cat felt hot and uncomfortable. It didn't seem natural picking over their relationship and she was half inclined to get up, but there was something desperate about the other woman, as if she had to know. As if her life depended on it.

'We went back to his flat near the Royal Albert Hall, the one he said he used when he was performing in London. He closed the curtains in the drawing room and we drank coffee and talked. That's when he told me about you and the children – and Maddy.'

'Didn't that shock you?' Victoria's face seemed to have turned an odd colour, like putty. 'Didn't you think it would be wrong to mess with someone else's husband?'

Cat knew this wasn't going to sound good. 'I was shocked, yes, and I wished it wasn't the case. But I suppose I respected him for telling me and he did ask if I wanted to go home but I said no. I'd never met anyone like him, you see. He was extraordinary. It didn't surprise me that he had a way-out personal life.'

Victoria took a long breath. 'But he was with *me*.'

'He told me that your love had died a long time ago,' said Cat gently. 'And he only saw Maddy because of the child.'

'He deceived you. Our relationship was very much alive.'

Cat wasn't having it. 'Then why would he want to go out with me? It doesn't make sense.'

'Like a lot of men he couldn't resist temptation. He had a strong sex drive—'

Cat felt tears pricking in her eyes. 'But it wasn't just about sex with us, it wasn't.' She wanted to lash out and hit something. Why couldn't she make this woman understand?

She rose unsteadily, suddenly stifled in that hot strange room. 'I have to go.'

'Wait,' said Victoria. 'I'm sorry for upsetting you. Let me at least make you a cup of tea?'

Cat hesitated before sitting down again.

Victoria returned with two mugs in one hand and two large slices of cake balanced precariously in the other. She passed a mug and plate to Cat and made to sit down again but nearly missed the edge of the chair, spilling tea on the carpet. 'Oops.'

Cat smiled despite herself. There was definitely something a little clumsy about her. Maybe the slippers were too big? Cat wasn't particularly into cake so she put her plate on the floor, but she took a sip of tea to keep Victoria happy.

Between mouthfuls, the older woman chatted a little about her job, Ralph and Salome. She was prattling but Cat was interested. She'd tried to picture Leo's other life so often. Victoria was good at asking questions, too, and Cat told her a bit about the bookshop and her flat with Tracy, the fact her father was dead and she was looking after her sick mother.

'It's weird,' she said, swallowing. 'Leo's death has made me think a lot about my dad again. It seems to have brought it all back.'

Victoria finished the last of her cake and put her plate on the floor. 'You haven't had any of yours,' she said anxiously, noticing Cat's lack of appetite. 'It's lemon drizzle. Salome and I made it earlier. It'll do you good.'

Cat shook her head. 'I'm not really into cake, sorry.'

Victoria settled back in her chair and sighed. 'How did your father die?'

Cat stared into her mug. She didn't like talking about it. Ever. Maybe it was the uneasy feeling in her stomach, the comfy chair, the warm room and smell of baking, or perhaps it was Victoria's encouraging voice, fluffy slippers and soft grey eyes. Whatever the reason, she found herself going back to her childhood when they seemed like a normal family.

'My dad was a teacher,' she explained. 'Head of languages at a big comp. Mum was a housewife. She was devoted to Dad, they were always laughing and teasing each other. We lived in Bethnal Green. It was only a small house, sort of two up, two down. But Mum had made it nice, with window boxes and potted plants, that sort of thing.'

Victoria listened carefully.

'I was an only child,' Cat continued. 'Mum couldn't have any more. I got so much attention it was stupid, really. No kid should get that much attention. We didn't have a lot of money but we still managed to have nice holidays, camping in Wales, mostly. The Gower Peninsula. We'd go body-surfing, even Mum. Sometimes Tracy came too, to keep me company. We've always been best mates, ever since we were tiny. When I got older I had all these grand plans – thought I was going to be an English teacher like my dad or even a writer.' She laughed bitterly. 'I liked writing.'

She paused and put her mug on the floor. 'Everything changed when he died.'

'Go on,' Victoria coaxed.

'I was fifteen when it happened. I went to the same school Dad taught at.'

'Was that difficult – being in the same school as your father?'

Cat shook her head. 'He was cool. Everybody liked him. He wasn't a pushover, I don't mean that. He could be strict when he needed to be. But he could have a laugh with the kids, too. They called him Hob Nob – that was his nickname.'

'Hob Nob?'

'Because he was always eating Hob Nob biscuits. He kept a packet in his briefcase. Sometimes he'd let the kids have one, if they were having a one-to-one with him after lessons or something. Course they made jokes about the nob bit behind his back but it was only friendly.'

Why was she telling her this? Now she'd started she couldn't seem to stop.

'I knew Dad was stressed with all the extra paperwork from the Government and that. He always seemed tired, he seemed to have lost his mojo, if you know what I mean. But I didn't really give it much thought, I was too busy with my own life, going out at weekends, having fun, that sort of stuff. Kids are so selfish, aren't they?'

Victoria gave a wry smile.

'Anyway, he was getting more and more stressed and then this girl, Kayleigh – this bitch in my year - decides to call rape.'

'What?' The other woman unfolded her long arms and shifted forwards on the seat.

'She claimed he raped her in the classroom one Friday afternoon after school when all the other kids had gone home.'

Cat could feel her heart pumping faster than usual. Thinking about it always had this effect on her.

'He was only helping her with something she didn't understand. No one believed her because she was a thief and a liar, she was always getting into trouble. But of course they had to call the police and Dad was suspended while they carried out investigations. All hell broke loose.'

Victoria made a sympathetic noise. 'What happened next?'

'He was off work for months. Luckily the bitch didn't show at school again – claimed she was traumatised.' Cat clenched her fists. 'Otherwise I'd have smashed her head in.'

Victoria flinched but remained silent.

'Mum tried to keep everything going, to keep Dad's spirits up, but he used to spend hours just sitting in his chair staring into space. Then one day I got back from school and...' Cat swallowed. '...and he'd topped himself.'

She glanced at Victoria, who was shaking her head.

'Found him in my bedroom. Mum was out. He'd hanged himself from one of the rafters in the roof – there was a trap door in the ceiling which was how you got into the loft. He'd kicked the chair away – the one I used for studying.' She screwed up her face. 'I tried to get him down but couldn't; he was too heavy. I called the ambulance but it was too late.'

Victoria leaned across and touched her knee. 'I'm so sorry.'

Cat pulled away. 'It's all right. I'm over it.'

'But you must have been—'

Cat laughed. 'I just wish he'd taken pills instead.'

'Did he leave a note?'

'Yeah. Lots of stuff about being sorry he let us down, that sort of thing. All a load of rubbish. He hadn't let anyone down, we knew he didn't do it.'

'And what happened to the girl, the investigation?'

Cat shrugged. 'She admitted she'd made it all up.'

'But why?'

'No idea. Well, I do, actually.' Cat leaned forwards, wrapping her arms around her knees and curling herself into a ball. 'Trouble is, it was my fault. She hated me, you see. Me and Tracy, we were the good little girls at school, popular, the teachers loved us cos we worked our little socks off. Kayleigh was always nicking stuff from the other girls and I caught her at it – pinching money from someone's bag in the changing rooms. I told her to put it back and we had a massive argument. She was screaming at me, calling me all sorts of stuff, and I gave as good as I got. We were sworn enemies after that.' She bit the back of her hand. 'Wish I'd kept my mouth shut...'

Victoria frowned. 'But she wouldn't have made up a terrible story like that just because you caught her nicking stuff?'

'You don't know Kayleigh.'

Victoria sighed again. 'I wonder how she feels about it now; I wouldn't want to have that on my conscience. But it's no way your fault. You did the right thing about the money. You had no idea your father would take such desperate measures.'

'It wasn't just his own life he destroyed either.'

Victoria looked at Cat strangely before bending forwards suddenly and picking up her untouched cake. 'Sure you don't want this?'

Cat shook her head. She'd never felt less like eating.

'Shame to waste it.' Victoria took a bite and looked at Cat seriously. 'Why didn't you finish school and go to university? You're smart, I can tell.'

'Because my mum went to pieces. She had a nervous breakdown didn't she? I couldn't exactly go poncing off to university leaving her like that. I'd lost one parent, I wasn't going to lose another. Besides...' Cat raised her chin '...I didn't want to. My dad thought education was everything – he always said if you got a good education you could do whatever you wanted. And look what happened to him. Don't know why I've told you this,' she added. 'It's old history.'

'I'm glad you have,' Victoria said quietly. 'I understand you better now. You've suffered greatly and now you've been let down by Leo, as have I. It's a lot to cope with.'

The women sat quietly for a moment, reflecting on the truth of these words.

It was Victoria who finally broke the silence. 'I know who's to blame, you know. For the money.'

Cat's eyes widened. 'Who?'

'Maddy,' the other woman hissed.

Cat was shocked. Victoria's soft sympathetic face had suddenly turned hard and ugly.

'She lives in some expensive house in London,' she muttered, 'and her child goes to a private school. She's got his money. She'll have wheedled it out of him and feathered her own nest.'

Cat hadn't thought much about Maddy but she was reminded now of the other woman's expensive clothes at the funeral and the immaculate makeup. She heard herself splutter. It had been hard to come here and even harder to talk about her father. She didn't want to be discussing Maddy now, or sitting opposite Victoria. And she didn't want to be understood.

She grabbed her parka and was going to leave without saying goodbye, but it was stupid to be mean. Victoria hadn't asked her to pour her heart out; she'd been like a bloody tap.

'Would you like a lift to the station?' Victoria asked, gulping down the last of the cake and wiping the crumbs off her chest.

'No.' You couldn't argue with Cat.

She walked quickly back along the darkened street, cursing

herself for making a big mistake. She'd been crazy to listen to Tracy and should never have come. She passed a particularly imposing house and kicked the fence hard a few times with her boot. The wood made a satisfying crack and she hoped she'd broken it.

'Oi! You!'

She didn't stop to find out who'd shouted at her but sprinted back towards Wimbledon Village, losing herself among the well-dressed people strolling in and out of restaurants and bars.

She wished now that she'd said something really mean to Victoria because she'd been with Leo all those years and probably didn't even realise how lucky she was. And Maddy had known him eight years compared with Cat's measly one. That wasn't fair either.

She glared at a few people on the train and gave a V sign to the city gent type in a pinstripe suit who'd looked her up and down. That made her feel marginally better.

CHAPTER EIGHT

Sunday December 20th

'C'mon. Let's go for breakfast.'

Tracy was standing over Cat, who was sitting cross-legged on the bed in her grey cotton jersey pyjamas.

'I just can't believe it,' Cat said, shaking her head. She was still mulling over the conversation with Victoria. Had been all week. 'How could there be no money? He was loaded.'

Tracy tugged at Cat's sleeve. 'Maybe he was a secret gambler or something. Must be awful for the wife and kids. C'mon, I'm starving.'

Cat rose reluctantly and went to open her curtains. Bright sunshine bounced into the room making her squint. It took a moment or two for her eyes to adjust then she looked down at the street below. Roman Road was normally bustling: women in traditional Muslim dress, some in the full niquab with only their eyes showing, going in and out of shops; men talking and arguing; children on their way to and from school.

Today, though, everything was shut, save for a halal grocery store, a discount shop selling everything from children's plastic potties to bins and brooms, and a Pound Store. She looked to her right and could just make out the soaring shape of the half-built Olympic Stadium in the distance.

There was a scuffling noise and Roddy poked out of his straw-stuffed house, sniffed the air and scuttled over to the wheel. She knew it was him because he was slightly smaller than his brother Cedric, who had a longer tail.

Cat crouched down to the mouse's eye level. 'Hello!'

'There's no time for mouse talk,' Tracy growled. She wasn't especially keen on mice. 'All the bagels will be gone.'

'OK,' said Cat, rising. 'Let me get dressed. I'll be quick, I promise.'

She pulled her black stretchy straight-leg jeans out of a drawer, along with a white thermal vest and a long sleeved black T-shirt, and yanked her grey hoodie on top. A glance in the mirror told her there wasn't a lot she could do about The Weasel, so she piled her hair on top and secured it with a tie. Then she put the silver hoop in her nose before splashing her face with cold water in the bathroom. She was ready.

Tracy was standing at the table flicking through the newspaper. She was wearing the weird black and pink ethnic skirt she'd got in Camden Market, with her tan suede cowgirl boots. She seemed to have forgotten about the upper half, though, because she was still in her pyjama top – the white one with pink hearts on. Her yellow hair was tied in two bunches which stuck out over each ear, a long thin line of pink scalp peeping through the neat central parting.

Cat leaned over Tracy's shoulder and read something about thousands of Brits trapped on Eurostar trains.

Tracy shook her head. 'Nightmare. They were stuck in that tunnel for hours in the boiling heat with no food or water. I wouldn't have stood for it.'

Cat smiled, momentarily forgetting her unhappiness. 'So what would you have done about it then, eh?'

Tracy closed the paper and swung round crossly, hands on hips. 'I'd have asked for the manager and demanded to be let out.'

Cat raised her eyebrows. Tracy's high and mighty moments amused her. She was convinced she could solve all the problems of the world; you just needed a bit of womanly common sense.

The two women strolled side by side to the bus stop, puffing on roll-ups. It was icy cold despite the sunshine; it couldn't have been more than two degrees. Tracy was wearing her bright red Peruvian hat with ear flaps and long dangly ties, which was a present from the on-off boyfriend, Rick.

The bus arrived and they found seats in the middle of the top deck; there was a family behind who were going to visit the Museum of Childhood on Cambridge Heath Road. The children were chatting excitedly, asking endless questions: 'Can we see the teddies? Can we have an ice cream?'

Cat felt a pang of nostalgia. She used to love going there when she was small; she remembered, especially, the glass cases full of old-fashioned dolls with their tiny rosebud mouths, white porcelain faces and frilly pantaloons beneath frothy frocks.

She'd never been particularly into dolls, but these were different. She'd longed to be able to take them out, dress and undress them and pop them in their funny old prams with the great big wheels and dusty fringed canopies.

Her mother loved them just as much as she did, probably more. 'Look at this one, Catherine!' she'd say excitedly, pointing to some exquisite doll with silky blonde curls and rosy cheeks. 'Isn't she beautiful!'

Then they'd stand beside each other commenting on each detail of the doll's features and clothes, right down to the miniature black leather Mary-Janes.

Back then, Cat's mother had been into lots of things: dolls, museums, books, cooking, gardening, crocheting. Cat would give anything to see her with her basket of brightly coloured wools and crochet hook, reading glasses perched on the end of her nose.

She pulled up the hood of her parka and stuck her hands in her pockets. Life was crap. What did she expect?

'Did you hear what I said?' Tracy had been rabbiting away and she hadn't listened to a word.

They got off the bus and walked slowly up the street towards Columbia Road Market, enjoying the familiar Sunday sight of people heading back to their cars carrying armfuls of brightly coloured flowers.

They passed one woman with a huge bunch of tall-stemmed pussy willow and what looked like eucalyptus, plus a giant amaryllis in a pot. Another man had a basket bulging with bright red poinsettias.

As they rounded the corner they could hear the comforting Cockney refrains from stallholders: 'Three for a fiver and a pound off for a sexy dozen!'; 'Four quid meant to be six pounds!' 'Have a look, Dell. Five extra large only a tenner today!'

There was a festive mood in the air, which made Cat feel weird. Some of the stallholders were wearing red Santa Claus hats and the little shops on either side of the narrow cobbled street were offering free mince pies and mulled wine.

There was also a street musician strumming carols on the guitar. Cat saw a tall dad in a blue bobble hat hoist his small son off his shoulders to put some coins in the bag in front of him. The guitarist waved his cap: 'Cheers guv!'

Tracy led the way across the throng and into a side street where they stopped for a moment outside their favourite bakery which looked like The Old Curiosity Shop. Its bow window with thick uneven panes jutted out into the narrow street and there was a variety of mouth-watering breads on display, ranging from organic spelt to German rye.

They rounded the corner to the cafe section at the back, narrowly avoiding tripping over a group of brave people sitting on the pavement, sipping hot drinks and eating croissants and bagels. Pushing through the door they were relieved to find seats next to each other on a trestle table beneath the window.

The room felt a bit like a farm kitchen with a stone floor and whitewashed walls. There was a makeshift counter at one end where the waiter made coffee and behind him, shelves were groaning with ornamental teapots and coloured tins. Cat normally loved the smell of fresh coffee but today she found it off-putting.

'I'll have organic salmon and cream cheese – and a Nicaraguan coffee,' said Tracy, eyeing the menu, her plump cheeks flushed red from the cold. 'I might have hot salt beef for seconds.'

Food usually perked her up. Cat wished her desires could be so easily satisfied. She went up and down the list of things to eat.

'I'll have orange juice. And a plain bagel with butter.'

'What about scrambled eggs and roasted tomato? You always have that.'

'Not in the mood today.'

While Tracy was away ordering, Cat peered at the notices on the wall to her left: there were ads for meditation, local yoga classes, piano lessons and a dodgy masseuse. The man on her right with a big bushy beard was having an animated conversation with the woman opposite about parking restrictions. Cat zoned out and Victoria's voice reverberated round her skull, making her brain ache: 'No will....no money...

he's let us both down...'

At last Tracy reappeared with two bagels on white china plates which she plonked on the table.

'This is nice,' she said, climbing over the bench seat and sitting down again.

Cat was silent and Tracy sighed, aware that her Pollyanna-ish 'being glad' strategy was failing.

'So, Leo's got no money. No holiday for us, which is a drag. But when did we ever have money, Cat? We always have a good time even when we've only got 50p in our pocket.'

'But where's it all gone?'

Tracy put an arm round her shoulders. 'Life's a bitch,' she said, in the manner of someone uttering a profound truth. 'Maybe it's a mystery he's taken with him to the grave. You've got to try to move on, hon. It'll take time, but there are lots more fish in the sea y'know.'

Now where had Cat heard that before? She was sure it's what her mother used to say when she'd had her heart broken by some spotty boy or other in Year 8 or 9.

They were interrupted by a loud voice behind them. 'Hola!'

Cat swung round and Tracy's face lit up in a wide grin: 'Rick!'

Rick was tall and well-built – maybe six one – with mouse-brown, shoulder-length hair and a goatee beard. He was wearing his regular black leather jacket and jeans. He was an artist, only he didn't seem to sell many paintings, and a musician in a rock band, only he didn't seem to get many gigs, so he earned his living as a pizza delivery boy.

Sometimes it would get him down and he'd become gloomy and uncommunicative, which was usually when things turned wobbly with Tracy. She couldn't stand it when he wouldn't talk to her. She liked to talk. A lot.

There'd be a blazing row followed by a few days of teary phone calls when Tracy was convinced it was all over. Then, to Cat's relief, the clouds would lift and they'd carry on as if nothing had happened.

'Fancy a bevvy when you've finished?' he grinned, eyeing Cat's virtually untouched bagel.

She passed him the plate and he polished off the food in a few short gulps.

Tracy turned to Cat. 'Shall we go to the pub just for an hour or two? It'll do you good.'

She and Rick hadn't seen each other since Thursday night because he'd been working. She was desperate to get her mitts on him, you could tell.

Cat wasn't going to play gooseberry. Besides, her head was in a muddle.

She stood up. 'Nah. You go. I'll catch up with you later.'

Which was a lie; she had no intention of joining them. She had things to do. But it kept Tracy happy, anyway.

***

'Look, Mum. A white Poinsettia.'

Cat had bought the plant, which was already in a gold pot, on her way back from the market. She put it in the middle of the table and admired it for a moment.

'Lovely,' said her mother, without looking up from the telly. 'Very Christmassy.'

At least she remembered it *was* Christmas-time.

Cat checked the kitchen and was relieved to see some evidence of food preparation: bread crumbs on the surface, a dirty pan in the sink. She opened the fridge and found that a couple of eggs had gone and the cheddar cheese had been opened, although her mother could only have had a tiny slice, barely enough to feed Roddy or Cedric.

She strolled back into the sitting room where her mother was still sitting, sniffed and wrinkled her nose.

'When did you last have a bath?'

'A bath?' The older woman tapped her temple with a forefinger. 'This morning I think.' She smiled. 'Yes, that's right. I had a bath and washed my hair this morning.'

Cat frowned. Her mother's shoulder-length hair didn't look washed, it was lank and greasy, pulled back off her face with a hotch-potch of criss-crossing hairpins. Cat went into the bathroom and ran a finger along the bottom of the bath. Dust. She thought so.

She turned on the hand-held shower and swooshed the tub clean. 'I'm running one right now,' she called.

Once the older woman was lying in the warm water, she seemed to relax. 'Smells nice,' she smiled, while Cat tipped a dollop of shampoo on her head and massaged it in. 'What flavour is it?'

Cat stopped massaging for a moment. 'It's not a flavour, Mum. It smells of almonds. Can't you tell? It's supposed to be almonds anyway.'

'Ah yes,' her mother said happily. 'Almonds. I like them.'

Cat found some clean clothes and helped her mother get dressed. She put the dirty laundry in the washing machine along with the towels she'd used, a couple of tea-towels and a few other items, then she washed the bath and sink out and mopped the floor.

Her mother settled back in her armchair and Cat brought her a cup of tea and a chocolate biscuit.

'I'll see you tomorrow,' she promised, bending down and brushing the top of her mother's newly combed and sweet-smelling hair with her lips.

'All right love,' her mother replied, staring contentedly at the screen. 'Now you have a good day in the office, won't you?'

***

While Cat walked towards the tube, Victoria was waiting on the other side of a quite different, tree-lined road, staring at a tall thin house with a smart dove-grey front door. There were few passers-by to wonder what she was doing; they were probably still asleep or reading the papers.

She was trying to imagine how much of Leo's money had been poured into this costly establishment and thought bitterly of her own front door, which needed re-painting. In truth it had never troubled her before; she'd been quite content with her warm, slightly shabby surroundings. But the elegant entrance opposite seemed to mock her.

Salome was playing all day at a friend's, which gave her the space she needed. She hadn't been sure whether to ring the bell or just bide her time; but now that she was here she was inclined to linger.

At last the dove-grey door opened and the woman, Maddy, stepped out in a navy overcoat and jeans, followed by her small blonde daughter. Victoria's stomach lurched as she felt her courage seep away. She took a step back, winded by the similarity between the little girl and her own Salome. Although Phoebe was a year younger, and shorter, she had the same slim upright build, the same long blonde hair tied back in a ponytail. From a distance you could easily mistake them.

Victoria breathed in deeply a few times to steady herself, watching Maddy bend down and start tying Phoebe's shoelace.

It seemed to be taking a long time; perhaps her fingers were cold.

Conscious, suddenly, of having a fleeting advantage, Victoria clenched her fists, drew herself up to her full height – it was now or never – and swept across the road, coming to a halt in front of the pair and looking down on them imperiously.

Maddy gasped. 'Oh!'

'Do you realise you've left us penniless?' Victoria barked, drawing strength from the other woman's alarm and her own sense of burning injustice.

'What do you mean?'

'He's left us nothing,' Victoria was aware out of the corner of her eye of the little girl, hovering and anxious, and felt a twinge of guilt. But it was her own children who were the real victims.

'He didn't make a will and there's nothing in his bank accounts,' she barked. 'You've taken everything.'

Maddy started to get up, holding her daughter tightly by the hand. 'Leo didn't give me a penny,' she said steadily.

Victoria gave a superior smile. How low to deny it! 'I'm not a fool, you know. What about that?' She tossed her head in the direction of the house. 'And her school fees,' she added, nodding at Phoebe.

Maddy was much shorter than Victoria but held herself well, with a straight back and shoulders down. 'I have a good job. I've never had to rely on a man to support me.'

Victoria gave a disbelieving 'hmmph'. But the woman was convincing, she'd give her that.

'And for your information,' Maddy went on, 'I paid for this house and I pay Phoebe's school fees. Leo always tried to give me the money but I wouldn't take it; I didn't need it.'

Victoria's eyes widened and she paused, momentarily lost for words. She didn't want to believe Maddy – but she seemed truthful. Either that or she was a consummate actress.

'But I thought—' she started to say.

'You were wrong.'

'Who is she, Mummy?' Phoebe's high-pitched voice cut through the icy atmosphere.

Maddy put an arm around her daughter and pulled her tight. 'Look,' she said, in a controlled voice, 'we can't talk here. Why don't you come inside and we can discuss this properly?'

Victoria, scarcely hearing, touched her temple feeling light-headed. 'But if he didn't give the money to you—'

'I don't know anything about it.'

Victoria watched, mesmerised, while Maddy bent down again, picked up a brown shoulder bag from the ground where it had been lying and started scrabbling around inside. At last she pulled out a tan purse, opened it and produced something with a triumphant flourish: 'Look.'

The older woman flinched, fearing that whatever it was might bite.

'Take it,' Maddy insisted, thrusting a piece of paper in her hand.

Reluctantly Victoria did as she was told. She glanced down and clocked that it was a cheque for several thousand pounds made out to 'Welbeck Girls' Preparatory School.' Underneath and to the right was a signature in bold artistic handwriting and black ink. Unmistakably Leo's.

Her stomach lurched again. It seemed as if she were holding something intimate that belonged to just the two of them. Tangible proof of their relationship, as if further proof were needed. She threw the cheque away as if it had scorched her and watched it flutter to the ground.

Maddy picked it up, ripped it in tiny pieces and hurled them in the gutter. 'I've had lots like this from him down the years and I've torn them all up, every single one. Leo used to say Phoebe was his daughter too and he wanted to pay her school fees, but it always annoyed me. I told him time and again that I didn't want or need his money. It wasn't why I was with him and anyway, I was the one who'd chosen to send her privately. But he continued to mail the money and I continued destroying the cheques. It became a bit of a silly ritual. I only kept this because it was the last thing he gave me. I had no intention of banking it.'

Victoria felt suddenly small and fragile and staggered a pace or two to the railings outside Maddy's house, needing support.

'I'm surprised he didn't make a will,' Maddy went on. 'I'm sorry about you and the children but I haven't got any of his money. And if it's any consolation,' she went on wryly, 'my finances aren't great at the moment. They've cut back my hours at work and I'm going to have to tighten my belt, too.'

Phoebe started hopping up and down, still holding her mother's hand. 'But you're not wearing a belt, Mummy, what do you mean?'

Victoria felt a flicker of sympathy for this single mother and her small, sweet daughter who looked like Salome. Until now she'd never hated anyone. Disliked, perhaps, but not hated. Then she thought again of her own children and her compassion faded.

'Well, it seems we're in the same boat,' she snapped, turning on her heels and marching away down road as fast as she could, conscious of Maddy and her small daughter staring after.

She managed to round several corners without registering which direction she was going in before stopping dead in her tracks, aware that her legs were shaking. Now that she was no longer in sight, all her anger and nervous energy seemed to have leaked away and she felt limp and wrung out, like spun washing.

She leaned against a garden wall for a few minutes, realising that she had no idea where the tube station was but it didn't seem to matter. She was replaying the scene that had just taken place over and over and one particular image tormented her: the bewildered face of Phoebe, so like that of her own daughter, clutching on to her mother.

An old tabby cat sauntered on to the pavement beside her, rubbing against her legs and mewing plaintively. Relieved by the distraction, Victoria stooped to pick it up and stroke it.

'There there,' she was saying, vaguely aware of the salty tears running down her cheeks, 'I did the right thing, you know. I had to find out.' But after a few moments the cat jumped out of her arms, over the garden wall and away.

Victoria was inclined to think Maddy must have been telling the truth. You wouldn't tear a big cheque up like that just to prove a point – would you? And she'd said that she was struggling financially, too.

This meant that Leo had abandoned all three of his women and all his children.

Which just left the wife.

***

Cat got off the Central Line at Leyton and turned right down the high street. The journey brought back memories because she used to make the trip with her father when she was a child.

He'd take her to watch the local football team, Leyton Orient, play on a Saturday afternoon. He was a big football fan and his enthusiasm would rub off on Cat who'd shout and cheer, even when she didn't have a clue what was going on.

Her mother would make white bread sandwiches and wrap slices of homemade cake in tin foil. They'd eat their picnic before the match in a little park called Coronation Gardens. It sometimes smelled a bit because there was a dump nearby, but Cat never minded.

She remembered the park was surrounded by a black fence and there were brightly coloured flower beds in spring and summer. When she'd finished her sandwiches, she'd dance down the snaking path to the little fish pond where she'd give her crusts to the enormous goldfish, who'd swim up from murky reeds and stare at her with open mouths and round glassy eyes.

The park was probably quite small but it seemed huge to her back then and full of interesting hiding places behind trees and under hedges. Her father would grin, pretending to be a giant – 'Fee Fi Fo Fum' – while he searched for her. She clenched her jaw and stared at her Doctor Marten boots, avoiding looking in any of the shops as she passed, taking care not to catch anyone's eye.

Gervaise's place was only a five minute walk from the tube, down a narrow one-way street lined with shabby terraced houses, and she glanced up now that she was safely off the main road. Bulging wheelie bins took up a large part of the tiny uncultivated gardens and quite a few of the curtains were drawn, even though it was still light.

She reached the door and knocked; there was no bell. She could hear footsteps and soon Gervaise was peering at her from his six foot three inch height, his face wreathed in smiles.

'You came!' he said, running a hand through his bushy black hair. 'I didn't think you would.'

Cat pushed past him down the narrow hall. 'I said I would if I could. How's it going?' The audition for the New York Jew part was tomorrow, she knew.

There was a slight whiff of fried food which turned her stomach, but she'd soon grow used to it. She started taking off her parka, relieved that the place was warm, and veered left into Gervaise's bedroom-cum-sitting room.

He rented the bottom half of the house and there was another tenant upstairs, some sort of salesman. It was a long rectangular room which had been knocked through. The wallpaper was a dull grey colour and a tatty blue border went all the way round the middle.

Gervaise's double bed was on the right under the window which looked onto a concrete backyard, and there were three brown armchairs and a TV at the other end in front of the bay. He'd thrown a maroon and gold Indian cover with elephants and pillars right over the bed including the pillows – to make it look more like a sofa, Cat guessed. There was a small white wardrobe against one wall with a guitar propped in the corner, and two black and white posters, of the young Sir Laurence Olivier and David Niven, were blu-tacked to the walls.

It was surprisingly un-messy for a boy and although the decor was tired – which wasn't his fault as he didn't own the place – it was cosy. Cat had been there before but not for a year or so as she'd been too involved with Leo.

'Will I take your coat, and can I get you a drink?' Gervaise asked in his strong Irish lilt. 'I've got some beers, or there's wine if you prefer?'

Cat handed him her parka. She was wrapped up to the nines while he was only in a black T-shirt, jeans and bare feet.

She noticed that his arms, though thin, were strong and wiry with long downy black hairs on them, and his biceps were hard round lumps.

'I'll have a beer, thanks.' She didn't want one but it seemed polite. She prodded one of his biceps. 'Have you been working out?'

He grinned sheepishly. 'Nah. It's just that you never see me out of that stripy sweater.'

It was true. The bookshop was so cold that they all came layered up. Even in summer you needed a sweatshirt.

They lit cigarettes and sat down.

'Shall I test you on your lines?' Cat asked.

Gervaise picked up a script from the floor beside him. 'I think I've got the accent taped, but I'm worried I'll forget it halfway through. I'm dead nervous. I reckon I could be in with a chance with this one.'

Cat smiled encouragingly and glanced at the script in her hand. 'Where do I start?'

He pointed to a place about halfway down the page. 'I'm called David. You do the bits highlighted in orange.'

'Ready?'

He put his hands behind his head, took a deep breath and nodded.

She started to read: '*Rose enters the room—*'

'You don't need to do the stage directions,' he interrupted.

'Sorry.' She began again: '*They're so apathetic, the lot of them. The universities could put fees up to £50,000 a year and they wouldn't do anything.*'

'*It's the same where I come from,*' said Gervaise. '*Students don't give a damn about politics.*'

Cat stared hard at the page. She didn't know much about accents but this didn't sound remotely New York to her. More

Caribbean, maybe – or Welsh?

'How was that?' Gervaise asked when he'd finished. 'Good, huh?'

She smiled. 'Fantastic.' There was no point bursting his bubble. He needed confidence-boosting at this late stage of the game.

She tested him several times to make sure he knew the words off by heart, then they agreed to watch Some Like it Hot. She took off her Doctor Marten boots and put them under the chair.

Gervaise's ginger moggy, Tamburlaine the Great, jumped on her lap and settled down, purring loudly. She chewed the back of her hand in that way she had, feeling her shoulders relax and her body sink into the chair.

The room was hot and she soon found her eyelids starting to droop. This is crazy, she thought, surrendering to drowsiness. I'm turning into an old woman...

'Cat, you're muttering in your sleep!'

She woke with a jump to find Gervaise kneeling beside her, poking her in the ribs, and she ran her tongue around her mouth which was very dry. She felt disorientated and troubled, aware that she'd had a bad dream but she couldn't remember what it was about.

Gervaise jumped up to turn off the TV and Cat started to protest.

'Ach, I was getting bored myself. I've seen the film that many times. Fancy a cuppa?'

He went into the kitchen and she hugged her arms around her, feeling chilly now the cat had disappeared, leaving a cold empty space in her lap. She glanced out of the window, realising that it was dark outside, and wondered how long she'd been asleep.

She felt that she ought to be getting back, though she wasn't sure what for. Tracy would still be out boozing with Rick. Either that, or they'd be shagging each other senseless in the flat.

'How are you feeling – about things?' Gervaise asked, returning with two steaming mugs and handing her one. He didn't usually mention Leo by name.

'Pretty rubbish,' Cat admitted, cupping her hands around the mug and glancing at her friend, which was a mistake. His eyes were bright blue, surrounded by thick black lashes like a girl's, and full of kindness.

'Wanna talk about it?'

'No.' She looked away quickly. She'd done enough talking with Victoria the other night and had learned her lesson.

Gervaise scratched his head. 'I've been thinking. How about coming to Donegal with me one weekend? We could stay with my folks. My mam's a great cook and she loves visitors.'

Cat's eyes clouded over.

'They live in a pretty little spot,' he said quickly, 'miles from anywhere. There's beautiful walks around and some smashing pubs. They wouldn't trouble you.'

He was watching her closely.

'Or if you weren't feeling sociable you could laze around at home and read and do your writing or whatever. I could give you a key so you could come and go as you please. I reckon some fresh Irish air would do you the world of good.'

Cat bit her lip. Gervaise talked a lot about his mum, dad and two younger sisters and they sounded lovely. She imagined the house smelled of freshly baked bread and the younger kids still ran down the hallway to greet their dad when he got in from work.

She shook her head. 'I can't.'

'Why not? I know you'd have a good time once you got there.'

'Because I can't. Full stop.'

He flinched as if he'd been slapped, and she hated herself. Why was she so mean? She leaned down and started to put on her boots.

Gervaise let out a long sigh. 'I wish you'd let me help you, Cat. I'd like to if I could.'

She finished tying her shoelaces, knotting them several times.

'Let me at least walk you to the tube?'

'I'd rather go on my own.'

It was a relief to get away from his bright blue eyes and seductively warm flat and out into the cold night air. If she'd stayed any longer she might even have accepted his offer.

Best to keep him at arm's length. Safer that way. At least you knew what to expect. No one got close to Cat Mason except Tracy. If you didn't let people get close, you didn't get hurt.

SECOND MOVEMENT

CHAPTER NINE

Monday December 21st

Victoria had decided to put in an appearance at work. It was only ten days since the funeral and very close to Christmas and Debs had advised her to wait till after the holidays at least. But she was afraid that if she left it too long she might never have the courage to go back at all and God knows, she needed her job.

The office was sandwiched between a bakery and a charity clothes shop. Its entrance was so inconspicuous that you'd hardly notice it was there unless you were looking for it, and nothing on the outside indicated what went on within.

She pressed the buzzer beside the black door and keyed in a series of numbers before climbing a steep flight of stairs to the first floor. She was dismayed to see Oliver Sands coming out of a door on the left and unfortunately, he spotted her. There was no getting away.

Oliver was a fellow relationship counsellor in his mid-forties. He used to run a successful design business and reportedly sold it for a handsome fee. He probably didn't need to work at all so he must have enjoyed it, though he didn't look as if he enjoyed anything much.

Victoria had heard that he was very good with clients but she wouldn't know. He always seemed rather arrogant to her and his presence made her nervous. She tended to blab to fill the silences, which she hated herself for. His speciality was domestic abuse.

'Hello!' he said, raising his eyebrows by way of a smile.

She pushed her hair out of her face. She was panting slightly, having walked so fast to get here, and smiled coolly; she wasn't going to waste a grin on him.

There was a pause while he just stood there and she shuffled from one leg to another. Why did he make her feel so *awkward*? Before she could stop herself her mouth opened and lo and behold, she was gushing like a fountain!

'I thought I was going to be late,' she said breathlessly. 'I shouldn't have worn these.' She raised a foot and pointed stupidly to her size eight black court shoe with the one and a half inch heel.

'I bought them in a sale. I thought they were such a bargain only it turns out they're really uncomfortable. I don't normally wear heels, I mean I wouldn't would I, being so tall? They used to call me Lanky Lou at school, well you can see why!'

Oliver, expressionless, remained silent.

'Any idea which room I'm in?' she said desperately.

He inclined his head to the right. 'Number Three.'

She put her hand on the door knob.

'I'm sorry about your loss.'

She hesitated, tears springing in her eyes. She was going to have to get used to people's sympathy, if you could call it that. He wasn't exactly dripping with compassion.

'Thank you,' she mumbled.

'If there's anything I can do...'

She shook her head and hurried into the room before she could embarrass herself further. In their job you got used to seeing women cry but she wouldn't feel comfortable doing it in front of him.

She had another five minutes before her clients arrived so she checked the coast was clear before scuttling into the galley kitchen to make coffee. The buzzer sounded and her friend Debs, a fellow counsellor, poked her head round the kitchen door and smiled.

'Your clients?' She hovered for a moment before coming in a little further. It was a tight squeeze as there was only really space for one person. Victoria nodded.

'Good luck,' said Debs. A small wiry woman in her mid-thirties, she mentored Victoria through her training and they'd become good friends. Victoria noticed that she was wearing trainers beneath her brown trouser suit. She was very sporty, always popping out for runs at lunchtime.

Debs cocked her head to one side. 'You OK?'

Victoria gave a wry smile. 'Bearing up.'

Debs reached into a cupboard above the sink and pulled out a tin. 'I made some cupcakes. Thought you might need one,' she said, opening the lid and winking at Victoria, whose eyes lit up.

She chose one with yellow icing and a pink rose on top and smiled gratefully.

Debs patted her arm. 'Let's catch up later.'

After gulping the cake down, Victoria took her mug and walked along the corridor to let her clients in. This wasn't going to be easy. She was fairly new to the game and still had a lot to learn. It wouldn't do to collapse in front of them, especially as they were new, too. That was the last thing they'd need.

***

'Welcome.'

Victoria wipes her mouth quickly with the back of her hand to check for any stray crumbs and mentally assesses the couple opposite. They're both in their early thirties – she knows this from the case notes Debs has passed on after doing the initial consultation.

He's a banker; she knows this, too. He's short and sturdy with a handsome, clean-shaven face and close cropped fair hair. He was soaking wet when he walked through the door – there must have been a sudden downpour – and carrying a bicycle helmet. He stripped off his waterproof clothes straight away and put them on a spare chair in the corner.

Underneath, he's wearing a well-cut black suit and pale blue shirt with the top button undone. No tie. He's leaning back in his chair with one leg over another, suggesting confidence, but his arms are folded defensively across his chest and his jaw's working.

Victoria can tell it was his wife's idea to come. It's usually the wives who initiate counselling. Right now she guesses that he'd rather be anywhere but here.

His wife has taken off her navy cagoule and put her open leopard-print umbrella by the radiator under the window to dry. She's short and dumpy, with a pretty round face and highlighted blonde hair cut in a sensible bob. She's wearing jeans, trainers and a tight black polo neck that doesn't flatter her top-heavy figure, and there are long grey hairs on her chest and shoulders that could have belonged to a dog or cat.

Victoria takes down a few details on a clipboard and smiles encouragingly. The woman puts her hands in her lap and glances at her husband, a worried frown on her face.

'It was her idea to come,' the man begins. No surprises there. 'I don't think we need-'

'Oh for God's sake, Don,' the woman interrupts. 'We've been through all this. You agreed.'

Victoria looks at the woman carefully. 'So it was your idea, Kate, to come for counselling?' It helps to repeat things, to slow the pace right down.

Kate nods.

Victoria turns to Don. 'And you're not comfortable with this, am I correct?'

Don is sitting on the edge of his chair as if he's about to leg it at any moment. 'There's nothing wrong with our marriage. I mean, we argue, sure, but no more than other couples.' A nerve twitches in the corner of his eye. 'I don't see what it will achieve anyhow. I've told Kate I'm sorry.'

Kate's eyes narrow and she purses her lips. 'Sorry isn't enough. It'll take a lot more than an apology to save our marriage.'

He turns and glares at his wife. 'I've told you, it meant nothing and it's over. What more do you want? Do I have to prostrate myself at your feet?' He laughs humourlessly. 'This is pointless.'

Victoria raises a hand. They've gone from nought to ninety miles an hour in minutes. 'Can we stop there? I can see that you're both angry.' Which is a bit of an understatement but it's important to exude calm. To her relief, Don sits back in his chair and crosses his arms again.

'I think we should start at the beginning,' Victoria goes on. 'So, Don, you don't accept there's anything wrong with your marriage?'

He shakes his head vigorously and Victoria takes a sip of coffee from the mug beside her on the table. There's also a box of white tissues which she glances at, guessing they might come in handy.

Kate opens her mouth to speak but Victoria raises her hand again. 'Let Don finish.' She likes the men to start because it puts them at their ease; they know, then, there's no question of the two women ganging up and not allowing them their say.

'There's obviously a discrepancy here,' Victoria continues. 'Kate's clearly very upset. Don, why do you think she's unhappy? What's your understanding of the situation?'

Kate narrows her eyes again and Don shuffles uncomfortably, rubbing his neck and craning his chin to one side in a way that looks quite painful.

'She's been miserable for a while,' he begins. 'I think she's depressed. Maybe it's because she's given up her job to look after the children. She gets bored at home. I've told her she should find something part-time but she won't listen.'

Kate clenches her fists, turning her knuckles white. 'It's got nothing to do with me giving up my job. That's just an excuse and you know it. Tell her the truth, Don. Go on, tell her.'

He cranes his chin again and clears his throat. 'It's true, I did have an affair but it's over now. She can't seem to accept it.'

Victoria nods, expressionless, determined not to

show bias. 'So you had an affair. When was this?'

He stares at the wall, refusing to meet her gaze. 'About six months ago. It only lasted a couple of—'

'Liar!' Kate's face is crimson and she looks ready to explode. 'I saw that text you sent. That was way after you said it was over.'

Victoria coughs. This isn't unusual. Couples are often furious when they first came for counselling. So much hurt and resentment has built up and you have to wade through all that before you can begin to make progress.

'Let me ask you both something – separately if you don't mind,' she says firmly. 'Don, do you want your marriage to work?'

He shoots her a disbelieving look. 'Of course.' More craning.

'You seem surprised but you must understand, counselling isn't just about keeping couples together. Sometimes it's about helping couples come to terms with the end of their marriage and helping them work out how best to proceed for the sake of the children.'

Don frowns. 'You mean we might end up divorced after this – no way! I'm not going through all this crap for that to happen.'

'Not at all,' Victoria says steadily. 'Counselling won't make you do anything. What I'm saying is that it's a journey and the outcome isn't always predictable...'

The session lasts fifty minutes and there's only a short break before the next client arrives, a tall thin man called Keith who enters the room looking nervous. It's his first session, too, and he's on his own because his wife has refused to come.

He sits opposite Victoria and fiddles with the zip of

his grey fleece. 'I've never done anything like this before,' he says, refusing to make eye contact. His face is long and pale. 'I don't know what to expect.'

Victoria has just started to take him through the process of counselling when the door bursts open and Keith looks up, dismayed, as a short man in a smart suit hurries in. It's Don.

'Forgot my trousers, sorry,' he explains, grabbing his waterproofs from the back of the chair in the corner. Victoria hadn't noticed that he'd left them there.

He closes the door and Victoria looks at Keith, who has gone even paler than before. He swallows and his Adam's apple bobs up and down.

'Will I...?' he splutters.

She wonders what on earth's the matter. He looks for all the world as if he's been told that his mother's had a sex change operation.

'Will I...' he repeats, squeezing the words out with difficulty, '...have to take off MY clothes?'

The penny drops. 'No,' she says, biting her cheek. 'He's on a bicycle. He took of his waterproofs when he came in – to dry them.'

***

Salome had broken up for the Christmas holidays and had been playing at her friend Lucy's house while Victoria was working. Whenever Lucy's mother, Joanne, saw Victoria her face became a picture of suffering. On a couple of occasions she'd been unable to hold back the tears and Victoria had been obliged to comfort her.

'Cup of tea?' Joanne asked as they strolled into her wide,

light, state-of-the-art kitchen. Salome and Lucy were bent over the oak table, colouring feverishly.

'Better not,' Victoria said hastily, noticing that Joanne was threatening to well up. 'Thanks so much for having her.'

'Any time, honestly. You only have to ask.'

Salome didn't want to leave. 'Can't I stay a bit longer?'

Joanne ruffled the little girl's hair in a melancholy fashion. 'By the way,' she said, glancing at Victoria, 'you're very welcome to spend Christmas with us, you know. But I expect you'll want to be at home for your first one without...' Her voice cracked.

Victoria nodded firmly. 'Home.'

In truth she didn't care what she did for Christmas, it was going to be horrible anyway. But where else would she be, for heaven's sake? Both parents were dead and she wasn't close to either her brother or sister. They hadn't cared for Leo and the feeling was mutual. They'd gone their separate ways a long time ago.

Plus, of course, she had no money to travel. Debs had invited her, which was very kind, but she had a husband and young children and Victoria felt she'd be imposing.

Salome dashed into the sitting room when they got home and turned on the TV. Victoria couldn't hear Ralph, but assumed he was upstairs with his bedroom door shut. His size twelve trainers were in the hall and his black padded body-warmer was on the coat stand.

She wandered into the kitchen and opened the fridge. There wasn't a lot there, apart from four salmon steaks and a cucumber. She used to enjoy cooking, though she was never anything like as accomplished as Leo. Since he'd died, though, anything other than cakes and puddings had become a chore. She'd eat out every night if she could afford to.

She started to peel some potatoes, shoving the peelings in the recycling container beside the sink. An idea had occurred to her but she'd have to do it straight away or she'd lose her nerve. She seemed to be doing so many things now that required vast reserves of courage she'd never known she possessed.

She put cling film over the fishcakes she'd made and stuck them in the fridge, before shutting the kitchen door and grabbing the phone. She needed to act fast, while Salome was engrossed.

The phone rang seven or eight times before a woman picked up. 'Oui,' she said abruptly.

Victoria swallowed. Leo's mother. 'Elsa, is that you?'

'Who is it?' Elsa had lived in Paris for many years and spoke fluent French, but her Austrian accent was still pronounced.

Victoria felt herself shrink and her legs were trembling slightly as she sat down. 'I'm glad you're in.'

She pictured the old woman in her elegant, echoey apartment in central Paris, surrounded by photographs of Leo. Victoria had never been there but she could imagine what it was like: spotless, stuffed with heavy mahogany furniture, silver and glass. Everything highly polished. Silent. She imagined the blue veins pushing through the pallid skin and the thin fingers knotted with arthritis.

'What do you want?' Elsa barked.

They'd never been friends but still, the hostility in her voice made Victoria wince. She straightened her shoulders, determined not to be intimidated.

'How are you?' she asked, fake-brightly.

'As well as can be expected. I'm ninety-five years old.'

'I'm glad.' Victoria was about to do a preamble about the

children, the weather, how she was feeling, but Elsa interrupted.

'You didn't call to inquire about my health. What is it?'

Victoria took a deep breath. Let her have it: 'Leo left no will.'

There was a pause, but only a slight one. 'It doesn't surprise me. He was totally impractical. He cared nothing about money and possessions, only his music.'

Victoria gripped the phone a little tighter. 'He had no money, Elsa,' she said quietly. 'I checked his bank accounts. There's nothing.'

'So?' Elsa's voice was harsh and tinny. 'What did you expect? That he had millions stashed away? Money trickled through Leo's fingers like water. He was desperately extravagant. You knew that, surely?'

Victoria wanted to scream at the old woman for not asking after her grandchildren, wondering what this would mean for them at least. But she bit her tongue. She wouldn't get answers by losing her temper.

'It leaves us in a very awkward position,' she continued steadily. 'Leo was the main breadwinner.'

Elsa snorted. 'Breadwinner? I don't think so. He was a child prodigy, a virtuoso on the violin, a world-famous conductor.'

Victoria sighed. 'I don't mean literally that he won bread, it's an English expression. It means he was the main earner in the household. He supported the children—'

'I know what breadwinner means,' Elsa scoffed. Victoria pictured her dry lips and the papery skin barely thick enough to cover her cheekbones. 'It wasn't his job to support you. It was his job to make beautiful music. That was why he was put on this earth.'

Victoria glanced out of the window at the bamboo swaying gently in the garden. 'He did love us, you know,' she said quietly.

'Don't fool yourself. He loved nothing but his music.'

Tears pricked in the corners of Victoria's eyes but she ploughed on regardless. She had received so many shocks recently that she felt almost inured.

'His wife,' she said, steeling herself. 'In Austria. I wondered if perhaps he'd been supporting her all these years, paying her alimony. Do you think that's where the money's gone?'

Elsa laughed, a thin cold hard laugh that seemed more brutal, more invasive than a slap or punch.

'There was no wife.'

Victoria felt light-headed and put her elbows on the table to steady herself. The old woman was playing games with her, surely?

'What do you mean?'

'This so-called wife was an invention, pure fabrication,' Elsa sang. 'So that he didn't have to marry you – or any of his other women for that matter.'

Another whack that made Victoria reel. She closed her eyes.

'He never wanted to marry,' Elsa went on. 'He wasn't the marrying sort.'

'But he told me—'

'He told you lots of things. Just to keep you quiet.'

Victoria's brain was a jumble of conflicting messages, bouncing around her skull and colliding with each other, making her brain hurt. She put the back of her hand to her cheek, which was on fire.

'But the children,' she said, grasping for something solid. 'He loved his children...'

'Of course,' Elsa said simply. 'In his way.'

Victoria found herself fiddling with her naked ring finger, feeling for something that wasn't there. She thought of all the times over the years that she'd begged him to marry her. It had been her dearest wish.

'I can't, my darling girl,' he'd say with a smile and a shrug. 'I'm so sorry. You know I can never divorce. It's against my faith.'

She knew that, but couldn't he go against the rules just once – for her? He wasn't even devout. He'd been born a Jew; he and his mother had converted after they came to England. He went to Mass at Christmas and Easter but never took Confession. And although he'd asked that the children be raised as Catholics, he never discussed religion with them. It seemed to Victoria that he just went through the motions.

Doubt crept through her and she felt suddenly insubstantial, as if she were made not of flesh, blood and bone but something light and inconsequential.

'Are you telling me the truth?' she whispered.

'Why would I lie to you? I lied for him because he was my son but he's gone now. There's no need.'

Victoria felt suddenly exhausted. As if she could sleep for a hundred years. 'Why have you always hated me?'

Elsa laughed again. 'I don't hate you, I pity you. You thought you were so important in his life but you weren't, none of you were. Leo was passionate about his music but like any red-blooded man he could be distracted. My task was to try to keep him focused, always focused. And mostly I succeeded.'

Victoria had a clear picture of Leo's wife. In her mind's eye, she was stuck at twenty-three or -four, the age when they married. She was of medium height, slim, with long dark hair tied back in a French ponytail. She had a pretty face and big brown eyes but her expression was always too bland for Leo, too sweet and simple. He'd needed someone with a dash of lemon.

Victoria had no idea if this is really what she looked like because Leo hardly spoke of her. Early on in their relationship she'd searched his belongings for old wedding photographs, letters, anything to satisfy her curiosity, but she'd always drawn a blank. Now she knew why.

The image of the wife started to break up and the pieces to scatter but she could reassemble them easily enough if she tried. She'd carried the picture around with her for so long.

'Will you cope – financially I mean?' she asked, meaning to underline her own circumstances and draw some thread of compassion, perhaps.

'Me? I'll be all right. Leo always took care of me. Anyway, I'll be dead soon.'

Victoria felt a twinge; she might loath the woman but she was still a link with Leo, one more strand that would soon be gone. She waited for something, some crumb of comfort, hating herself for it and knowing that she'd be disappointed.

'Au revoir,' said Elsa.

Victoria sat for some time staring into the distance, seeing nothing but grey. The sky, the trees, the grass, even the holly berries on the bush at the end of the garden, all had merged into one murky shade as if she'd gone colour blind.

Did he ever love her or was it all an illusion? She felt as if the very foundations on which she was built were subsiding and no amount of underpinning would ever make them safe again.

'I'm hungry Mum.'

It was Salome, a voice from a previous life. Victoria continued to stare at the greyness.

'What's the matter?' The little girl was anxious and wheedling, wanting reassurance.

Victoria turned and stared at her daughter who was beside

her now, her eyes wide with alarm. She looked peculiar. Those dear features that were once so recognisable – the dark eyes and eyebrows that didn't seem to match her thick fair hair, the dainty, slightly arched nose, the creamy beige skin that hinted, perhaps, at some foreignness.

She looked unfamiliar, now. Victoria thought she'd never met her.

She looked like Leo.

CHAPTER TEN

Monday December 28th

It was a Bank Holiday and Maddy rose late. Wandering into the kitchen where Phoebe was eating a bowl of cereal, she glanced at the pile of unopened letters on the black granite worktop under the window. Bills and more bills. Well, she wasn't going to open them now.

She found herself going over yet again what Blake had said about the business, which had come as a complete surprise. She'd known that things were grim, but everyone was having a tough time. As far as she was concerned they needed to hunker down, work like stink and grin and bear it until the climate improved, whilst all the time looking for new outlets.

He was being negative and cowardly and she couldn't quite believe that he hadn't shared what was on his mind. She supposed she had been preoccupied, but she'd only taken one day off for the funeral.

It wasn't personal, she knew. The others were in the same situation. She just wished that he'd shown her the books before it became a fait accompli.

She was angry – with herself for not twigging sooner but most of all with Blake. She'd never thought of him as a quitter, but that's what he was. Well, she'd show him. She'd secured the Tequila Tease contract for starters and she'd already started on a charm offensive, setting up lunches in the New

Year in a bid to pull in new names. She'd also begun to put out feelers for freelance work. It didn't matter whether she was working for Blake or someone else. In fact she might earn more if she touted herself around. She knew her worth.

At last the bell went and her stomach fluttered. Phoebe pushed her chair back ready to race to the door.

'Stay,' Maddy commanded, pointing to the half eaten cereal. 'Finish your breakfast first.'

Maddy had felt jittery all week about Ralph's visit, but curiously excited, too. She was worried, though, about Phoebe. She'd told her daughter that Ralph was the son of a friend she hadn't seen in a long while. Under no circumstances must she find out the truth.

It was also terrifying to think that Victoria might discover what Ralph was up to. She already hated Maddy and her fury would know no bounds. Maddy pictured the older woman outside her house, wild with rage and still, apparently, clinging pitifully to her delusion that Maddy meant nothing to Leo. Well let her cling; she knew the reality.

Ralph was on the doorstep, clutching a cheap box of chocolates which he thrust in Maddy's hands. He looked on edge again, just as he was when he first came to the office. He towered above her but his shoulders were hunched, cutting inches off his height. She was tempted to give him a hug to put him at his ease, but stopped herself. It wouldn't be appropriate.

She took him into her elegant drawing room that ran almost the entire length of the house. She'd bought a small Christmas tree for Phoebe which she'd put in the far corner beyond the grand piano, beside the French doors that opened out onto steps leading down to the small walled garden.

Normally they'd have a great big tree which filled the room with the smell of pine when the heating was on, but the little one was all she could manage this year. Other than that, the place was bare of decorations.

He seemed to have made an effort to look smart and she noticed that he'd shaved. His handsome face was pale olive and smooth, apart from a red spot on his chin that reminded her he was still a boy, really.

He was wearing a well-ironed blue and white striped shirt, open at the neck and tucked into low-slung jeans, with a navy blue cardigan on top and a thick shiny black gilet. On his feet were well-worn, dirty white trainers.

'Phoebe's finishing breakfast,' Maddy explained, putting the chocolates on the glass coffee table in front of the sofa. One of the white wooden shutters on the bay window that faced the road was jutting into the room and she pushed it back. 'She'll be with us in a minute. Can I get you something to drink?'

He shook his head and perched on the edge of the pale blue sofa, his elbows resting on his lap, while Maddy picked the armchair opposite. She'd chosen to dress casually in jeans also, her favourite Rock & Republic ones, with a round-necked pale pink cashmere jumper. She was wearing no jewellery, apart from little round diamond studs in her ears, and her blonde hair was tied back in a ponytail.

She'd put on minimal make-up; she wouldn't be seen dead without any. Only face powder, a touch of blusher, a dab of blue-grey eye shadow on her lids and beneath her eyes and a slick of pink lipstick. She wasn't wearing shoes – just thick grey cashmere socks. She felt pretty.

'How was Christmas?' she asked politely, fishing around for something to break the ice.

'Not great,' Ralph admitted. 'Yours?'

'The same.'

She caught his eye and they laughed grimly.

'Mum's not good,' he went on. 'I think she's depressed.'

'I'm not surprised,' Maddy replied, crossing her legs. 'Grief's a weird thing. It hits you like a sledgehammer at unexpected moments. I'm pretty low myself.'

'Me too.' He sat back and ran a hand through his hair. She caught the outline of his jaw, the curve of his slightly aquiline nose, the smooth, full bottom lip.

'How's your work going?' she said quickly. 'You've got exams coming up?'

He frowned. 'A-levels. It's been hard to concentrate these past few weeks.'

'Mummy?'

Maddy turned. Phoebe was standing shyly in the doorway, one foot on top of another, swaying from side to side. She looked very cute in a baby blue cardigan, pink flippy skirt, black leggings and bare feet. Her thick blonde hair was tied back in bunches.

Maddy felt a swell of maternal pride. 'Come here.' She opened her arms and the little girl ran into them, plonking herself on her mother's lap and staring curiously at the visitor who smiled broadly back. He was obviously good with children and soon he and Phoebe were playing Snakes and Ladders on the rug while Maddy prepared lunch.

They sat, the three of them, round the black lacquered kitchen table and picked at her fish pie. No one seemed that hungry. She'd opened a bottle of good white wine and poured glasses for herself and Ralph.

Phoebe kept asking him questions: 'Do you like school?'; 'Do you have brothers or sisters?'; 'Where do you live?' If he found her irritating, it didn't show.

Once or twice Maddy's heart missed a beat when it seemed

he might be sailing too close to the wind.

'My Dad died,' he said in answer to yet another enquiry.

Phoebe's bottom lip quivered. 'So did mine. He's gone to heaven now.'

Maddy eyed Ralph but she needn't have worried.

'It's sad, isn't it?' he said. 'But at least we know our dads are at peace now. What's your favourite lesson at school?'

Maddy was at the head of the table with Ralph on her left and Phoebe opposite him. She sat back, took another sip of wine and surveyed them both for a moment in profile. There was a resemblance, she thought, but only a small one. After all, Phoebe was so blonde and he was dark. It was something to do with the lower halves of their faces, she decided; the narrow gap between nose and mouth and the way their upper lips protruded very slightly when their mouths were shut. In truth, though, Phoebe was far more like Victoria's daughter. They could be twins.

After lunch they went for a walk along the river by Hammersmith Bridge. It was a gloomy day, drizzling slightly, but Maddy felt strangely comfortable strolling beside Ralph while Phoebe raced ahead on her silver scooter.

'How did you and Leo meet?' he asked, hungry for facts.

She found herself opening up. What was the harm? He deserved some answers. He'd never had any from his mother.

'At my tennis club,' she said, smiling a little at the memory. 'I was waiting in the cafe for my partner to turn up. Leo had just finished a match and come out of the shower.'

'Tennis?' Ralph said incredulously.

Maddy raised her eyebrows. 'Yes. We used to play a lot.'

He fell silent.

'We started chatting, mostly about the game,' she went on. 'My partner was really late so we had a good half hour together.

In the end he asked if I'd like to go for a drink one evening. It seemed quite natural as we'd got on so well and things went from there.'

Ralph rubbed his chin. 'When did you find out he was married – or with my mum? That he had kids?'

He was trying to be strong but really he just sounded hurt.

Maddy swallowed. This must be so hard for him. 'Pretty soon,' she admitted. 'I think he told me on our second or third date.'

'Didn't it bother you?' Ralph's pace had quickened and he was staring straight ahead.

'Not really.' She might as well be truthful.

'Why not?'

She shrugged. 'I guess I didn't really think of the other woman – Victoria. As long as I didn't have to meet her she didn't seem real.'

She looked at him wryly. 'I've always had a wild streak, been a bit of a risk-taker. I'm not particularly proud of it. It wasn't until we began to get serious, until we fell in love, that I wished things were less complicated. Initially I thought we were just having a fling.'

Ralph frowned. He was concentrating very hard. 'But didn't you feel guilty knowing there was another family involved?'

Maddy nodded. 'A bit. But you see, Leo told me it was over with him and your mother and had been for years. He said he was only staying with her because of you and Salome.'

Ralph stopped and stared. 'And you believed him? Isn't that what all married men say to their mistresses?'

Her heart fluttered. That word – mistress. She didn't like it. What did he, a mere seventeen-year-old, know about such things?

'Why shouldn't I believe him?' she said coldly. 'We had a child together. I knew his heart was with me.'

Ralph shook his head. 'I don't believe it was over with Mum. It suited him to have different homes, different families.'

Maddy felt hot all over. She should have known that things would get tricky.

Phoebe had put down her scooter a little way ahead and was trying to climb a tree.

'What about the other one?' said Ralph. 'That young girl at the funeral. The one who was crying outside. You know he was having an affair with her as well?'

The blood drained from Maddy's face. She'd heard it from Victoria, of course, but at a time when she was upset and vengeful. Hearing it from him, too, gave it more credence.

She shook herself mentally. 'I don't know about that. Maybe they did have an affair. I've no idea. All I know is that Leo and I loved one another deeply.'

She was keen to change the subject and get on to less contentious ground. 'How are things between you and your mum?' she asked, remembering how angry he'd been in the Italian pizza place.

He paused. 'Pretty bad. All she seems to care about is my exams. That's her sole focus. She's desperate for me to go to university but I don't even know if I want to. We're not getting on at all.'

Maddy thought it must be tough for both of them, being at loggerheads on top of everything else they were going through. They should be supporting each other. And she knew how furious Victoria could be, having experienced it herself. She felt sorry for Ralph, who must feel so alone and confused.

Suddenly he stopped, turned and seized both her arms clumsily, gazing into her eyes with a shy intensity. She wanted to pull away but couldn't; she was caught, a lobster in a pot.

'I don't blame my father for falling in love with you,' he said quietly. 'But I'm angry that he tried to hide it from me. And most of all I'm angry Mum tried to keep up this pretence that everything was all right.'

Maddy didn't know what to say.

He was still staring at her, talking to her with his eyes, and the hairs on the back of her neck stood on end. She turned away and focused on Phoebe, who was sitting on the lowest branch of a tree, swinging her legs and looking pleased with herself.

'We should be getting back,' she said, half to Ralph, half to herself.

She pulled up the collar of her coat and he jogged towards Phoebe, who was grinning and waving, loving the attention. Maddy watched as he lifted her down gently from the tree making sure she didn't scrape herself, just as Leo would have done. He looked back and smiled but she pretended not to see.

Phoebe wanted to walk home in the middle, between them, and grabbed their hands. They went a couple of paces before Maddy pulled away and strode ahead.

'Wait Mummy!' The little girl had to run to catch up.

When they reached the house they hovered awkwardly outside the gate and Phoebe started tugging on her mother's sleeve. 'Can he come inside? Please?'

She started trying to drag Ralph up the front path.

'Stop!' Maddy shouted, her voice shrill and panicky.

Phoebe froze.

'I'm sorry but Ralph needs to go now,' Maddy said more

gently, stroking Phoebe's hair, finding its softness comforting. 'He has things to do, don't you Ralph?' It was more of a statement than a question.

She glanced at him and noticed that his shoulders were hunched and he was fiddling with the zip of his gilet. He'd turned back into a gauche schoolboy which made things easier, somehow.

'Don't worry,' he said, giving Phoebe a high five. 'I'll come and see you again soon.'

The little girl grinned. 'Will you? When?'

'It's up to your mum.' He looked hopefully at Maddy.

She hesitated, knowing what she ought to say, but somehow the words tumbled out before she could catch hold of them.

'Yes, yes you can.'

***

'Oh my God.' Tracy clutched her stomach and raced off to the ladies' again.

Rick frowned. 'D'you think she's all right?

'Yeah,' said Cat. 'She's got the runs, that's all.'

'But she's had them for days.'

They'd been in the pub all evening which was more crowded than usual, being a bank holiday. Gervaise's audition for the New York Jew part hadn't gone well so Cat had invited him along to cheer him up. He'd forgotten his lines and, when prompted, slipped into Lancashire, he thought, or was it Yorkshire? He couldn't remember. The casting director hadn't been encouraging.

'Anything else on the horizon?' Cat asked, switching the subject from Tracy's bowels.

Gervaise, who was in his stripy jumper as usual, took a

swig of beer. 'We-ell. My agent's asked me to audition for this part, but I'm not sure.'

Cat stared. It was unlike him to turn anything down. 'What is it? What's the role?'

He frowned. 'It's a made-for-TV drama. Great cast and director.'

Rick leaned forward, his long hair flopping over his face. He was wearing a tight black T-shirt with a picture of Ozzy Osbourne on it, and there was a tattoo on his left arm that said Rock Rules. 'So what's the problem?'

Gervaise huddled over the table so no one else could hear. 'It's set in nineteenth century France,' he whispered. 'I'd be this gay boy, see.'

Cat giggled. 'That's all right, you can do gay.'

'I'm not worried about the kissing bit, it'd be a challenge, good experience.' He gulped his beer.

'Well come on, spit it out man.' Rick was getting impatient. 'What's the issue here?'

Gervaise grimaced. 'It's the fact I'd have to do the can-can. I don't know if I could cope with that.'

Rick and Cat roared with laughter while Gervaise pursed his lips.

'Why not?' Rick jeered. 'Look, it's easy!' He eased his sizeable bulk out of the chair and did a demonstration, complete with singing – da da, dada dada, da da – much to the amusement of the other customers.

Tracy returned from the ladies looking sheepish and smelling of soap. She sat down beside Cat on the bench and the men got up to play darts next door.

'Bad?' Cat asked.

Tracy nodded.

'Why don't you take something to stop it?'

141

Tracy leaned closer. 'It's these Mexican diet pills. I got them from someone at work.'

'Stupid girl,' tutted Cat. 'You don't need to lose weight. Stop taking them.'

Tracy sipped her Bacardi and Diet Coke. 'Not until I've finished the bottle. They're expensive.'

'How many have you got left? I don't think I can stand it.'

'Six weeks' worth.'

Cat gasped. 'You'll be a skeleton by then. And you don't even know what's in them.'

'I don't care. So long as they make me thin.'

Tracy drained her glass and glanced at Cat's lager, which was almost untouched. 'What's the matter? Why aren't you drinking?'

Cat smiled weakly. 'To be honest I don't feel great. I might go home soon.'

Tracy frowned, as if she were pondering something. 'You haven't felt good for ages.'

'It's Leo. I can't stop thinking about him.'

'It's not like you not to drink,' Tracy persisted. 'And I've noticed you haven't been smoking much either. You keep lighting them and stubbing them out.'

'Fuck,' said Cat.

There was a pause while Tracy took a deep breath and drew herself up. 'When was your last period?'

'It's late.'

'How late?'

'A month.'

'A *month*?'

'I'm upset about Leo,' Cat said desperately. 'It gets mucked up when you're upset.'

'Jesus, Cat,' Tracy said seriously. 'You might be pregnant.

You've got to take a test.'

Cat put her head in her hands. 'I can't be. I mean, I suppose I could but—'

Tracy pulled on one of her yellow plaits, coiling it round her finger. She'd switched into practical mode. 'When did you and Leo last have sex?'

Cat thought back. 'There was that time he took me to the opening of the Aztec exhibition at the British Museum and I stayed at his flat afterwards.'

Tracy stared at her glass. 'That was October, wasn't it? But you're on the Pill. I know you are.'

'Yeah, but I might have forgotten to take it a few times.'

Tracy suddenly pushed herself up. 'I need another drink.'

Cat watched her shove her way to the bar, ignoring the dirty looks, and return with a large glass of white wine before plonking down again. 'You'll have to get a test tomorrow.'

Cat nodded miserably.

Tracy patted her arm. 'Don't worry, it'll be all right.' She sounded less than convinced.

Cat swallowed. The thought of being pregnant terrified her. She'd been ignoring the symptoms for weeks, trying to convince herself it was grief that was making her feel so tired and sick. Now Tracy had uttered the dreaded word, it felt frighteningly real.

She clenched her fists, suddenly furious, and put her face up close to Tracy's. 'Don't tell anyone, OK? Not a soul.'

'Course I won't.' Tracy crossed her arms in that headmistressy way of hers that Cat found both irritating and endearing. 'But don't think you can ignore this. It won't just go away y'know.'

The men reappeared. 'Fancy a game?' Gervaise nodded at Cat who shook her head.

They drained their glasses, though Tracy's was already

empty. Cat had never seen a massive glass of wine disappear so fast.

'How about a nightcap?' asked Rick, putting on his black leather jacket, which was covered in studs, and grinning at Gervaise. 'I've got a bottle of fine Irish whiskey tucked away at home.'

Gervaise picked up his denim jacket and wrapped his long yellow scarf around his neck several times. 'How can I resist an offer like that? Coming, Cat?'

She rose. 'I'm going to head back. I'm knackered.'

'Will I walk you home, then?'

'No.'

He looked disappointed.

'Look,' said Cat, 'I've told you before, I can walk myself home.'

Tracy touched her arm. 'Come on, he's only being nice.'

Gervaise shrugged but he was obviously hurt; he was missing a few layers of skin, that boy. Cat grabbed her parka and left the three of them still standing in the warm pub, Tracy's arm linked in Rick's.

'What's got into her?' she heard Rick mutter.

She imagined Tracy saying something conciliatory. She wouldn't spill the beans, for sure. She was dead loyal like that. She'd probably say Cat had PMS or something. Ironic.

If only Cat could talk to Mum. If only she could talk to Leo.

She gritted her teeth as she approached the door of her flat and stared at her boots, aware of Ali waving and grinning through the shop window and determined not to catch his eye. The last thing she needed was for him to come out, laughing and cracking stupid jokes. She might even thump him.

CHAPTER ELEVEN

Tuesday December 29th

She opened her eyes and blinked in the early morning half-light, a feeling of dread washing over her. *I'm pregnant.* It didn't seem real. She squeezed her eyes shut again, hoping when she repeated the exercise that things would be different. But they weren't.

She did the test in the bathroom with Tracy, who had a handy pregnancy kit stored away for emergencies. She stood there gibbering inanely until the result came through, clear as day.

'Bleedin' heck, Cat,' she said, her face draining of colour. 'You've only gone and got yourself up the duff.'

Cat had to sit on the end of her bed, fear and confusion mixing with waves of nausea.

'What are you going to do?' Tracy whispered.

Cat shook her head.

'You can't have it,' Tracy said, aghast. 'I mean, where would we put it?' She glanced round the room, which was crammed with stuff: books, furniture, clothes strewn across the floor. Cat wasn't exactly tidy.

'I suppose you could fit a cot under the window,' Tracy said doubtfully. 'You'd have to get rid of the mice, though.' She perked up a bit.

'I'm not putting a cot under the window.'

Tracy shrugged. 'Just a thought.'

Cat started chewing the back of her hand.

'Look,' Tracy said, gently pushing the hand away, 'it'll be all right. I mean, my mum's good with babies. Maybe she'll have it for a couple of days when you're at the bookshop. She's good at knitting, too.' She brightened. 'She makes lovely bootees for the church bazaar.'

Cat glared. 'I don't want any bootees.' Tears were springing in her eyes which she wiped away angrily.

'You'll have to decide what to do,' Tracy urged. 'You need to see the doctor. I'll come with you now if you want.'

'No. I'll make an appointment.'

'Today,' Tracy said firmly.

Cat jumped up. 'I have to check on Mum. I'll call the surgery later.'

Tracy was doubtful but she was keen to get back to Rick, who was ensconced in her bed. They were both on holiday still and they'd be at it like rabbits soon, Cat thought gloomily.

'Promise me you will,' Tracy said sternly as Cat started to get dressed.

'I promise.'

* * *

She let herself in as usual and was hit by a blast of cold air. It was still only 10 a.m. and the windows were wide open and the curtains had gone. The rug in front of the electric fire was rolled up in the corner, furniture had been moved and there was a smell of polish and disinfectant.

'Mum?' she called, dismayed. 'Mu-um?'

Her mother emerged from the kitchen with a frown on her face.

'Take off those boots please, Catherine. Can't you see I'm

146

trying to clean the place up?'

Cat stared. Her mother's hair had turned vibrant red, so dazzling that it was almost fluorescent. It made a statement, all right, but quite what it was trying to say was another matter.

She was wearing a yellow apron over her thin cardigan, which was rolled up at the sleeves. Her eyes were shining too brightly and her cheeks were rosy from exertion.

'Boots,' her mother commanded.

Cat bent down to take off her Doctor Martens, anxiety creeping through her. 'What's brought this on?' she asked nervously.

'The place is a tip,' her mother snapped. 'Filthy. It needs a proper spring clean.'

'But it's not spring.'

Cat's mother shot her a look before disappearing into the kitchen again and returning with a bucket of hot soapy water and a mop.

'I've done it once,' she said, stopping to wipe her brow. 'But it needs another going over.'

Cat finished taking off her boots and stared at the fluorescent locks again. 'What did you do to your hair?'

Her mother patted the back of her head in a self-satisfied way. 'I bought some special shampoo from the chemist.' A look of confusion flitted across her features. 'Yes, I'm sure I did.'

Cat wandered into the kitchen to put the food away and when she returned, the older woman was standing on a chair dusting the top of the display cabinet. It was normally laden with objects – china vases, ugly bowls, photographs in frames – which she'd put on the table.

'Be careful, Mum,' she said. 'That doesn't look very stable.'

Her mother brushed a strand of bright red hair out of her eyes with the back of her hand, leaving a dirty streak across her cheek.

'You can't expect me to live in this mess,' she said crossly, rubbing furiously at something on the shelf.

'Let me do it.' Cat helped her mother down. 'You go and make us a cup of tea.'

The drink seemed to do the trick. At last the older woman settled in her usual spot in front of the telly, and Cat put everything back in its place and closed the windows. Unfortunately her mother had put fabric conditioner rather than powder in the washing machine and the curtains would have to be done again.

'Didn't you notice what you were using?' Cat asked when she discovered the mistake.

Her mother looked up from the TV and frowned. 'But I always put that in,' she said, pointing to the large pink bottle of liquid that Cat was holding.

'Yes, but you need powder, too.'

'Of course. Powder and pink liquid. I know that.'

Cat sat for a moment beside her mother, fiddling with the sleeve of her sweatshirt.

'There's something I need to tell you,' she said at last. 'I need your advice.'

Her mother laughed at the TV.

'You see,' said Cat, swallowing. 'I've got this problem—'

'Look at this, Catherine,' said the older woman excitedly. 'That man's pretending he can't speak English but really he understands everything.'

'I'm in such a fix,' Cat said desperately. 'I don't know what to do.'

Her mother patted the empty space beside her without

removing her eyes from the screen. 'Sit down here. You'll enjoy it.'

Cat sighed and rose slowly. Her body felt heavy and her eyes were stinging. 'I'll see you tomorrow,' she said, squeezing her mother's arm. 'And don't you go climbing on any more chairs, all right?'

'Now why would I do a silly thing like that, dear?' said the older woman, turning up the volume.

***

Cat hovered on the pavement outside for quite some time, unsure what to do. She didn't fancy going home and facing Tracy again. She'd only nag her about the GP, but Cat didn't want to ring. Not yet, anyway.

She found herself heading towards the tube and crossing through the barrier, stopping for a moment to think which direction to choose. For some reason she picked west, and jumped on the train that would take her to Waterloo and then the overground to Wimbledon.

She didn't know what she was going there for or what she hoped to achieve. But her body seemed to be propelling her up the hill towards Victoria's house for the second time in two weeks.

What to do? Of course she couldn't keep it. The last thing she needed right now was a baby.

But then...she'd just lost Leo. Did she have it in her to destroy the part of him that was growing inside her at this very moment, only tiny now, but getting bigger every day? Wouldn't that destroy her, too?

She reached the end of the older woman's road and realised that she was shaking. It was no good. What had she been thinking of? There was no point talking to *her*. What could she possibly say that would make things any better?

She hovered for a few moments, confused and disorientated. Her brain seemed to be sending out conflicting messages to her limbs, which were poised to obey but couldn't decipher the instructions.

She managed a step down the tree-lined street before stopping dead, then turning swiftly back in the direction of the shops. At least there, among the smart clothes boutiques and posh delis, she could mingle unnoticed. A faceless nobody in the crowd, with no past that anyone was interested in and no discernible future.

***

Victoria didn't like to think about the future, either. She was just relieved that Salome had been invited to a friend's house again. She was finding it incredibly difficult to act normal and keep going but she knew she must. Really all she wanted was to curl up in a darkened room.

No wife...no wife. The words had been crashing around her brain leaving her with a constant headache. She needed to talk to someone about this, probably Debs. It was too big for her to handle alone. But it was the wrong time between Christmas and New Year. Debs was having a break with her family.

She set off across Wimbledon Common towards the windmill in her thick coat and wellies. She walked very fast, almost unaware of her surroundings, conscious only of the occasional dog in her path, the odd shout of other ramblers, the drizzling damp settling on her hair and face.

She had a vague feeling that if she were to wear herself out physically she'd be better able to sleep, because for the past few days it had almost entirely eluded her. She'd spent the nights listening to the radio, wandering around the house, staring at the TV and taking nothing in. She was desperate for rest; she'd go mad otherwise.

At last, when she must have been gone a couple of hours, she strolled along the High Street thinking she might buy a loaf of bread and a sticky bun for lunch. It was after 3p.m. and she was feeling light-headed.

Across the road from the deli she spotted a small, slight young woman staring in the window of a clothes shop. No one else appeared curious, but Victoria's interest was roused immediately. The young woman seemed to be lingering and there was something pitiful about her, as if she were only pretending to be absorbed by the shop's display, as if she had other matters entirely on her mind.

It took a moment to be certain, then she called out Cat's name. The young woman turned, a haunted look on her face. It seemed as if she might bolt like a wild animal, but Victoria jogged on long legs across the road and was soon alongside smiling carefully, attempting to calm, to reassure: 'What brings you here?'

Cat's eyes were wide and her face was ashen. Victoria wondered what on earth had happened. Had someone else died? She gestured to the cafe a few doors up, anxious to detain. 'I was going to get something to eat. Can I buy you a coffee?'

To Victoria's relief the young woman allowed herself to be guided meekly into the shop, where they sat in a corner as far from the door as possible. Sensing that Cat wouldn't feel like consuming anything, Victoria ordered cappuccinos, sandwiches and some apple tart to share. She shouldn't be going to cafes really, she hadn't the money, but Cat looked as if she could do with nourishment and they needed somewhere to talk.

'How was your Christmas?' Victoria asked, spooning froth off the top of her drink and putting it in her mouth. She noticed that Cat's hands were trembling and wasn't surprised when she failed to answer the question. It was only supposed to break the ice anyway.

She seemed unable to form words and looked confused, as if she'd walked into the wrong exam room and been handed a paper on Applied Mathematics instead of English Literature.

When she finally spoke, the words came out in a messy jumble. 'I tried to tell Mum but she doesn't understand...it's Leo's...I did a test...'

Victoria sat very still, attempting to make sense of it all. She felt as if Cat were speaking a foreign language, expecting her to understand when she'd never learned the vocabulary.

Finally the younger woman managed to blurt it out: 'I'm pregnant.'

There was silence for a moment while both women waited for a clap of thunder, or for the building to cave in on them. But nothing happened.

'I don't know what to do,' Cat said, gnawing the back of her hand. 'I wish Mum could help. I don't want a baby but I don't know if I can get rid of it either.'

Victoria took a few deep breaths, her hunger gone. She was aware on some level that she ought to be furious and ranting, sickened by the other woman's treachery. Crazy with rage and weeping, as she had been all those years ago when she'd found out about Maddy's pregnancy.

Then, she'd wanted to slash Maddy's throat and cut off Leo's balls, until he'd somehow managed to convince her that the baby was just a terrible mistake. But Cat was small and alone; she had no father, Leo was dead and she couldn't even turn to her own mother.

Victoria drew herself up. 'Look,' she said, attempting to hide the shake in her voice and force herself into practical counsellor mode, 'you do have a choice, you know. You can keep the baby, if that's what you want, or have a termination. It's your call. No one can make that decision for you. But I can help with numbers if you like, find people for you to talk to who are very experienced. They're used to dealing with this sort of situation, they'll be able to guide you through.'

Cat's shoulders seemed to relax a little but her brow was still a mass of wrinkles. Victoria could almost see the fug of conflicting emotions clogging her tired brain. It was an agonising decision for any young woman, and even worse given that Leo, who should have been here to assist, had just died. She found herself trying to imagine how she'd feel if her own daughter were in this situation. It didn't bear thinking about.

'This must be the last thing you need,' she heard Cat whisper.

Victoria was strangely touched. It was surprising that she could think of anyone other than herself right now. 'Don't worry about me,' she found herself saying. 'I'm getting used to body-blows.'

She thought about Leo, safe in his urn at the back of a cupboard. She hadn't been able to face scattering his ashes; she'd thought that maybe she'd wait and ask for hers to be mingled with his when the time came. Fury welled up, taking her by surprise. She wouldn't want that now. No way.

'I've got news, too,' she said. The barriers had disintegrated and surely she deserved to unburden herself a little as well?

Cat's eyes widened. 'What news?'

Victoria summarised the conversation with Elsa. 'You may as well know,' she said at last.

'He never mentioned a wife in Austria to me,' Cat replied. 'But I s'pose I never asked. Are you sure she was telling the truth? Elsa, I mean. She sounds like a cow. Why would you trust her?'

Victoria shrugged. 'I have no reason to but something tells me that on this occasion, she was being truthful. It makes such sense, you see.' She rubbed her eyes. 'I realise, looking back, that there never was any evidence of a wife; no pictures, letters, nothing. I always thought it was strange but, well, I believed him.' She shook her head. 'Fool that I was.'

She glanced at Cat. 'Are you sure he never mentioned the Austrian woman?'

'Never. But why would he lie to you?'

'So he didn't have to marry me?' Victoria imagined that she'd never be able to say it out loud but now she had, she realised that it hadn't been so very hard.

'It's funny, you know,' she added, 'but despite everything, I still love him. I can't help it. It makes no sense, does it?' She frowned. 'I can't believe I'm saying all this to you.'

Cat gave a weak smile. 'I guess there aren't any rules, not now Leo's gone. It's up to us to make them. I don't suppose there's a book on the subject,' she added wryly.

Her thin little shoulders were hunched in on her, making her body seem concave. And yet there was something big about her, bigger than her physical self. Victoria realised that she liked her. She shivered, sensing a thread of connection running through them. Whatever else was true, here, in front of her, was a young woman in a lot of distress.

They finished their sandwiches in virtual silence. It gave Victoria a strange sort of pleasure to see the girl eat, and drink her milky coffee. It was the mother in her. Cat wouldn't touch the apple tart though so Victoria polished it off.

At last she asked for the bill. 'You do need to see your GP.'

Cat nodded.

'But first,' said Victoria, handing her bank card to the waitress, 'I'll go and look up those phone numbers.'

The two women rose slowly, reluctant to leave the warmth of the cafe and head out into the cold late-afternoon. They hovered for a few moments on the pavement and Victoria was relieved to see that a little colour had returned to Cat's cheeks, making her appear less other worldly. She'd been of some use to the girl, then, even in their heightened emotional states.

'Go home,' she said, 'and have a warm bath. You looked half frozen to death when I bumped into you. If you want to talk some more you know where I am, OK?'

Cat smiled properly for the first time that day. 'OK.'

CHAPTER TWELVE

Wednesday December 30th

There was an air of fretfulness in the office which Maddy could feel the moment she arrived. Even Jules, the receptionist, seemed subdued. Normally her wild afro hair was loose around her face but today she'd tamed and clamped it into two fat neat plaits and she wasn't wearing any of her usual bling.

She looked up briefly at Maddy. 'Good Christmas?' But she didn't even wait for a reply before turning back to the computer.

Lola was on her way up to the third floor, cup of coffee in hand, when Maddy reached the landing. She knew Lola and her husband had recently bought a new house and that she'd be worrying about having her hours cut.

Lola smiled thinly. Her skin looked dry and there were red stains around her nose and mouth, as if she had a cold.

Blake was in a meeting with his accountant and his door was shut. Maddy took off her coat, sat down and stretched her arms above her head. Great welcome, she thought grimly. It seemed like most of the world was off work between Christmas and New Year, but they'd all shown willing by coming in today. She surveyed the walls of her office, which were grubbier than she remembered, and felt resentful. She should have stayed away.

She gave herself a mental shake and checked her desk diary, aware that she had a meeting with the Tequila Tease people at 3 p.m. They were hard at it, too. She'd kept up to date with emails on her BlackBerry during the short break and decided to use the next couple of hours to make a few exploratory phone calls about freelance work. It was a bit naughty but her loyalty to Blake had been severely tested and she had to look after Number One.

'Hi Mads! What can I do for you?'

She'd known Hazel, from Freewheel Expo, for years. They worked at DPP Events together for a time.

'I'm looking for freelance work,' Maddy said, going on to explain about her three days a week with Blake. She made out it was her choice and that she wanted to work from home and see more of Phoebe. But something in Hazel's voice told Maddy that she didn't believe a word. She knew how bad it was out there and was probably worried about her own job.

'Sorry, Mads,' she said regretfully. 'There's really nothing doing at the moment. There's not enough work for our own guys, y'know.'

Maddy leafed through her address book and rang half a dozen other contacts. It didn't feel good, touting herself around like this. She was used to hustling for business but always from the vantage point of having the weight of the company behind her. She'd never been on her own.

It was the same story everywhere: cut-backs, cancelled events, redundancies, companies struggling. She put down the phone and took several deep breaths. OK, so finding work wasn't going to be as easy as she imagined, but that didn't mean there wasn't any. She'd just have to try harder, get in touch with people she didn't know, think laterally, act smart.

She stared out of her window at the street below and the strangers bustling by in warm coats and hats, keen to get in from the cold. It was extraordinary to think that only a few weeks ago she'd been up a mountain skiing with Leo.

She was so glad they'd gone. But she could do with the money now that she was contemplating a far smaller pay cheque next month. She supposed that she'd have to economise, though the very word made her shudder. She hadn't watched what she'd spent for years, hadn't needed to. And where would she begin anyway?

She had to pay the mortgage, Jess the nanny and Phoebe's school fees; they were givens. Plus heating, lighting and so on. She could give up her gym membership and buy fewer clothes. After all, she had so many. And she could cancel her monthly membership with the beauty salon, forgoing the regular massage and facial.

She logged onto her bank account and checked her statement. There were other standing orders she could cancel, too, like her membership to various museums, her charitable donations (she felt bad about that, but charity begins at home), her Sky membership.

She worked all through her lunch break, making phone calls, leaving messages on answerphones and writing letters. By the end, she felt a certain sense of achievement. She'd be saving herself several hundreds a month and she'd get to see more of Phoebe into the bargain. Maybe working three days a week – for the time being at least – wouldn't be so bad after all.

Her stomach rumbled and she realised that she hadn't had lunch. She'd grab a sandwich on her way to meet the Tequila Tease people then head for home. Her phone rang just as she was putting on her coat. Damn.

'Maddy? It's Jules. Blake wants to see everyone in the conference room now.'

'But I've got a meeting-'

'You'll have to cancel. He says it's important.'

Maddy frowned. 'OK.'

She took off her coat again, made the call and walked slowly downstairs, surprised to feel her heart fluttering. It was all right, she told herself, bit odd but these were strange times. Maybe he'd lost another contract and wanted to give everyone a bollocking for not getting enough work in.

Jed, Steph and Ben were in a huddle around the reception desk. They looked up when they saw Maddy but none of them spoke. Jules, who wasn't here, appeared from the conference room at the back of the office and grabbed her chair before disappearing again.

'What's all this about?' Maddy whispered, but there was no time for a reply.

'Come this way please,' Jules said in her most efficient voice. 'Blake's ready for you now.'

***

Maddy didn't like the way Blake was perched on the very edge of the table, the dark-suited accountant hovering beside him like a bad conscience. She was also dismayed to see the post boy and various freelance set and lighting designers, sound people, carpenters, choreographers, the ones they used regularly. There must have been forty people crammed into the smallish, low-ceilinged room which was tacked on the main building years ago.

There was nowhere to sit so she stood at the back, resting against the plain white wall. There were no pictures or furniture, save for the white table at the front and six metal chairs. They didn't use the room often and for some reason, it had never been done up and made welcoming; they usually took clients out.

Maddy felt suddenly hot and undid another button on her white shirt. She was furious that Blake hadn't told her about this beforehand. They were supposed to be *friends*.

A smartly dressed woman in a navy trouser suit with a neat dark bob and fake pearls entered the room and took her place beside Blake. Maddy recognised her as the freelance human resources consultant they brought in from time to time, and felt sick. The last time they'd met was when she and Blake needed advice on how to get rid of a particularly useless employee. The woman was very helpful, Maddy remembered. Ruthless.

Her palms felt sweaty and she glanced round and noticed that everyone was standing very still, no one speaking a word. The woman in the suit turned and whispered something to Blake, who nodded.

She walked over to the door and closed it, before resuming her place beside him. She looked serious but the corners of her thin, pale pink mouth turned up ever so slightly in what Maddy decided was a mocking fashion. She couldn't bear the fact that this woman knew something she didn't.

At last Blake rose and Maddy noticed that his face was drawn and his hands were trembling.

'Thank you all for coming,' he began, looking as if he were about to burst into tears.

There was a cough from the other side of the room but otherwise everyone remained silent.

'I'm afraid I've got some very bad news,' he said falteringly. 'As you know, the company has been in serious trouble for quite some time and I've had to cut people's hours. In the last few weeks we've lost several valuable contracts which have tipped us over the edge. Inland Revenue has now made the decision to pull the plug. This morning I received a date for a bankruptcy hearing.'

There was a collective gasp of disbelief followed by a series of groans. One or two people covered their faces with their hands.

'I knew it,' muttered someone to Maddy's left. 'Christ,' came another voice. 'What the hell does this mean?'

Blake remained glued to the spot, his hands hanging limply at his sides. When the hubbub showed no signs of quietening, the accountant in the dark suit held up his flattened palms.

'Please let Blake finish. We're going to explain everything.' He was raising his voice so that everyone could hear.

The room hushed again and Blake cleared his throat. 'Obviously I'm devastated, not just for me, for the company that I founded and love, but also for all of you who have put so much in over the years.'

He wiped his eyes with the back of his sleeve. He could have been removing the sweat but it was more likely tears, and Maddy felt curiously indifferent. She was thinking – bastard, how could you do this? The Revenue must have been snapping at his heels for months. He must have thousands, maybe hundreds of thousands of unpaid tax but he'd never told her that things were quite this bad. And she thought they shared pretty much everything.

'What are the chances that you'll be able to sort things out at the bankruptcy hearing and save the company?' It was Ben speaking. Good question. Maddy felt a shiver of hope.

'None at all,' said Blake, shaking his head. 'I won't lie to you. There's no way we can pay the debts in full. I'm afraid that bankruptcy is inevitable.'

Any semblance of formality dissolved and people started shouting questions from all corners.

'What does this mean for our jobs?' said one. It was Lola, who was on the verge of tears.

The human resources woman stepped forward. 'I'm here to answer all your questions,' she said calmly. 'I can give you all the advice you need.'

'But what does it mean – are we out of our jobs?' Lola persisted. She wanted the truth now, not in a half an hour or this afternoon or tomorrow morning.

The human resources woman stood up very straight, maddeningly serene. Well, she would be. It wasn't her facing disaster. She'd be profiting from their misfortune.

'It means,' she said, 'that if – and nothing's set in concrete until after the hearing next Wednesday – but if the company is declared bankrupt, as it most likely will be, it will be closed down pretty well immediately and all assets will be seized. All employees will be listed as creditors in the bankruptcy and you'll be able to make a claim for wages owed.'

'That's no help to us freelancers!' someone cried. Maddy glanced round. It was Louis, the carpenter who made wonderful sets. He was a real pro, one of the best. He'd never been on the company payroll but he'd worked for them pretty much full-time for years. He was well liked and into his fifties now with kids at university. She noticed that he was shaking.

The human resources woman removed her jacket and put it on the table behind. She was looking a little less tranquil now, Maddy noted with some satisfaction. She wanted to see her sweat.

'Freelancers will be able to claim for unpaid wages too,' the woman continued. 'I'll be here for the next two weeks to answer everything you need to know. After the meeting I suggest you make individual appointments to see me. Go to Jules and she'll book you in one at a time. I can explain all this in detail and tell you exactly what you must do and what your options are.'

Someone laughed humourlessly. 'Options? What options. We're all on bloody skid row.'

Blake shifted from one foot to another and glanced at the door. Probably thinking he'd like to do a runner.

'I'm in this with you,' he said shakily. 'I stand to lose everything – my house, car, savings, pension funds. Don't think I've got a nice little lump sum stashed away because I haven't. Everything's tied up in this business.'

'Why the hell didn't you warn us sooner?' Maddy was surprised to hear her own voice, shrill and accusatory. 'We could have looked for another job.'

He searched her out through the various heads, his eyes pleading. 'How could I? I was doing everything I could to ensure this didn't happen. As I said, I only found out today—'

'But you must have been getting warning letters for months.' She wasn't going to offer any sympathy; she was too angry.

'I didn't want to worry you in case I could sort this out.' He looked lame and defeated, his pale blue jumper and khaki trousers dangling limply from his hanger of a body. 'I was hoping right till the end that something could be done...'

Maddy felt light-headed and couldn't believe that she'd failed to see this coming. There again Leo died only, what, three weeks ago? She was still reeling from the shock. She'd hardly been focused on the state of the company. And anyway, Blake had always been prone to gloominess, it was part of his make-up. She'd been aware he was worried – but not that worried. She realised that she didn't know him half as well as she thought.

The questions were still coming thick and fast but Maddy was scarcely listening. She was remembering the conversations she'd been having with her business contacts and the fact that there was no work.

She'd been paid for December but presumably there'd be no January cheque and she had no idea how long it would take to get back what she was owed. She wished she'd been more sensible and put money away.

She needed to think. The house had gone up substantially in value and was in a highly desirable area. She was pretty sure that she'd be able to sell it fast and move somewhere smaller. Maybe she could pay off the loan she'd taken out for renovations and even buy something almost outright if she moved far enough from London.

There again, it wouldn't make sense to go too far from Phoebe's school. How would she get her there? She could say goodbye to Jess, but then how would she be able to look for work without a nanny? No, that would be short-sighted and stupid. She was panicking. She needed to go somewhere quiet and ponder.

'I know this is a big shock,' she heard the accountant say. She glanced at Blake, who was sitting crumpled on the desk as if his limbs weren't strong enough to support him. 'I expect you'd like to go away and think about it.'

The noise level rose again and the human resources woman clapped her hands. 'Please make appointments to come and see me. Jules will be at her desk...'

Maddy was aware that someone had opened the door and people were starting to file out. It crossed her mind to tackle Blake but she didn't have the energy. She was exhausted, numb with disbelief. She followed the others, sheep-like, into the reception area and started to tramp slowly upstairs.

'Maddy! You coming to the pub?' She turned and saw Jed standing beside Jules.

'C'mon, I need a drink,' someone shouted. The atmosphere had changed and people seemed feverish, almost excited.

Perhaps they imagined they could do something, fight for their rights, start petitions and persuade the taxmen to change their minds.

They were deluded. Maddy knew the game was up. In a week or so's time, they'd all be out of a job and there would be no more Blake Smith Event Management. She found herself wondering, for a moment, what Blake and his wife would do. Move abroad? Start up another company somewhere? Well, she wouldn't be going with them even if they asked her. As far as she was concerned, she and Blake were finished.

'You coming?' Ben said again, more urgently this time. She was still hovering on the stairs and snapped out of her reverie.

'I need to go home and think.'

'Don't forget to make your appointments,' Jules shouted above the throng. 'She's in there waiting.'

'Alcohol first,' Ben cried, still looking expectantly at Maddy.

Someone laughed. She noticed Lola, leaning over the reception desk and supporting herself with her hands, looking as if she might be about to throw up. Maddy felt a twinge of sympathy but it quickly faded. She hadn't time to think of anyone else right now; she was in enough trouble herself.

'I'm going home,' she said again to Ben. 'I'll ring later.' She trailed upstairs to fetch her coat and bag and left the building as quickly as possible, pushing past a gaggle of colleagues on their way to the pub in her eagerness to reach the tube.

* * *

Why did Leo die? How could he? If he were here he'd be able to get her out of this mess. He'd tide her over financially until she could find another job or set up as a freelance.

For the first time she felt really scared. He should have made sure that she and Phoebe were properly provided for when he died. After all, he wasn't a young man. It made her wonder if he cared. She gave herself a mental shake. Of course he did. He'd wanted to buy a house in the mountains for them. It wasn't his fault that he had a heart attack.

Besides, he knew that she had a good salary and she'd never relied on him financially. She was always more than capable of looking after herself. He wasn't psychic; he couldn't foresee that her company would go bust and nor, more to the point, could she.

It was still only 4.40 p.m. She'd probably just be finishing her meeting with the Tequila Tease people now. Maybe she could persuade them to employ her on a freelance basis, though it would sound odd explaining that her company has folded. Wouldn't exactly inspire them with confidence.

She realised she was shaking. She wouldn't phone them now. She needed to shore herself up and think very carefully about what she was going to say.

Instead of descending the steps to the underground, she hung around outside the entrance to Leicester Square tube for a few moments debating what to do. She needed to talk to someone, she needed help. She wished so much that Leo could wrap his arms around her and hold her close.

Verity, her sister in Scotland. She was practical, she'd have some good ideas. Maddy's fingers trembled as she scrolled for the number and it seemed to take forever for the other woman to answer.

'Maddy? Is that you?' Verity sounded more shocked than pleased and Maddy's heart sank. It had been a stupid idea to call. Verity was the good girl. She'd never been wild like Maddy. She'd gone into teaching, had a sensible husband and visited their parents frequently. She almost matched up to their mother's impossibly high standards and threw all Maddy's shortcomings into relief. They'd never really got on but they were sisters, after all. Surely she'd have some words of comfort?

Maddy poured out her problems.

'Oh God,' Verity kept repeating.

Finally, when Maddy had finished, there was a pause.

'Well you did choose to go into a very competitive, unstable industry,' said Verity, sounding just like their mother. 'And as for Leo...'

Maddy heard a buzzing in her ears and felt sick.

'I shouldn't have rung,' she started to say, aware that Verity was talking to someone else, her son: 'Just a moment, David...'

'I have to go,' Verity continued. 'David needs help with his homework. I'll call you back some other time. I'm sorry about all this...'

Maddy hung up before she could finish.

She glanced around and all she could see were streams of purposeful people going about their business. People who knew what they were doing, who hadn't just lost their jobs and weren't facing ruin.

She thought of everything that she'd worked so hard for, all those years of grafting so that she wouldn't have to return to that cold childhood home where she'd never really felt loved or understood.

She remembered Phoebe, who relied on her completely. A total innocent whose safe little world was about to crumble.

Her mind flitted to Victoria and the way she'd marched up to her so imperiously outside her house and accused her, in front of a frightened Phoebe, of stealing Leo's money. The injustice of it now seemed all the more scalding.

She grabbed her phone from her bag again and called Leo's

Wimbledon home; she'd had the number in there for years but had never needed to ring it.

Victoria herself answered almost immediately.

'I thought you'd like to know,' Maddy said, her voice wobbling, 'that I've lost my job. My company's gone bust and I've got nothing. I expect I'll have to sell my house.' It didn't sound like her. Surely this was some other wretched individual speaking?

There was a long pause.

'So you see,' Maddy went on, filling the silence, 'I'm in just as bad a position as you, if not worse.'

'Why are you telling me this?' Victoria sounded angry and defensive.

Maddy was trying hard to sound strong but she felt cold through to her bones. 'Because I didn't want you to be under any illusions; I want you to be absolutely certain that I never had a penny from Leo.'

'You told me that.'

There were hundreds of people milling around but Maddy was scarcely aware of them. She was bent over and wrapped around her phone as if her life depended on it.

'I think *you* should know that I've found out Leo never had a wife in Austria – it was all a lie,' Victoria blurted.

Maddy's heart started thumping and she had to ask for the words to be repeated. Leo had mentioned the wife but it hadn't troubled her; she'd never wanted or expected marriage in the way that Victoria had. But the fact that he'd deceived them both...

'What?' she found herself saying. 'Why would he do that?'

'So he didn't have to marry me?'

Maddy didn't know what to say.

'There's another thing,' Victoria went on.

Maddy didn't like her tone; she wasn't sure she could take anything more.

'Cat's pregnant.'

Maddy's knees buckled and she backed towards a wall close by for support.

'Who's the father?'

'Leo of course.'

'You're lying.' But she knew it was the truth.

She stood in stunned silence while the crowds jostled past. She didn't know what to do with herself or where to go. She found herself wandering in a daze around Covent Garden, past the Royal Opera House where Leo had performed so often, and through the central square.

She stopped for a moment and hovered on the fringes of crowds watching street performers doing juggling acts and robotic dancing, but she barely took anything in. All she could think about was the thin, waif-like girl who was now carrying Leo's baby.

She thought that, perhaps, if she could speak to Leo right now, he might somehow be able to explain, to put everything right. He'd been so good at smooth-talking her in life. But he was gone, along with all his glittering shine, leaving nothing, it seemed, but fear and despair, rusting metal and bitter ashes.

CHAPTER THIRTEEN

Same Day

Ralph was at home while Maddy and Victoria were talking, watching TV in the sitting room, his feet on the antique coffee table, several empty mugs scattered around.

He could hear Victoria in the kitchen but couldn't discern the words. He could tell that she was speaking quietly so he wouldn't hear. He was used to it. There had always been secrets and whispering in the house, for as long as he could remember.

That old sensation of helplessness washed over him. Sometimes, when he was younger, he'd catch his mother staring out of the window or listening to a piece of music and he'd feel her sadness like a pain in his gut. But there was nothing he could do.

He'd go up to her and hold her hand or stroke her cheek wanting to make it better, but he never could. She'd smile, pretending that she had something in her eye. But he knew.

He balled his fists, forcing the uncomfortable feelings out. He was too old to worry about that now. She'd chosen to shut him out and it wasn't his problem. He had his own life to lead.

He could hear her coming down the hallway and she entered the sitting room, strode over to the window and closed the curtains. They were in virtual darkness for a moment until she turned on one of the sidelights in the corner.

'Can you switch that off?'

Ralph's eyes remained glued to the screen and the volume was up very loud. 'I like watching in the dark.'

Victoria, ignoring him, took a deep breath and sat down beside him.

'Ralph, there's something I'd like to tell you.'

His heart pattered but he didn't look round.

'Can you turn off the TV for a moment?' she repeated.

His eyes narrowed. Why should he do what she wanted? He was sick of being pushed around.

He looked at her and, seeing that she was serious, did as she requested. His feet were still resting on the coffee table. Normally she'd ask him to remove them but her mind was on other things.

'You might have noticed that I've been a bit down just recently,' she began.

'No more than usual.'

'I've discovered something – about your father.'

He flinched. 'What?' He was staring straight ahead, trying not to show interest.

'I spoke to Elsa,' she went on quietly. 'Leo – your father – never married. There was no wife.'

Ralph turned and stared at her. 'So, what difference does that make?'

He knew it wasn't what she'd expected. She seemed to hold her breath for a few seconds and her cheeks started to burn red.

'It's made me very upset,' she said slowly. Massive understatement, obviously. 'It means we could have married but your father didn't want to for some reason.'

The 'for some reason' dangled in the air for a few seconds. He contemplated reaching out to comfort her, then he remembered the whispering and lies and clenched his teeth.

'It's pretty obvious isn't it? Why he didn't want to marry you? He had another woman, another whole life. More than one woman.'

Victoria cringed and he looked at her expectantly, waiting for some acknowledgment of the third. Even the second. She knew what he was asking but she wouldn't, couldn't level with him.

'They were nothing,' she said steadily. 'He was a man of many passions, you know that. Men like that always have affairs, it's in their nature. But they didn't mean anything—'

'Don't give me that!' Ralph took his feet off the table and leaned towards her, his big shoulders thrust forward.

'You don't understand,' she replied, shaking her head. 'I've never lied to you. You were too young—'

'Understand what?' He was spitting with rage and frustration. 'That Dad was having it off with another woman? That they had a child – my half-sister, no less? I understood all right.'

She bowed her head, her hands in her lap. 'I'm sorry. I didn't know you knew. I wanted to protect you.'

Ralph got up. 'I can't take any more of this. You know the saddest thing?' She shook her head, willing him to stop. 'The saddest thing is that you believe all this stuff about him loving you. He was a man-whore, Mum. Face it.'

She sprang up herself, suddenly strong and powerful. 'Don't you dare call your father that.'

'Sorry for bursting your bubble, for telling you the truth,' he sneered, refusing to be intimidated.

'Go to your room now!' She was shaking with fury. 'And don't come down until you apologise.'

He laughed. 'That's right, treat me like a ten-year-old, just like you've always done.'

She didn't seem to hear. 'And don't mention any of this to Salome. She loved her father very much.'

'Don't worry.' Ralph was pacing towards the door, his back turned. 'She'll figure it out for herself soon enough – like I did. Then I suppose you'll feed her the same lies and mess her up just like me.'

'Please Ralph?'

He was at the front door now.

'Can't we sort this out? I really need you right now.'

There was a blast of cold air and he slammed the door so hard that the stained glass rattled and the ground shook.

* * *

Maddy waited a long time before heading home until she knew Phoebe would be asleep and Jess would mostly likely be watching TV in her room. She was gripped with confusion and panic and felt as if something nasty and crawling had taken up residence in her intestines.

She tried to tell herself that she was being silly about the job. She was clever, resourceful and talented and of course she'd find more work. But a vicious little voice in her head would keep reminding her that they were in the middle of a recession and jobs were like gold-dust. Then there were the unpaid bills...

And worse still, Cat was pregnant. In fact it couldn't be much worse. So Leo had betrayed her as well as Victoria, yet all along she'd foolishly imagined that she was different.

At least she and Phoebe had each other – and their health. She must try to cling to the positives and get through this nightmare somehow. She was no quitter, never had been. But was she strong enough now?

She was taken aback to find Ralph on her door-step and, she realised, a little pleased.

'What are you doing here?'

He was in his trademark grey hoodie and jeans, looking pale and slightly uncomfortable.

'I've had a row with my mum,' he said hanging his head.

Maddy wasn't surprised. Emotions must be sky high in that house.

He followed her down the hall into the kitchen and watched as she made mugs of tea. Her hands were trembling as she poured boiling water into the cups and she turned her back on him, hoping he wouldn't notice.

She knew Victoria wouldn't have told him about Cat because she didn't tell him anything, so there must be something else. Maddy wasn't exactly an expert counsellor and had no experience of teenagers but listening, she supposed, would at least take her mind off her own troubles for a while and give her something else to focus on.

They sat in the half-light round the kitchen table sipping their drinks. Maddy had turned off the overhead spots and the room was illuminated only by downlighters; she'd had a dull headache ever since this morning and preferred to be in semi-darkness. That way Ralph wouldn't see her puffy frightened eyes either.

'It sounds as if you were very hard on Victoria,' she said at last, thinking how shocked she herself was to learn of Leo's treachery. Quite why she was bothering to defend the woman, though, was a mystery. It had been a low blow to blurt out Cat's pregnancy; mean and cruel. 'I agree she shouldn't have tried to hide things from you but she's been through an awful lot, remember.'

He took her observations on board and seemed grateful. Victoria was his mother, after all, and he must love her despite everything. He probably just needed someone to talk to. Maddy noticed that he had the same handsome smile, the same look of Leo, and she felt anger and misery bubble inside. He should have provided a strong, stable role-model for this man-boy, his only son, but he'd let him down big time. Let them all down, including Phoebe.

And yet, and yet...she missed him so much.

She took another sip of tea and sighed. 'My company's gone bust. I heard today. I'm out of a job.'

Ralph stared at his mug, embarrassed. She waited for some words of comfort but he just seemed awkward and the silence between them made her twitch with upset and frustration.

Finally he mustered something: 'You must feel like crap.'

It was hopeless, inadequate, and she cursed herself for expecting anything more from a not yet eighteen year old boy. Leo was experienced and wise. He would have put his arms around her and explained it all away and made her feel safe. 'It'll be all right, my darling girl,' he'd have said, kissing her hair.

She fought back tears. It seemed wrong to cry in front of this youth with a skinny body and an inability with words.

She gulped down her drink and rose. 'I'm sorry, I shouldn't have mentioned it.'

He looked confused and got up too, his arms hanging limply at his sides. Then he took a step forwards into her body space so that they were very close, just a couple of feet apart. She could smell tobacco on his clothes mingled with fabric conditioner.

She was aware that he was much taller than her, a long lanky streak of a boy with a deep voice and a trace of stubble on his chin. He leaned forward so that she couldn't see his face and she thought he was going to peck her on the cheek, relieved, no doubt, to be saying goodbye.

Instead, he wrapped his arms around her, crushing her against his chest. Startled, she made to pull back but something stopped her. She could sense his heart pumping and feel the warmth and strength in his muscles. Her arms snaked around him as if by their own will and she felt her energy drain, her sense of self dissolve. It was a profound relief, almost dizzy-making, like easing into warm seawater and allowing yourself to float away.

They stayed like that for a few moments, her limbs so heavy that she could scarcely move. She felt as if she were drowning under the weight of her burdens. She couldn't cope on her own any more. Maybe she wouldn't have to.

Instinctively she raised her face towards his, feeling his hot, vital breath on her forehead and cheeks. She was tiptoeing to meet him, aware that his mouth was close, so close that she could...

Her eyes snapped open and, horrified, she stepped back. 'You must go.'

It was cold out of his embrace and she felt suddenly frightened and alone again.

'Are you sure?' he asked. 'I can stay if you want?'

His voice sounded deep and slightly mysterious.

'You need to get some sleep.' It was 1.40 a.m. after all. What had she been thinking of? 'Go home and make up with your mum. She'll be really worried about you.'

They were a few feet apart now, a safe distance.

He pulled a face, which made him look young again. 'Serves her right.'

Maddy was tempted to agree. Victoria didn't deserve this

beautiful sensitive boy who had been through so much. But he was hers, not Maddy's.

'I'll order you a cab.'

'I can get the night bus.'

'I insist.'

They waited for a few moments in the sitting room, perched awkwardly on the edge of chairs, not knowing what to say. At last her mobile pinged, making them jump. They were a bag of nerves. *'Your taxi is waiting outside.'*

He rose and a thought occurred to her. 'Can you do something for me when you get back? Tomorrow's fine.' It wasn't too much to ask, surely?

She explained what she wanted and he nodded before following her down the hallway.

He'd been doing his best to console her, she was telling herself. That's what it was. In his own gauche, wordless, teenage way he'd been trying. Nothing more than that.

'When you see Victoria give her a hug like the one you've just given me,' she said, opening the front door quickly. The wind whooshed in making her shiver.

He hovered expectantly and the air between them crackled with meaning. She wrapped her arms around herself tightly, pretending not to notice, and watched him walk down the steps and into the waiting cab.

'Thanks,' he said, winding down the window.

'You're very welcome.' *But thanks for what?*

'Can I see you again?'

She thought of Leo and the silent house awaiting her. Blake's crushing announcement, her financial nightmare, Cat's growing baby and Phoebe and Jess fast asleep, still blissfully oblivious.

'I'll call you,' she whispered, aware of his big brown eyes

focusing on her in the dark. She glanced left and right anxiously as if something – or someone - might be watching. But no one was.

* * *

Victoria was worried sick. It was the early hours of the morning and she had no idea where Ralph was.

He'd been so cruel but now she felt guilty for losing her temper. She paced around the sitting room unable to concentrate on anything. She missed Leo so keenly that she didn't know how her body could withstand the pain.

Then she remembered that, were he still alive, he'd no doubt be distracted by Cat's pregnancy. This thought tortured her almost as much as the grief. And the truth was that she was anxious about the girl because she hadn't heard from her for several days. She wondered why she should feel any responsibility. And yet she did.

Ralph made her alternate between anger and despair. She was angry with him because she couldn't quite believe that he'd disappear like this. Didn't he think that she had enough worries? His selfishness took her breath away.

Then panic set in. What if he'd been run over or mugged or done something stupid? She knew about the suicide rates among teenage boys. Ralph was in a vulnerable state, suffering, too, after the death of his father. His mind must be teeming with black thoughts and his behaviour was likely to be unpredictable and scary.

Whatever he felt about her, she was the person who loved him more than anyone in the world, who would lay down her life for him no matter how he behaved.

Despite the time, she picked up the phone and rang Debs,

sensible, calm Debs who, though younger than Victoria, seemed to have lived for a thousand years.

'I don't know where Ralph is,' she found herself saying mechanically, as if she were talking about some other strange woman who'd carelessly lost her son. 'I don't know what to do.'

Debs was practical and level-headed, as Victoria knew she would be. 'He'll have gone to a friend's house, they'll have had a few drinks and he'll have crashed there and forgotten to call....he'll be back in the morning with a hangover and his tail between his legs....'

She was right. He was probably snoring at this very moment on someone's sofa. But...but...Victoria picked up her mobile and rang him. Again no answer.

'*Call me now,*' she texted. No response.

She couldn't sleep so she turned on Radio 4 and half listened to a report on schoolchildren in China having lessons about healthy eating. She dozed off briefly and was woken by a woman making loud ghostly noises during story-time at a school in India.

Snapping the radio off she lay on her back, staring at the dark and feeling like the only person awake in the entire world. It reminded her of when Ralph and Salome were babies. Ralph, in particular, was a very bad sleeper. He didn't go through the night until he was nearly a year old.

She could see herself now, wrapped in her warm dressing gown, tip-toeing into the small room at the front of the house that was now Salome's and lifting him out of his cot. When Leo was home she'd leave him sleeping; she was always careful not to wake him.

Ralph was a big strong round baby with lots of dark hair. She remembered that baby-scent of sweet skin and talcum

179

powder and nappy cream. He'd be hot, sticky and crying, furious at having woken to find himself alone.

She'd sit on the wooden rocker in his room with the door open just a fraction so that there was a shaft of light from the landing, not enough to make him think it was day but just enough to enable her to see.

She'd undo the buttons of her nightdress and put him to her breast, tipping backwards and forwards ever so gently as he suckled. His breathing would slow and he'd become heavy and limp, a dead weight of precious flesh and blood and bone. But as soon as she'd put her little finger in his mouth to unlatch him, his eyelids would flutter open and he'd shriek, enraged.

Victoria sighed at the bittersweet memory. Often she'd resign herself to her fate as willing slave to this small tyrant. She'd rest her head on the back of the chair and nod off herself, so tired that even when her head lolled forward onto her chest it wouldn't wake her.

She'd open her eyes and find herself staring down at her son with a painful crick in her neck and her own dribble on his cheek. He'd still be attached to her, sucking occasionally, draining every last drop of her milk and drawing, it seemed, all liquid energy from her numb body. She'd have a roaring thirst and her mouth would be dry like sandpaper.

She felt then, as now, as if the earth stood still, buried beneath a blanket of dark, all sounds muffled, waiting for daybreak to melt the blackness and life to begin again. Desperate for a cup of warm milky tea.

She was still lying there, thinking these thoughts, when she heard a key in the front door. The clock on her radio said 2.30 a.m. She rose quickly and hurried downstairs, her heart racing, to find Ralph in the hallway taking off his shoes.

She stood on the bottom step staring at him, her boy. She wanted to cover him in kisses, to feed him, bathe him, fetch him clean ironed pyjamas and put him to bed.

'Where have you been?' is all she could say.

'A friend's.'

'Why didn't you call?'

She opened her arms and he walked into them. His body was straight and brittle but he allowed her to rest her head on his heart for a moment or two before pulling away. She didn't care that he failed to reciprocate with a hug; it was enough.

'I'm sorry for saying those things,' he said.

'Forget it.' Her voice was shaking. 'I'm sorry, too. Shall I make some cocoa – or a cup of tea?'

He shook his head – 'just water'– and walked slowly past her into the kitchen. Her heart fluttered. There was something different about him and she felt as if he were hiding something from her.

She trailed after him, looking for reassurance. 'What friend have you been with? Who?'

'No one you know,' he replied vaguely.

CHAPTER FOURTEEN

Wednesday January 6th

DON IS WEARING CASUAL *clothes. His body language is a little less uptight, perhaps, although he cranes his chin as he sits down in that nervous way he has.*

Kate looks weary. Her blonde hair's greasy and she's wearing the same unflattering black polo neck, complete with animal hairs. She's made some effort and put on a little make-up, but her blue eyeshadow is smudged and she's overdone the blusher.

That's what small children do to you, Victoria thinks, remembering her own utter exhaustion. Don, on the other hand, is positively jaunty, in navy chinos and a crisp white open-necked shirt, with a racy black blouson jacket on top.

'How was Christmas and New Year?' Victoria asks. Kate waits for Don to answer, which may be a good sign. Previously she's waded in angrily at the first opportunity.

Don admits that it's been tiring - for Kate – as one of the children had a chest infection and was cranky and demanding. It's clear that this relationship is run along traditional lines.

The session starts calmly enough, with Don claiming he's had no contact with the other woman. But then he turns to Kate.

'I can't understand why you feel so threatened,' he says, craning. 'I told you it meant nothing. It was just a stupid mistake.'

Kate's body tenses and her blue eyes flash. 'Can't you get it into your thick skull that it makes me feel totally undermined? I feel like I'm second best in your life, like you have all the fun with someone else and I'm just left with the boring tired Don who can't even be bothered to play with the children when he comes in from work.'

There's a catch in her voice. 'I thought we were equals. But it appears I'm just the drudge at home who looks after the house and kids. Well, I'm not prepared to be second best any longer.'

Don, who's sitting next to her, tries to touch her hand but she pulls away. 'I've said I'm sorry. It won't happen again.'

Kate opens her mouth but Victoria interrupts. 'I hear what you're both saying. I think it would be helpful to examine the reasons why you had the affair, Don, if you can tell us about it.'

She glances at Kate, who looks fearful. 'I know this is going to be painful but you need to listen. Your turn will come.'

Kate nods.

Don proceeds to recount how he met the other woman, what he felt about her and how the affair had begun. He admits it seemed exciting and secretive, that Kate was always tired and never wanted sex anymore.

'Even your clothes...' he says.

Kate swallows nervously.

'You used to be so glamorous. Now you wear the same thing every day. You've put on weight and

183

sometimes you don't even bother to wear make-up.'

Kate can't contain herself. 'What do you expect when I'm at home with the kids all day? I'm knackered all the time. Looking after a four and a one year old is incredibly hard work, in case you haven't noticed. If you helped more maybe I wouldn't be tired all the time. Maybe I'd be able to go to the gym and get fit and buy nice clothes.'

Victoria is drained by the end of the fifty minutes. The atmosphere has been so highly charged and she's been on a knife-edge, afraid that Kate might bolt at any minute.

The couple leave, however, agreeing that it's been useful to get certain issues out in the open. Moreover, Kate says she's prepared to finish the course of counselling before making any decisions about their future.

***

Victoria picked up her coat and bag, having finished for the day. She couldn't wait to get home and hurried down the narrow flight of steps, opening the main door on to the street. Right in front of her, waiting to come up, was her colleague Oliver Sands chomping on a baguette sandwich.

Surprised, she tripped over the final step and nearly floored him.

'Woah!' he said, opening his arms to catch her but she righted herself just in time. 'I didn't realise I had such a powerful effect on you.'

She glanced at him and noticed that he was smiling which made her blush, and curse her stupid big feet for landing her in trouble.

'I was just leaving,' she said unnecessarily, smoothing down her coat and pretending not to have heard his comment.

'I can see,' he replied, still amused. 'What's the rush?'

She found herself blabbing again, telling him about her daughter's penchant for peculiar flavoured crisps. Why did she do that? He gave a wry look, which made her feel even more stupid, and she was about to excuse herself when he interrupted.

'Just a thought. Are you busy tonight?'

She was so surprised that for once she was lost for words.

'I've got two friends coming for supper,' he went on. 'Rosanna and I have known each other since university. She's a widow, too. I thought you might like to meet her.'

The floodgates opened. 'A widow? Oh. I haven't really thought of myself as that. It sounds like an old lady doesn't it?'

He remained expressionless.

'But I suppose I am. A widow I mean,' she said hastily, 'rather than old. Well, not too old, anyway, although to someone of 21, I must seem absolutely ancient. I remember when I was at school one of my teachers turned 40 and I thought she was positively prehistoric.'

Her cheeks flared once more and she stared at her shoes, wishing the ground would swallow her whole.

When she raised her eyes she realised that he was smiling again, a mischievous, open sort of grin that lit up his face and made him look quite boyish. She'd never seen him smile like that before and she was startled.

'Well you certainly don't look prehistoric to me. But you haven't answered my question.'

'Why not?' she said in spite of herself, clamping her mouth shut before anything else could escape.

'Good,' he replied. 'Eight-ish? I can't guarantee the quality of the cuisine but I hope you'll enjoy the company.'

* * *

It was kind of him to try to cheer her up, she thought, staring at herself in the mirror. She had made herself put on a dress that she hadn't worn since well before Leo died. It was deep purple, almost black, and it wrapped around her and tied at the back. She'd liked it when she bought it but somehow it didn't look as flattering now.

The problem was that she was too heavy. Too many cakes and puddings. She examined herself critically, hating her broad shoulders and wide hips and that horrible cushion of fat that had settled round her middle. Leo always said that she was statuesque and womanly, like a Greek goddess. Middle- aged frump more like.

She straightened up and pinned her hair off her face, which badly needed de-frizzing. At least now you could see her dangly silver earrings that twinkled in the electric light.

She huffed, feeling like throwing the whole lot off and climbing into bed. Why did she say yes? She must have been mad. But she'd committed herself now. Still, she wouldn't stay late. Oliver would understand. It was a weekday, after all.

She was surprised when she reached his house as it was much bigger and grander than she'd expected: a solid, red brick, double-fronted Victorian building a stone's throw from Richmond Park, with a welcoming light in the porch that cast a warm glow.

She parked her old Vauxhall Astra and stood outside the iron gate for a moment or two, gazing at the black and white tiled front path leading up to the handsome black front door, the ornamental trees on either side that cast interesting shadows all around.

Walking slowly up the path, she was aware that her nerves were failing. She'd been a fool to think she'd be able to cope with meeting new people; it was far too early. She was tempted to turn right round, jump back in the car and drive off. Then she remembered that Oliver had invited her expressly to meet his widow friend and she couldn't let him down. She pulled the ringer on the old-fashioned brass bell which jingled melodically.

He answered almost immediately and she handed him a bottle of red wine, before taking the opportunity to gaze around while he helped her off with her coat. The hallway was just as impressive as the outside of the house: wide and spacious, with polished wooden floorboards and a sweeping curved staircase.

His walls were covered in art; some black and white etchings, some paintings, and her eye was drawn to one canvas in particular which she stopped to look at more closely. Deep blue flowers, the shape of poppies, were painted on a dark green background of stems. The blue was so vibrant, yet also cool and bottomless, almost purple, that it seemed to drag you in.

'Andy Warhol?' she asked. 'I love it.'

He seemed pleased. 'I bought it in New York a few years ago. I'm very fond of it.'

'It's original? I thought it must be a print.'

He shook his head. 'It was one of those impulse buys. You know when you see something and you just have to have it?'

She thought about it for a moment. She'd never been into possessions particularly, though she was sure she'd enjoy buying art if she had that kind of money.

'I don't know. I'd certainly like it on my wall. I'd sit and stare at it for hours and hours on end then stare at it some more.'

He laughed. 'It was hanging in my bedroom for a while. It was nice waking up and going to sleep looking at it but I tend to move everything around – paintings and furniture. Bit restless I suppose.'

She followed him into the drawing room, dismayed to discover that she was the first one there. While he went to fetch wine glasses, though, it gave her time to take in her surroundings which struck her as an Aladdin's Cave.

The room was large, high-ceilinged and square, with old wooden shutters at the end overlooking the front garden. The walls were painted chalky white and the floor was bare polished boards again, scattered with exotic looking rugs in deep reds, greens and golds. A log fire burning in the cast iron grate made everything glow.

On either side of the fireplace were built-in shelves which reached right up to the ceiling, lined with rows and rows of books of different sizes, interspersed with various objects: a white plaster-cast bust of somebody; a trio of interesting looking cut-glass containers with silver tops, and a small piece of smooth, pale, oval-shaped marble with a round hole in the middle. It was just begging to be picked up and stroked.

Everywhere her eye fell there was something to spark interest or sooth the soul, but it wasn't a show-house, it was eminently liveable-in. He'd left a pile of newspapers on the floor in front of the fireplace and a beige sweater across the arm of a chair.

He was clearly a man of immense taste, she thought. Extraordinary how she'd never realised. It seemed like an awfully big house, though, for someone on their own.

He returned with a tray of glasses and champagne in an ice bucket.

'You have a beautiful home,' she said, glancing around again and noticing for the first time a cello propped in the corner next to a metal music stand. 'Do you play?'

'Badly,' he replied, uncorking the bottle and pouring her a glass. 'I had lessons as a boy but I'm really not up to much. I take it out from time to time and mess around.'

'I play too, or used to. That's how I met Leo. It was the music that drew us together. I was a professional musician for a while.'

'Were you?' He looked interested.

She nodded. 'But I haven't touched my cello for years. I stopped when Ralph was a baby and I've hardly picked it up since. It's gathering dust in the corner of my bedroom.'

'Why's that, then?' he asked. 'Why don't you play just for pleasure?'

He was beside her on the sofa and took a sip of wine. He was in loose dark blue jeans with a white collarless linen shirt, rolled up at the sleeves, and she noticed that his dark hair, slightly grey at the temples, was damp, as if he'd just come out of the shower.

She fiddled with one of her dangly earrings. 'I can't. I don't know why. My fingers are clumsy and the music comes out wrong. I got so angry and furious with myself that I decided to stop.' She shrugged. 'I lost it, simple as that.'

'But don't you miss it? I would.'

'Not really. I guess there are other things in my life now.'

There was a pause. 'Tell me about you,' she said, keen to deflect attention. She was feeling uncomfortable under the spotlight. 'You're divorced, right?'

He nodded.

'Do you get on all right – with your ex-wife I mean?'

He took another sip of champagne and she noticed that his

189

wrists were strong but also delicate, like his hands. He seemed quite sympathetic and not at all intimidating. Why did she never realise? Maybe he just took a while to get to know.

'Not at all, I'm afraid,' he replied, scratching his head. 'She's living with someone else now. We used to talk when our boys were younger because we had to, but not now.'

Victoria remembered something Debs had told her about his marriage having been tempestuous, the split bitter and drawn-out.

'It took about five years to get over the break-up,' he went on, as if reading her thoughts, 'but I can truly say I'm through it now.'

'Why do you think the marriage failed?'

'Oh, we had multiple problems. The fact that I had an affair didn't help.'

She tried her best to disguise her disapproval. These days, she found that she had less and less tolerance for faithless men.

'I'm not proud of it,' he continued, 'but there were, shall we say, mitigating circumstances.'

Victoria pretended to understand but she didn't. She remembered the obligatory interview she'd had with Debs before embarking on couples counselling training. She'd done her best to explain why her relationship with Leo was different; why she could deal with his affairs whilst for other women, the situation could be highly damaging, intolerable even.

Debs had been very tough on her, examining her motives and issues of self-esteem and pulling her apart. She'd questioned whether Victoria was the right person to be a counsellor, and Victoria had had to admit that part of the reason why she was drawn to it was that she was looking for answers herself.

Debs seemed to accept this and had agreed that in the end,

it's not about saying one marriage is right while another is wrong. Victoria, meanwhile, had conceded that for some couples, sustained infidelity simply wouldn't work. But, she'd argued, not everyone lived with a genius like Leo.

Mitigating circumstances? The only one she could think of was genius. If Oliver were a genius like Leo, well then. But he wasn't.

'Is there anyone else in your life?' she asked, taking a crisp from the bowl that he offered her. She found her cheeks flaring again, which was absurd. She was more than used to asking personal questions; it was part of her job.

He tilted his head to one side. 'Not really.'

'Go on,' she teased. 'What sort of answer is that? Is there or isn't there?'

He looked her in the eye. 'I have been seeing someone occasionally but I'm a bit wary of relationships now, to be honest. I don't want to get hurt.'

She nodded, surprised again by his openness. She'd misjudged him; he wasn't aloof at all, just shy, defensive or cautious – or all three. She could understand caution. She doubted that she'd ever trust enough to love again. In any case, Leo was irreplaceable. Like a swan, she'd mated for life.

The doorbell rang at last and Oliver rose to answer. Glancing again at his cello, she found her mind wandering back to her childhood. The days when she'd shut herself away in the family dining room, pick up her beloved instrument and lose herself in her music. It had meant everything to her then; it was her refuge, her sanctuary, the only place, it seemed, where she could escape from the unhappiness of home and feel truly at peace.

She was never allowed to hide for long, though. Soon one of her younger siblings would burst in, asking for something:

Can I have a drink? Will you make me a sandwich? I've cut my knee.

Her mother would be shut away in her bedroom with the curtains drawn and the television blaring. She was always ill, or claimed to be. It was one thing after another: the flu, exhaustion, conjunctivitis, fed up with life-itis, you name it.

And her father, the great surgeon? He was at work, of course, or doing whatever it was he did in the evenings. Seeing private patients, he said, which made her mother snort. Victoria never did understand why she pulled that face and made that noise – until later.

She sighed, thinking of Leo. Funny how history had a habit of repeating itself. But she was so different from her mother. Victoria had made a conscious decision to keep Leo's affairs in their proper place, to afford them no more attention than they deserved. Her mother, on the other hand, had behaved as if her husband's flings were the end of the world and made the whole family suffer. Anyway, it was all in the past now. They were both long gone.

The other two guests arrived at the same time. Victoria immediately took to Robert, who informed her that he worked closely with Oliver at the creative design agency he'd founded in his twenties. Rosanna, though, whom he'd met at Oxford, she wasn't sure about.

A tall slender woman with dark shoulder length hair and a big red mouth, she struck Victoria as scary. Which surprised her, given what Oliver had said. Rosanna was too good-looking and well-dressed, too clever, too confident, too *sorted*.

'So, are you getting out?' she asked, leaning across the supper table to address Victoria. 'It's no good sitting around moping. You should always accept people's offers and say yes to absolutely everything. I didn't want to move when my husband died. I was distraught, inconsolable, but I forced myself out of the house. It paid off, it really did.'

'Well, you see—' Victoria started. She was about to say that it was only a month since Leo's funeral. Four little weeks after twenty years together. A drop in the ocean. But Rosanna, who was 'Something in the City', wasn't listening.

'And it's terribly important to get dressed every day even if you don't feel like it, and wear nice clothes and make-up. I wore the same jeans and grubby old sweater for ages until one morning I looked in the mirror and thought: Rosanna, what have you *become*?' She gave a dramatic pause. 'Whatever happens, you MUST NOT let yourself go.'

Victoria imagined that Rosanna had been eyeing up her frizzy hair and badly put on mascara, her two year old frock. She probably thought she spent all day slobbing round the house in her dressing gown, which sounded rather more appealing right now than listening to this litany of no doubt well-meaning advice.

The men were discussing Robert's job with a new design company. They must have thought the widows wanted to be left to their private chat.

'When did you lose your husband?' Victoria asked tentatively, assuming it was a fairly recent event.

'God, ten years ago now,' Rosanna said with a far-off look. 'I'm a different person these days. Much stronger and more independent. I've travelled the world on my own since my husband died, you know.' She gave a superior little smile.

'I've also run two New York marathons – never used to run before. Had to learn from scratch. I love it now. I get positively twitchy if I don't run five or six miles at least every other day. And I've learned to cook properly. Oh, and completely gutted my house. It takes a lot to faze me.'

193

Victoria felt herself shrivel. She couldn't imagine running one mile, let alone a marathon.

'I've learned to be happy in my own company,' Rosanna continued, 'but that's not to say I wouldn't like to be with someone. I feel ready for commitment in a way I wasn't before.'

She gave Victoria a strange look that she didn't know how to interpret.

'If you take my advice,' she went on, patting Victoria's arm, 'you should wait a few years before you get into another relationship. It wouldn't work out; you'd still be grieving. You need to get yourself into a healthy mental space before you start dating again.'

Her voice had risen and Victoria started to feel dazed and slightly peculiar. None of what Rosanna was saying seemed to relate to her. Another relationship? What was she talking about? Victoria could still smell Leo's scent on her pillowcase. His shoes were still in the hall where he'd left them, his clothes hanging in the cupboard waiting for his return.

Oliver seemed to sense her discomfort. 'What are you going on about, Ros? I hope you're not overwhelming Victoria.'

He turned to her and smiled gently. 'She can be a bit bossy and she likes the sound of her own voice,' he said in a stage whisper. 'But she's coped incredibly well since Matthew died.'

He got up to clear the plates and brought the next dish – chicken in some sort of tomato sauce and vegetables, which they helped themselves to. Victoria tucked in, happy to focus on putting food in her mouth.

'What do you do?' Robert asked after a while. He was a big man with a kind round face and alert blue eyes. It seemed that his wife was away on business and the children were old enough to look after themselves.

'I'm a relationship counsellor – the same as Oliver,' Victoria said, replacing her knife and fork at last and feeling uncomfortably full. 'I'm fairly new to it, actually, still finding my way.'

Rosanna dabbed her mouth with her napkin. She'd left most of her meat and all her potatoes. Therein lay the difference, Victoria reflected glumly, eyeing her own clean plate. At the first sign of middle-aged spread Rosanna would be down the gym doing two hundred press-ups before you could say 'profiterole.'

'Really?' the other woman picked up the conversation thread. 'How interesting. 'I bet you meet all sorts of weird and wonderful people. Oliver tells me the most amazing stories.' She glanced at him fondly before turning back to Victoria. 'Tell me about your customers.'

'Clients,' she corrected. 'Well, yes, you do see all of life I suppose.'

'Go on,' Rosanna begged.

'Well...' Victoria looked doubtful. 'I'm not allowed to discuss individual cases.'

Rosanna laughed. 'Oh you counsellors, you're all the same. You're all so obsessed with *confidentiality*. I won't shop you for being indiscreet, I promise.'

Victoria felt silly and awkward. 'I do see quite a lot of couples where they've met at university and started off as equals,' she said hesitantly. 'Then they have kids and she stays at home to look after them. She's harassed and tired when he gets home and he's living in this different world at work. They drift apart and quite often she discovers that he's having an affair. That's when they come to us.'

Which wasn't strictly true. In fact it was more common to

meet couples whose marriage was under immense pressure because money was tight and they were both working all hours. But she was thinking of Kate and Don, of course.

'Bastards,' Rosanna said suddenly. 'I wouldn't put up with it. I'd never stay with a man who'd had an affair.'

Victoria glanced sideways at Oliver, who shuffled in his seat. Didn't Rosanna know about his affair? You'd think he'd have told her as they were such good friends. She might be more sensitive.

'It's complicated,' Victoria offered, trying to put Oliver at his ease and feeling the need to defend her own position, too. 'You have to look at the reasons behind it and also what is and isn't acceptable to the other partner. Sometimes—'

'Excuse me,' Rosanna butted in. 'Are you saying an affair is *ever* acceptable? I'm sorry. I don't think so.'

'There may be circumstances—'

'Look at it this way. Imagine if those women you're talking about have girls. Would they want their own daughters to put up with unfaithful husbands? Surely not! Then why would they accept it for themselves? It suggests to me they must have very low self-esteem.'

Victoria swallowed, remembering Salome, and something Kate said earlier in the day came back to her: *I'm not prepared to be second best any longer.*

Did she, Victoria, put herself second best throughout her marriage? Perhaps. But there was no one like Leo. That was the whole point. He was an exception. He needed her total, undying love and support in order to carry out his life's work.

Oliver cleared his throat, nudging Victoria out of her reverie.

'I think you're rather jumping to the conclusion, Ros, that all the women in these cases are blameless. I'm not saying infidelity is desirable, but there may be reasons.'

Victoria noticed an odd look pass between them.

'You misunderstand,' Rosanna said more gently. 'Of course not all women are saints but the way Victoria described it, the women in these cases she's talking about *are* the innocent party.'

Victoria, conscious that she'd already said too much about Kate and Don, remained silent.

'Isn't that right, Victoria?' Rosanna said, turning to her. 'I mean, what are these women like? Are they total doormats with nothing to say for themselves? Surely even that doesn't justify the man shagging other women?'

Victoria had had enough of the conversation and glanced around for a way out. Luckily, Oliver suddenly rose. 'Cheese anyone? I'm afraid I didn't get round to making pudding.'

Seizing the opportunity, she pushed back her chair a little too abruptly. 'I really have to go. I promised the babysitter I wouldn't be late.'

She could feel the other guests' eyes on her but she didn't care, mumbling a quick goodbye before scurrying down the hallway, followed by her host.

'I do hope you're not—'

'I'm fine, just tired. Thanks for inviting me.'

She glanced at Oliver who was frowning, his dark eyebrows nearly meeting in the middle.

'I thought Ros would be helpful. I don't know what got into her tonight. She was so – strident. She's not normally like that. It was stupid.'

He opened the front door and she tumbled onto the doorstep in her eagerness to get away.

She could tell that he was watching while she fumbled with her car keys and clambered in, but she didn't look round. She managed to get round the corner out of sight before the tears started to fall.

It was bringing Salome in that did it. Her own darling girl. Horrible thoughts were swirling round her mind, thoughts of patterns of behaviour, lessons learned – legacies.

She realised for the first time that there was no way she'd want Salome to be treated as she was treated in her marriage. Yet for so long Victoria had believed the love she had with Leo was perfect, or as near perfect as you could ever hope for.

She slapped the steering wheel hard. She wouldn't have it. She was furious with Rosanna for churning up dirt like a filthy eel, sliding along the riverbed looking for muck to ingest.

It was no business of hers or of anybody's. How would they understand? The only solution was to put that woman and the whole evening right out of mind. To walk away and never look back.

CHAPTER FIFTEEN

Thursday January 7th

'I've told you if you go then that's it, we're finished.'

There was a crash and Cat winced. Tracy was having a row with Rick, which began last night just before they turned in. He wanted to go to a Black Sabbath concert in June with his mates. Tracy didn't approve of Rick's mates who were losers, she said, and anyway she wanted to go with him to Lake Garda in July.

The whole world planned their holidays in January, according to Tracy, but he couldn't afford two holidays and he'd had this booked for months. The likelihood of compromise seemed bleak.

Tracy's bedroom door was shut and she was already late for the dry cleaners. Emotions were high and Cat could hear everything.

'Look, Cupcake—'

Another crash.

Cat hurried out of the flat closing the door gently behind her.

'Good morning!'

She groaned. Ali – Mr Yum Yum – was on the pavement outside his shop grinning from ear to ear.

'Why the glum face?' he asked. 'Eees beautiful day, no?' It was true, the sun was shining for once and it was quite mild.

He peered at her strangely. 'You look a leetle peaky. Too much partying?' He winked. 'What are you girls like!'

'I'm late for work.'

He raised his hands. 'Sorree.'

'The shower's not working properly. It keeps going hot and cold.'

Ali's face clouded over. 'Ahh, ees problem'.

He moved closer to Cat and whispered in her ear. 'Mrs Ali, she want new vacuum cleaner with root cyclone technology – no bags, no fuss, see? She says old one ees no good, no mattress tool for easy removal of dirt.' He assumed a tragic face. 'Ees no good for allergic sufferers.'

Cat narrowed her eyes. 'Does she suffer from allergies, then?'

Ali shook his head mournfully. 'No allergies. But new vacuum will prevent them, see? She ees very determined, my wife. She will not take no for an answer.'

***

Gervaise was busy making pyramid displays on the front table when Cat walked in and his face lit up when he saw her, but his smile soon faded as she got closer.

'You OK?' He put down his pile of books for a moment and made a sympathetic noise.

'Yeah, late night, that's all.'

She hung her parka on the peg in the back room and started unpacking a box of books.

'When you've finished, can you do a stint on the till?' Rachel said. 'I need to make some important calls.'

Cat was suspicious of Rachel's important calls. They tended to go on for a very long time. If Cat ventured into the tiny office with the phone and computer, Rachel usually had a cup of coffee, a packet of chocolate biscuits by her side and Facebook on screen. No wonder she'd got that enormous backside, sitting on it for so long.

Gervaise bounced over while Cat was tidying the till area. 'I've signed up for some private voice coaching. Reckon I need a spot of help with accents after the New York Jew fiasco. And my agent's put me up for a pilot TV series.' His eyes were shining. 'It'll be a six parter if it gets commissioned. The business.'

Cat felt light-headed and had to perch on the edge of one of the display tables. 'Fab,' she said, 'tell me more.'

He scratched his chin. 'It's kinda sci-fi. I'll be this alien, see, who crash-lands on earth with various alien mates and they can't get back so they have to pretend they're human and try to fit in.' He waggled his fingers in front of her and made a scary face.

'Sounds ideal,' she said drily. 'You'll make a good alien.'

He looked at her strangely, not quite sure how to take it.

She checked her mobile when she went to make coffee and there was another message from Victoria with more numbers to call for pregnancy advice. '*Ring me if u need to*' she said. '*You must make a decision soon.*'

The truth was that Cat hadn't rung any of the numbers yet, despite having promised she would. She hadn't been to the GP either, though she'd told Tracy that she had. She was still thinking.

She was very grateful to Victoria, she really was. It was extraordinarily big of her to be offering help. There was something special about her, Cat decided. She wasn't like other people. Most women in her situation would probably rather slit her throat.

She was serving a customer when her eye was drawn away by a small, blonde, upright woman who'd just walked into the shop. Her back was turned and she was looking at some books on the first section of shelves. She seemed strangely familiar.

She turned and looked at Cat, whose stomach rolled. Maddy, Leo's other lover. What the hell was she doing here? Something in her expression warned Cat this was no accident and she remained rooted to the spot, aware that her hands were clammy and her heart was racing.

Gervaise noticed. 'Cat, are you all—'

'Shh.' She warned him away as Maddy approached. She was wearing a smart navy overcoat over jeans and trainers. Her hair was tied back in a ponytail and she had little makeup on, much less than at the funeral. Only eyeshadow and a bit of pink lipstick. She looked ill at ease.

'Cat?' she asked tentatively.

Cat nodded, unable to speak because her mouth was so dry.

'Can we talk?'

Gervaise was still hovering beside Cat and she wished he'd make himself scarce.

'What about?' Her voice came out as a squeak.

'You. Leo.'

'How did you know where I work?'

'Ralph,' said Maddy. 'He found the name of the shop for me in Leo's address book. I've seen him a couple of times.'

It seemed odd but Cat let it pass. There were other more pressing problems. She felt her body relax just a little. The other woman looked vulnerable, despite her carefully coloured hair and smart overcoat. A bundle of nerves.

'I'm going out,' Cat said, climbing shakily off the stool and looking at Gervaise. 'I won't be long. Tell Rachel it's an early lunch break or something. Tell her I'm feeling sick – whatever.'

There was no arguing with her and Gervaise stood back and let her pass. She was aware of his eyes boring into her back until they left the bookshop and disappeared from sight.

Cat lit a cigarette. She didn't want one but it was something to do.

'Where can we go?' Maddy asked. 'Are there any quiet places round here?'

Cat decided to head to the canal, thinking that she'd be able to breathe there; she couldn't bear the thought of sitting in a hot cafe, assaulted by smells that would make her feel more ill.

They walked through the backstreets in silence, passing row upon row of tall elegant terraced houses with black iron railings and steps up to the front door. Finally they reached the edge of the grey water and Cat turned to Maddy.

'I haven't got long so you'd better ask away.'

Maddy focused on a point in the distance and took a deep breath. 'I know you're pregnant.'

Cat's heart fluttered. 'How?'

'Victoria told me.'

'What? That was private, between me and her.'

Cat thought of Victoria's big soft grey eyes, the way she inclined her head so sympathetically when she was listening, drawing things out and making you feel safe. An empty hole lodged in her chest. Cat had trusted her. She'd thought they were on the same side. She clenched her fists, determined not to cry. Why should she be surprised? Didn't everyone let her down – apart from Tracy?

'Wait,' Maddy said, sensing she was about to bolt. 'Please

don't get the wrong idea. It was me who phoned Victoria because I've lost my job. I wanted to put things straight, because she thought I'd stolen all Leo's money. But I've got nothing. I never had anything from him.'

Instead of taking off, Cat kicked a pebble on the towpath with her foot and it plopped into the water. 'She shouldn't have told you,' she repeated, scarcely registering the news about the job. 'It's nobody's business but mine.'

Maddy's arms were crossed and she was staring hard at the ripples that the pebble had made, spreading across the water.

'Victoria hates me,' she said. 'She knew your pregnancy would upset me. She wanted to hurt me.'

Cat took another cigarette out of her pack and lit the match savagely. 'Well I'm very sorry. I'm not exactly over the moon either.'

Maddy turned to look at her. 'What are you going to do?'

Cat noticed that her eyes were hollow and surrounded by dark circles. She looked sad and exhausted, like she needed a hug, but Cat wasn't going to waste any sympathy. She could use a hug herself – and there was no way on God's earth she was going to get one.

'Don't know,' she replied bitterly. 'I can't pretend having a baby was exactly on my agenda.'

Maddy frowned. 'Will you be able to manage – if you keep it I mean?'

'Well, I live in a tiny two-bedroom flat with someone else and earn crap money in a dead-end job. And my mum's sick and I'm the only one to look after her. Oh, and Leo's not paying my rent any more so I'm even more broke than usual.' She laughed nastily. 'Does that answer your question?'

Maddy walked over to a bench and sat down. Cat followed, despite herself.

'Why did you get involved with him?' Maddy asked. She didn't sound threatening or aggressive.

'I could ask you the same question.'

Maddy put her hands on her lap and fiddled with the red ring on her finger, twisting it round and round. Cat found herself staring at it, mesmerised.

'We loved each other very much,' Maddy said quietly.

'So did we.'

There was a pause. The conversation was going nowhere.

Cat straightened up. 'Look. I didn't come here to argue about Leo. One more question then I'm off. I'm busy, in case you hadn't noticed.'

'Did he tell you about me?' Maddy was wincing slightly at her own question.

Cat lit yet another cigarette and took a few puffs before stubbing it out. 'Yeah. He said he felt guilty about your kid and the other children, Victoria's. He couldn't just dump you.'

Maddy was silent for several minutes. 'He never mentioned you to me.' There was pain in her voice but she wasn't crying.

'Well maybe he had lots of secrets,' said Cat, 'like the will and everything – and that wife who never existed. You were lucky. At least you had eight years or whatever it was with him. I only got just over one.'

'I can't understand it. We were so close, we loved all the same things. Long walks, tennis, skiing, antique decanters.' Maddy gave a half laugh. 'We spent hours trawling funny little shops for those. We had quite a collection.' Her voice trailed off.

Cat stared at her before picking up where she'd left off. 'Art...' She was remembering how patient he was, explaining why this or that painting was so much better than another. '... old movies, rock music. Chinese takeaways—'

'He hated takeaways. And rock music.'

Cat shook her head. 'No he didn't. And he never struck me as the sporty type either.'

Maddy looked as if she'd like a discussion but Cat had had enough. She rose and both women were silent as they retraced their steps, lost in their own thoughts. Finally Maddy stopped a few doors down from the bookshop.

'Look,' she said, 'I felt sick when I saw you at the funeral; it was a terrible shock and I hated you, just as Victoria hates me. I think you were wrong to get involved with Leo-'

Cat laughed unpleasantly. 'I could say the same about you.'

'But,' Maddy went on, ignoring her, 'you're in a fix. If there's anything I can—'

Cat pulled a face, which shut her up. The sun had gone now and it was spitting with rain. She could see Gervaise peering at them through the shop window. She yanked up the hood on her parka and swallowed.

'Victoria thinks she's been helping already, chucking loads of numbers at me like I couldn't look them up for myself. Then she turns round and gossips to you about me behind my back.

'I don't want your help or anyone else's for that matter. I don't trust you and I wish I'd never set eyes on either of you. I'll deal with this on my own.'

* * *

The bleeding started at around 4 p.m. Cat went to the loo and noticed three or four dark brown spots and wondered what they were. She and Gervaise were alone at the till while Rachel made an 'important call.' He bent down and took something out of a backpack on the floor.

206

'I've had new headshots done,' he said cheerfully, brandishing several sheets of paper with hundreds of thumbnail photos on them. 'Will you have a look and tell me which one you think's best?'

'Sure,' she said wearily, realising that she wasn't feeling sick anymore and her breasts weren't so sore.

She took the sheets from him and peered at the rows and rows of pictures. They all appeared the same to her. In some, he was wearing a blue shirt, in others a black V-neck, but other than that they were virtually identical.

'This one's nice,' she commented, pointing at one of the middle pictures, scarcely able to focus.

Gervaise pulled a face. 'One of my eyebrows is higher than the other.'

'Hmm. Well, what about this one?' She pointed to another shot, about two thirds of the way down the page. 'I like the expression – kind of mean, moody and magnificent. And you can see the dimple in your chin.'

Gervaise took the sheet of paper from her and examined it for a long time, his head on one side.

'Ye-es, but I don't look very approachable. I need to look sexy and friendly at the same time, and also kind of blank, so they know I can turn my hand to any role.'

When Cat went to the loo again there were more brown spots and by the time she left for home she was feeling pretty grotty: cold and shivery and her back was aching.

'Wanna come to the movies?' Gervaise asked, but she shook her head.

'I need to visit my mum. She's acting really strange at the moment, getting up at dawn to clean the flat from top to bottom and cooking these massive meals. She used to eat like a sparrow and now she can't seem to stop.'

'Maybe it's her hormones?' Gervaise said helpfully.

She didn't go to her mother's, she went straight home, taking off her clothes and jumping in the bath. The warm water eased her back slightly but as soon as she got out, the aching began again. She didn't want to eat anything. Instead she fed the mice, made herself a hot water bottle, put on some Mozart, climbed into bed and curled up like a foetus, cuddling the warm bottle tight.

She was woken by the sound of Tracy coming in. She could hear a man's voice, too: Rick. They must have made up already, then. She checked the clock beside her bed and saw that it was past midnight. She'd been asleep for hours but now she was wide awake and alert and probably would be half the night.

She thought she'd get up and make herself a cup of tea, then she remembered. The backache had gone, to be replaced by dull, period-like tummy cramps. She reached down between her legs and felt that her pyjama bottoms were wet. She understood, intellectually of course, what was happening, but emotionally it was harder to grasp.

She rushed to the bathroom and sat on the loo. The cramps were much worse suddenly, really painful. Bright red blood was gushing out along with big dark clots. She felt tears trickling down her cheeks and realised she was devastated.

This was Leo's baby that she was losing, the baby she didn't even think she wanted and couldn't afford, that was going to mess up her life and have to sleep in the corner where the mouse cage was. This baby that would cry and have smelly nappies and stop her going out and drinking and having fun.

Fun. She wasn't having much of that now. She thought she wanted the baby more than anything, that noise and smelly nappies and all, it would make her life complete. And now, unlike Victoria or Maddy, she'd never be whole, she'd always be this unfinished thing, waiting for something – someone – to complete the circle.

She sat there, praying to a God she didn't even believe in that it wasn't so, but the blood continued to flow, a ball the size of a small orange. She peeked at it but daren't look closer. Her stomach hurt so much and she screwed up her eyes with the pain.

Tracy banged on the door. 'Are you all right? You've been in there ages.' She sounded giggly and excited; she'd obviously been to the pub.

'Yes,' Cat managed. 'I must have eaten something.'

'Eeuuw! I won't bother to clean my teeth then.'

She heard Tracy's door click shut and waited until the bleeding slowed before padding back to her room feeling infinitely sad, not just for herself but for the entire world.

This was an unlived life, a person who might have been and a relationship she'd never have. She felt that a precious, no, a priceless thing had been taken and no one would ever now see its beauty or know its worth.

CHAPTER SIXTEEN

Saturday January 9th

Victoria was still in her dressing gown when the doorbell rang. She'd been leafing through the Saturday morning papers and was halfway through her third cup of tea and second shortbread biscuit.

'Salome! Can you get it?' she called from the kitchen. She knew that her daughter was watching cartoons next door and it was high time she turned the television off. Standards were slipping; she was never allowed so much TV when Leo was alive.

She heard Salome thunder down the hallway and open the door. There was a man's voice and Victoria's ears pricked.

'Mu-um, postman!'

She rose, sighing. Why couldn't he have shoved everything through the letterbox? She wasn't expecting any deliveries.

She felt slightly embarrassed greeting him in her nightwear and crossed her arms tightly over her chest. It was gone eleven and he must have been up for hours. He passed her a pile of letters and a heavy brown paper parcel and handed her a slip to sign. The parcel was addressed to 'Mrs Victoria Bruck', care of Leo's agent. From its shape and weight, she guessed it might be books.

She took the parcel and letters back into the kitchen.

'You'd better get dressed quick young lady,' she told

Salome, who was following her. 'And can you bring down your swimming things? We need to leave in twenty minutes.'

Intrigued, she opened the parcel first. Inside was a card with a soothing picture of the sea on the front and three books about bereavement. It was from one of Leo's fans, a woman from Portsmouth. 'I know how you must be feeling, she said, because I recently lost my husband, too. I found these books very helpful. I hope you will as well.'

Victoria was touched and resolved to reply this afternoon. She'd had so many letters and messages of condolence and support, forwarded on by Leo's agent in batches. Mostly she found them comforting as they reminded her of the special place that Leo occupied in so many hearts.

She had a green and gold box, decorated with an Arabic design, which she put them all in and which she'd pass on to the children one day. Some of the notes, however, annoyed her. It was the ones that went on about Leo's achievements with no recognition of the fact that, whilst the world had lost a prodigious talent, she'd lost her husband and the children, their father. Some people had no sensitivity.

She checked the postmarks – Morpeth, Taunton, Reading – and put the letters down again. She needed to get ready and could read them later. She was about to place the last letter, unopened, with the others when something made her stop.

The writing was clearly foreign. Small, neat, flowery and rather old-fashioned, it was quite different from any English script that she'd seen. She checked the stamp, which was from the United States, and knitted her brows.

Her curiosity roused, she slit the letter open with her special bone handled knife. The letter was on two sides and she glanced down at the signature first. It was from someone called Rudolf Hirsch and she started to read.

He began by offering his condolences, then went on to tell her that he met Leo when he was a child.

'I too,' he wrote, *'was lucky enough to escape the gas chambers as a Kindertransport child. Your husband and I travelled on the same train from Vienna and, being the same age, took great comfort from each other.*

'I remember how we distracted each other from our sorrows and tried to make ourselves laugh with silly boyish jokes. We were both very scared and homesick, having left our families behind.

'After we arrived in London, I was sent to the north of England while Leo went to Guildford in Surrey. I was cared for by a kind enough farmer and his wife who had three children of their own.

'Leo and I wrote several letters to each other but then life got in the way, I suppose, and we lost touch until our late teens. I happened to be on a visit to Surrey and read something about him in a local newspaper. The article said he was a violin prodigy, still living with his English family and destined for great things. It didn't surprise me because I could tell that he was passionate about music, even as a little boy.

'I wrote to Leo and we met up. It was a wonderful meeting, we had so much to discuss and catch up on. But then there was the nasty business with the English family and I'm afraid that he stopped writing after that and we never saw each other again. It has always been a sorrow to me.'

The letter went on to tell Victoria about the author's life in New York, where he emigrated after the War, his job as a doctor and his wife, now sadly deceased, two children and six grandchildren. Victoria skimmed through but didn't really take it in. 'The nasty business with his English family' he said, as if she knew all about it, yet she had no idea what he meant.

She knew, of course, that Leo was one of the first Kindertransport children, rescued by a special British Committee. It was they who'd persuaded the Government to allow Jewish children seventeen years old or younger into England. This way, some nine to ten thousand Jewish children from Germany, Austria, Czechoslovakia and Poland were saved.

She knew, too, that he was taken in by a wealthy cultured English family in Guildford, Surrey, and that he lived with them in their converted boathouse by the river until several years after the end of the War.

They were very good to Leo. They recognised his talent and paid for him to take violin lessons with the top people in the country, later encouraging him to apply to the Royal School of Music. Without them, he would almost certainly never have become a great violinist and then a conductor.

She also knew that his father was killed by the Nazis and that the kind family managed to get his mother to England on a domestic service visa a few months after Leo arrived. She, too, stayed with the family, ostensibly as a cook, until the end of the War.

All this much Leo had told her though he never wanted to dwell on it. She recognised that his past must, on some profound level, have been very painful to him and respected him for his courage and lack of self pity. But she also wished sometimes that he'd open up because she'd have liked to help him. She thought that she could have.

The letter unnerved her and she found herself wondering

again why Leo lost touch with the English family who did so much for him. She'd always assumed that it was because he was so busy, so wedded to his work, but now it seemed there was something more, something 'nasty'.

She tucked the letter under the others and went upstairs to dress, thinking that she'd have plenty of time to reflect on what to do while she watched Salome thrashing up and down the pool during her lesson.

* * *

Maddy was in the supermarket, putting a sparkly pink frock firmly back on its hanger.

'No,' she said with exasperation, 'you may not have that. We can't afford it and anyway it's disgusting.'

The notion of not being able to afford something was entirely alien to Phoebe. She'd never been to this particular supermarket before and as far as she was concerned, it was girlie heaven. She was surrounded by more pink, silver, baby blue and lilac clothing than she'd ever seen before and Mummy was saying she couldn't have one single thing. It wasn't fair.

'But I want it,' she said, stamping her foot.

'Stop being a monster,' Maddy replied through clenched teeth, 'and help me with the shopping.'

It had been a bad few days. Maddy had now been on the phone to every company that she knew and respected and followed it up with an email. The message was the same everywhere: staff cuts rather than new appointments, little or no freelance work but by all means send us your CV and we'll put you on file, blah blah.

She'd been updating her CV for the first time in years but there seemed little hope of immediate employment. With the recession still in full swing it might be a long wait.

She could hardly believe that only a short while ago she'd been casually internet shopping for items she didn't need and wondering where to go on holiday next. Now, already, she was desperately trying to scale back.

'Hmm. What do we need?' she pondered, examining her shopping list. 'Fruit.'

Phoebe was sulking but the sight of a large pineapple raised her spirits.

'Can we have this?' she said, picking it up.

'We'll stick with apples and oranges today,' her mother replied, almost popping an enormous navel orange in her plastic bag before glancing at the price and replacing it quickly.

Next stop was the estate agents. Maddy parked her BMW round the corner, took off her belt and leaned round to talk to Phoebe in the back.

'Darling, I've some important news.'

She'd made the decision that selling the house was the most sensible – possibly the only course of action. It was the only way that she could pay off her debts and contemplate a jobless, or semi-jobless few months.

To her relief Phoebe took things quite calmly. 'Will I have a new bedroom?'

'Of course.' Maddy wanted to add that Phoebe could choose lovely wallpaper and bed linen to match but stopped herself, realising that redecorating, unless she did it herself, was going to be out of the question.

'And will we have a big garden?' Phoebe wanted to know. She'd often complained about the small paved area at the back of their Brook Green house.

Maddy swallowed. 'No darling. I expect we'll be in a flat. You know, in a big tall building with a lift that we get in to go up and down. We'll be able to watch all the tiny people below. It'll be fun.'

Phoebe was silent for a moment. 'But I won't have anywhere to play.'

'We'll go to the park,' Maddy replied as brightly as possible. 'It's more fun at the park anyway, with swings and things.'

The estate agent was a weasel of a man who looked slyly at Maddy when she explained that she wanted a quick sale and was after a flat nearby.

'It's a bad time,' he nodded knowingly. 'I've got lots of customers like you needing to downsize.'

'I don't need to,' Maddy said quickly, 'I'd just like somewhere smaller, that's all.'

'Of course,' he said, lowering his eyes fake-respectfully, 'A nice flat for you and the little girl. Just the two of you is it?'

'Ideally I want three bedrooms.' Maddy was damned if she was going to discuss her personal arrangements with him.

'I'm not little, I'm seven,' Phoebe chipped in. Maddy smiled, grateful for the distraction.

'Little? Of course you're not,' said the man winking at Maddy, who pretended not to notice. 'You're quite the young lady, I can see that.'

Phoebe beamed, showing off enormous front teeth which her face still needed to catch up with. 'I'll be eight in September,' she said proudly.

Maddy was exhausted by the time she reached home but felt a certain sense of achievement. They were coming to value the house later this afternoon and all being well, it would go on the market early next week.

She was underwhelmed by the description of the flats she'd been shown but the estate agent had assured her they'd be doing more viewings over the course of the weekend and he was sure they'd be able to fix her up.

He'd warned that prices were depressed and she might have to accept a lower offer than she hoped for. The upside, though, was that property in the area was still selling well and anything she bought, of course, would be cheaper, too.

She drew up outside the house and sat for a moment staring into the distance. It wasn't what she wanted. She was doing her best, but she couldn't quite believe that it had come to this. She felt a lump in her throat and was relieved when Phoebe snapped her out of it.

'Come on Mummy, I'm hungry.'

After lunch, Phoebe went upstairs to play and Maddy sat at the kitchen table, nursing a mug of coffee and staring into space. Since meeting Cat in the bookshop two days ago she'd been trying to put all thoughts of this other child, a new Bruck baby, out of her mind. The younger woman had made it quite clear she didn't want any further contact, after all.

Maddy had wanted to talk to her, needing answers, and had hoped that this would be enough to satisfy her. Yet she couldn't escape the feeling that whatever Cat said to the contrary, this baby was very much her business as well.

Her thoughts returned to Ralph and she wondered how he was getting on. She'd phoned the day after he'd turned up unexpectedly on her doorstep and he'd wanted to visit again, but she'd put him off. She knew he was keen; he could scarcely hide his eagerness. She rose quickly, thinking she must clear away the lunch dishes and get on with some work.

The phone rang just as she was taking a dishwasher tablet out of the packet and she knew immediately who it was.

'What are you up to later? Can I come and see you and Phoebe?'

He was persistent, she'd give him that.

She thought of the long evening ahead with just the two of them. She used to be quite sociable when Leo wasn't around and would often go out with friends. Since his death and losing her job, though, she hadn't wanted to do anything.

'We've no plans,' she found herself saying. 'Come for supper if you like.'

But hadn't he made arrangements with his mates?

'No. I'd rather see you.'

She shivered and put on the cardigan on the back of her chair, thinking that for some reason the temperature seemed to have suddenly dropped.

***

It seemed strange to be Googling her own husband; she'd never done it before. Victoria skipped all the newest articles and went right back, dozens of pages, to earlier reviews which she felt were more likely to go into his background.

There was one from the Times which spoke briefly of the Gannon family who took him in during the War. But it didn't refer to any children and of course, the Gannon parents would be long since dead.

Victoria knew that there were children because Leo had told her, but he'd never mentioned them by name. Her best hope, she decided, was to try to find out who they were and track them down. She didn't want to contact Rudolf Hirsch, who'd written her the letter; he might only know half-truths or falsehoods. Leo had never spoken of him and she didn't know if she could trust him. No, it was the Gannons she must speak to.

She pushed her glasses up her nose and continued to read. There was so much about Leo's career, his style of conducting and his greatest triumphs but little about his personal life. This wasn't surprising because he'd always been notoriously wary of the press and had rarely given interviews. When he did, he would refuse to answer questions about anything other than his music, which meant that journalists had been obliged to scrabble around in old clippings and repeat what had been written before in order to provide some sort of biography.

Her search yielded nothing that she didn't know already. She leaned back in the chair and scanned around the room, hoping for inspiration which didn't come.

Frustrated, she wandered upstairs to his study and stared at the rows and rows of books and music scores and CD's, until at last her eye was drawn to a blue file on the very bottom shelf beside a music dictionary.

She took the file out, opened it and a wodge of musty, yellowing newspaper clippings tumbled out. Most of the clippings repeated much of the information she'd just read but there was one, from the Guildford Advertiser, that was more promising.

The date was July 1949 and there was a faded black-and-white picture of a Leo with very short dark hair in a dark suit playing his violin, a small smile on his lips. She skimmed through the article which said that local boy, seventeen-year-old Leopold Bruck, had won a scholarship to the Royal College of Music.

She paused, reflecting that he was the same age then as Ralph was now. Ralph, who seemed so secretive and unmotivated, who had no idea what he wanted to do in life. How different they were!

She read on. The article mentioned The Gannon Family of Guildford who took Leo in just before war broke out and to whom he was greatly indebted. There was nothing at all about the children. Victoria sighed. Dead end. Elsa would know more but it was unlikely that she'd reveal anything.

Victoria looked at the photograph one more time, taking in Leo's wide intelligent brow, the close-set eyes, curved nose and sensitive mouth. It tugged at her heart strings. Her Leo. Then she noticed that there was a fair-haired girl in the background sitting on the corner of an armchair. The image was blurred but it was a person all right. She looked about twelve or thirteen, perhaps. It was hard to say.

Victoria glanced at the caption. 'Leo in the front room of the Gannon home playing to Maeve, the eldest daughter.'

Victoria's heart jumped. Maeve Gannon. She might have married and changed her surname, but it was something to go on. She rushed back downstairs to her computer and tapped in the words. To her delight an entry came up: 'Maeve Corcoran, née Gannon, member of the Royal College of Psychiatrists, wife of James Corcoran, one son, one daughter.' It must be the same person, surely? It wasn't a common name.

She repeated her search, this time keying in Maeve Corcoran. There were full biographies on Linkedin and Wikipedia and more on the Royal College of Psychiatrists' website. She was born in 1937 so she was five years younger than Leo. She'd had a distinguished career and lived in North London, but they didn't say where.

Victoria stuck a pen in her mouth and thought. She could write to her via the Royal College of Psychiatrists but she might not reply. Without a road name, directory enquiries wouldn't help with the home address. She needed something more.

She scrutinised the Google entries for Maeve again and on page four spotted something interesting: Maeve was a governor at a secondary school in Highbury. Quickly, Victoria pulled up the school's website and saw that there was a full governors' meeting on January 19th. That was only ten days away but it seemed a long time to wait. Could be her best option, though.

She got up and made herself a cup of tea, thinking all the while about this unknown woman, trying to picture her in her mind's eye.

Her stomach fluttered. She felt as if she were on the brink of a discovery of some kind. She didn't know where her investigations would lead her or how she would cope with whatever she discovered. She just knew that she had to do it.

CHAPTER SEVENTEEN

Monday January 11th

She was a bit late for the counselling session and Don was pacing up and down the corridor while Kate was nowhere to be seen.

Debs appeared from the kitchen with a mug of coffee. 'Have this,' she said, offering the mug to Victoria. 'I'll make another one.'

'Would you like a drink?' Victoria asks Don, who shakes his head. She can tell that he's eager to start and opens the door of the consulting room. 'Come on in.'

She takes off her coat and sets the mug on the table beside her chair. Don is still pacing.

'No Kate today?' she asks evenly. It doesn't do to express surprise.

'She wouldn't come,' he replies, running a hand through his hair. 'Said there was no point.'

Victoria takes a sip of coffee and smiles encouragingly. 'Sit down. You'll be more comfortable.'

He perches on the edge of the chair opposite, his legs wide apart in that way that men have, his elbows resting on his knees, his head hanging.

'Tell me about it,' says Victoria. 'Why wouldn't she come today?'

Don explains that they had a massive row last night after he admitted the affair Kate found out about wasn't his first. In fact he's had several.

'I honestly didn't think it would make much difference,' he says, staring at the ground. 'I mean, I was being totally truthful for once. I admitted I was unfaithful and accepted it was wrong and now I was telling her there was a bit more to it. But she went beserk, chucking stuff round the room and screaming. She woke the children who were really upset. It was awful.'

Victoria looks at him. It's her job to remain neutral but she realises that she'd like to slap him. The irony of her situation isn't lost on her. If Don knew what her relationship with Leo was like, he'd probably laugh in disbelief. 'And she thinks she can counsel me,' he'd scoff.

'She says we're finished,' Don says hopelessly. 'I know it's all my fault and I can understand why she's upset but there's so much at stake. I mean the children...' He cranes his chin. 'I suppose we'll have to sell the house. I can't afford to pay for that as well as somewhere for myself.'

'Slow down,' says Victoria. 'It's never a good idea to do anything sudden. Kate's had a shock. When things have cooled a bit, you and she need to talk seriously about where you go from here, whether a split really is what you both want and if so, how you can make it easiest for the children. I can help you with that.'

She pushes her hair back off her face. 'But we're not there yet. As she's not here today, I suggest we use the next forty-five minutes to look at ways that you can encourage her to talk without having an argument. I can give you some useful strategies. I also think it would *be good to talk about you. To go back to your childhood and examine some of your early influences, if you're OK with that?'*

Don seemed happier and less twitchy when he left and promised that he'd try to persuade Kate to come next time. It was 12.15 p.m. and Victoria had an hour and a half to kill before she saw her next clients. She'd got a pretty heavy schedule this year but was grateful to Debs, who knew she needed the money. She'd reduced her own appointments so that Victoria could have them.

She turned on her mobile to check for messages, relieved there were none. As far as she knew, Ralph was at school and had agreed, in his angry offhand way, that he would up the ante as A-levels loomed closer. Salome, thank heavens, was going happily to lessons though she was more clingy and needy in the evenings.

It was hard, of course, for them both having to adjust to their change of circumstances on top of the loss of their father. Victoria had reluctantly had to stop Ralph's allowance, which he'd not been happy about, but what choice was there? She'd said if he needed money for going out he'd have to get a weekend job. And she'd managed to get the cash back for Salome's after-school clubs.

She'd told them there would be no more holidays for the time being, no new clothes, no restaurants. She'd contemplated selling their old car but decided that she'd see how things went. She'd get so little for it, anyway.

She'd never been extravagant but when Leo was around, money simply hadn't been a worry. There had always been enough. Now she was having to watch every penny. She'd made a rule about no heating during the day, taking showers

224

not baths and eating only at mealtimes because they could no longer afford expensive snacks. She was trying not to think about what would happen if the washing machine broke or the roof needed mending. She had nothing put by for a rainy day.

She poked her head round the door of Debs' consulting room but she wasn't there. Oliver, though, was in the kitchen taking something evil-smelling out of the microwave.

'Hi!'

He turned and smiled. She hadn't seen much of him since the dinner party last week though he'd apologised again for Rosanna's insensitivity. He didn't need to, really. Victoria had been very upset but she'd forgiven him now. After all, Rosanna was the one to blame.

Peeling back the lid of a plastic container, he dumped something on a plate and showed her.

'Looks awful,' he said, prodding the contents with a fork. 'Shall we go for a sandwich – on me?'

She laughed and it crossed her mind that she'd stopped that stupid habit of burbling to fill the silences. It must be because she'd got to know him a little better.

They found a table in the basement of Starbucks, in a corner where they couldn't be overheard, and somehow started on the subject of an otter-spotting weekend he'd had in Northumberland last spring with a group of male friends.

'Great fun,' he said, catching her eye, an amused self-mocking smile on his lips. He opened a bag of crisps and offered her one, which she took. 'We saw one very early on with binoculars, about thirty metres away.' He was sounding like one of the presenters on the BBC's Springwatch. 'We were willing it to come closer then it dived for several minutes and surfaced just a little distance from where we were. It was dipping and diving against a backdrop of reeds, catching fish and rolling on its back to eat them.'

Victoria sipped her cappuccino. 'I like otters,' she said, playing along. 'I adored Ring of Bright Water as a child – though it made me sob.'

'We might be foolish enough to go back to the same place again this year. Come with us if you like.'

She wasn't sure if he were joking but smiled, trying to imagine herself on holiday with a bunch of otter-obsessed men. 'Wouldn't I cramp your style?'

He took a bite of sandwich. 'Not at all, I think you'd make an excellent addition to our club. Wives and girlfriends are always invited...and women friends,' he added almost imperceptibly, though Victoria noticed, 'but for some reason they choose not to join us.' He gave a wry smile and she noticed the firm jaw and dimple in his chin.

'Modern art, otters. Your interests are certainly eclectic,' she teased.

He scratched his head, suddenly serious. 'To be honest, it's my friend Simon who's the wildlife nut. I just tag along. But don't tell him that.'

She found herself wondering again if he were a bit lonely. But he seemed to have plenty of friends. And Rosanna, of course.

He talked a bit about his clients that morning and she mentioned Kate and Don.

'Doesn't sound too promising.'

'I'm not sure,' she replied, biting carefully into a baguette, praying that the filling wouldn't squirt out and hit him in the eye. 'You know, there's a lot of hurt and anger but I think there's plenty of love and commitment, too. I just hope she can be persuaded to come back to counselling. I reckon I can help.'

One of her hands was resting on the table and Oliver leaned across and touched it lightly. She started, unaccustomed to physical contact, and he took it away again.

'How are you coping? You and the children?' he asked gently.

She was sorry for being jumpy and realised how much she wanted to talk. She found herself telling him a bit about the will, the empty bank account, Leo's mythical wife and Cat's pregnancy. Then she went on to describe the strange letter and how she thought she might have tracked down Maeve Gannon. He listened carefully.

'You must feel very hurt that he lied to you,' he said at last. 'It's clear he couldn't be faithful and had a huge fear of marriage, some sort of commitment phobia. Yet he *was* committed to you. You were together all those years, despite the other women. You mustn't forget that.'

Victoria smiled. 'It's true, and I do still love him. He's the love of my life. But it's such a shock.'

Oliver nodded. 'But are you sure you want to know what this nasty incident was? It's in the past now, Leo's dead. Isn't it time to move on?'

Victoria fiddled with a silver dangly earring. 'I can't. Not until I know. I suppose, looking back, that there always was a mystery about my husband. It was part of what made him so attractive. Maybe I'd be happier living in ignorance but once Elsa told me there was no wife that wasn't possible. I've opened a Pandora's Box and I can't rest until I know what's in it. You can understand that, can't you?'

Oliver fixed her with troubled eyes. 'I'll come with you if you like. I can drive you to the school and wait in the car while you speak to her. I wouldn't mind. Let me do that for you.'

She was touched. 'It's kind of you, but no. This is my journey and I'll make it on my own.'

She pushed back her chair, aware that she'd been here far longer than intended. The time seemed to have flown. 'I must go or I'll be late for my next session.'

'Let me know how you get on.'

She nodded, feeling embarrassed suddenly though she wasn't quite sure why. Perhaps it was that sense that he was watching her as she slipped out of the shop in front of him. She was hoping that her shoulders didn't appear too wide in the old trenchcoat that she'd pulled out of the cupboard this morning, that she wouldn't trip and that the back of her hair wasn't too frizzy.

* * *

'It's you!' Maddy sounded anxious.

Ralph was walking slowly across the Common, phone to his ear. He didn't want to get home too early or Victoria would be suspicious. He'd bunked off afternoon lessons and had a smoke with his mates. He'd made the mistake of mentioning Maddy and they'd teased him a lot, asking if she was fit, that kind of rubbish. He tried to explain it wasn't like that but they didn't believe him. 'Does she fancy you?' they'd joked. He was glad to get away.

He'd tried her a couple of times earlier in the day but she hadn't replied and he didn't want to leave a message. Anyway, she'd know that she'd missed his calls.

'When can I see you and Phoebe again?' He didn't want to sound over-keen but they hadn't fixed another time when he'd been to see her on Saturday. She kept going on about how she was really busy looking for a new job. He supposed she must be pretty worried about that.

'Look, Ralph.'

He swallowed, not liking her tone.

'I'm not sure we should meet again. I don't think it's a good idea.'

This wasn't happening, surely? His face and neck were burning. He liked her so much and she was the only person who understood what he was going through. She was beautiful, too, but that was totally irrelevant.

'Why not?' There was an empty feeling in the pit of his stomach. 'What's wrong with it?'

'It's your mother,' Maddy sighed. 'I mean think about it. If she found out she'd go ballistic.'

'But she won't. She doesn't need to know a thing.'

'And there's something else,' she said hesitantly.

'What?'

'It's not normal, is it, for a woman my age to be spending time with you? You're only seventeen. What would people say?'

Ralph stopped walking and stood there in the middle of the Common. It was cold and grey and the collar of his dark blue school mac was turned up.

'I'm nearly eighteen. Anyway you're my stepmother, kind of. And Phoebe's my half-sister. What's wrong with that?'

Maddy wasn't having it. 'I'm sorry Ralph.'

His heart sank into his black school lace-ups. He was losing her, he could tell. He wished he didn't care but he did.

'It's not quite like that, is it?' she ploughed on. 'I'm not officially your stepmother and Victoria certainly wouldn't allow your visits. We're skating on extremely thin ice.'

Ralph clenched his hand around the phone and his voice came out funny. 'But I'll miss you.'

'You need to find someone else to talk to,' Maddy said gently. 'Your friends. Or a counsellor. There must be someone at school – a pastoral care officer you could speak to?'

'I don't want to talk to anyone else.'

Maddy, who was sitting at her computer, rested her head in one hand. She was feeling slightly dazed. She'd been busy all day, fiddling with her CV and trying to make it as good as possible. She'd also been calling accountants, trying to find a decent one. She still hadn't told the Inland Revenue that she was now self-employed but it didn't really matter as she hadn't any freelance commissions yet. She was just praying that it wouldn't take too long.

She glanced at her screen and a thought popped into her head, distracting her from her train of thought. 'Shouldn't you be at school?'

'I couldn't concentrate.'

She circled her shoulders and rocked her head from side to side. Her body seemed to have seized up over the past few weeks, she was so tense, and the conversation was making it worse.

'So you bunked off?'

'Yeah.'

She clicked her tongue. But she wasn't his mother, for heaven's sake. It wasn't her job to tell him off.

'What's up? Why couldn't you concentrate?'

He paused. 'I know this is going to sound stupid—'

'No it won't,' she said more softly. 'Tell me.'

'I was thinking about something you said.' He hesitated. He'd been going over it again and again in his mind. 'About how you played tennis with Dad.'

'Yes?'

'I wish he'd played with me. We never did anything like

230

that together.'

She bit her lip, not knowing what she could say to make it better for him.

'It's all right,' he went on bravely, jumping in to fill her silence. 'I know it's not your fault—'

'Well it sort of is.'

He needed something, she knew. Words of comfort that she couldn't find. She drew herself up in her chair. 'Where are you now?' She felt that this was urgent and she shouldn't mess about.

'On the Common.'

'Do you want to come over?'

'Are you sure?' He sounded so relieved.

Victoria's face, those big grey eyes, flashed in front of Maddy but she quickly brushed the picture away. He needed her. 'Phoebe will be home from school soon. She'd love to see you.'

She left her work and went upstairs to her bedroom, where she slipped off her baggy old jumper and put on a clean black figure-hugging top. She found herself gazing in the mirror, examining herself critically, noticing fine lines that she'd never spotted before. She dusted her face with powder, put on some mascara and brushed her silky hair. For some reason her cheeks were burning hot and her eyes were bright as crystals.

Poor Ralph, she told herself, squirting on her favourite scent. He was going through such a tough time – and there was no denying that she was in part responsible for having become involved with his father. She owed it to him to talk things through some more.

She applied her pink lip gloss and gave herself a quick once over in the full-length mirror before strolling back downstairs to await him.

Wednesday January 13th

Cat hadn't been to work since the miscarriage six days ago. Tracy had told her she must visit the GP and get checked out but she didn't see any point. The baby was definitely gone and all that was left was a big black empty hole.

'Hey, it's probably a blessing in disguise,' Tracy said, passing her a cup of sugary tea and sitting down beside her on the bed. It was dark outside now and Cat's curtains were drawn. She'd hardly stirred all day, apart from a quick visit to her mother this morning. She took the tea and continued to stare at a point on the far wall.

'I mean, there might have been something wrong with it,' Tracy continued. 'A lot of people miscarry because the baby's not quite right, deformed. It might have had Spina Bifida or something. It's nature's way, you know.'

Cat grunted. She knew Tracy was trying to be helpful but there was no way that something was wrong with her baby, Leo's baby. It was her stupid body which had failed to do what it was supposed to. Story of her life, really – messing things up.

'Listen, I'm going to pop out with Rick,' Tracy said. 'Just for a couple of hours. Will you be all right, do you think?'

Cat noticed that Tracy was all dressed up; she hadn't registered before. She was wearing a very low cut black top which showed off the tiny angel tattoo on her left boob. Her yellow hair was loose and she'd done her eyes in that cat-like Cleopatra way that she favoured, rimming the top and bottom lashes with kohl which extended upwards beyond the corner of each eye. It was kind of mad but it suited her.

'Of course,' Cat said wearily. 'I'm not going anywhere, I'll be fine.'

Tracy sprang up off the bed, relieved. She was like Tigger. You couldn't keep her down for long.

Cat rested her tea on the bedside table and walked over to the mouse cage by the window, which smelled a bit because it needed cleaning. Roddy was sniffing his food bowl expectantly.

After opening the cage door she pulled him out, placing him gently in the palm of her hand and stroking his soft white fur. It was comforting to feel his warm little body and the tiny heart beating gently within his ribcage.

She kissed the top of his head – 'at least I've got you' – before climbing back on the bed, curling up like a ball and cupping him carefully in both hands so he couldn't run away.

She didn't feel too bad physically. The bleeding had lessened quite quickly and it was just like the end of a period now. In a few more days, she supposed, she'd get up, get back to work and carry on as normal. Except that she knew she'd never really be the same again.

It was like a second loss. Leo was gone and now the part of him that she'd been carrying inside was dead, too. It was hard to believe that not long ago she'd been contemplating a termination. Maybe this was her punishment. She felt as if she'd been given a life sentence.

She thought of Victoria and found herself wondering what she'd say. For some reason Cat would like to have told her what had happened. The older woman had tried to call so many times but Cat had ignored her. Then she remembered Victoria's fake concern and bit her lip. It just showed you couldn't trust anybody.

She was dismayed when the doorbell rang and sat stock still, intending not to answer, but it kept on ringing and ringing, like it was urgent. She got up slowly and put Roddy back in his cage. If it weren't for her mum she'd pretend she wasn't here, but there was always this dull worry that her mother might have done something stupid, slipped and fallen – or worse.

After pulling on an old green sweatshirt, Cat walked slowly down the dark flight of steps to open the door. Gervaise was looking down at her from his huge height, brandishing a bunch of tired-looking flowers in one hand and a see-through bag of grapes in the other.

'Hey!' he grinned, 'Something for the patient.'

Cat smiled thinly. She'd have to ask him in. 'I'm not very good company.'

'Ach, you don't have to be,' he said cheerfully in his Irish lilt. 'I'll do the talking for the both of us.'

There was one beer in the fridge, which she gave him, and she made yet another cup of tea for herself. She'd be turning into a tea bag at this rate.

'So, how're you feeling?' he asked, plonking himself on the sofa. 'We've missed you at work.'

Cat sat down beside him and pulled her knees up, nursing her warm mug. 'Not too bad. Nasty stomach bug, that's all. Probably something I ate. I'll be fine by Monday.'

He glanced at her strangely. 'You look bloody awful.'

'Thanks.'

There was no way she was going to tell him about the miscarriage. It was her own private business. And to cap it all she'd had yet another rejection from a magazine this morning for her latest short story. Just what she needed. She wouldn't mention that either.

He told her about his preparations for an audition. He'd play the part of a student doctor and he said he'd been watching old episodes of Casualty.

'Problem is,' he said, knitting his brows, 'I'm not keen on needles or operations or anything. Every time there's any blood and guts I feel like I'm going to faint.'

'Can't you make that part of the role?' Cat asked. 'I mean, you'd only be a student. Maybe student doctors do go funny when they see blood at first, then they get used to it. You could say you're going queasy deliberately, that you're method acting or something.' She looked doubtful.

Gervaise took off his long striped jumper. Cat had the heating up full blast and it must have been very warm, though she couldn't feel it. It was like that when you'd been sitting around for hours.

He swigged his beer and rubbed his chin. 'Hmm. That's not a bad idea actually.'

She'd left the flowers on the table and he got up to fetch a tall glass from the kitchen.

'There,' he said, setting them down on top of the television. 'Pride of place.'

They were white and red stargazer lilies with a deep pink inside. Cat knew their name because her mother used to like them. They looked a bit sad but they'd probably perk up now they were in water. 'They're lovely, thank you.'

Gervaise was perched on the edge of his seat. 'I've been thinking.'

'Oh yes?' Cat wondered what was coming next. She picked up a cushion and hugged it to her chest.

'You once told me about that place you used to go on holiday when you were a kid – the Gower Peninsula?'

She nodded, squeezing her eyes shut. She wished she'd never told him; she hated being reminded of the past.

'Well I wondered...' he was staring at his red canvas boots

'...I wondered if we should go there for a few days instead of Ireland. On holiday I mean. For you to get better. We could take your mum, too, if you like. See the sights. It might do her good. And you could get on with some writing.'

Cat felt her body go hot. 'No!'

'Why not?'

'Because there's no way I ever want to go there again. I left that part of my life behind a long time ago. I'm a different person now and I don't need reminding. It's done, finished.'

Gervaise bit his lip. His black hair was sticking up and the thick black lashes round his blue eyes were very long and curled at the ends.

'I'm sorry.' She touched his arm. 'I know you're trying to be kind.'

'I'm not,' he replied petulantly. 'Well yes I sort of am. But I'd like to go with you. I thought it would be fun.'

His voice trailed off and Cat felt guilty. She was a cow, she really was.

'I'm sorry,' she said again, 'I did tell you I was bad company. Maybe we can go somewhere different, a bit nearer. Southend for the day – when the weather gets nicer?'

He brightened. 'Really? That'd be great.'

He jumped up. 'Here's me full of self-pity because you won't come on holiday and I'm completely forgetting you're the invalid and I'm supposed to be looking after you. Can I get you another cup of tea, or some cocoa – or how about some grapes?'

'Just what I fancy,' she lied.

She didn't like to shoo him away when he was being so good to her, so they sat chatting and listening to music and he made her laugh with stories of drama school.

'We had to do combat training,' he told her.

She'd heard it before but didn't mind being told again. It was kind of comforting.

'You know, with swords and stuff,' he went on. 'One of the lads was over-enthusiastic and did the splits by accident and damaged his groin. It was quite a nasty injury actually. Put him out of action for quite some time. Another lad refused to wear his codpiece because he thought it looked silly. Let's just say he lived to regret it.'

He was still there when Tracy and Rick – or Trick and Racy as Cat had taken to calling them – returned after midnight. Tracy staggered in, clutching Rick's arm.

'Shouldn't have had that last Bacardi and Coke,' she said ruefully, plonking herself down on a chair and hiccupping while Rick went to make black coffee.

'How're you feeling?' Tracy asked Cat, fixing her as best she could with her glazed eyes. 'Any better?'

Cat pursed her lips and shot her a meaningful stare. Tracy had never been known to blab even when pissed, but there was always a first time.

Gervaise seemed to notice Cat's discomfort and smiled gently. He was sensitive like that.

'Time for my bed,' he said stretching. 'I'll give you a tinkle tomorrow – see how you're doing.'

He let himself out of the flat and was gone by the time Rick emerged from the kitchen with two mugs of coffee – and a tea for Cat. Rick winked at her. He didn't seem half as drunk as Tracy, which made a change.

'He's mad about you,' he said to Cat, meaning Gervaise. 'You know that, don't you?'

Tracy nodded her head slowly several times as if moving it any faster would make it drop off.

'He is, Cat. Absolutely besotted. Anyone can see that. Me

and Rick think you could do worse, you know, than get together with Gervaise. He's a good kind man and he loves you.' She emphasised the point by slapping a hand on her thigh, which made her spill coffee on the carpet.

Cat frowned. She'd never really thought about it before but now they'd said it, she supposed that Gervaise did like her. She liked him too, sure. But not in that way.

'Rubbish,' she said, kicking Rick with her foot. 'You're drunk, the both of you. We're just mates, that's all. People who are thrown together at work and get along. As soon as he gets an acting job he'll be off, you'll see.'

'I wouldn't be so sure,' Rick said, ruffling Tracy's hair affectionately, which made her spill more coffee. 'I'd say he's too far gone for that. I know the signs. When a bloke's that far gone there's nothing much he can do about it.'

CHAPTER EIGHTEEN

Tuesday January 19th

Victoria knew there was no point asking Ralph to babysit Salome, so she recruited her neighbour's daughter instead.

She was worried sick about the fact that he was going out repeatedly in the evenings after school when he should be studying. He wouldn't tell her what he was doing and she was often on her way to bed by the time he returned.

She felt so helpless and alone. Although Leo was frequently away when he was alive, she could still talk to him on the phone and ask him to speak to his son. Of course it wasn't the same as having him there on the spot, but he'd had a lot of authority and Ralph was a little scared of him.

She knew she should probably book up to see his teachers. They might tell her to impose a ban on weekday outings and a curfew at weekends. But since that row after Christmas when he'd failed to return until the early hours of the morning, the truth was that she'd been treading on eggshells, afraid that if she said something to annoy him he'd disappear again.

Besides, she had so much else to think about. She tried to tell herself that he was nearly eighteen, after all, and old enough to accept responsibility for his actions. She must learn to let go. Salome was her priority, Salome and herself, because she was the one keeping a roof over their heads and food on the table. To a degree, she felt that Ralph would have to learn to take care of himself.

It was extraordinary, she reflected, as she put on her warm purple sweater, knee-length checked skirt and black boots, how much her thinking had changed in the past few weeks. Only a short while ago, the most significant things in her life, apart from Leo's work of course, were Ralph's exams, Salome's performance at school and her violin practice, plus who was or wasn't being mean to her in the playground. She almost marvelled at how narrow her horizons had been.

Now, the violin lessons had been scrapped due to lack of money and Ralph's exams had faded into the background. Cat's pregnancy, among other things, seemed to be of far more importance. It troubled Victoria that the young woman wasn't answering her calls but she'd keep on trying.

The canvas had become so much bigger and more frightening but also, in a way, more interesting. This realisation surprised Victoria. She'd never felt in any way cramped or small or restricted when Leo was alive; she'd thought that she was perfectly content with their unusual arrangement and that she had just about everything. Or was she merely imagining this?

She looked at herself in the bedroom mirror and noticed that she seemed altered in some way that was hard to define. The wild untameable curls were the same, the big grey eyes (her best feature), the strong nose and jaw. She decided the difference was that she didn't look like someone's wife anymore.

This made her sad, but she was also quietly proud of the fact that she was still here, holding herself together and even delving into something she'd have ignored before, pretending it wasn't there. She felt that, perhaps, six weeks on and in some very small way, she was making progress.

She decided not to tie her hair back but to let it hang loosely round her face. She chose a chunky silver necklace from her jewellery box, put on a dab of mascara and lipstick and kissed Salome goodbye at the door.

'Bed at eight Poppet,' she said firmly, tapping her daughter gently on the nose.

'Thanks, Sara.' She smiled at the babysitter who was standing behind. She'd agreed to look after Salome tonight for free. People were being very kind like that. 'I won't be too late.'

Victoria was nervous but curiously excited, too, as she drew up outside Moorcoat Secondary School in Highbury. It was 8.40 p.m. and she didn't know how long these meetings took, but it had started at seven-thirty. She'd wait another ten minutes or so, keeping the engine running and the heater on to stay warm.

The school appeared dark and imposing from the outside, an old Victorian building with thick heavy iron railings and an austere concrete forecourt. But a small gate to the side of the locked main entrance was open and there was a bright welcoming light in the reception area. She hoped that she'd be able to find her way to the meeting without bumping into anyone who might ask awkward questions.

When the ten minutes were up, she walked slowly into the school and stopped to listen. She could hear distant voices and the occasional burst of laughter. Turning left down a long corridor that had that familiar school smell of paint and disinfectant, she followed the sound up a small flight of steps to the first floor.

The voices were getting louder now and Victoria felt her pulse quicken. She couldn't quite believe how brave and brazen she was being, but there didn't seem to be any other option. If she waited outside until the meeting finished and everyone started to leave the building, she wouldn't know who to approach. Maeve might be half way home before it dawned on Victoria that she'd missed her.

The noise grew louder still and she stopped outside a closed grey door and took a deep breath. The worst that could happen, she told herself, was that Maeve would refuse to speak and she'd go home none the wiser. The other woman was hardly going to create a scene in front of all these people, surely?

Victoria opened the door and walked boldly in, casting an eye around the gathering. It was a large room, painted pale blue, with garish overhead strip lighting. About twenty people perhaps – men and women – were sitting on either side of a long wooden table and they all looked up.

She pulled back her shoulders. 'Is Maeve Gannon here?' she said loudly, trying to disguise her apprehension.

A voice came from the left. 'Yes, that's me.'

Victoria turned and saw an elderly woman stand up. She had short white hair and a shrewd intelligent face. She might be in her seventies but didn't look weak or bowed. Her back was perfectly straight.

Victoria felt her mouth go dry. 'I'm Victoria Bruck, wife of the late Leopold Bruck. There's something I need to know.'

There was a shuffling and a scraping of chairs but no one spoke.

Maeve walked slowly towards Victoria, clutching her coat and a small black bag. She was small and strong with the sprightly, confident gait of a much younger person.

'Ah,' she said. 'I wondered if I'd hear from you.'

She turned to the face the meeting. 'I apologise for the disruption. There's an important family matter I must deal with.'

She swivelled round and addressed Victoria again, who marvelled at her sang froid.

'You'd better come with me,' Maeve said, taking control of both the situation and Victoria and leading her by the arm towards the exit.

***

They strolled in silence towards the main gate then Maeve stopped. 'There's a pub round the corner called the King's Head. We can go there.'

She was a tiny woman, little more than five feet tall, and Victoria towered over her. But her voice was low and commanding and she didn't seem at all nervous.

The pub was fairly quiet and they found a table in the corner beside an open fire. Victoria bought a gin and tonic for Maeve and a glass of red wine for herself and sat down opposite the older woman.

'What do you want to know?' Maeve asked. Her smile wasn't unfriendly and her eyes, an unusual shade of green and partially obscured by heavy wrinkled lids, were sharp and inquisitive.

'You know Leo died?' Victoria asked.

'I read about it. I'm sorry for your loss.'

Victoria took a sip of wine. She recognised that this might be her one and only chance to gain the information she needed and she didn't know how much time she had.

'Since his funeral I've discovered all these things about him that I never knew,' she began. Maeve watched carefully. 'He told me he'd made a will and he'd look after me and the children. There was no will and no money. He said he had a wife in Austria which was why he couldn't marry me, but there was no wife. He had other women too, you know, at the same time as me?'

Maeve nodded. 'Of course. Go on.'

Her certainty was disarming. Victoria paused to regain her composure before continuing: 'I knew he'd lived with your family during the War but he never spoke of you.'

Maeve put her head on one side and continued to scrutinise Victoria's face. She felt uncomfortable under the spotlight, as if she were being analysed.

'All this doesn't surprise me,' Maeve said. 'Now ask me what you came for then I want to go home. I've had a very long day.'

'Yes,' Victoria said quickly, cutting to the chase. 'I had a letter – from someone who met Leo on the train to England in 1939. He referred to a 'nasty business' with your family.'

For the first time Maeve's mask fell. Her eyes clouded and she gave a humourless little laugh. 'Nasty business? That's one way to describe it.'

Victoria waited to see if she would elaborate but her thin lips were clamped shut. She leaned forwards, bringing her face close to the older woman. 'What did he mean?' she asked. 'Please tell me.'

Maeve took a sip of her drink, her eyes narrowing as she examined Victoria again. 'Why do you want to know?'

'Because he was my husband in all but name, my friend and partner for over twenty years and the father of my two children. There was so much about him I didn't question when he was alive but now...' She was aware that her voice was shaking but was determined not to crack '...now I want to solve the mystery once and for all. I want to understand the real Leo. I feel I can't move on in my life until I've got all the pieces of the jigsaw and put them together.'

She sat back, praying that she'd have got through and her plea wouldn't have fallen on deaf ears.

Maeve crossed her arms and sighed. 'Ah,' she said, closing her eyes for a minute, 'I don't think any of us will ever get to the bottom of Leo. But yes, I will tell you about the nasty business and then, I hope, you'll leave me alone. I'm old and it all happened a long time ago and I've dealt with it in my own mind and laid it to rest.'

Victoria nodded. 'I promise I'll never bother you again.' She meant it.

Maeve put her hands around her glass. They were small and neat and covered in brown liver spots. She had two wide gold rings on her wedding finger, one with a single white diamond.

'When Leo came to live with us,' she said, looking down at her drink, 'we were all so happy. I loved him. I had four younger siblings who could be very annoying but he was older. He took care of me and I looked up to him hugely.

'We'd moved to the boathouse near Guildford because my parents thought it would be safer than London during the bombing. It was idyllic, really. We children had a wonderful time playing by the river and messing around in boats and having picnics. We were scarcely aware that there was a war on at all.'

She sipped her drink and sighed, suddenly looking older and less in control. 'My parents adored him and treated him as their own son. They spotted straightaway that he was a musical genius and were determined to help him achieve his full potential. They were passionate about music themselves and paid for the best tutors available and gave him a special room to practise his violin in. Although we loved him, sometimes we children got a little bit jealous, I think. My parents seemed to give him more attention than the rest of us put together.'

Victoria listened intently. She was trying to imagine how Leo must have felt, plucked from his life and everything he knew in Vienna and put down in a new family, surrounded by strange children speaking an unfamiliar language, in a boathouse on the river. It must have taken some getting used to.

'Leo picked English up very quickly,' Maeve went on, as if reading her thoughts. 'He begged and begged my parents to help his mother, who was still in Vienna of course, and eventually they managed to get her a visa and she came to live with us too, as a sort of cook and housekeeper.

'We didn't like her much and my parents thought she drove Leo too hard with his practice. But I think she was a little scared of my father and she knew it was his house and he'd always have the final say.

'When the war ended, my mother said it was time for Leo and his mother to leave. I think, by then, she'd grown a little tired of Elsa and besides, she wanted to move back to our house in Pimlico and resume her old life and there wouldn't be enough room for two extras. But my father said no. We must continue to support Leo or his musical talent would be wasted. He didn't want him to have to go out and get a job. So we remained in Guildford and Leo applied to the Royal College of Music and won a scholarship. We were all so proud of him.'

Maeve paused for a moment, staring into the distance. Victoria scarcely dared breathe in case she changed her mind and decided not to go on.

At last the old woman picked up her story: 'My father was a very devout man. Roman Catholic, like my mother. His religion was very important to him but he didn't wear it on his sleeve; it was a very private matter to him.

'He never tried to convert Leo and Elsa, that wasn't in his mind at all when he took them in. He did so out of pure compassion; he could never bear to see human suffering and was deeply moved by the plight of the Jews. However, he was pleased and surprised when Leo said he wanted to join our faith and started to go to classes with the local parish priest. Soon, Elsa went too.

'It was around this time, after he got his scholarship and just before he started at the Royal College, that I became aware of a different atmosphere in the house. My father worked long hours in the City – he was a lawyer, a very good one – and it was my mother who really brought us up.

'Leo seemed to go into himself a little. He became distant with me and we didn't speak as much as we used to do. But he and my mother were always talking and laughing together, having cosy little chats, disappearing into the kitchen and closing the door. I felt angry and hurt – jealous, I suppose, of their relationship. Shut out. I was a teenager by then and I thought myself quite grown up though I'm sure I was still rather babyish really. I wanted to be part of their discussions not excluded from them.'

Victoria felt her pulse quicken. They'd both finished their drinks but she had no intention of going back to the bar.

'One day,' Maeve went on, 'my father came back from work early. I think I was doing my homework. I don't know where Elsa was, or the other children. Outside playing, perhaps. I heard a terrible commotion upstairs – shouting and banging and crying.' She swallowed.

'My father had walked in on my mother and Leo.' She turned her face away. 'They were making love in my mother's and father's bed.'

Victoria's heart missed a beat. 'That's horrible,' she cried before she could stop herself.

Maeve looked at her again and nodded. 'It was horrible – for all of us. After that, nothing was ever the same again.'

Two young men sat down at the table next to theirs and started talking but Victoria scarcely noticed or heard them.

'Do you want me to go on?' Maeve asked. Victoria nodded.

'My father was devastated,' Maeve said quietly. 'He threw Leo and Elsa out, of course. He felt so betrayed, you see, by the woman he loved more than anyone in the world and the boy he'd cared for as his own son. And to make matters even worse, Leo admitted he'd never really wanted to convert at all. It was a ploy to win favour with my mother. And it had worked.

'As far as my father was concerned, Leo had not only stolen his wife but trampled on his faith, on the beliefs he held so dear and everything that he stood for. Can you imagine? It was an almost fatal blow.

'My father blamed them both. My mother was old enough to know better and Leo was no longer a child either. He was a young man who'd been through a lot. In some ways he was far older than his years and must have known what he was doing and what the consequences would be. In my father's eyes they were equally culpable.

'My father moved back to London, taking us with him, while my mother stayed in the boathouse. I don't think either of them ever recovered. They managed to keep the story out of the papers but there was local gossip, of course. Separation was still frowned on in those days. My father would never listen to classical music again. He threw out all our records and banned us from playing our musical instruments. We were allowed to see my mother, but only during the school holidays and with our nanny present.'

She fiddled with the silver brooch at her neck. 'I think the day my father discovered Leo and my mother together was the day I left my childhood behind. Once Mother was gone, it seemed I was now responsible for the younger children, who missed her dreadfully. They were still quite little, some of them, and I became their mother – as well as nursemaid to my father who was bitter and angry, a broken man. He could never talk of her, though he'd once been so devoted, or of the boathouse or our old life in Guildford – or of Leo.

'We knew Leo had become famous – how could we miss it? But we never went to a single one of his performances.'

Victoria was frowning. 'But he did convert.' She was thinking hard. 'I wonder why, after all that had happened. Perhaps he felt guilty and was seeking some sort of atonement. I'd like to think so.'

She glanced at Maeve, who was shaking her head, and felt her stomach lurch. 'No. He never became a Roman Catholic. Of that I'm absolutely certain. My father remained true to his faith despite everything and was very active in the church, right up until his death. He would have known if Leo had taken that step. He would have been told.'

Victoria found herself shivering. She was thinking of Leo's protestations down the years. That sorrowful look in his eye: 'I can't marry you, my darling girl. I'm sorry. It's against my religion.'

So he'd lied about that, too.

She crossed her arms tight across her chest, aware that her teeth were chattering. She was outraged, not only for herself but also for Patrick Gannon, the man who'd shown such kindness. He must have felt as if he'd invited the devil himself into his home.

A thought occurred to her. 'But Leo still took up his place

249

at the Royal College of Music? I know he had a scholarship but there must still have been expenses. How did he manage that?'

Maeve nodded. 'As far as I know, Leo and my mother continued to see each other for a while. I presume she must have supported him. Eventually, of course, it fizzled out. Perhaps she could stand no more of his philandering.' She laughed bitterly. 'Ironic, yes? I never saw or spoke to him again.'

Maeve looked into Victoria's eyes and smiled sadly. 'So now you know,' she said. 'And you'll understand why I wasn't surprised to hear your late husband had other women.'

Victoria nodded. 'But why?' she said, her brain working overtime. 'Why would he betray the family that had given him so much? As you say, he must have understood the consequences.'

Maeve shrugged. 'Excitement, temptation – my mother was a very good-looking woman – the thrill of the risk, the need for admiration and approval, a sense of entitlement, perhaps? Leo was handsome, as you know. He was always seeing some girl or other, long before my mother set her cap at him. We used to tease him about it. We called him Casanova. I was rather jealous but fascinated, too. In my silly teenage heart I think I believed I was the one he loved really. He just didn't realise it yet.'

She smiled, drawing back her shoulders, before continuing her story.

'I'd say,' she said eventually, 'putting on my psychiatrist's hat for a moment, that he had a touch of narcissistic personality disorder. Looking back, I think he craved admiration, you see, and had perhaps a rather unhealthy opinion of his own uniqueness and importance.

'Of course we were all guilty of encouraging this, to a degree, especially my parents and his mother. They were always telling him how wonderful he was, how exceptional.

'It's possible that his particular problem was sexual narcissism,' she went on thoughtfully, almost as if she were talking to herself, now. 'An egocentric pattern of sexual behavior that involves both low self-esteem and an inflated sense of sexual ability and sexual entitlement. This would help to explain the many sexual exploits in the form of extramarital affairs that you say he had. These can tend to compensate for low self-esteem and an inability to experience true intimacy, you see.'

Victoria was thinking hard, too. It seemed to fit somehow, to make sense. It was true that he was egocentric, that he craved admiration and he was certainly a sexual predator.

'But why,' she asked, 'why would he be unable to experience true intimacy? So many people loved him, including me.'

Maeve looked at her shrewdly. 'Now that,' she said, 'I cannot answer. Remember I've never analysed him myself. All I can say is that he suffered a great deal of trauma in his childhood from which, perhaps, he never fully recovered.

'Imagine. He was there on Kristallnacht, The Night of Broken Glass, in November 1938, when most of Vienna's synagogues and prayer-houses were destroyed by the Nazis. They broke windows and plundered Jewish shops and businesses, including his father's, and he was taken away never to be seen again. Probably beaten to death. It must have been absolutely terrifying for a small boy, devastating.

'Then, of course, he was despatched to a strange family in England and expected to adopt a new language, school, friends, way of life.' She shook her head. 'It's a wonder, really that any of the Kindertransport children survived and even more extraordinary so many of them did so well.'

Victoria nodded. 'But I still don't understand about the intimacy thing. Why, in all those years we shared, would he never really let me close? I knew there were things he didn't tell me about his past and I could have helped him, I wanted to. It's only now, since he died, that I realise I hardly even knew him.' She wiped away a tear. 'In fact I wonder if he ever loved me or the children at all.'

Maeve picked up her bag and coat and shuffled along the bench seat to the space between their table and the next.

'That, I'm afraid, is also something you'll have to work out for yourself,' she said not unkindly. 'I have my own burdens to carry.' She stood up. 'Now, if you'll excuse me, I must go home.'

Victoria rose too. She held out her hand to shake Maeve's then, thinking better of it, bent forward and kissed her lightly. She flinched slightly but didn't resist. Her cheek was soft and she smelt of roses.

'Thank you,' Victoria said, 'for being so honest. And I'm sorry for all the pain he caused. I wish it had never happened.'

Maeve gave a half-smile. 'You deserved to know. And you have a gentle face. I wish you and your children well.'

Victoria stood watching as she walked towards the door, a tiny woman with a remarkably straight back and firm step. She turned just as she was about to leave, as if she'd remembered something, and beckoned to Victoria. Surprised, she hurried quickly to the old woman's side.

'You know,' said Maeve quietly, 'that there was a sister, don't you?'

Victoria's eyes widened. 'A sister? No. Leo said he was an only child.'

Maeve shook her head. 'He had a sister. He told me once.

His mother left her behind in Austria.'

More mysteries. Victoria's mind was racing. 'Left her behind? But why?'

Maeve shrugged. 'I don't know. He wouldn't say and I was never allowed to tell Elsa I knew. It was supposed to be a secret, our secret. No one was ever to speak of her. I don't think even my parents had any idea.'

'What became of her?' Victoria wanted to know. 'Is she still alive? Did they keep in touch? Where is she now?' So many questions.

Maeve opened the door and took a step out into the night.

'I've no other information,' she said. 'I've told you all I know. The rest is up to you.'

And with that she turned and disappeared into the darkness.

THIRD MOVEMENT

CHAPTER NINETEEN

Thursday March 4th

For the next few weeks Victoria was extremely busy working, looking after Salome and tidying the house. She decided to do a massive clear-out, mainly of Leo's things but also of all the junk they'd accumulated over the years. She was a hoarder by nature; she could never bear to throw anything away. She'd kept all the children's old books and toys that they'd long since grown out of and her own room was groaning with clothes she never wore and piles of magazines she never looked at.

The hardest part was getting rid of Leo's clothes. One morning when she wasn't at the office, she opened his wardrobe and threw everything on the bed: suits, jackets, shirts, cashmere sweaters, silk ties and cravats (he was quite a dandy) and about ten pairs of handmade leather shoes. She didn't allow herself to look at them too closely, still less feel them, smell them or hold them to her.

That evening, when Ralph came in from school, she asked him to take a look and see if there was anything he wanted. He came away with a few ties, three pale blue shirts, one with a thin purple stripe, and a couple of sweaters, nothing else. He didn't want any of the suits, saying they weren't his style and he'd never wear them.

He didn't seem particularly moved by the exercise, behaving as if it were the sort of task his mother might ask him to perform any day of the week. But Victoria knew he was trying to upset her and found herself surprisingly unruffled. She'd grown accustomed to Ralph's indifference and in some ways this was a relief; he couldn't hurt her quite so much.

When he left the room, she folded up all the clothes and put them in black bin bags. She didn't ask Ralph or Salome to help. Later, she sifted through her own wardrobe and removed anything she hadn't worn for a year or so. She was amazed how many clothes were lurking at the back that she'd forgotten she even had.

By the time she'd finished, her wardrobe was three quarters empty and she had only two full drawers instead of five. Looking at her own and Leo's bare rails and vacant cubby holes made her curiously elated.

She put all the bags in the dining room. Leaning for a moment against the polished wooden dining table, she cast her eye around the walls and shelves and realised there was no reason why she shouldn't also chuck out some of the ornaments and pictures she'd never really liked, starting with the ugly silver candlesticks that Elsa had given them one Christmas. There was also a porcelain tea service from Leo's mother that she'd hardly ever used. But she left them where they were, deciding she'd done enough for one day.

Ralph was in the kitchen making something to eat. The fridge door was open and beeping and there was a smell of something just starting to burn on the grill.

'I bought some steak,' she said amiably, shutting the fridge door and filling the kettle. 'I thought we could have it for supper.'

Ralph took two pieces of cheese on toast from the grill and sat down at the table, pushing Victoria's laptop to one side.

'I'm going out,' he said, without looking at her.

She raised her eyebrows. 'Again?'

'Yeah,' he replied, cutting into his food and putting a forkful in his mouth. 'Again.'

***

Maddy, too, was sorting through her house, throwing things out and beginning to pack everything into the giant cardboard boxes provided by the removal firm.

She'd made a quick sale, which she was grateful for. She'd had to lower the asking price but she'd still been able to buy a small light two bedroom flat just off the Goldhawk Road with only a small mortgage.

It had an open-plan reception room at the front, a modern fitted bathroom in the middle and two bedrooms to the back. Patio doors from what would be her bedroom lead out onto a paved backyard of about thirty foot, so Phoebe would have a garden after all.

She'd snapped it up, not least because there was no chain so they were able to move almost immediately. They'd already said goodbye to Jess. It had been a painful decision but in the end, the only option. Maddy simply hadn't the money for a three bedroom place in the area and besides, she didn't need Jess any more. What little freelance work she was getting she could fit round Phoebe's school hours and Jess had become a luxury she could ill afford.

With no regular salary coming in, her life had started unravelling frighteningly fast. She'd sold the BMW, replaced it with a battered red Fiesta and used the extra to help pay off her credit card bills.

But she was also behind with the gas, phone, council tax, water and electricity bills. She couldn't wait now to get the cash from the sale of the house in the bank, then she could settle her debts with what was left over after she'd paid for the flat.

This prospect was so beguiling that she decided she no longer really cared about leaving her beautiful home. Being in debt and constantly fearing a knock on the door from her creditors was worse. She'd already been receiving letters and phone calls. It hadn't taken them long to latch on to her changed circumstances. She felt as if she were just a few short steps away from disaster and was determined, for Phoebe's sake, to ensure they stayed afloat.

She'd been trying to avoid the question of her daughter's school fees but the issue simply wouldn't go away. She was paid up until the end of the term but Easter was fast approaching. It had become her dearest wish, as she sifted through the chaos that her life seemed to have turned into, to keep Phoebe in the little prep school where she was so happy until she reached eleven. By the time she went to secondary school, with any luck Maddy's circumstances would have improved.

Now, however, she was beginning to have doubts. She was no longer confident, in the way she had been, of finding a new well-paid job soon. And a little part of her, she realised, had also started to question whether paying fees was the right thing to do anyway.

She'd found that, despite all her worries, she rather enjoyed being at home with Phoebe and looking after her on her own. It was hard work, of course, but also rewarding and she felt she and her daughter had become closer.

If Phoebe remained at the prep school, Maddy would have no choice but to get another well-paid full-time job, or make a real success of freelancing. But if she removed that burden altogether then the pressure to earn would be lessened. A mad idea had also implanted itself in her mind and seemed to be gathering strength. She had no idea where it would ultimately lead, but it interested her.

She remembered Ralph. With luck he'd be here in half an hour or so, just in time to see Phoebe before she went to bed. He was becoming such a regular fixture in the evenings and at weekends that the little girl had started complaining if he wasn't there. He was very good with her and seemed quite happy to sit for ages playing Junior Scrabble or Monopoly. He had far more patience than Maddy.

Phoebe still had no idea that she and Ralph were related. He and Maddy had been very careful. He clearly enjoyed spending time in their company, though, and she could understand why: it was an escape from the tricky atmosphere in his own home and he felt able to talk to Maddy in a way he obviously couldn't with his mother.

She blamed Victoria for having driven him away but to her surprise, Maddy also felt a little sorry for her. From what Ralph had said, his mother was struggling. And she undoubtedly loved her son and would be so hurt if she knew where he was going. It was imperative she should never find out.

Sometimes Maddy tried to persuade Ralph to be kinder to her and would suggest strategies for opening up a non-confrontational discussion. But he was too bitter and angry.

'She's a fool,' he'd say, 'there's no point trying to talk, we just end up arguing.'

Maddy knew Ralph had A-levels coming up and found herself worrying about his future. She'd taken to nagging him about his studies just as she imagined his mother did, and she neither wanted nor felt in any way comfortable in that role.

He said he was doing enough work but she doubted he

could be, given that he was round at her house three or four times a week. And he'd stopped mentioning university, which made her anxious. But she was afraid of telling him not to visit so often because she knew he was vulnerable and had come to depend on her. And besides, she looked forward to seeing him.

Often, after Phoebe had gone to bed, they'd sit and watch TV together for a while on the sofa or just chat. She found herself talking to him as she'd once talked to Leo, telling him what she'd been up to and how she was feeling and so on. His presence comforted her. She supposed it was because he reminded her so much of his father.

Strange, she thought, that no one knew about their friendship when it had become such an important part of both their lives. She wouldn't dream of telling her parents, of course, because they'd been appalled enough about her relationship with Leo. They certainly wouldn't understand about Ralph. And she wouldn't make the mistake of calling Verity again.

It was silly, really. After all, whatever it was that she and Ralph had was rather sweet and innocent. Since that moment of madness when she'd almost lost her senses in her kitchen, they'd only hugged. Nothing wrong with that. She was helping him out, for heaven's sake. Doing him a favour. But Verity was blinkered.

He was late. She read Phoebe another chapter of 'Matilda' and kissed her goodnight.

'Can't I wait for Ralph?' she begged but Maddy shook her head.

'You smell nice, Mummy,' the little girl smiled, lying back on her pink pillow, her soft blonde hair spread out around her.

Maddy realised that she'd reapplied her make-up and put

on her favourite scent without registering.

Later, when he still hadn't arrived, she strolled downstairs and poured herself a glass of white wine. She took a sip and pulled a face. She'd stopped buying her favourite Pouilly-Fume and started getting the supermarket's cheapest; you could tell the difference.

She wandered with her glass into her airy drawing room and looked out of the tall picture window over the window box. She'd planted it only recently with deep blue pansies and pale green ivy, hoping to attract buyers. They looked so pretty.

The street was very quiet and she knew she'd miss its leafy tranquillity. The evenings were drawing out and it would be the start of British summertime soon, which was a strange thought. Somehow all through winter she'd felt that Leo hadn't quite gone. But now spring was approaching, a spring he'd never see, she had that sense of time rolling on without him.

It was often the little things that made her sad now. Like a spring flower, or the fact that Phoebe had lost another baby tooth and Leo would never see her with her funny gap or watch the big tooth coming through.

Thinking about these things made Maddy want to cry so she tried not to. But on balance, she decided, she was doing OK. Whatever life threw at her, she was just about coping and he'd be proud of her. 'Well done, my darling girl,' he'd say, stroking her cheek or hand.

She glanced out of the window and saw Ralph walking up the steps to the front door. He smiled and her heart hurt; it was such a hesitant yet hopeful smile. He might be ferocious with his mother but with her, he was a lamb. She thought he'd follow her wherever she chose to go and her power over him frightened her.

'Hi!' He handed her his gilet and sweatshirt. He was wearing a navy blue polo shirt underneath and smelled of his mother's washing powder.

They stepped into each others' arms and had one of their bear-like squeezes which made them both laugh. It had become a bit of a joke because Phoebe gave big crushing hugs like that.

There was something magnificent about his tense, finely tuned frame, his glossy hair and glittering dark eyes. He reminded her of a young male cat, all sleek and sinewy.

'I'll make supper,' she said, pulling away and walking swiftly into the kitchen where she picked up a recipe book. He was right behind her.

'Do you like risotto?'

He nodded.

'Come and talk to me while I cook.'

She chatted a little about this and that: her work, Phoebe, the new flat, but she had an agenda tonight and was keen to get started.

'Which lessons did you have today?' she asked.

Ralph scowled. 'Don't want to talk about it.'

'No, go on,' Maddy persisted. 'I'd like to hear about it. I did A-levels too, remember.'

He told her that he'd enjoyed Philosophy but couldn't stand his French teacher.

'Why not?' Maddy gave the onions and garlic one more stir before adding the mushrooms.

'She's a cow,' said Ralph. 'She hates me and the feeling's entirely mutual.'

Maddy picked up her glass, which was beside the cooker, and took a sip of wine. 'Do you feel on top of it – the language I mean?'

Ralph was standing beside her, his arms crossed, leaning against the granite work surface. 'Not really.'

'Tu aimes parler francais?' Maddy smiled.

'Pas du tout.'

'But it's a wonderful language. I did French and Spanish at University, you know. And I spent a year in France in my third year.'

She added the rice, wine and stock, waiting for the liquid to be absorbed.

'I'll tell you what!' She was twitching with excitement at the brilliance of her own idea. 'Next time you come, bring your French books and I'll help you.'

Ralph frowned and she punched him playfully on the shoulder. 'Don't give me that. How long have we got till your exams?'

He shrugged. 'My oral's at the beginning of May but the rest start in the middle of June or thereabouts. I haven't got the timetable yet.'

Maddy did a mental calculation. 'Early May? So we've got about six weeks.'

She added more stock and stirred. The rice was beginning to plump up.

'Look, I don't want—' he started to say, but she was having none of it.

'I'll be your tutor,' she said gleefully. 'We'll do an hour every time you come. I'll make it my mission to get you an A.' She was being carried away on the crest of her brainwave.

'It's burning,' Ralph said, nodding at the risotto.

Maddy quickly added more stock.

'Look,' she said more seriously, 'I want to do this for you and I won't take no for an answer. Bring your books next time and we'll make a start.'

They ate supper then watched a detective programme on the TV but Maddy couldn't really concentrate. Her brain was whirring and for once she was anxious for him to be off so that she could start to progress her plans.

When he left at around 10.30 p.m. she sprinted up to her study on the second floor, logged on to her computer and started to print out the entire French A-level syllabus. Meanwhile, she typed in some key words and surfed around a bit, checking out various websites and investigating grants and loans. Her other little scheme was no longer just a blip on the radar, it was beginning to have shape and form.

By the time she'd finished she was exhausted. She tiptoed out of the study and past Phoebe's bedroom, taking care not to trip over the packing cases on the landing. They were moving in under a week but it no longer felt like a tragedy, more of an opportunity, a new beginning, even. This was something she would never have predicted back in chilly December when it all started.

***

Friday March 6th

'What are you doing here?'

Cat hadn't been in work more than ten minutes. She had a heavy pile of books in her hand which she was about to arrange on the table in an attractive, come-and-buy-me display. She scowled at Victoria and glanced left and right to check the whereabouts of Rachel and Gervaise. He was at the till and looked curiously at Victoria but remained at his post. Rachel was nowhere to be seen.

Victoria looked different from how Cat remembered. She

was wearing nice clothes, for a start, and she'd maybe lost a little weight and her face looked younger and prettier.

'I wanted to see how you are,' she whispered.

'That's nice of you.' Cat plonked the books down and put her hands on her hips.

Victoria frowned. 'You didn't answer any of my calls. I was worried.'

Cat tucked a strand of hair behind her ear which had sprung loose from her ponytail.

'Yeah, well, I've been kind of busy,' she sniffed. 'And I've got stuff to do now, in case you didn't notice.'

She wondered if Victoria had clocked the discreet silver stud which was in her nose, on the other side from the ring. She'd also got one through her tongue, though Rachel wouldn't let her wear it in the shop.

She noticed Victoria lower her eyes and glance quickly at her tummy. She couldn't hide her shock.

'I lost it,' Cat said simply, hands still on hips. 'Tragic isn't it?'

Victoria swallowed. 'I'm so sorry, how did it—?'

'Miscarriage.' Cat shrugged. 'It happens.'

Victoria's eyes clouded. 'When?'

Cat started to fiddle around with the pile of books, though she wasn't concentrating.

'Ages ago. I'm over it now.'

She glanced at Gervaise, who was serving a female customer, peeping over her shoulder at them at the same time. She flashed him an insolent smile and he looked away quickly.

'Why didn't you ring me?' said Victoria. 'I tried and tried to get hold of you.'

Cat pulled a face. 'Because you went and told that other woman – Maddy.'

A flicker of understanding crossed Victoria's features and she frowned, embarrassed.

'How could you?' Cat hissed. 'That was supposed to be private, between you and me.'

Victoria hung her head and fiddled with the edge of her cardigan sleeve. 'It was terribly wrong, I know. I was furious with her. I let anger get the better of me.'

'Yeah, well, you didn't need to go blabbing about me to get back at her.'

'I feel so ashamed. You told me in confidence. You trusted me and I let you down.'

Cat stood there glaring, her arms across her chest. She noticed Victoria's face had gone very pale and she felt glad.

The older woman started rummaging in her handbag. 'Look.' She pulled out a brown paper bag. 'I've got something for you. I want you to have it.'

Cat was curious, despite herself.

'I did a big sort-out,' Victoria explained, passing over the package. 'It was one of Leo's favourite bow-ties. I thought you might like it.'

Cat took the paper bag and peeked at the silky black and gold tie inside. She remembered Leo wearing it and was too choked to say anything.

'I've got more of his belongings at home if you'd like to go through them.'

Cat remained silent, lips pursed.

'And I've been going through some of my things, too. Mainly clothes. I wondered if there's anything you'd like for your mother, maybe? There are a few nice cardigans and skirts. I don't know what size she is?'

'My mother doesn't eat,' Cat said. 'She's tiny and frail. Your stuff will be far too big.'

'There's also a tea service – cups and saucers, and little plates,' Victoria persisted, ignoring the snub. 'They're good quality, bone china. Leo's mother gave them to us. I never use them.'

Cat thought of her mother's motley collection of chipped mugs. She'd probably love bone china, it would be just her sort of thing.

'Well she might—' she said hesitantly, hating herself for wanting anything this woman had to offer.

'They're Royal Doulton with little flowers on. Quite pretty. There's a matching tea pot, too. I could bring them over in the car. I'd like them to go to a good home.'

Cat was in a dilemma. 'Well...'

Spotting the glimmer of possibility, Victoria seemed grateful. 'I can drop them at your mother's later if you give me the address?'

Cat was going to put her foot down but checked herself. She was picturing her mother playing with the cups and saucers like a kid with a toy tea set.

'If you want,' she said grudgingly.

'I might bring one or two other things, too. You can always give them to Oxfam if you don't like them.'

Cat had had enough and guided Victoria towards the exit, where she stopped.

'I apologise from the bottom of my heart,' she said, looking Cat in the eye. She was begging for forgiveness. Strange woman.

Cat managed a tight smile. 'I guess it doesn't make any difference now anyway.'

She paused, wondering whether to get her own back. Why not? Victoria deserved it.

'She came to see me, you know. That's how I know you

told her about my pregnancy.'

Victoria had forgotten to ask but remembered now and her eyes widened.

'What for? Why did she come?'

Cat shrugged nonchalantly. 'To get some answers. She seemed pretty cut up about everything – Leo's death, losing her job. Me.'

Victoria's expression hardened. 'I should imagine she has a lot of regrets that I wouldn't want to have to live with. I just thank God, now Leo's gone, that she can't hurt me or my family any longer.'

CHAPTER TWENTY

Same day

Cat ignored Gervaise's inquisitive eyes all day and scurried home, via her mother's, as quickly as possible. Victoria was already waiting in her car outside the block of flats when she arrived.

It seemed strange taking the older woman into her mother's territory. The atmosphere was hot and oppressive, as usual, and Cat instinctively hurried to the window to open it.

The TV was up very loud and Cat's mother was watching an old episode of Dad's Army.

'I've brought someone to see you, Mum,' Cat said, but the old woman didn't look up.

Cat noticed Victoria glancing round and taking everything in: the excess of furniture, the messy carpet and dirty kitchen floor next door. If Victoria hadn't been here she'd have whipped out the vacuum, mop and bucket and given it a good clean.

'I'm sorry,' she said, annoyed with herself for feeling embarrassed. 'Mum's not very communicative.'

Victoria put down the cardboard box she was carrying. It must have been heavy.

'Please don't apologise.'

She walked over to Cat's mother and squatted beside the armchair. 'Hello,' she said gently, 'my name's Victoria. I've brought you something.'

Cat's mother looked at her vaguely. 'Who are you? What have you brought?'

Cat and Victoria unpacked the dainty cups and saucers and put them on the table. They really were very pretty. Then Victoria hurried downstairs to fetch a few more things, returning with a rug and several woollen cardigans. They'd be too big for the old woman but she might appreciate them in winter.

'I also brought a cake,' Victoria said hesitantly, producing a tin from the bottom of one of the bags. 'It's banana cake. I made it this afternoon. I hope your mother likes it.'

Cat felt her anger diminishing. The woman was making a big effort, having come all this way when she didn't need to. Maybe she really was sorry for what she'd done, but Cat wouldn't let her off the hook yet.

They sat at the table sipping tea out of the china cups and nibbling on cake. Even Cat had a little.

'Nice,' said her mother appreciatively, spilling crumbs on her lap. 'Look, Cat, look at the little daffodils round the edge of the teapot.'

'They're roses, Mum,' Cat said softly.

Her mother tapped her forehead lightly with a forefinger. 'Roses? Yes. I know that.'

'Can I come and see you again?' Victoria asked when at last they'd finished and tidied the plates and cups away.

'You may,' Cat's mother replied imperiously.

Cat smiled, wondering if the 'Royal' in the Doulton had rubbed off on her.

It was past eight when she reached home. Rick had virtually taken up residence in the past few weeks and he and Tracy had taken to cooking exotic meals which they'd eat by candle light around the sitting room table.

They tended to use every saucepan in the kitchen and, although Cat was always invited to join them, she felt a bit of a gooseberry. She'd been hoping to see her mum, get home early and make herself something to eat first, leaving the way clear for them, but it hadn't quite worked out like that. They'd be sure to be back by now.

Mr Ali was outside his shop, picking up crumpled paper bags and old drinks cartons.

'Look at this,' he said, thrusting a polystyrene container half full of ketchup-smeared chips under Cat's nose. 'They are animals. They have no respect.' He waved the carton around and she had to dodge the flying food. 'This country ees going to the cats.'

'The dogs,' Cat said helpfully. 'I think you mean the dogs.'

Ali's brows were thick angry caterpillars. 'Dogs, cats, chimpanzees, what does it matter?' he ranted. 'Ees all the same. People have no respect, no manners anymore.'

'I agree,' she said quickly, hoping to assuage him. 'No manners at all.'

She wondered whether to raise the issue of the leaking shower and newly wonky lavatory.

'Mrs Ali all right?' she asked tentatively. 'And the children?'

He broke into a huge smile. 'Children very well, little Atan, he ees walking now.' He did an imitation baby walk, all bandy legged and wobbly. 'Hee heeee heee heee hee.' Cat couldn't help laughing, too.

Suddenly Ali went serious. 'But my wife, Mrs Ali, she not well,' he shook his head mournfully.

'Oh?'

'She have bad back. She say she cannot live without seventeen hundred by seven hundred Acqua Viennese six jet Jacuzzi bath tub with multi massage therapy seat.'

Cat trudged upstairs, feeling cross, and put her key in the lock. She was relieved that the flat was in darkness and she'd beaten Trick and Racy to it after all. She turned on the light, put down her bag and blinked for a moment or two. A dozen faces, some familiar, some not, were grinning at her, raised glasses in their hands. 'Surprise!'

Tracy came forwards, teetering on high heels and brandishing a full glass of something fizzy which she gave to Cat. Her hair was pinned up off her face, she had a big pink flower over one ear and was smiling widely.

'Guess what?' she said, eyes shining, red lipstick smeared. 'Rick and I are getting married!'

Cat blinked again. She could see Rick's tall shape behind the shorter, dumpier figure of Jaz from the pub. To her left was Dermot, Rick's band mate, and beside him, his girlfriend Bo.

'That's fantastic,' Cat stammered, feeling as if she'd been shot with a stun gun. 'I mean, wow! When did you decide this?'

Tracy flung her arms around Cat and planted a hot sloppy kiss on her cheek.

'He asked me on Sunday. You know? The day we went to Greenwich on the boat. He got down on one knee.' She lowered her eyes and there was a giggle from the guests and someone said 'pansy' and shoved Rick, who stumbled forwards, a sheepish grin on his face.

'I thought I was going to explode with excitement,' Tracy went on. 'I was desperate to tell you only I wanted to wait till we had the ring. Look.'

She flashed a white gold ring with three small glittering diamonds in the centre. 'Isn't it beautiful?'

'Oh Tracy.' Cat hoped no one would notice the catch in her voice. 'It's absolutely lovely.'

274

This time it was Cat's turn to put her arms around her friend. She could feel Tracy's pumping heart and smell her familiar sickly-sweet perfume.

'I'm getting *married*!' Tracy whispered. 'Can you believe it? I'm going to be Rick's wife! I'm going to be Mrs Meech!'

Cat hugged her tight, knowing that things would never be the same again. No more Cat n' Trace, Tracy and Cat. No more nights in front of the telly, drinking wine, smoking fags and moaning about boys and life and stuff. The end of an era. She wondered what she'd do about the flat. She'd be lonely on her own. Find someone else to move in, she supposed. She wondered how she'd cope without the person she was closest to in the whole world.

She was a selfish cow; she hated herself for thinking bad thoughts on her best friend's special day.

'Rick can come and live here properly can't he Cat?' Tracy said, as if reading her mind. 'We'll be one big happy family!'

Cat pulled away from the embrace and looked into Tracy's round shining face. 'It's brilliant news, I'm so happy for you both.' Most of her drink had spilled on the carpet but she raised her glass anyway. 'To Tracy and Rick,' she said loudly, 'Trick and Racy.'

'Trick and Racy!' everyone chorused. 'Mr and Mrs Meech.'

Cat went into her bedroom and changed quickly into her denim mini skirt, black T-shirt and leggings. Someone had turned up the music full blast and the floor was vibrating. Boom, boom, boom. She hoped the mice wouldn't have heart attacks.

She glanced at herself in the mirror, registering the tired sad eyes, and fixed a smile on her face. You can do it, Cat, she told herself as she rejoined the party, smile still firmly in place.

'Where's the drinks?' she shouted, spotting Rick beside the

window and walking towards him. 'Come here and give us a hug.'

There were tears in his eyes. 'I love her so much,' he blubbed.

Cat gave him a squeeze. 'Ya, you big softie. Thank God you're going to make an honest woman of her at last.'

***

Monday March 8th

Kate and Don were late for their counselling session and Victoria went to make herself a cup of coffee, bumping into Debs in the kitchen.

'You look well!' she said, examining Victoria from top to toe. 'What have you done to yourself?'

Victoria reddened. 'I was fed up with the grey in my hair. I tried out this home dye kit.' She patted her head. 'D'you think it looks all right?'

Debs grinned. 'All right? It looks great. Slightly coppery. And your hair's so shiny. I like the brown eye shadow, too.'

The kettle had boiled and Debs put two spoonfuls of powder in two mugs and filled them with water. She was wearing white trainers under her dark trouser suit, Victoria noticed. Going for a run at lunchtime again. Must be super-fit. Maybe Victoria would join her one day to see what it was like. It wouldn't cost anything, after all, not like expensive gym membership.

'Is it just us today?' she asked nonchalantly, adding some milk from the fridge to each cup.

Debs looked at her curiously. 'I think Oliver's in shortly.' She frowned. 'You should be careful.'

Victoria stirred her drink slowly. 'What do you mean?'

'I mean,' said Debs, 'that you should be careful of Oliver.'

Victoria opened her mouth to object.

'Look,' said Debs seriously, 'Don't try to deny it. I know you've been seeing a bit of each other and in any other circumstances, I'd be all for it.'

Victoria swallowed, feeling like a child caught with its hands in the biscuit tin. 'We've only had lunch a couple of times,' she protested. 'And he invited me for dinner once at his house with other people. That hardly constitutes seeing each other, not in the sense you're talking about anyway.'

The two women were standing with their backs to the sink, resting against the white melamine worktop. Debs took a sip of her drink and looked seriously at Victoria.

'You know what I mean,' she said. 'I can tell he's keen on you.'

Victoria looked at the ground, embarrassed. It seemed so odd to be discussing Oliver in these terms. She'd never thought of him in that way – or had she?

'Rubbish,' she said hotly. 'He just feels sorry for me, that's all. He's a kind man and he's been trying to cheer me up since Leo died.'

'Not that kind,' Debs said darkly.

Victoria stared at her. 'I don't know what—'

'Look,' Debs interrupted, 'I shouldn't tell you this but as my friend I feel I must. Oliver once told me in confidence there was violence in his marriage.'

Victoria gasped. 'I can't believe it. He doesn't seem the type.'

Debs nodded. 'It's true. You know he had an affair, too?'

'Yes. He told me.'

'Well as we know,' Debs went on, 'domestic violence is something else. If a man's hit a woman once, he'll do it again.'

'But he seems so gentle.' Victoria started to snivel, she wasn't sure why, and Debs put an arm round her shoulder.

'I'm so sorry to have to tell you this, hon. I wouldn't have upset you. But I was worried that you might just...' she paused, 'that you might be getting into something that would only cause you more grief and heartache. You don't need it and you certainly don't deserve it. I'd keep a wide berth if I were you.'

Victoria took a piece of kitchen roll from beside the microwave and wiped her eyes. 'You're quite right. Thank you,' she said, trying to pull herself together. She felt winded and unsteady, as if she'd been punched in the stomach. She wanted to go and sit down.

'There was nothing between us but...' she hesitated, 'but I suppose I did like him. In time we might have...it's just possible...you know.' She blew her nose, feeling suddenly stupid with her coppery hair and new brown eyeshadow. She wished she could wash it off.

Debs gave her a squeeze. 'I know. No need to say anything else.'

The buzzer went, making Victoria jump. Her clients. But she was wobbly and leant against the work surface for support.

'I'll get it,' Debs said quickly. 'You go and powder your nose or whatever.'

She took her still almost full mug. 'How about going to a film one night? I haven't been to the cinema for ages.'

'That would be lovely,' said Victoria forcing a smile. She was taking this so badly...she'd had a lucky escape. Anyway, she'd had no intention of getting involved with Oliver Sands.

She caught Debs's eye. 'And thanks again, I appreciate it.'

Kate and Don look flustered and Victoria can tell something's up. The counselling had been going well, since the last debacle when Don revealed he'd had more than one affair. Victoria was feeling hopeful they could pull their marriage back together. She wonders what's happened now.

Don's pacing round the room, craning his neck more than ever, and Kate starts crying. Victoria passes her the box of tissues and looks at Don.

'Please sit down. I can't think.' Her voice is sharper than intended but it does the trick; Don plonks himself in the chair next to Kate, who makes a big show of shuffling as far from him as possible.

Her action doesn't go unnoticed. 'You seem very upset today, Kate,' Victoria coaxes. 'Can you tell me why?'

Don thumps the palm of his hand with a clenched fist, his face crimson. 'She's been up all bloody night shouting and screaming at me, that's why. I'm knackered.'

Victoria relaxes her shoulders and rests her hands in her lap, wanting to calm the atmosphere. 'Can you tell me about it?'

Kate shakes her head, too upset to speak, and Don glares at her. 'All right I'll tell her.' He turns to Victoria, eyes blazing. 'She's been poking around in my emails.'

Kate gives a little mew of protest and weeps some more.

'She discovered something I'd written to someone,' Don goes on. 'OK, I shouldn't have done it, it was stupid. But if she hadn't snooped she'd have been none the wiser. It didn't mean anything—'

'You always say that!' Kate shouts, suddenly animated. 'Again and again you tell me it doesn't mean anything, so why do you do it? Why did you write to this woman if it didn't mean anything?'

He's silent.

Kate turns to Victoria, her face wet with tears. 'They

279

were disgusting emails. Filthy, sexy stuff about what he wants to do to her. I can't stand it anymore. I've told him I want a divorce.'

Victoria takes a deep breath. 'I can see this has been a terrible shock for you, Kate. Who have you been writing to, Don?'

He runs a hand through his close-cropped hair. 'Just a girl from work. One of the secretaries. She started sending me these silly flirty messages and I replied. I know I shouldn't have but it was just a lark. We never actually did anything.'

Victoria can feel anger bubbling and fizzing inside her and crosses her arms, hoping to contain it.

'Don,' she says through gritted teeth. 'If you think there's any real difference between sending sexy emails and shagging another woman you need your head examined.'

He raises his eyebrows, momentarily stunned.

'Haven't you learned anything since you started coming to see me?' Victoria continues. 'Can't you see that every time you lie to your wife, every time you send sexy emails or sleep with another woman you're investing your emotional and sexual energies elsewhere and a little part of her dies? Just look at her.'

Don hangs his head.

'Look at your wife, Don.'

He does as he's told. Kate's face is red and blotchy, her shoulders slumped, her body crumpled like a piece of discarded wrapping paper.

'You're destroying her. What's she done to deserve it?'

Don shoves his chin forwards and tries to straighten up. 'I thought you were supposed to be impartial. I *thought you weren't supposed to be on anybody's side.'*

Victoria, ignoring him, touches Kate's knee.

'Sometimes,' she says, 'it's impossible to be impartial even in my job. Sometimes the case against someone is so damning and clear-cut there's really no argument.'

* * *

She knew she'd overstepped the boundary and would need to bring it up with her clinical supervisor, and that Don might make an official complaint. Still, Victoria didn't care. He was a lying little toad and Kate deserved better. She was glad she'd let rip, although it went against every rule in the counselling book, and she fervently hoped Kate would stick to her guns and start divorce proceedings. He was never going to change. Some men didn't.

She thought of Leo and was filled with a sense of regret so overwhelming that it made her gasp. Luckily she was on her own still in the consulting room, so no one could see her stagger and reach for the arm of the chair to steady herself.

If only....if only she'd left him after the children were born. She couldn't ever say she wished that she'd never had them; they were her life. But all those years she'd wasted, hanging on for him, waiting, hoping that one day he'd grow tired of his affairs and come home to her. Give her all of him, not just the little portion that he saved, like a scrap of meat for a starving dog.

She cursed herself for being his slave for so long, for allowing herself to believe that genius was entitled to play by other rules. Genius, however great, did not absolve him of moral responsibility for what he did. The truth was that he was a liar and a serial adulterer, a user of women.

She felt a wave of sympathy for Cat. Even, surprisingly, a little for Maddy. For they, too, had been victims in a way. They'd put up with his deceit, just as she had. They must hurt like hell, too.

There was a knock on the door. 'Are you all right?' She realised she must have been in there for quite some time.

'Fine,' she said weakly, wishing she could be left alone.

The door opened and Oliver walked in. 'Difficult session?' Was it that obvious? She nodded.

He checked his watch. 'Lunchtime. D'you fancy a bite to eat?'

He looked very handsome, Victoria thought, in a white, open-necked shirt and dark blue trousers.

'I can't,' she said quickly.

He stuck his hands in his trouser pockets. 'I've got two tickets for a piano and cello recital on Friday. It's a charitable thing at the local church but it should be quite good. They're playing Chopin, Schubert, Tchaikovsky and Mozart, I think. Would you like to come? Maybe we could have dinner afterwards?'

She shook her head. 'I'm busy that night.'

'Oh.'

'Why don't you ask Rosanna?' she asked suddenly, her voice dripping with sarcasm. It was the devil in her speaking.

He looked confused and scratched his head. 'I hadn't thought of that. I could do. I don't know what she's up to.'

Victoria gathered up her things. 'I have to go.'

She swept past, leaving him standing in the middle of the room staring after her. The thought that he'd be trying his best to figure out what on earth he'd done wrong gave her no small satisfaction.

CHAPTER TWENTY-ONE

Thursday April 29th

Parked in front of her laptop in a corner of the new bedroom, Maddy rubbed her tired eyes and stretched. It would soon be time for the babysitter to collect Phoebe from school. She didn't know where the day had gone. She'd been so absorbed in what she was doing that she'd scarcely noticed the hours ticking by.

She was thrilled with what her old friend, John, had done. She'd asked him to design a website for a new internet business venture – MumSkills – and he'd come up with something really fresh and different. She'd warned him that she wouldn't be able to pay much but he was happy to accept far less than the going rate so long as his wife, a sub-editor, could become involved.

The idea behind MumSkills was this: Maddy reckoned there were thousands of highly qualified women out there, like herself, who wanted to work but also wanted to raise their children.

Her site would be a way for employers to access those qualified women and employ them, say, for a few days a month or for an individual project. Obviously childcare would be a problem and she was well aware that many of these women would only be able to do certain days a week, depending on who was around to look after their kids. But if she had a big enough pool of, say, marketing or public relations consultants, she could give the work to whoever was available on that day. And naturally she hoped the site would bring in events work for her, too.

She got up and glanced around her room at the half a dozen or so unopened packing crates still stacked against the wall. With its low ceiling and view out over the paved backyard of other people's brick walls and corrugated garden sheds, the room had none of the splendour of Brook Green. But she and Phoebe had settled in OK.

It was nearly May now and everything looked nicer in spring anyway. Pale pink Clematis Montana was climbing over her wooden fence hiding the broken slats, and a white lilac bush in the corner was coming into bloom.

She hadn't yet got round to planting her terracotta pots but she would, then the outside would look prettier. Inside she hadn't needed to do any decorating, though she'd had to have the curtains altered to fit the smaller windows. The problem was, she'd got rid of masses of stuff when she moved but there was still more that she didn't know what to do with; there simply wasn't enough storage.

She had a quick shower and changed into her old nude silk dress with gold and pearl beading. It had a round neck, plunging back, asymmetric hem and reached, at its lowest point, almost to her ankles.

It had cost several hundreds and she remembered how she'd fallen in love with it in a shop window and simply had to have it. She marvelled, now, at how she'd ever been able to afford it. The days of impulse purchases had long gone; in fact she couldn't remember when she'd last been clothes shopping. Luckily she had so much in her wardrobe that she didn't need to.

Her tummy was fluttering. She'd been working on the

launch of an old contact's new bar on the King's Road and the day had finally arrived. He'd given her the job because he knew she was desperate for work and she was grateful and didn't want to let him down.

She was also nervous because it was Ralph's French oral exam next week and they wouldn't be able to do any revision tonight. She'd been helping him, as promised, for an hour or two three or four times a week. He'd been reluctant at first but once he'd realised she meant business, he'd knuckled down and come on in leaps and bounds. She desperately wanted him to do well mostly for his own sake, but also, she had to admit, for hers. If he failed his A-levels she'd feel responsible.

Once they finished his work, he'd been helping her in return with ideas for her website and also with tonight's event. He had a good phone manner and had made calls and done bits of research.

She'd wanted to use her old associates from Blake Smith Event Management but they were mostly too expensive so instead, she'd assembled a new, younger team. It had been Ralph's idea to approach students from Central Saint Martin's College of Art and Design. He guessed they'd be keen, full of ideas and they'd cost less, and he wasn't far wrong. He was the one who'd talked to them initially, explaining the project and persuading them to come on board. Then Maddy had taken over to discuss the finer details – and money.

Some of their ideas had been impractical and outlandish but some were really good. She just hoped everything would go all right on the night.

Maddy was meeting Ralph at 4 p.m. at the bar. It was to be his last night off revision, she said, before the exams. And no arguing. He was to man the door, welcoming guests and ticking their names off the list. She was paying him. She knew that he'd built up debts, smoking weed and going to the pub. She reckoned he'd quit the drugs now, which was a relief, and she wanted him to settle what he owed. She was trying to teach him about budgeting, which was a bit of a joke considering her track record. But it was like a crash course in prudence for her, too.

Spotting various students inside the bar putting the finishing touches to the set and testing the hydraulic platform, she teetered through the door in her high heels and looked around.

The bar was called Wild Thing and she'd come up with a jungle theme for tonight. The drinks were brightly coloured cocktails with names like Jungle Juice, Monkey Gland and Snake Screwdriver. She'd borrowed tropical plants from a special supplier and bought vases of brightly coloured rainforest flowers which were on every table.

The waiters and waitresses, mostly out-of-work actors, were dressed in skimpy leopard and zebra print outfits made up by a local seamstress. But the pièce de résistance was the hydraulic platform on a raised area at the back. Around it, the college students had built a fabulous set, at least eight foot high, painted with green fluorescent palms, pink and orange parrots, purple flowers, frogs, monkeys and a lurking tiger.

Maddy gazed and it and smiled. 'Perfect.'

'Hi!'

She felt hands on her shoulders and swung around. Ralph. He gave her a bear squeeze.

'Not here,' she whispered, pushing him away.

'Sorry. Love the dress.'

He was looking gorgeous. Tall and clean-shaven, in an expensive pale blue shirt with a thin purple stripe and dark

286

blue jeans. He seemed so different from the embarrassed youth at the funeral. He'd grown up.

She glanced at the shirt again to check and her insides tugged. 'I recognise it; it was your father's wasn't it?'

Ralph nodded. 'Do you mind?'

'No. It's nice that you're wearing it; he'd be pleased.'

She tried to disguise the sadness that had washed over her with a big smile, but Ralph wasn't fooled. 'You'd rather he was here than me, wouldn't you?'

'Don't be silly.'

'But you would, wouldn't you? I can never live up to your expectations because I'll never be him, the great Leopold Bruck.' There was hurt in his voice, masquerading as a sneer.

Maddy's eyes flashed. 'Don't say that. You're every bit as good as him.' She was aware of people milling around, moving bits of furniture slightly to the left or right, getting out glasses. 'Your father was a great man but he had many faults. He was incredibly proud of you. Don't ever forget it.'

She squeezed Ralph's arm and he seemed to relax a little. 'We need to get our skates on. The guests will be here in just over an hour.'

A lorry pulled up outside the bar with 'Exotic Animal Co.' written in large orange letters on the side. Miles, who owned the bar, came down from his office to watch the animals troop in.

In his mid-forties, Miles already owned several successful restaurants in London and another bar, called Tiny Dancer, on Kensington Church Street.

He looked at the animals and frowned. 'I hope this is a good idea.'

Maddy, who was standing beside him, laughed a little too loudly. 'It'll be a roaring success, just you wait and see!'

She had asked for two chimps, a boa constrictor, an orang-utan and her baby, a couple of toucans and, most importantly, a tame tiger. They all belonged to Reggie, a former circus trainer who'd bought them when the circus folded and started up a company hiring the animals out for film and TV and events such as this.

His team of handlers took care of the smaller animals while Reggie himself held tightly on to the tiger's lead as he led him downstairs to the basement, bending his head as he did so as the ceiling was so low.

'He's absolutely enormous,' Miles whistled, following on behind. 'Are you sure he's safe?'

At the bottom of the steps Reggie stopped to grin and pat the animal, who was wearing a black, crystal-studded collar. 'What, Terence? Safe as houses. Wouldn't hurt a fly.'

Someone switched the music on upstairs and the basement started to vibrate to the sound of Brazilian jazz. It was hot and dark and Maddy couldn't wait to get some fresh air. She settled Reggie and his tiger in a small dressing room and was about to leave when one of the waitresses appeared in a zebra print bikini.

'Where is he, then?' she asked, nearly tripping on the uneven floor in her perilously high heels. She had thick make-up and long yellow hair tied up in a leopard-patterned scrunchie.

The tiger, who was sitting quietly in a corner licking his big paw, shook his mighty head and yawned. On catching sight of the giant pointed teeth the waitress let out a scream.

'I'm not going anywhere near that thing!' she said, backing towards the door.

Maddy tried to calm her. 'He's called Terence and he's lovely.' She was tentatively patting the tiger on the back as she'd seen Reggie do. 'Just like a big pussycat. You have a go.'

The girl, looking doubtful, stretched out an arm and took a few wobbly steps towards Terence before pulling back.

'Go on,' Maddy coaxed. 'He's so soft.'

The girl tiptoed forwards again and touched Terence's coat with one finger. The beast seemed unperturbed. Emboldened, she moved a little closer and stroked him with her whole hand.

'See,' Reggie grinned. 'Told you he wouldn't bite.'

Maddy left the waitress having a quick lesson in tiger handling and went upstairs to the ladies', where she brushed her hair and applied more pink lipstick. She hoped the girl would hold her nerve. Otherwise Maddy herself might have to take over and she had to admit that she wasn't that keen on animals, especially the wild variety.

Emerging from the bathroom, she wrinkled her nose.

'What's that smell?' she asked a passing waiter with a bare oiled chest carrying a tray of empty glasses.

'No idea, darling.'

He sauntered off and Maddy, catching sight of his pert round bottom bulging out of a leopard print thong, frowned. She didn't remember asking the seamstress to make male cheese cutters but it was too late to do anything now.

The smell seemed to be growing worse and time was getting on. All they needed was a problem with the sewage pipes. Exasperated, she followed her nose, pushing her way through the green streamers and vines made from twisted crepe paper that were hanging from the ceiling, and came to a halt beside the chimps. They seemed to be agitated, screaming and waving their hairy arms around and chattering their teeth.

'What's the matter?' Maddy asked the young woman in

khaki trousers, a green T-shirt and baseball cap, who must be their trainer.

'Careful,' the young woman shouted, pointing to the floor.

Maddy glanced down and did a sideways hop, narrowly missing something nasty.

'Blossom's got a bit of an upset tummy,' the trainer apologised. 'Someone's gone to find a mop and bucket.'

'Get it cleaned up – quick,' Maddy barked, muttering under her breath: 'If I'd wanted a chimp with diarrhoea I'd have asked for one.'

The first guests arrived bang on time at 5.30 p.m. Ralph was at his post at the door while waiters and waitresses hovered with full trays of drinks and nibbles including slices of mango, coconut and guava, chocolate covered crickets and barbecue flavoured worms.

Others held brightly coloured silk leis which they threw over peoples' heads as they entered. Miles knew a lot of people and the guest list included a number of B and C-list celebrities as well as the usual hangers-on, national and local journalists, PR people and friends. All in all around two hundred people were expected.

Maddy wandered around, untouched cocktail in hand, talking to people and checking that everyone's drinks were topped up and the waiters were clearing away the used glasses. When the room was full and the atmosphere suitably buzzing, she caught Miles's eye. He nodded and she walked over to the hydraulic platform to give the order.

The music changed to a steady insistent jungle beat and slowly, slowly the platform started to rise. There was a hum of excitement when people turned and realised that a pretty girl in a zebra bikini and high heels was rising from the bowels of the earth with a real live tiger at her side.

The platform stopped moving and the room fell silent, save for the odd shriek from the chimps standing in a corner with their handlers.

'Welcome to Wild Thing!' said the girl in the zebra bikini, giving a theatrical bow. 'We hope you have a wonderful evening and go away and tell all your friends about us.'

She gave a 'hup' and nothing happened. She said it again, more loudly this time, and Terence got up on his hind legs and gave a fearsome growl, which made the audience scream. The girl smiled, pleased with herself, and repeated the instruction for good measure.

Suddenly the orangutan pulled away from its handler, dashed across the room, its baby hanging on for dear life, grabbed onto a palm tree in a container and raced to the top chattering loudly. The tiger, already confused by the heat, noise and volume of people, spotted what had happened and made a giant leap off the platform.

The girl in the zebra bikini lost hold of the long black lead and tumbled to the floor, which fortunately wasn't too far down so she was able to get up immediately, helped by one of the waiters. The crowd screamed and started bolting for the door.

'The tiger's escaped!' they were shouting, as if anyone hadn't noticed. 'Call the police!' 'Ring the RSPCA.' 'Fire!' 'Emergency!'

In the midst of the panic, Maddy looked around wildly for Reggie, the only person who would know what to do, and spotted him scrambling along the bar, knocking off drinks and bottles, trying to clear a path to his precious pet.

'Don't hurt him!' he was hollering. 'He's harmless!'

Maddy wished at this moment that she were anywhere but here. Timbuktu would do fine.

'Calm down,' she was crying, 'there's no need to panic.' But no one was listening.

The room cleared and everyone gathered on the pavement outside, furiously texting, calling and taking pictures with their mobile phones. Maddy could hear police sirens in the distance and her heart sank.

Terence, meanwhile, glad of a bit of space at last, had settled down beside the palm tree, his head resting on his big soft paws, while the orangutan and its baby calmly surveyed the chaos from the top branches.

Reggie grabbed hold of Terence's lead and knelt at his side, arms around his neck, their heads touching. 'It was the music that upset him,' he was muttering mournfully. 'Poor old fellow. Scared the life out of him.'

Maddy stared at the pair of them. 'Poor old fellow? What about me? My career's ruined.'

She was standing there wondering what to do when Ralph came up and put an arm round her shoulders. 'It's not your fault.'

She laughed grimly. 'Oh yes it is. I'll be looking for a new job in the morning. I'll never work in events again.'

It was several hours before they'd answered all the police questions, spoken to reporters, paid the staff for the night and cleared up the mess. Finally, when the last glass had been put away, Maddy found herself alone with Ralph in the darkened bar.

'We may as well go,' she said miserably. 'We won't be getting paid, that's for sure. I'll write and apologise to Miles in the morning. Fat lot of good it'll do.'

She and Ralph collected their coats and were walking slowly towards the door when Poppy, one of Miles' assistants, called from the other side of the room: 'Miles wants to see you in his office.'

Maddy's stomach turned over and she glanced at Ralph. 'Will you come with me?' He nodded. At least she wouldn't have to face the music alone. She quickly applied her favourite pink lip gloss, hoping for some courage.

Poppy, who had orange hair and purple glasses with big round frames, took them in a mirrored lift to the fourth floor where they stepped out into what felt like a jewelled cavern. The black painted walls were lit by disco lights that shimmered and sparkled and the dark carpet was soft and squishy underfoot, like the underbelly of a sea serpent. Maddy felt her nerves give way as she followed Poppy towards a half-open door at the end of the corridor.

Miles was leaning back in his private room behind a black kidney-shaped table, his arms behind his head. He had removed his jacket and tie was wearing just a white open-necked shirt with the sleeves rolled up. His face was hard and expressionless.

Maddy and Ralph stood in front of him, heads bowed, feeling liked the condemned. Maddy, deciding that it would be preferable to get in first, blurted: 'I'm so sorry. It's all my fault, I should never have—'

Miles, who had a mass of curly collar-length black hair, raised a hand. 'Don't say anything. It was total and utter chaos. I had a tiger on the loose in my club, terrorising guests, celebrities, journalists, some of my closest friends.' He glared at her. 'Someone could have been seriously hurt or even *killed*.'

'I know,' said Maddy, wincing. Ralph, beside her, shuffled miserably.

Miles paused, studying the pair for what seemed like an

age. It was torture without nooses or manacles.

'But,' he said at last.

Maddy glanced at him, astonished to see the flicker of a smile on his face. Or was she imagining it?

'But,' he repeated. 'There was a room full of reporters. This'll be all over the papers and on TV tomorrow. Thanks to you I'm going to get the best publicity I've ever had.'

He stood up, came round from the back of the table and patted Maddy on the back, who was too stunned to say anything. Then he handed her a cheque, which was slightly larger than the sum she'd asked for.

'It's was a massive cock-up, Mads,' Miles continued, grinning widely, 'but well done! Just don't book any wild animals next time, eh?'

***

Once outside, back in the cool night air, Maddy and Ralph stood on the pavement for a moment discussing the extraordinary turn of events. Neither could quite believe their luck. They'd thought the business was doomed.

She rested her head against his chest. 'I'm so tired,' she mumbled happily, 'I feel like I could sleep for a week.'

'Me too,' he said, putting an arm round her shoulder. They stayed there for quite some time, breathing in and out slowly, enjoying the warmth of each other's bodies and contemplating the velvety night.

Finally she pulled away and waved down a black cab for him. It was high time she got him home; his mother would be frantic.

'Some evening!' she said, kissing him on the cheek as he climbed in the car. 'Thanks for all your help.'

She was about to slam the door shut when she thought she heard him mumble something. Her ears pricked, but she wasn't certain.

'What?'

'I think I love you.'

Her heart fluttered. 'Don't be silly.'

'I mean it.'

'No you don't.'

She glanced in his eyes as the car pulled away and thought she could see right into the centre of his soul; she was holding it in the palm of her hand, like a ripe peach.

At last the car rounded the corner and she was alone.

She must have misheard, surely? Either that or he'd had too much to drink.

She wanted to shout from the rooftops; she wanted to hide under the duvet.

She imagined the towering figure of Victoria before her, booming: 'Black heart. Confess your sins.'

CHAPTER TWENTY-TWO

Victoria was pacing around the sitting room when Ralph walked in. She was so tired she didn't even have the energy to be angry.

'It's two-thirty in the morning. You've got school tomorrow.'

'I know. I'm sorry.'

She noticed his eyes were shining and his cheeks were flushed. She closed her own eyes and swallowed. 'Have you been drinking?'

He laughed, not in a nasty way, and her eyes fluttered open again.

'Mu-um.' He plonked himself down on the sofa, his long legs straight in front of him. 'I've been working.'

He took something out of his pocket and showed her. A wodge of money.

'Where did you get that?'

'I told you, I've been working.'

He couldn't fail to notice the dismay on her face.

'It's not what you think,' he said, amused. 'I've been helping a friend who runs—' He paused and checked himself. 'Who runs a business.'

'What kind of business?' Victoria asked suspiciously.

'Just a business, OK?' He was starting to get annoyed now. 'It's all above board and it went very well tonight. You should be pleased I'm doing something useful.'

Victoria frowned. 'I am but – oh Ralph!' She sat down

beside him. 'Now's not the right time. Your exams—'

His eyes clouded. 'Exams, exams. It's all you ever think about. Look,' he said, softening slightly, 'they're under control, all right? I took tonight off but I know what I'm doing. I'm not going to fail.'

She looked doubtful. 'You don't seem to me to be doing any revision. You're always out.'

He rose and stretched. 'I work round at my friend's. I can concentrate better there. Just chill – OK? You've got to trust me.'

Trust. Victoria felt she'd ceased trusting Ralph a long time ago. He was so secretive. She had no idea what he got up to or what he thought, really. Except that he seemed to hate her and blame her for everything that wasn't right in his life.

She sighed. 'You'd better go to bed.'

She was going to kiss him goodnight when she noticed something on his cheek.

'What's that?'

She rubbed the smudge and it came off on her fingers. Pink lipstick.

'Dunno where that's from,' Ralph laughed, embarrassed, scrubbing the remainder away quickly.

A worried frown crossed Victoria's features and he wouldn't look at her.

'I think you do.'

***

Friday April 30th

She rose early and dropped Salome at her friend's house before catching the train from St Pancras. She'd been gearing herself up for months for this and saving her pennies, ever

297

since her meeting with Maeve Gannon, and she was feeling extremely nervous. It didn't help that she'd hardly slept last night; she'd been too busy worrying about Ralph, wondering what on earth he was up to.

The last time she'd visited Paris was seven or eight years ago when Leo was performing at the Paris Opera House. She'd spent some time then wandering about on her own while he was rehearsing, and she found that she could still remember her way about and how to use the metro.

Clutching her map just in case she needed it, she alighted at Saint-Germain-des-Prés on the Left Bank and walked the few hundred yards up the Boulevard to the apartment block.

It was a classic monumental nineteenth-century Parisian Haussmann building – in total harmony with all the others around it. She stood back and gazed for a moment at the thick walls and arched entranceways on the ground floor, the gorgeous balconies on the second storey and perfectly aligned cornices. It spoke of empire, efficiency, regulation and uniformity. It was impressive certainly, and beautiful, too, in its own way.

Taking a deep breath, she stepped inside the building and took the lift up to Elsa's apartment on the fourth floor. It was a gamble turning up uninvited, but Elsa was very old and infirm. Where would she go on a Friday morning? Anyway, in the unlikely event that she were out Victoria could hang around. She had all day.

She was anxious but excited, too. She felt as if she were approaching the end of a journey that had begun when Leo died. Although in a way the true beginning was when she first met him all those years ago and fell in love and quickly learned not to ask too many questions.

She pressed the brass buzzer. The door was so thick that

she could hear nothing inside and she had to wait for what felt like an eternity until at last, an elderly woman in a white blouse and grey cardigan came to the door.

'I'd like to speak with Elsa, please,' Victoria said, trying not to betray the fear in her voice. 'I'm her daughter-in-law, Victoria.'

The elderly woman, whom Victoria took to be the housekeeper, said nothing. The door closed again and Victoria found herself pacing up and down the landing, examining paintings on the walls that were of no merit, desperate to find something to interest and distract.

At last the door reopened and the housekeeper beckoned her in. 'Madame is not feeling well,' she said in faltering English. 'You must not stay long.'

She led Victoria through a wide hallway along a wooden floor to a drawing room right at the end. It was an imposing room, high-ceilinged with two large French doors that must have looked out over a balcony onto the Rue Saint-Germain, but the view was obscured by voile curtains.

Elsa was in a high-backed armchair by the marble fireplace, a small table by her side with a gold bell on it. She was wearing a crimson velvet dressing gown, but you could see that the shoulders beneath were thin and hunched and there was a tartan rug on her knees.

Her hair was pure white and so thin that pink scalp peeped through. She was tiny and shrunken, the grey skin across her wrinkled face so papery that it looked as if it might peel off and flutter away. Victoria wasn't sure she'd ever seen anyone so old.

Elsa looked up at the younger woman and waved the housekeeper away.

'Why are you here?' she asked. Her eyes, though small and

half buried beneath the folds and wrinkles, were sharp and interrogating.

'I need to know something.' Victoria said as steadily as she could.

'I have already told you everything,' Elsa replied in her strong Austrian accent. 'Leo is dead and I shall soon be joining him. What more do you need to know?'

Victoria was suddenly aware of how tall and ungainly she must seem to this minuscule woman amidst her dainty furniture. She sat uninvited on the edge of a gold chair on the other side of the coffee table, settling down carefully so as not to break it.

'What happened to Leo's sister?' she asked.

Elsa hesitated for no more than a couple of seconds; Victoria was watching closely.

'I don't know what you're talking about.'

Victoria folded her hands in her lap. 'Yes you do. I spoke to Maeve Gannon, now Corcoran. She told me everything. She said there was a sister and you told Leo never to speak of her. What happened to her?'

Elsa started to push herself up on the arms of her chair, opening her lips wide as if to call out, but she thought better of it and slumped down again.

'Why should I tell you?' There was spittle in the corners of her mouth. 'What business is it of yours?'

Victoria felt surprisingly calm, knowing that she had right on her side. 'Because Leo was my partner, my lover, the father of my children. And because I won't be able to move on until I know the truth.'

Elsa's thin lips puckered. 'Why should I care whether you *move on*? I do not even know what it means.'

Victoria refused to be angered. 'If you won't tell me I'll find out some other way. I'll ask questions, dig around. The Internet has made it so much easier to track people down and there are records of children who went missing during the War.

'Why don't you make it simple for me? Why don't you save me having to probe, to unearth old acquaintances of yours, perhaps?' She glanced slyly at Elsa. 'People who were around when Leo was a little boy in Austria, maybe. People who knew his sister, or who knew about his affair with Mrs Gannon...'

Elsa's face was blank but her veiny hands were trembling in her lap. Witnessing the old woman's scarcely concealed panic, Victoria suddenly understood why she'd been so insistent on a quiet cremation for her son with no pomp and circumstance. It had seemed peculiar at the time but she'd been in no state to argue.

Now, though, it was so obvious. Elsa must have been desperate to escape the glare of publicity and ensure that her son's precious name should remain untarnished. Victoria felt a fool for not realising.

'All right,' Elsa said. 'I'll tell you.'

Victoria sat very still, every nerve, every fibre on alert.

'There was a sister,' the old woman went on slowly. 'She was younger than Leo. Anna she was called.'

Anna? Now she had a name she seemed more real to Victoria. She was a person, a girl.

'There was something the matter with her,' Elsa explained. 'She was always sick, especially in the winter, always coughing. Cough, cough, cough. She'd always been like that, ever since she was a baby.' She scrunched up her thin wrinkled face at the memory.

'Before the War, I took her to see doctors. I did all I could.' She looked at Victoria sharply. 'They told me she had a weak

301

chest. She was born like that and there was nothing they could do. They said a different climate might help, somewhere hot like Southern Spain. But how was I to get her to Southern Spain? It was ridiculous. Besides, I had Leo and his music to think of.' Her eyes lit up. 'I knew he was extraordinary, from the very first moment that he picked up a violin.'

She glanced at the door. Victoria turned and saw the housekeeper hovering but Elsa waved her away.

'When I heard about the Kindertransport I knew that Leo must go,' Elsa continued. 'It was imperative to keep him safe.'

Victoria raised her eyebrows. 'And Anna?'

Elsa shook her head. 'She was too weak. She might have fallen ill on the journey and made Leo do something stupid. He might have turned around with her and tried to come home. I couldn't risk it. And then I thought, if she did make it to England what family would want her? Who would take in a sick little Jewish girl who was always coughing?

'She would have hindered Leo's chances of finding a good family. And he did, didn't he?' She glanced craftily at Victoria. 'They looked after him, didn't they? They recognised his talent.'

Victoria took a deep breath. She wasn't going to raise the issue of his betrayal of the Gannons again. Now wasn't the moment. She wanted to know more about Anna.

'What happened to her?' she asked quietly.

Elsa shrugged. 'She was taken away like all the others, like my husband and all the rest of the family. Her and my niece, who looked after her. The soldiers came and took them away to Auschwitz and gassed them.'

She betrayed no emotion. Victoria couldn't decide if this meant that she really had no heart, or that she'd been through so much and become so hardened she'd buried her feelings where they'd never be found.

'You left her behind when you followed Leo to London?'

Elsa nodded.

'But why? Why didn't you bring her then? The Gannons would have helped. They would have done everything they could to get you both out.'

Elsa clicked her tongue. 'Foolish girl, have you not listened to me? Don't you understand? Anna was sick. She needed medical attention. The family were already paying for Leo to go to the best school, to have the best tuition. Anna would have been a distraction. They would have put their resources into making her better and Leo's music, his genius, would have suffered. I could not let that happen.'

Victoria was silent for a moment, absorbing the information. She thought of her own children, Ralph and Salome, and knew for certain that she loved them equally, that nothing would persuade her to put one before the other.

'How could you do it?' she whispered, 'as a mother? How could you leave your little girl behind to what you knew would be an almost certain death?'

It wasn't a rhetorical question. She was genuinely mystified and wanted an answer. She was looking steadily at Elsa as she spoke. The old woman touched her forehead lightly with a papery hand.

'You don't understand,' she said again. 'They were terrible times, unique circumstances. It wasn't a decision I made lightly—'

'But you knew Anna would die.'

'I hoped, of course, that she and my niece would be lucky, that somehow they would escape. Some of them did, you know. Unfortunately it was not to be.'

Victoria felt a painful lump in her throat but was determined not to waste precious time crying. She dug her nails into the palms of her hands.

'Poor Anna. Did Leo know? Did he find out what happened to her?'

'I don't know,' said Elsa, her eyes glazing over. 'We never spoke of her. From the moment we left her, the moment we got in that cab to Vienna station, I warned him never to speak her name again. It was the only way.'

'Were they very close – as children I mean?'

Elsa pulled the tartan rug, which had slipped, over her knees again. 'They played together like normal children. He was protective of her because she was sick. She looked up to him.'

'I suppose,' Victoria said in a small voice, as much to herself as to Elsa, 'that he never got over her. He was probably always looking for her, in a way. But he never found her.' She put her face in her hands, she couldn't help herself. 'It's so sad.'

'You waste too much emotion on things that are done and over,' Elsa said coldly. 'You were never hated and spat at and ostracised and murdered. You never had to face the Gestapo or watch your livelihood destroyed. Your husband wasn't taken away in the middle of the night never to return. You don't know what it is to stare death in the face, to fight for your very survival. Many impossible decisions were made at that time that we would rather not have had to make. You were never a Jew. You don't understand.'

The two women looked deep into each other's eyes. There was a ferociousness in Elsa's stare that made Victoria shrink, but she held her gaze with a question and beneath the multiple layers of rage and defensiveness she thought that she might have detected a glimmer of something else. It looked to her very much like shame.

It was enough. Victoria glanced away, exhausted.

'You must go now,' Elsa said.

'Yes.'

'What will you do with this information?'

Victoria thought for a moment. 'I don't know.'

The old woman was silent until at last she picked up the gold bell on the table beside her and rang it. The housekeeper appeared at the door.

'Show Madame out.'

Victoria stood up. The space between her and the old woman was only a few feet but it could have been a hundred miles.

'Goodbye Elsa,' she said, knowing that they'd never meet again.

The old woman nodded.

Victoria was about to turn her back when Elsa crooked an arthritic forefinger and beckoned to her. Surprised, the younger woman took a few steps forwards and bent right down so that Elsa could whisper in her ear.

Victoria could feel the dry lips crackling on her skin and the hot breath made the tiny hairs in her ear canal stand on end. It took a few moments after Elsa had finished speaking for her to collect herself enough to stand up. Now, at last, it all made sense.

Tears were coursing down her cheeks as she walked back down the long corridor to the front door. She was glad that Elsa would never see her cry. She wanted her to remember the strong, steady gaze, the gossamer thin shaft of light that had penetrated, she hoped, deep into the old woman's dark soul. Albeit so fleetingly that no one watching would guess it had even happened.

***

She couldn't read or sleep or do anything but think on the journey home. Her mind was filled with images of Anna. She would have been five or six years old to Leo's eight, almost certainly dark like him. Pretty, Victoria was sure, but pale and thin because of her illness.

She didn't want to imagine how she must have suffered but her thoughts kept returning to the moment when she said goodbye to Leo, then to her mother. She must have been so frightened and bewildered.

And then her journey to Auschwitz. Victoria wanted to scream. It was a horror so unimaginable that it didn't seem possible. And yet...and yet...it had happened in Leo's lifetime. It had happened to the little girl who was his sister and her children's aunt.

She wished with all her heart that Leo had been able to share this with her. To carry a burden like that with you all your days must have been so hard. He must have been tormented. She wondered what his dreams were like – did he dream of Anna night after night? Did he search for her in the eyes of all his women – in the eyes of his own daughters, too?

To know that he had been chosen over his sister, that his genius was more important than her life. The guilt must have been suffocating. And the need to succeed, to fulfil everything that his mother wanted of him in order to have made the sacrifice worthwhile. It was a weight that no boy should have to carry, no man either.

She knew for certain now that she'd never really known Leo and she felt a fool for imagining once that she did. His feelings must have been so complex, his mind so turbulent that she doubted if he himself understood why he behaved as he did towards her, the children and all the other women in his life. No wonder he chose, above all, to focus on his music.

It must have seemed so simple, a welcome escape.

For several days she found that she didn't want to speak to anyone. She went about her business doing what needed to be done and avoiding anything other than mundane conversations about the weather, where people were going on holiday and so on. She saw Oliver a few times at work and he invited her for lunch twice, but she had excuses ready.

One afternoon he asked, half joking, if he'd done something wrong and she laughed, pretending not to register the hurt in his eyes: 'Of course not. I'm just busy.'

Ralph had his French oral exam and said it went all right. Salome won a prize at school for the best self-portrait, done in the style of the pointillists. It was a mess of pink and purple and yellow and brown blobs and Victoria said it was lovely and stuck it on the kitchen wall. Debs rang and asked her to go out for a drink but she claimed she couldn't get a babysitter.

Then one evening, exactly a week after her visit to Elsa, she picked up the phone and rang Maddy first, then Cat.

'I want us to meet up,' she said. 'There's something I need to tell you.'

Maddy hesitated. Was this a trick? Did she know about her and Ralph? Cat was anxious. Would there be some sort of show-down between the two other women?

'It's about Leo,' Victoria said calmly. 'He wasn't who we thought he was.'

The arrangement was made and Victoria felt surprisingly relieved. She slept better that night than she'd slept in months. She had no dreams at all.

CHAPTER TWENTY-THREE

Wednesday May 5th

'This creek's as dry as a dead dingo's donger.'

'What?' Cat wasn't sure she'd heard right.

Gervaise repeated himself, with extra emphasis on the 'donger.'

'I reckon I've got the accent nailed,' he grinned. 'Been getting lessons from my Aussie mate.'

He was up for a part in another TV series. He'd play the Australian barman.

'What's a donger?' Rachel asked innocently. She had tell-tale biscuit crumbs round her mouth. As far as anyone knew she'd never had a boyfriend. She could be a bit naive.

Cat and Gervaise gave her a funny look.

'Oh,' Rachel said, blushing slightly. 'I see.'

A man was browsing in the cookery section but otherwise the place was empty. It was nearly time to shut up shop.

'I'm on a course tomorrow afternoon,' Rachel said, changing the subject quickly. 'I won't be back. I'll need you two to close up for me.'

Cat was pleased. She'd started writing again at last; for a while she hadn't felt like it at all. It was another short story – a love story – and she knew it probably wasn't any good but she was really into it and wanted to finish. It would be easier to sneak some time without Rachel breathing down her back, giving her unnecessary jobs.

'What are you doing tonight?' Gervaise asked casually as they collected their things from the cloakroom.

'Meeting someone for a drink,' Cat replied, tying the shoelace of her black Doctor Marten boot and picking up her rucksack. 'You?'

'Who are you meeting?'

Cat couldn't help noticing the suspicion in his voice.

'A female friend, *silly*,' she said, smiling. He attempted to hide his relief by scratching his nose.

'You look different,' she said suddenly, taking a step back. She hadn't noticed before. 'What have you done?'

His sideburns weren't shaved off anymore and his black hair, which usually stuck out around his head like a halo, was longer over his ears and wavy. It showed off his bright blue eyes.

He ran a hand through his fringe. 'I haven't had a haircut for ages. I probably should.'

'Don't. It suits you longer.'

He looked pleased. 'D'you fancy doing something this weekend? We could take a bus. Sit by the river in Barnes or somewhere, if the weather's good. Have a few drinks.'

Cat frowned, remembering what she was really doing tonight. She'd managed to put it to the back of her mind during the day but suddenly, she wasn't sure that she'd ever felt as nervous.

'Look, I can't think about the weekend now. My mother—'

'S'OK.' Gervaise picked up his bag, too. 'It was just an idea.'

Cat touched his arm. 'Don't be like that. It's a nice idea. I'll let you know tomorrow, all right?'

Maddy switched off her computer and sighed. She couldn't believe it was time to go already. Thanks to the surprising success of Wild Thing, she'd secured several more jobs, including a couple of Bar Mitzvah's in North London. Bizarrely, she'd also been asked to help with the soft launch of a new brand of condom called Mr Smooth.

The idea was to have several small roadshows in Brighton, Leeds and Reading. A Love Bus, complete with Jacuzzi, would tour around, handing out free condoms to teens, mainly, and twenty-somethings. The idea was that an early adopter would stick with the same brand for life. If the soft launch was a success, they'd go nationwide later in the year. It was a great opportunity.

She was relieved to have some money coming in at last but it was hard work and because she now had no childcare, she was quite often having to labour late into the night after Phoebe went to sleep.

MumSkills was also up and running. She was paying Ralph to help out for a few hours at weekends but if it took off, she realised that she'd need to employ someone full-time. At the moment she was still doing most of it herself.

She'd taken the painful decision not to send Phoebe back to her prep school next term. She didn't have the money upfront and in truth, she couldn't bear the financial anxiety anymore. It had almost broken her heart to break the news and Phoebe had taken it badly.

'But I don't want to leave,' she'd wailed. 'I like it there, I like my friends.'

'I know,' Maddy said, trying to sooth. 'But your new school's nice, too, and you'll make other friends very soon.'

It was an awful lot for Phoebe to have to cope with and adjust to, on top of the move and losing Jess, not to mention her father's death only five months before. Maddy felt terribly guilty. But, she reasoned, it would be worse to build up massive debts again and live with constant worry. The local primary had a reasonable reputation and she just hoped that Phoebe would settle in.

Maddy took off her T-shirt and put a black silk shirt over her jeans. She wasn't going to dress up but didn't want to look scruffy either.

She strolled into the kitchen, where Ralph had his head in a History text book. His brown fringe was sticking out in front from where he'd been pulling it. He tended to do that when he was concentrating.

'How's it going?' she asked.

He glanced up and smiled. 'OK. Can't wait till it's all over.'

She took her pink lipstick out of her bag on the chair and put it on without looking in the mirror. 'Keep focused. Not much longer, then think what a lovely summer you'll have.'

They hadn't mentioned again those five little words that he'd uttered as he climbed in the cab, but something between them had changed. Their conversations had become more intimate, somehow, their body language more significant. They both knew, and they were both waiting.

Phoebe was supposed to be in bed reading, but Maddy could hear her chatting to her dolls and went in to check on her. The little girl was sitting on the carpet, four or five dolls arranged in a circle in front of her. She'd changed them into their nightclothes and there were several cups and saucers and a toy baby bottle in front of them.

Maddy couldn't help smiling. Phoebe was in her yellow

nightie with ducklings on and looked all clean and fresh from the bath.

'I'm giving them their milk,' she explained, tipping a cup into one doll's mouth.

'All right. But as soon as they've finished you must hop into bed. Ralph'll come and turn out your light.'

Maddy went back into the kitchen and put on a pair of black wedge sandals.

'Are you absolutely sure Victoria doesn't know?' she asked Ralph, who was chewing the end of a biro.

'Yeah. There's no way she's found out.'

'Then why does she want to see me?' she asked for the umpteenth time.

Ralph rocked back on the legs of his chair. 'I don't know. Honest. She hasn't told me anything.'

Maddy picked up her black jacket and handbag and swung it over her shoulder. 'Don't forget Phoebe. I won't be late.' She bent down and kissed him on the cheek. 'Work hard. Oh, and wish me luck.'

'Good luck,' he replied.

* * *

A small slim scarily glamorous blonde in jeans, a black jacket and blouse walked in and looked left and right. Victoria's heart started hammering. She felt so sick that she wondered if she'd be able to go through with it. She might have to dash to the loo.

She took a swig of wine and wiped her mouth on a paper napkin. Deep breaths, she told herself. Be brave. You can do it.

She caught Maddy's eye and the younger woman made her way towards the back of the wine bar. Victoria was relieved to note that Maddy, too, was nervous. You could tell by her tense shoulders and the way she was clutching on to her black handbag, turning her knuckles white. She gave a tight smile and sat down facing the wall, opposite Victoria.

'Thank you for coming,' Victoria said stiffly.

Maddy cleared her throat and nodded, then they waited in silence while the waiter brought her a vodka and tonic.

Victoria checked her watch. 'I hope Cat turns up.' She glanced up just in time to see the young woman weaving her way around the tables towards them.

She was wearing a pale blue T-shirt that looked several sizes too small, skinny black jeans, a silver studded belt and enormous black bovver boots. Her hair was bunched up on top of her head and as she came closer, Victoria spotted the silver nose ring and nose stud, as well as a small, multi-coloured tattoo on her right upper arm. She hadn't noticed before; it must have been covered.

Cat looked pale, thin and slightly grubby as usual in that cultivated grunge sort of way, and her eyes were circled with black kohl. The overall effect ought to be aggressive and off-putting Victoria thought, as if seeing her afresh, but she was in fact curiously attractive. She might even be beautiful if she took out the nose ring, got rid of the tattoo and bought herself some half-decent clothes. You'd never guess in a million years, though, that such a tender heart beat beneath the tough exterior.

The bar, beneath the railway arches near Waterloo Station, was dark and atmospheric, with plenty of shadowy spots behind pillars in which to hide. Victoria didn't go to wine bars much but she'd remembered that she liked this one and had hoped it wouldn't be too busy once the theatre-going crowd had cleared off.

Cat sat down beside Maddy and ordered a pint of lager. Victoria noticed her chewed nails and every now and again, she'd bite the back of her hand in that odd, compulsive way. As soon as she realised what she was doing, she'd put her hand back in her lap only for it to flutter up again a few seconds later.

Victoria took another gulp of wine and tucked a strand of hair that was getting in her eyes behind her ear. They were all a bundle of nerves; she might as well get straight to the point.

'I went to Paris to see Leo's mother,' she began.

Maddy's left eye twitched.

'I'd discovered something about him, about his past,' Victoria went on, 'and I needed Elsa to give me the final pieces of the jigsaw.'

'What things?' Maddy asked. Cat was silent and listening, her face as white as a ghost.

Victoria glanced at them both. 'He had a sister.'

Maddy's eyes widened. She had no clue, then.

'She was called Anna. You know Leo came to England on the Kindertransport?'

Both women nodded.

'Well, I'd heard from someone that there was a sister and that Elsa left her behind when she joined Leo in England. The sister died in Auschwitz. She was about three years younger than Leo. Elsa said she was sick, always coughing, although she didn't seem to know what was the matter. Basically, she chose to leave her behind with a niece, knowing that the odds of her surviving in Austria were poor. Above all, Elsa wanted to protect Leo and his genius.'

Maddy put her elbows on the table and rested her head in her hands as if her neck could no longer support the weight. 'Why didn't he tell me?'

'Or any of us,' Victoria pointed out.

'And she died, this Anna?' Cat needed to hear it again.

'Anna and the niece and all the rest of the family, as far as I can make out,' said Victoria. 'The awful thing is, Elsa told Leo never ever to speak of Anna again. It was as if she'd never existed. And Leo had to live for the rest of his life with the knowledge that he'd been chosen over his sister.'

A tear trickled down her cheek and Cat pushed a paper napkin towards her, which she picked up. 'Thanks.'

'A sort of Sophie's Choice,' Maddy said thoughtfully.

'In a way,' Victoria agreed. 'But there's a fundamental difference. Sophie was forced to choose, whereas Elsa could have sent Anna with Leo and most probably both would have survived. The point is, she valued his talent over her daughter's life. She was determined not to let anything – or anyone – stand in his way.

'I pity him,' she went on. 'Despite everything he's done. Because he carried this burden and was unable to share it with anyone. Perhaps if he had, we'd all have understood him better. Perhaps he wouldn't have told so many lies.'

She hesitated, waiting for the information to sink in. 'I wanted you to know.'

'Why?' Maddy asked suddenly, sitting up straight and crossing her arms defensively. 'Why did you want to tell us?'

Victoria blew her nose. 'Because it made me understand so much. It was as if a veil had been lifted from my eyes. And there was something else.' She went on to describe his affair with Mrs Gannon, the fake desire to convert to Catholicism that had so rocked Patrick Gannon, the break-up of the family, the subsequent shame, Leo's banishment and her meeting with Maeve. The other women listened in silence.

'You see,' she said sadly, 'I don't believe he loved any one of us more than the other. In fact I'm not sure what he felt. I don't think he knew himself.'

Maddy's eyes narrowed, while Cat chewed the back of her hand and stared at the table.

'Do you remember,' said Victoria, 'at the funeral, how Maddy said Leo's pet name for her was 'my darling girl' and we found out that he called us all that?'

Cat nodded but Maddy remained tight-lipped, ramrod straight.

'I was shocked at first, then I did what I'd always done, I simply refused to believe it. As far as I was concerned Leo loved only me – while you two,' she glanced from one to the other, 'were just inconveniences, silly little distractions that he'd one day grow tired of.'

Maddy cleared her throat. 'He would have left you if it weren't for the children.'

Victoria waited, scarcely daring to breathe. Hadn't Maddy heard what she was saying? Victoria had been banking on the fact that her words would somehow cut through the defensive layers of suspicion, hatred and jealousy. But maybe it simply wasn't possible. Perhaps they'd always be bitter enemies.

'As we're having this confessional,' Maddy went on coldly, 'I may as well tell you that I was shocked to find out about Cat. But I suppose I did the same as you.' She looked straight at Victoria. 'I refused to believe she meant anything.'

The older woman's shoulders relaxed a little. It seemed she had got through. Maddy was prepared to accept some errors of judgment, anyway.

'But what are you saying?' Cat interrupted. 'That he loved none of us? That's rubbish. I don't care about the money or the fact that he never made a will. And I don't care about Mrs Gannon, or whatever she was called. I know he loved me, I wasn't imagining it.' There were tears in her eyes now, too, which she brushed away with a fist.

Victoria leaned over and touched the young woman's arm.

'I'm not here to hurt either of you or score points,' she went on, fixing Cat with her soft grey eyes. 'I think he probably did love us all in his own, inadequate way. I couldn't, wouldn't believe that at first but I can now.

'I also believe, though, that a part of him could never really commit because he was always searching for Anna, afraid that if he gave his heart to one person, that person would be snatched away as Anna was. He couldn't risk it. He couldn't risk losing that one person again. Everything he did, every relationship he had, was coloured by what had happened to his sister. It was what drove him.'

'I didn't know you were a psychiatrist,' Maddy butted in, her voice laced with sarcasm.

'A counsellor – not a psychiatrist,' Victoria replied.

Maddy pursed her pink lips.

Cat gulped her lager. 'What, we were a sort of insurance policy?' She made a peculiar sound. 'His mum has a lot to answer for.'

'Yes,' Victoria agreed. 'She's a dreadful, cruel woman, ruthless. I know I couldn't have done it. I couldn't have sacrificed one of my children on the altar of another's talent, even in Nazi-occupied Austria.

'I think deep down she may feel remorse. I thought I saw a glimmer of it in Paris. But she'd never say. She's buried her feelings too deep and admitting her guilt and acknowledging what she did would destroy her.'

The waiter came over and, seeing that the women hadn't finished their drinks, moved away again. Victoria was aware that they were attracting stares from the man and woman a few tables away but she ignored them.

'Poor Anna,' Maddy said suddenly.

'And poor us,' said Cat. 'If what you say's true, we've all been affected by this horrible decision of Elsa's and we didn't even know it.'

Maddy suddenly glared at Victoria, her face and neck red and blotchy. 'I wish you'd never told me. I don't believe you're telling the truth. I think you're trying to get back at us, to get revenge.'

Victoria felt herself shrink. Perhaps Maddy was right. Maybe her motives were selfish.

'No,' she cried, rallying. The man and woman a few tables away turned and stared openly. 'I understand why you might think that but you're wrong. We've all been living a dream, an illusion. I feel better, cleaner, now I've found out the truth. I wanted to help you.'

She swallowed, feeling as if this were the hardest thing that she'd ever done in her life. 'Like it or not,' she went on, 'we're all linked, all part of the story. It's important that we know the reality. For our children's sakes as well as our own. For their future as well as ours.'

Maddy fell silent again and Cat's face had taken on a greenish tinge.

'What about the fact that he was so different with all of us. I mean...' she said, looking at Victoria, 'I remember you saying he didn't like rock music but he did, we listened to it all the time. And Maddy,' she went on, turning, 'You said he hated takeaways but we often had them. It's so odd.'

Victoria's mouth puckered, which made her face appear lop-sided and peculiar. 'It's as if he was three men, living three separate lives.'

'Yes,' Maddy said thoughtfully, remembering how often they'd played tennis, too, though she didn't say. It was Ralph who'd revealed that Leo never did any sport with his first family.

Victoria's brow was a mass of furrows. 'It's extraordinary, I know. And there's something else, too.'

Maddy and Cat stared, as if there couldn't possibly be more.

'The money,' Victoria went on. 'I know Cat says she didn't care about it, but I couldn't comprehend why he didn't provide for us, for his children. Why he left us penniless. Elsa told me that he gave most of it away in great chunks – to a charity which educates young people about the Holocaust. That's where it went.'

'Ah,' said Maddy, as if a switch had been flicked.

Cat rubbed her eyes several times, as if something were stuck in there.

'That's it,' Victoria said simply, raising her hands, palms upwards. 'I've finished. That's what I wanted to tell you.'

'Thanks,' Maddy said sarcastically. 'I think I'll stick to my own interpretation of events if you don't mind.'

Victoria sighed. Her armpits were damp and her mouth felt dry. She wished she'd ordered water as well, but now the waiter was nowhere in sight.

'Don't be like that,' came a small voice. Both women looked at Cat. 'It's better that we know. I'm glad Victoria's told me.'

Maddy's chin jutted forward. 'I know how we felt about one another.'

She paused and her shoulders drooped. 'He cared more about what happened in the past than about Phoebe, his own daughter. It was all lies. But maybe...' she added, uncertainly, '...maybe ignorance would be worse.' She glanced at Victoria, who gave a sad half smile.

Cat pushed her chair back and rose unsteadily. 'I need to go home. I feel a bit weird.'

Victoria looked at her anxiously. 'Will you be all right?'

'Are you going to the station?' Maddy asked and Cat nodded.

'I'll come with you.'

Maddy turned to Victoria and caught her gaze. There was something in the younger woman's eyes that Victoria didn't understand and that troubled her. She watched Leo's two other women walk quickly towards the exit as if they couldn't wait to be out of there, out into the cool night air. Maddy went first while Cat followed close behind, which was what you'd expect, somehow. The younger following the older. Experience leading the way.

Victoria felt, for a moment, strangely wistful. After all, they had each known another side of Leo, one that she'd never be familiar with. They had held a little piece of his damaged heart, however tenuously, that she could never have.

But she must put all that behind her and look to the future now. She straightened her shoulders, knowing that she wouldn't sleep tonight, that she'd be going over and over what had been said, every nuance, every change of expression. But her overriding emotion, she realised, was one of relief.

She'd said it, it was done and she'd made a sort of peace, or tried to. She thought that it was one she could learn to live with anyway.

CHAPTER TWENTY-FOUR

Same day

'Go – now,' Maddy said.

Ralph pulled a face. 'Can't I just—'

'No! Your mother will be home soon. She'll worry. And your exams—'

Ralph knitted his dark brows. 'All anyone ever goes on about is my exams.'

Maddy handed him his bag. 'But they're important. I want you to do well.'

They were in the kitchen and she hadn't yet taken off her jacket or shoes.

'You haven't even told me what it was about.' Ralph's bottom lip was sticking out like a sulky child. Maddy couldn't deal with this now.

'She'll tell you if she wants to. It's not my place—'

'Christ,' he said. 'You're treating me like a kid.'

'How was Phoebe?' Maddy asked quickly, hoping to divert him.

'Went to sleep straight away. Didn't hear a squeak.'

'Good.' She noticed with a pang that he hadn't shaved in a while and his beard was getting darker and stronger. She wanted to kiss his cheek but stopped herself. 'No more late nights until they're over, OK?' The A-levels started the following Tuesday.

When he'd gone, she opened the fridge and poured herself a large glass of white wine, which she took into the sitting room before putting a CD on.

She chose the last part of Mahler's eighth symphony, one of Leo's recordings. It tore at her heart strings every time but it was also uplifting, speaking of an optimism, a confidence in the return of the human spirit that she needed right now. She sat down and closed her eyes for a few moments, allowing the fusion of song and symphony to seep through her soul.

Meeting with Victoria had unsettled her in more ways than she could ever have imagined. It wasn't just the information about Leo – the full extent of his lying and subterfuge, though that was shattering enough. It was also coming face to face again with the woman whose partner she had shared and whose son she was seeing behind her back.

She thought of Leo's disastrous affair with Mrs Gannon, the older woman, and shivered. It had been so wrong and had wrecked so many lives.

She must stop Ralph's visits, but how? She felt so protective of him, such a responsibility towards him. When he was poring over his books he seemed totally absorbed, oblivious to anything or anyone around him. If he could only find something that he loved, some passion, then he might start looking outwards and away from her.

The music finished and the CD went back to the first movement. Maddy tried to imagine Leo there, conducting his orchestra with that precise mix of passion and control that he was famous for. She wondered if he'd thought of Anna often when he was at work, trying to imagine what sort of woman she would have grown into and what she'd have done with her life. Maddy had never met Elsa but she hated the old woman. Her decision was unbelievably cruel, however dreadful the circumstances in which she'd made it.

She'd been angry with Victoria this evening but also knew for certain, just a few short hours later, that she was glad she'd been told. She'd never been one to shy from the truth; she always wanted to have the full facts to hand.

Reluctantly she found herself agreeing with Victoria's conclusion – that Leo loved them all equally and, in truth, none of them much at all. Once again, her foundations had been shaken and she was going to have to work hard to shore herself up – for Phoebe's sake as well as her own. It was a tough order.

Unable to sleep, she decided to finish her wine and do a bit of work. Plans for the new condom launch were going well but the logistics were pretty difficult. And one of the Bar Mitzvah boys wanted to dry ski into the hotel where the event was to take place. It wasn't going to be easy.

She decided to have a quick shower before settling down to her computer. She'd be exhausted tomorrow but it was better than pacing around or watching rubbish TV. At least she'd be doing something useful.

***

Cat hoped Rick wouldn't be round tonight because she wanted to talk to Tracy on her own, but she was out of luck. He and Tracy were on the sofa leafing through a wedding magazine.

Tracy was in her Snoopy pyjamas, her bare feet with blue painted toenails on the seat beside her. 'Rick wants to get married in black but I think that's a terrible idea,' she said, frowning. 'What d'you reckon Cat?'

Rick shifted away from his fiancée. 'I never said I definitely wanted it.'

'Don't lie,' said Tracy, turning to her friend. 'What do you think?'

Cat shrugged. 'It's up to you guys.'

Detecting storm clouds gathering, she scuttled into the kitchen to get herself a glass of water before turning in. Tracy could be a Rottweiler when challenged. Cat didn't want to be around to witness the carnage.

The mice were sniffing around in their cage. She took one of them out, gave it a stroke and put it back again.

'Sorry Cedric,' she said, 'I don't feel great.'

She got into her pyjamas and lay on her bed, wondering how she could banish the negative images and horrible thoughts that were swirling around her brain, making her dizzy. Leo and Anna, Anna in Auschwitz, Leo and that woman who took him in, the lies about Catholicism, the family's shame and misery, Anna dead. And Maddy and Victoria. She wanted to believe they had nothing, really, to do with her, especially Maddy. That they were a thing apart. And yet she couldn't escape the feeling that they were, as Victoria had said, all linked, all part of the story.

She clenched her fists. That was a lie. She, Cat, was alone, always had been and always would be. No one dictated to her what to do, think or feel. In any case, there was no point picking over the past. Leo had gone just like her father and nothing whatever would bring them back. She was sad about Anna, it was a horrible story, but sad things happened all the time. She needed to forget – if only she could.

Her head swam. She wasn't strong enough and couldn't cope with this on her own. She rootled around in her bag for her mobile and pulled it out.

'Gervaise, is that you?'

'Cat?' It was comforting to hear his familiar voice.

'Can I come over?' she said. 'I'll get a cab. It won't take long.'

'Course.' He sounded anxious. 'Are you all right?'

'Um.' She tried to swallow her tears. 'I really need to talk.'

'I'll put the kettle on. Or maybe you need something stronger?'

'Something stronger,' she replied.

* * *

They started off on Gervaise's sofa. Cat did almost all the talking and he listened, making observations every now and then. She found it easier to open up than she'd thought. She even told him about the miscarriage.

'I guessed,' he nodded. 'I was worried about you.'

'Were you?' She was astonished that he cared. She'd felt so bad before she came here. Leo's third best woman and he'd never really loved any of them anyway. Her whole life was a mess. But Gervaise didn't appear to agree.

'You're beautiful you know,' he said, brushing a strand of hair out of her eyes.

'No I'm not.'

He put his face close up to hers. 'You are. You just don't realise.'

She was about to protest again when he placed a finger on her lips. 'Shh'.

They were on their second bottle of cheap red wine. She'd almost given up on sleep. They'd be zombies in the morning.

He lit a cigarette and passed it to her. He'd done it often enough but it seemed strange, suddenly, taking something that had been in his mouth. Intimate. He lit another cigarette for himself and looked at her through the smoky haze. She thought she could see two of him; she really was drunk.

'Cat Mason?' he said, one eye watering slightly from the smoke, 'do you want to come to bed with me?'

She swallowed. 'I'm not sure—'

The next thing she knew, he'd made a lunge and she'd tipped back on the sofa and he was on top, covering her face in smoky kisses.

'Stop,' she laughed, holding her cigarette in the air. 'Do you want me to set fire to your flat?'

'I don't care,' he mumbled through his kisses, 'we can go out in a blaze of glory.'

Somehow they made it to the bed. When Cat woke, the sun was filtering through the curtains and her head felt as if it had been squeezed in a flower press. She couldn't remember an awful lot except that their lovemaking had been good and comforting and wholesome and unembarrassing.

She glanced over at Gervaise who was lying naked on his stomach, spread-eagled across the mattress and facing the other wall.

He must have sensed that she was awake. 'I love you Cat Mason,' he muttered. She couldn't see his expression.

'What?' Had she heard right?

He turned over and whispered in her ear, moving her hair out of the way. 'I said I love you, you big dope.'

She didn't know what to reply so she kissed his chest and his neck and his tummy button and they made love again and it was still only 6 a.m.

He made mugs of tea and they had two pain-killers each and ate toast and jam on their laps on the end of the bed.

'Will you take the first shower?' he asked, getting up, opening the wardrobe and taking out a white towel, which he threw at her.

It was hard and scratchy but she appreciated the gesture. 'Thanks.'

When it was his turn, she watched him pad naked across the floor towards the door. His skin was very pale, almost luminous, and he had dark hair on his long legs and broad shoulders and a perfect little bum.

She laughed and he turned to look at her, self-consciously covering himself with the towel.

'What?'

'It's just so weird. All these years we've known each other. I can't believe I'm staring at your naked backside!'

He gave a sheepish grin. 'Me neither. You don't regret it, do you?'

She shook her head and could hear him whistling as he sauntered into the bathroom before the water drowned out his tune.

It was the oddest thing, travelling into work together by tube and bus. They passed a few people that Gervaise recognised in the street on the way to the station and he waved at them merrily. He seemed in a very good mood, despite the hangover.

She was hardly aware of what she was doing that day or who she spoke to. She was living totally in her head. Maybe this is it, she was thinking: first Leo, now Gervaise. He loves me properly, not like Leo. He's straightforward and kind. Tracy's getting married. Now I'm fixed, too. It's all sorted.

She felt bewildered, as if she were being carried along on something that she had no control over. But maybe this was good, this was what she'd needed all the time. Just to go with it, stop worrying and let someone else take care of it all. She wondered what her mum would think. Nothing. She was living in her own little world. So long as Cat popped in to see her as usual she wouldn't notice any difference.

'Let's go for a drink – to celebrate,' Gervaise said at the end of the day when they were cashing up.

Rachel overheard. She had extraordinarily acute hearing as well as eyes in the back of her head.

'Celebrate what?' she asked suspiciously.

Cat frowned at Gervaise but he didn't notice.

'Cat and I,' he said grinning, 'we're, well,' he blushed, 'put it this way. We're more than just friends.'

'Oh!' Rachel was startled. 'You mean you're *going out* together?'

Gervaise, scarcely able to contain his excitement, put an arm round Cat's shoulders and squeezed. 'Don't worry, it won't affect our work or anything.'

'I should hope not.' Rachel gave a small smile. 'But I'm pleased for you.'

Cat swallowed, wishing Gervaise hadn't done that. But what was the harm? She'd decided to go with it so she gave him a hug and smiled back.

They went for a few drinks in a pub on Upper Street, then a few more in a bar round the corner. Cat's headache had gone though she still felt delicate, but the alcohol lifted her mood.

'Will we go back to yours or mine?' Gervaise asked as they stood on the pavement at the end of the evening, swaying slightly. It was still warm and they didn't need coats. Cat had just a sweatshirt on and Gervaise was in a T-shirt.

Cat chewed her lip. She hadn't really thought about it but of course, now they were going out they'd be spending lots of nights with each other. That's what normal couples did. It was only her and Leo who'd been different.

'Er, mine?' she said, thinking she'd like to have a shower and put on clean clothes in the morning.

'Great.' Gervaise leaned down and kissed her on the mouth, his arms twining round her like a vine. His breath was warm, sweet and beery and she felt safe, comfortable and loved. There were worse things. Much worse. This was good; she was lucky.

She was hoping Rick and Tracy would be in bed when they got home, having recovered from their little contretemps last night. But they were very much awake. The sitting room was strewn with bits of card and Tracy was standing up, her chin in her hand, head on one side, examining each of them on the floor. Rick was on the sofa looking slightly dazed.

'What do you think, Cat?' Tracy said as they walked in. She didn't seem to notice Gervaise.

'It's a selection of wedding invitations. They've done some different designs for us. I like the one with pink and yellow roses in the corner. I think they're really cute. But Rick says they're too girly. He wants the one with the guitar and cowboy boots because he says it reflects who we are.'

Cat stood beside Tracy and tried to focus on the pieces of card on the floor. They all seemed a bit soppy to her.

'Um,' she said, concentrating on staying upright, 'The flowers are nice but I like the cowboy boots, too.' She beckoned to Gervaise, needing help. 'What's your opinion? Which is your favourite?'

Rick jumped up, delighted to have found an excuse to escape. 'Gervaise, my good fellow! Fancy a beer?'

Gervaise muttered something about being 'pretty tanked up' but Rick was having none of it and dragged him into the kitchen to choose an exotic bottle from his collection in the fridge.

Tracy sighed. 'Rick's just not that interested.' She looked at Cat tearfully. 'D'you think he's trying to tell me something? D'you reckon he doesn't really want to get married, but if

329

that's true, why doesn't he tell me?'

Cat started gathering up the invitations. 'Course not, he's just tired. Anyway, guys aren't interested in this sort of thing. All they care about is beer and music and sex and fast cars.'

Tracy smiled, squatting down and helping Cat put the invitations in a box. 'Yeah. I reckon I'll just have to decide myself.' She winked at her friend. 'The pink and yellow roses.'

Cat grinned back. 'Lesson one. Always get your own way!'

They sat down and Tracy studied Cat for the first time. 'You look knackered, what have you been doing? I didn't see you this morning.'

Cat stared at her fingernails. 'I went over to Gervaise's.'

'Did you now?'

Cat didn't like the tone in Tracy's voice.

'It's not what—' she started to say, but she was interrupted by Rick who'd appeared from the kitchen, beer bottle in hand, followed by Gervaise.

'Guess what?' Rick said, a huge smile on his face, 'Cat and Gervaise have only got it together at last!'

'No!' Tracy put her hands to her mouth and stared. 'Is it true? Why didn't you tell me?'

Cat shifted in her seat.

'Oh Cat!' said Tracy, leaning over to hug her, 'that's wonderful! I'm so happy for you!'

She glanced up at Gervaise, who was swigging from his bottle, a look of dreamy contentment on his face.

'I need to get some sleep,' Cat said quickly, ignoring Rick's and Tracy's winks.

'Sleep,' echoed Gervaise, stretching happily. 'Sounds like a very good idea.'

He padded after her into the bedroom and closed the door behind them.

CHAPTER TWENTY-FIVE

Friday June 25th

Pale yellow sunlight filtered through the open window and illuminated the battered white case in the corner of the bedroom.

Victoria walked over to it, snapped open the eight latches down the sides and undid the case before stopping for a moment to look. Her cello was just as it had been, a rich golden brown, scored with numerous small, deep scratches that signified years of wear, resting there in the dark, waiting to be brought back to life.

She lifted the instrument out, sat on the edge of her bed and dusted it down with a clean cloth. There were traces of rosin on the strings from when it had last been played, what, more than fifteen years ago? A lifetime away.

She tightened the bow, breaking off a few frayed hairs, put the instrument between her knees and tuned the strings, which were flat and sad. Then she massaged her cello lovingly, feeling with her fingertips for the familiar marks on its belly from centuries of use, the worn down section of ornamental border round the edge, in the place where it sits on your chest, close to your heart.

It had been her pride and joy, this cello, bought for her by her parents and worth a small fortune. Made in 1780 by Joseph Hill, it had always given her a thrill to think that somebody might once have played it in a wig and britches, that it had a life well before she did and that one day another person would become its caretaker. Would he or she, too, wonder and speculate about its previous owner?

It had travelled all over the world with her when she'd played professionally and she knew it in the way that she knew her children's faces: each blemish, the shape of the bridge, the sound of its voice. If you lined it up in a room with six others she'd be able to pick it out, no trouble. And it had its own distinct personality.

'I'm so sorry I've neglected you,' she whispered, holding it close and stroking its glossy scroll and the smooth tuning pegs.

She positioned herself correctly and struck the first open D string of the Prelude from Bach's Second Cello Suite. It was a piece of music that she held dear to her heart and she knew every note. The deep, intense, melancholy sound sent goose bumps up and down her spine. It was the open string in its purest form, the ultimate resonance.

She breathed out – 'Aaah' – as the memory of that glorious sound world that was once hers to make and inhabit came flooding back.

She continued to play, at first a little self-conscious and clumsy, but before long it just returned, that sense that she and the instrument were one. She forgot what her fingers were doing and felt that she'd reawakened her cello's very soul.

Tears started to trickle down her cheeks but they were tears of happiness, not sorrow. She could still play! She hadn't forgotten. To think that she'd denied herself this pleasure for so many years! And now, as she moved on to the more rumbustious Prelude from the C major suite, she felt something deep in her stirring that had been almost dead, a creature in hibernation.

After a while, her fingers and the muscles in her arms started to ache. It had been beginners' luck, perhaps, that she'd played so well. The next time there would be more tension in her shoulders and neck, more frustration at how rusty she'd become.

Reluctantly she propped her beloved cello back in the corner of her bedroom where it had languished for so long, and stretched. The pads of her fingers were sore, having become soft through lack of use. But she'd be back, she knew. The instrument had spoken to her; it seemed to have become a part of her again like a limb that's been re-attached. It might never work quite as well as before – but it was hers.

She checked on herself quickly in the mirror and went downstairs to join Salome, who was eating Rice Krispies at the kitchen table. 'Time to go sweetheart,' Victoria said, 'quick tooth-clean and get your shoes on please.'

She didn't bother to lock when she left the house as Ralph was still in bed. He had just one more exam, then it was a question of waiting for the results in August. Victoria dreaded the possibility that he might fail to get his place at university because she wasn't at all sure that he'd agree to re-take.

She remembered that mystery smudge of pink lipstick on his cheek and shuddered. If she could only get him to college in September she felt that he might, yet, find his way in life. But if he flunked, who knew what would happen? She stopped outside the school gates and gave Salome a kiss. 'Work hard – and have fun!' She always said that.

It was warm and sunny and had been for days, which made a change from the wash-out of the previous summer. Victoria was wearing a new slate-grey T-shirt with little puffed sleeves and a knee-length denim skirt and flat leather tan sandals. She hadn't bought anything new for months – not since Leo died

– and had decided she deserved a treat.

She usually opted for loose baggy clothes which hid her tummy, but the girl in the shop had persuaded her the T-shirt suited her. 'You've got the figure for it, you may as well show it.'

Victoria supposed she was a little trimmer these days, having made a conscious effort to cut back on the cakes and puddings. As she strolled along the High Street towards the bus stop she realised that, despite her worries about Ralph and money, she felt good. She straightened her back and was secretly pleased by the occasional admiring glance from passers-by.

She was starting with new clients today: a pair of GP's with three children who were on the brink of separating. It was the same old thing, she thought resignedly. If only they'd come sooner when the cracks had first started to appear, then the odds of saving their marriage would be far higher.

When the fifty minutes were over, she decided to grab a sandwich and pick up a few groceries before her afternoon sessions. Oliver came out of his consulting room at the exact same moment as she left hers. She couldn't help thinking that this was deliberate and was quickly making up excuses in her mind when he spoke.

'It's you,' he said, fake-surprised.

He was wearing a dark navy polo shirt and khaki chinos. She caught a faint whiff of sandalwood aftershave and was struck by his clean handsome features, but rapidly suppressed the thought. She gave a cool little smile.

'Can we go for coffee?' There was an urgency in his tone that surprised her. 'There's something I must clear up.'

She was about to say no, reminding herself that she didn't socialise with wife-beaters, when he took her lightly by the arm.

'Please Victoria. Just this once.'

It was hard to refuse.

They sat in the window of a little coffee shop on the main street. Victoria was hungry and found her gaze straying to the fudge slice at the other table, but she was determined to get this over with as quickly as possible and wouldn't order food.

Oliver must have sensed that he didn't have long and got straight to the point. 'I couldn't help noticing the change in you.'

She started to protest but he shook his head. 'Don't pretend. We both know the truth. It's been puzzling me obviously, then the penny dropped. I want to get something straight.'

His directness was disarming and Victoria sighed, feeling that she probably did owe him some sort of explanation. 'Debs—' she started.

He nodded. 'She told you about a conversation we had when I said there was violence in my marriage.' It wasn't a question, it was a statement.

'She was trying to protect me.'

Oliver ran a hand through his short, well-cut hair and fixed her with penetrating grey eyes. 'She's wrong. She jumped to conclusions. I didn't tell her the whole story.'

Victoria frowned. Her cappuccino was virtually untouched. Violent husbands were always coming up with excuses for their behaviour and clearly Oliver was no exception.

'You don't need to tell me,' she said tightly. 'I'm not your counsellor.'

'I do,' he insisted. 'Because I didn't beat my wife – she beat me.'

Victoria's mouth fell open. 'You mean...?'

He nodded. 'It started quite early in our marriage. She'd throw pots and pans around and shout a lot when we had an argument, that sort of thing. I didn't think much of it. I knew she had a temper and it always blew over.

'But gradually her rages grew more frightening. She started literally laying hands on me, punching, biting, kicking. I realised this wasn't right but like many men in these circumstances, I blamed myself. If I could only do as she asked, be more accommodating and stop annoying her then she wouldn't get so angry.'

He sipped his coffee and continued to look candidly at Victoria. 'Our love died but I stayed with her for the children, more than anything. And also because I was worried about her. I didn't know what she'd do if I left; she was so irrational.'

Victoria listened in silence, feeling guilt seep through her. Thinking back, it was true that Debs had used the phrase 'violence in the marriage,' presumably repeating the same words that he'd used. Why hadn't she questioned him further, given the slightly strange terminology? Why, more to the point, had Victoria just accepted Debs's mistaken conclusion?

'Was she violent towards the children as well?' she asked, her mind racing.

'Thankfully, no. If she had been I'd have got them out of there immediately.'

'What about when you had the affair? Did that tip things over the edge?'

Oliver sighed. His body was very upright and still as he spoke. 'No. She didn't find out for a long time and when I finally told her, I'd decided to go anyway. Not to be with the other woman – that had ended. We only got together because I was confused and a bit desperate, to be honest. The other woman was going through a tricky divorce and I think we were both craving human comfort. What actually tipped things over the edge, as you put it, was the fact that my wife's behaviour had escalated. She was totally out of control.'

Victoria fiddled with the Perspex salt grinder on the table, twizzling it round and round. It was something to do. Realising that she'd made a mess on the table, she swept the salt grains on to the floor.

'What happened?' she asked.

Oliver laughed grimly. 'She threw a kitchen knife at me which hit me here.' He pointed to an area on his upper left arm. 'A few more inches to the right and it might have killed me. I knew then that I had to get out.'

Victoria winced but said nothing.

'There's not a lot of sympathy for battered husbands,' he went on. 'Many people think – but men are stronger. Why would they let a woman brutalise them? It's not possible.' His eyes narrowed. 'Well it is possible. She's a very bright woman, my ex, highly educated and manipulative. And there's no way I would have ever laid a hand on her. Besides, as I said, I spent many years hoping she'd change and that I could help her. I wish now, of course, that I'd left sooner.'

Victoria took a sip of coffee and wiped the froth off her upper lip with a paper napkin. 'Why didn't you?'

He gave a small smile. 'I believed in our marriage vows. I'd promised to look after her in sickness and in health and I realised she was sick, although she couldn't see it and wouldn't seek help. At least one positive thing has come from it – it's made me a good counsellor. I expect you can understand why I chose to specialise in domestic violence?'

Victoria nodded, lowering her eyes. 'I'm so sorry I judged you. It's unforgiveable.'

'In my experience, people are all too quick to judge, although I must say I thought you were different.'

She was stung, but knew she deserved it.

'It's such a little understood area,' Oliver went on. 'But battered husbands aren't as uncommon as you'd think.

Apparently a third of victims of domestic violence are men.'

He sat forwards slightly, warming to his subject. 'It's still a taboo and people need to be better educated. A lot of men don't want to admit what's happening because they feel stupid and inadequate. And often the police don't take them seriously, either. There's very little help around, you know.'

Victoria wished that there were somewhere to hide. She felt as if he could see right through her veneer of cleverness and sophistication to the seething mess of bone-headed stupidity and prejudice within.

'I'm as bad as everyone else,' she stammered. 'I shouldn't have listened to Debs. I should have asked you myself, not accepted second-hand information. Especially when you've been so kind to me.'

'Don't beat yourself up.' He gave a humourless little laugh. 'If you'll pardon the pun. At least now you know the truth.'

Victoria felt dumb with misery when he signalled to a waiter to bring the bill. He put his hand in his pocket to find change but she insisted on paying. Damn the family finances. 'It's the least I can do.'

They walked in silence back to the office. She was blaming herself, wholly, for being ignorant and judgmental. Debs had meant no wrong, but wrong had been done and now Oliver would quite rightly want nothing more to do with her.

She thought of how kind he'd been when she'd gone for dinner, how he'd stood up for her when Rosanna was bossy and loud-mouthed and how he'd invited her to go otter-watching with him. He'd never ask her to do anything again and it was all her fault.

They said goodbye when they reached the office and she knew that he'd be gone for the day by the time she finished her next two sessions.

'I really am sorry,' she said again. It sounded so inadequate.

'Forget it. I'm glad it's off my chest.'

She wanted to ask how she could ever make it up to him but decided against it. She'd given him enough trouble already and should leave him alone. After his terrible marriage, he needed to be around people with more sensitivity and intelligence.

Besides, by the time she opened her mouth to speak, he'd disappeared into his consulting room and shut the door.

***

There was a strange atmosphere in the house that evening which made her uneasy. She was feeling really down about Oliver and wanted comfort, but even Salome was behaving badly.

'How was netball practice?' Victoria asked.

Salome frowned and started picking bits of onion out of her vegetable stir-fry. 'Boring.'

'Don't mess with your food,' Victoria said gently.

'I hate onion.'

Victoria sighed. 'Did Naomi behave today?' Naomi was the naughtiest girl in the class. There was usually some story or other to tell.

Salome scowled. 'Why do you always ask about Naomi?'

She must be tired, Victoria decided. Early night tonight. She ate a forkful of rice and turned to Ralph.

'Have you got everything you need – for your exam, I mean?' His final A-level was the following week and he said they'd been going all right so far, but what would she know? 'Pens, pencils, that sort of thing?'

He scraped his chair back and rose. 'Yeah.'

'Where are you going?' she asked, alarmed. He'd left half his food and she didn't like the look on his face, sort of hard and distant.

'Out.'

She felt her breathing become shallower. 'Ralph, you're always out. You should be revising—'

He stood up straight and glared at her, his eyes on fire. 'I'm going out, it's arranged. I've told you, my exam's under control.'

He moved towards the door and Victoria followed. Her head told her to leave him be, but her limbs seemed to move of their own accord. She was aware of Salome still sitting at the table perfectly still, watching.

'Stop!' Victoria said, standing ramrod straight. They were in the hall now. 'I've had enough of this. You're not going anywhere.'

Ralph turned and stared and she was shocked by his hard expression. Couldn't he see that she was upset after a bad day, tense as a coiled spring ready to fly open? All she really needed was an arm round the shoulder.

'Mum, you're being—'

She felt something snap and took a step forwards into his body-space. 'Don't tell me what I'm being.' She was frightening herself.

He veered off into the drawing room and she strode behind; she'd switched to auto-pilot now and couldn't go down a gear if she tried.

'Stop shouting,' he said, maddeningly superior. 'Are you trying to pick a fight? You're being hysterical.'

She saw him close the door to prevent Salome hearing her rave, which only enraged her more.

'Where the hell d'you think you're disappearing to?' she

barked, hands on hips and glaring. 'I'm sick to death of all this secrecy. I should have put my foot down months ago.'

He ran a hand through his hair. 'You don't want to know.'

'Yes I do.'

'OK then. I'm going to see Maddy.'

Victoria's heart missed a beat.

'Maddy who?' She knew the answer already.

'Maddy Barclay.'

That name. Those pink lips in the wine bar. He seemed to be a great distance from her, speaking across a wide open plain. She slumped on the sofa, unable to support her own weight.

'I've been seeing her a lot. It's her house I go to in the evenings.'

She looked up at her son, whose mouth twitched. His hostile posturing seemed to have vanished to be replaced by facts, which were altogether more alien and frightening.

'I found her office number and rang after Dad's funeral. I wanted to talk.' His voice trailed off into nothing.

Victoria hugged her arms close to her chest and pulled up her knees. 'In what sense have you been *seeing* her?' She felt sick but needed to know the truth.

Ralph had gone very pale and the skin seemed to be pulled tight across his face. Victoria glanced at the door, relieved now that it was shut and Salome couldn't hear, her mother's protective instinct kicking in despite everything.

He wouldn't look her in the eye.

'Tell me,' she whispered. 'You can show me that much respect, at least.'

He was standing very still, his arms crossed over his chest. 'We get on really well. We talk about things and I enjoy her company.'

Victoria felt terribly cold and was aware that her teeth were chattering. The world seemed to have stopped turning. They were the only ones left on the entire planet.

'How *could* you?'

Ralph put out a hand but she shrank away. 'Don't touch me.' He was a snake uncoiling in front of her.

'I can't believe it,' she went on, still trying to decipher his words. 'You're saying you've been seeing the woman who had an affair with my husband? You're disgusting.'

Her head was suddenly filled with lurid images and her mind was darting this way and that, unable to focus.

'How could *she* possibly...?' She squeezed the bridge of her nose with finger and thumb. 'I don't know how she can live with herself. I feel totally and utterly betrayed.'

Ralph put his hands in his pockets. 'It's not what you think. She's a good person. She understands me.'

Victoria snorted but he ignored her.

'She's helped me a lot. She's really caring; she listens.'

Victoria's body tensed. She was one taut muscle. She wanted to smash something, anything.

'If she cares about you so much, how come she's happy for you to throw away your future? That doesn't seem like the act of a caring person to me.' She was surprised that her words made so much sense.

Ralph seemed to have diminished in height. His body was almost concave. 'You don't understand. She's been helping me with my exams—'

'Oh yes?' She wasn't really listening, couldn't listen, she was smearing her own interpretation across everything like rancid butter. 'And what else has she been helping you with, I wonder?'

'It's not like that. Look, there's no point talking now. You twist everything I say. I said I'd go tonight and we can talk tomorrow. She's very upset about whatever it was you told her at that meeting you had. I know it was something about Dad—'

Victoria rose to face him again. He was taller than her, but only by a couple of inches. Her hand shot up and she slapped him hard on one cheek, then the other, until he gripped her wrists and all her strength seemed to dissipate. He took a step back and put his hands up to cover his burning skin.

'She's upset?' Victoria was screaming. 'What about me? He was my husband...' Her body was shaking with sobs. 'Have you no feelings at all?'

The door opened slightly and Salome poked her head in, her face white, her eyes wide with fright. 'What is it? Are you all right?'

Seeing her mother weeping, she ran to her side and buried herself in the folds of her top while Victoria put a trembling arm around her shoulders.

'I'm sorry darling,' she said to her daughter, stroking her hair mechanically. 'Mummy's upset. Mummy's had a shock.' She was trying hard to regain control.

'What shock?' Salome said, looking from one to the other. 'What's happened?'

Victoria's eyes fixed on her son's. He was still nursing his cheeks and looked frightened of her, which made her glad.

'There's nothing to worry about,' she told her daughter. 'Ralph's just packing his bags now, aren't you Ralph?'

He gave a start.

'He's going to live with a friend.' She was still holding his gaze.

'What friend?' Salome chipped in, but Victoria ignored her.

'It won't take long, will it?' she went on, 'to pack your

343

bags?' Her voice was dark and heavy, ready to burst at any moment like a rain-laden cloud.

He looked at her squarely. 'Do you really want this?'

'Yes.'

She saw his thin shoulders droop and for a split second she thought she was going to reach out to him, her boy. Then she remembered Maddy.

'Go to her,' she spat. 'Go now. And give me back my keys before you leave.'

CHAPTER TWENTY-SIX

Soon after he'd gone she hurried next door to her elderly neighbour, citing an emergency, and asked if she could babysit Salome for a couple of hours. After all, she'd offered plenty of times before. It took Victoria less than half an hour to drive to her friend's house in Clapham, where she picked up the keys to the cottage and a list of instructions.

'Are you sure you're all right?' her friend asked, concerned. The two women had met at university and although they saw little of each other now, they'd kept in touch.

'Honestly I'm fine,' Victoria replied. She realised that she must look white and shaken but she couldn't talk now. 'I just need to get away for a little while. You know how it is?'

'Of course,' said her friend, frowning. 'Everything should be working. Call me if you need anything.'

Back home, Victoria hustled the neighbour out as politely as possible and rang Lucy's mother, Joanne. She felt a bit guilty, knowing that the other woman had a lot on her plate and wouldn't feel able to refuse. But, Victoria reasoned, she'd do the same in return and Salome would be happiest staying at Lucy's. She didn't know any other family quite as well.

Victoria didn't want to sleep; she wasn't tired. She seemed to have found a hitherto untapped source of energy and packed her bag hurriedly, unable to sit down or stop moving.

She felt shaky and her mind was constantly working.

She needed to look after herself for Salome's sake most of all, she knew that. Getting away for a while on her own seemed the best way of sorting her head out. Here, in Wimbledon, she couldn't think straight.

In the morning she dropped her daughter at Lucy's house with her bag and drove straight to Deal in Kent, which took just under two hours. Concentrating on the road ahead whilst listening to the radio left less room for black thoughts. It was a relief to escape them for a short while.

She felt her spirits lift a little as she approached Dover and the white cliffs and passed the ferry terminal, feeling the same small prickle of excitement that she always experienced near ports, airports and international railway stations. They reminded her of holidays past, of strange lands – and adventure.

The Deal road quickly narrowed into a windy route flanked by green fields. The sky ahead was filled with wispy cotton wool clouds tinged with pink and the sight of a black windmill with white sails made her feel, suddenly, a million miles from London.

Arriving just before 10.30 a.m., she found a parking space on the sea front, as her friend had directed, and stopped and looked around her for a moment. It was a lovely spot, no doubt about it. She'd been here once before years ago, when Ralph was little, but she'd forgotten how pretty it was. Her friend had bought the weekend cottage with some money left her by a grandparent and she and her husband used to come often, but rarely used the place now.

Victoria stared across the long ribbon of pebbly beach that sloped downhill to meet the dirty grey sea. The tide was high and the waves were slapping against the shingle and throwing up curling white spume. Seagulls were wheeling overhead in the watery blue sky in ever increasing circles making eerie crying noises.

To her right, just a few blocks up, she could see the criss-crossing structure of the concrete pier, newly restored to its former glory and stretching far out to sea. Behind her, the street was lined with bow-fronted Georgian and early Victorian buildings, a mixture of the jaded and gentrified, some newly painted in pinks, creams, sparkling whites and pale blues, others faded and calling out for attention.

There were few people about, just the odd person walking their dog, a fisherman several hundred yards down the beach to her left, a couple of small wooden fishing boats pulled up along the pebbles and lying half on their sides.

She stretched her arms above her head and took in several deep breaths before fetching her bag from the boot. Then she walked slowly up the narrow winding street which led away from the beach and stopped outside Number Five.

It was a thin terraced house, painted pale blue, with one large-ish oblong window downstairs and a sort of crow's nest, an extension, in the roof. Unlocking the dark blue door, she stepped straight into the sitting room which felt almost like a ship's cabin because the ceiling was so low. The thick walls were painted white and to the left was a large brick inglenook fireplace with a cast-iron grate surrounded by heavy black wooden beams. A pungent, smoky odour made her wrinkle her nose.

She dropped her suitcase and handbag in the middle of the floor and wandered into the kitchen at the back overlooking a courtyard. It was small and simply kitted out, with little more than a stainless steel sink, hob, cooker and fridge. But it was clean and had everything she needed, really.

Opening a few cupboards she was pleased to find tea bags,

salt, pepper, olive oil and a few other essentials, including washing powder. She could pop out for milk and bread and any other items she might want later.

Pausing to listen, she was amazed to hear nothing but the sound of her own breathing and tried to recall when she'd last been totally alone like this. She felt herself sway slightly and took a few deep breaths, her inner voice whispering: be kind to yourself. Take care.

Rallying, she opened the back door to let in some fresh air before carrying her bag up the stairs, which ascended sharply to the bathroom on the right before twisting equally sharply to the left into the main bedroom. Fortunately this was a good size, painted white like downstairs and simply furnished with a double bed, a square mirror over the small fireplace, a wooden wardrobe and chest of drawers.

She pulled back the cream cotton throw and was grateful to discover crisp white bedlinen. She was inclined to draw the curtains and jump in straight away, pulling the duvet over her head, but resisted the urge. Oblivion wasn't the answer, tempting as it seemed. Somehow, she was going to have to find a way through this. At least Ralph had no idea where she was and wouldn't be able to contact her. She wanted nothing more to do with him.

After unpacking a few things, she decided to head off straightaway for a walk, shoving a little cash and her debit card in the back of her pocket. Other than that all she needed was a jumper, which she tied around her waist, and her grubby old trainers.

Haughty seagulls perched on top of red flood alarms seemed to watch her as she strode past, their shrill cries mocking her efforts. She hurried through the entrance to the pier, vaguely registering a few elderly couples on wooden benches and several fishermen on canvas chairs, stacks of equipment beside them. They were chatting and making cups of tea on primus stoves and nodded as she walked past, but didn't speak.

After strolling as far as the cafe at the end, she stood for a few moments staring down at the sea. It was muddy brown and, much as she loved swimming, it looked dark, cold and uninviting. Shivering, she forced her eyes back towards civilisation and the outline of the houses on the seafront, which only made her feel even more alone and frightened.

Leo's death and everything that she'd learned about him since had shocked her to the core, yet somehow she'd survived. Now, however, she simply wasn't sure that she had it in her to endure any more.

She imagined that she were looking down on herself from high above, a tiny speck of a person, comically small against the backdrop of the vast, rolling waves. How could she ever hope to ride the relentless swell of the wind and tides? It would be so much easier to give in.

She pulled on her jumper and glanced back along the pier at the little figures huddled round their primus stoves, taking pleasure in the small things. No, she thought, she wouldn't surrender. She headed back towards the shore, her hands firmly in the pockets of her jeans. Keep moving, she told herself. Perpetual motion. It was the only answer.

Leaving the pier, she noticed how warm the air felt back on shore and the town appeared to have woken up. People were coming in and out of the little shops and cafes and one or two smiled at Victoria who glanced quickly away, afraid they might try to engage her in conversation. Continuing past pubs and guest houses with window boxes brimming with brightly coloured geraniums and lobelia, she finally reached the thick grey stone walls of Deal Castle.

An image flashed into her mind of Ralph, who must have been about five at the time. He was rushing excitedly through the dark tunnels of the symmetrical Tudor fortress. He was so full of enthusiasm then, convinced that he would become a soldier when he grew up and live in a place just like this.

A little blonde girl passed by, holding her mother's hand, and Victoria felt a shock like an electric current race through her. Phoebe, Maddy's daughter. She'd hardly given any thought recently to the child whom Leo had fathered and who was not much younger than Salome. But of course Ralph must have met her, spent time with her and got to know her. This sudden realisation was almost as painful as the knowledge that he'd forged some strange relationship with her mother.

What kind of relationship? For a moment Maddy's face and that of Mrs Gannon seemed to merge into one horrible, scornful image. Victoria sank down with her back against the fence surrounding the castle wall, oblivious to any stares, and put her head between her knees. She was still breastfeeding Salome when Leo was bedding Maddy, planting the seed in her womb that was to become Phoebe, Ralph's half sister. And now Ralph...

'Are you all right?'

She glanced up and saw through her tears an elderly gentleman with white hair peering down at her anxiously. She rose unsteadily.

'If I can—?' the gentleman started to say, but she shook her head and resumed walking, relieved to feel the wind on her face again, allowing the roar of the waves to drown her thumping heart.

Once out of Deal town centre, she continued her journey through Walmer. Here, the coastal path narrowed and she passed a long row of fine old houses which looked out over a stretch of glossy green grass and then the beach.

She stopped again for a few moments to read the wording on a stone plaque which marked the landing of Julius Caesar and his legions in 55 BC. Britons reputedly met them at the beach with a large force, including warriors in horse-drawn chariots. What was going through their minds as the Roman ships hove into view? A mixture of fear, dread and excitement too, perhaps, at the prospect of war.

She wished that she could summon up one ounce of the courage and adrenaline that must have been coursing through their veins as they smelled battle and prepared their weapons. She must fight back, she thought, and stand up for what she believed in. But how?

It crossed her mind to jump in the car, drive straight to Maddy's house and lie in wait until she appeared. Then what would she do? Stab her? Throttle her? This was insane. Victoria had no wish to deprive a child of its mother however wicked that mother might be. But she'd like to hurt her badly if she could think of a way.

And what of Ralph? She wondered whether she hated him and decided that no, she couldn't. He was her flesh and blood and she would always love him no matter what he'd done. But she wanted to punish him and show him how cruel he'd been. The best way she could think of doing this was by harming Maddy.

She shook her head. What was she thinking? Never in her wildest dreams would she have imagined, before all this happened, that she'd find herself plotting sadistic revenge on a fellow human being. She loathed what she had become almost as much as she detested Maddy.

She set off again and after a while turned right off the

coastal path, soon finding herself in the village of Upper Walmer. She wandered around for a bit not knowing what she was looking for until she spotted a small, ancient-looking flint church with an old yew tree near the porch.

The door was locked so she strolled around the empty graveyard, crammed with uneven headstones, some covered in moss and lichen and ivy, the engravings barely visible now, others newer and clearer.

She found herself half smiling at the names that she could read: Phyllis and her beloved husband Arthur, Edith Musgrave, Abraham Gribble. Who was called Abraham now? She tried to imagine her own name there – Victòria Royce, not Bruck. That wouldn't be correct. But who was Victoria Royce?

It crossed her mind that here, she was just an anonymous stranger. She could, if she wanted, invent any story that she liked and become someone else altogether. She felt like someone else. All the assumptions and expectations that she'd had about herself were wrong. She felt as if she'd been stripped bare and was standing, naked, in the middle of the graveyard, an alien washed up on the seashore.

Suddenly she was scrambling around the headstones and bushes, slipping on grassy mounds and uneven patches until she reached the church walls. She laid her palms on the flinty stones, resting her cheek against the hard unyielding surface, and slid down, down, onto her knees, aware of the softness and fragility of her own bulk beside that of the centuries-old building.

She closed her eyes and prayed that there was a way back, waiting, hoping for something. But there was no blinding flash of light, no voice that cracked the firmament and spoke her name. Only the sound of birdsong and the rustling of indifferent leaves.

***

Monday June 28th

Maddy had been thinking. It was Ralph's final exam in two days and they hadn't discussed what would happen afterwards. He loped into her bedroom wearing a crumpled T-shirt and torn jeans.

'I've got brain overload,' he said, running a hand through his fringe, which needed a trim.

He looked terribly handsome. Maddy was at her desk again and frowned. He'd arrived three nights ago with a big holdall and a teary expression and what could she do? She couldn't exactly turn him away so she'd made up a camp bed for him in the sitting room. But she was deeply uneasy.

She thought of Victoria and her stomach keeled. Maddy was appalled that Ralph had told his mother about their relationship but she hadn't had it out with him. He was upset enough and she didn't want to jeopardise his last exam.

She wished so much that she could explain things and put Victoria's mind at rest, but Ralph said there was no answer at the house and she wasn't picking up his calls on her mobile.

'When are you going to eat?' he asked, hanging around near the door.

'I need to finish this,' she said, more sharply than intended. 'You'll have to make your own lunch.'

Seeing his face fall, she immediately regretted her tone.

'I'm sorry. I'll join you as soon as I can.'

He brightened a little. 'OK. I'll make poached eggs. D'you want any?'

She shook her head and he made to leave.

'Ralph?'

353

He turned to face her again.

'Have you thought about what you'll do after your exams?' It was maybe too soon to be asking him this; it had just slipped out.

A strange looked flashed across his face and he shuffled from one foot to another.

'What is it?' she asked.

'Well, I...'

'Come on, spit it out.'

'A few of my friends have been talking about getting an InterRail ticket and travelling round Europe. I've got a bit of money saved up now, thanks to working with you, and before all this happened I wondered—'

'That's a wonderful idea!'

He bit his lip.

'So what's the problem?'

'Well, Mum obviously.' His eyes clouded. 'I wish I knew where she was.'

Maddy made a sympathetic face.

'Also, I thought you might not want me to go,' he went on. 'I thought you'd feel like I was abandoning you or something.'

She hesitated. Of course she'd miss him – too much. Straightening her shoulders, she looked at him squarely.

'You must go travelling if you want to. You're only young once and it'll be a great experience. I'm sure your mother's fine and she'll get in touch soon. She'll encourage you, too. She'll say it's a fantastic opportunity.'

She saw that his brow was still furrowed; he must have been thinking about this and worrying for some time. She wanted to run a cool hand across his forehead to smooth the wrinkles away but stopped herself.

'And what about university?' she asked brightly. He had

his place at Birmingham to read History in September – if he got his grades – but he was still showing no enthusiasm or signs of wanting to go.

'Dunno,' he said, his expression darkening again. 'Can't think about it now.'

He left the room and she sat for a while, resting her elbows on her desk and cupping her chin in her hands. This was welcome information about travelling, wasn't it? Maybe her campaign was working. She'd deliberately been acting a little cool and perhaps his feelings towards her had changed. What did love mean, anyway, to a teenager? They were all fickle and finding their way.

She just needed to keep him focused until the exam and somehow reconcile him with his mother – though it wasn't going to be easy. Then she could help him plan his travels if he needed it. With luck a month or two away from her would give him more space to think practically about his life and what he really wanted.

She scrolled through the numbers on her mobile phone and found the one she wanted. She'd been mulling over an idea ever since that evening with Victoria and Cat and it seemed to make good sense, especially now that Ralph might leave.

Yes, she hoped that it would be some sort of atonement, but she had something genuinely positive to offer. Surely her suggestion wouldn't be misconstrued?

She'd talked to Cat for quite a while outside the train station after they'd left the bar on the night that Victoria had told them about Leo – and Anna. They'd stood chatting by the entrance, neither bothering about missing train after train, and Maddy had gleaned a lot of information. She had a pretty clear idea of the lie of the land.

Cat was bored at the bookshop and wanted to write but

didn't think she was good enough; she needed to move on and do something different, something that would give her more confidence. She was a project in the making. Victoria had grown very fond of her and would surely be pleased if someone tried to help, whoever that someone was.

Maddy pressed the call button and waited nervously for Leo's youngest lover to pick up.

CHAPTER TWENTY-SEVEN

Sunday July 4th

'Why you so happy? You win Lottery?'

Ali was practically in Cat's face, grinning as she opened her front door. He was cleaning the street outside Mr Yum Yum's Tasty Kebabs, picking up bits of paper and polystyrene cartons. It was a mess as usual, last night having been Saturday when the shop stayed open till the small hours.

'I wish,' she smiled. 'But guess what? I've got an interview for a new job!'

Ali put down the black bin bag he was holding, allowing its contents to spill out over the street.

'Ees wonderful news!' he cried, raising his hands heavenwards in a prayerful gesture. 'What ees you going to do?'

'I might be going to help this woman who's set up a new internet business. It's a recruitment business for working mothers, really. My job would be to handle the website and also help my boss with her separate events company. I'd be her girl-Friday. I'd have a lot to learn as I know nothing about business, really. But it'd be a challenge and I'm sick to death of the bookshop.'

Ali scratched his head. 'Internet business? Hmm. Ees big money? You make lots of cash?' He rubbed fingers and thumb together.

Cat shook her head. 'The salary would be pretty rubbish to

start with I think, but if the company's a success I'd get more.'

'Small salary ees no good. You should go for something with beeg profits.' He brightened. 'I have idea. You come work for me. I pay you small salary but you learn about kebab business. My shop always busy.' He pointed to the mess that surrounded them by way of evidence. 'Mrs Ali, I buy her new silver Land Rover Discovery for her birthday. Ees brilliant on and off road. Classy cabin has space for seven, plus superb versatility and excellent levels of refinement.'

It must have taken ages to learn the sales pitch.

'You see!' he said triumphantly. 'Ees good money in kebabs. You come work for me and one day maybe you have kebab shop of your own. You call it "Kat's Kebabs" with a K.' He made a gesture over his shop, to show how the sign might look. 'But no here in Roman Road,' he added quickly. 'You go somewhere nice like Willesden. I hear good property in Willesden.'

Cat laughed. 'Thanks very much for the offer but I think recruitment's more my style.'

Ali shrugged. 'Suit yourself. But maybe you make beeg mistake.'

Cat took off her jacket. Today was shaping up to be really hot. She'd dug out the Primark suit that she'd worn for Leo's funeral and ironed a clean white shirt. She wasn't exactly keen on ironing and there were a few creases down the back, but she'd make sure she stayed facing Maddy throughout the interview.

Her call had come totally out of the blue and at first Cat had been very wary. But the more Maddy talked, the more it had seemed to Cat that this was a genuine offer, a real olive branch, and she'd be a fool not to check it out.

The idea of working with Leo's other girlfriend was totally

weird, but then everything had been weird since he died. Besides, she'd warmed to Maddy on their walk to the station after the meeting with Victoria. She thought that she might just be all right after all.

Her nerves gave way as she arrived at the door of the flat but Maddy spotted her through the window so she couldn't run off. The older woman was looking very casual, in jeans, a white T-shirt and bare feet, which made Cat feel silly and over-dressed. But Maddy was so friendly and welcoming that Cat soon forgot her embarrassment.

Maddy made coffee and they sat in her sitting room, which was still full of unopened boxes. As interviews go it was very informal and at first Cat couldn't concentrate properly. She was too busy gazing around, checking out the furniture and pictures, staring at Maddy and trying to imagine her and Leo together. Meeting her at the bar had been one thing, but seeing her in her own environment was different.

Cat knew that Maddy hadn't lived here when Leo was alive, that he'd never have come here, but still he must have sat on the same sofa, drunk from the same cups, enjoyed some sort of domestic life with Maddy in the same way that he'd relaxed and pottered with Cat in his own flat in Kensington.

Had he done with her lots of the things that he'd done with Cat? Sipping tea – Lapsang Soushong was his favourite? Watching movies? Sex? She shuddered. Course he had. She expected to feel angry and bitter and was surprised to discover that jealousy had been supplanted by something else, something akin to fellow feeling. They were both missing him. They'd both been lied to and abandoned.

Maddy explained the business to Cat who, once she began to focus, started to feel really excited.

'I can't cope on my own,' Maddy said. 'I need a right-hand

person. It won't be like boss and employee, we'll be more like partners.'

She took a sip of coffee and eyed Cat. 'I know I'm taking a risk because we haven't worked together before and, more importantly, you have no experience. But I'm willing to train you up and tell you everything I know. My instincts tell me that you're a bright woman with good writing skills and a lot to offer. Besides, I want to help you. And I think you can help me.'

Phoebe wandered into the sitting room and squashed in beside her mother on the armchair. She was wearing a pink T-shirt and little denim shorts with appliqué flowers. Her feet were bare and her blonde hair, unbrushed, dangled round her face in messy waves.

Cat had felt a pang. Phoebe represented a part of Leo, a living legacy that Cat would never have. But it was for the best, really. She hadn't been ready for a child. There were things she wanted to do first. She pushed the dark thoughts away.

'When are you going to be finished?' Phoebe whined. 'I'm bored.'

'We won't be much longer,' Maddy replied, stroking her daughter's hair. 'Go and play for another ten minutes then I'll take you to the park.'

'Sorry,' she said, returning to Cat. 'It gets a bit dull for her, being an only child. We would have liked more...'

She stopped herself, which was a relief. Perhaps one day they'd be able to talk in depth about their relationships with Leo but not now.

'I'll pay you the same salary as the bookshop,' Maddy went on.

Cat's face fell.

'I guess you were hoping for a rise?'

Cat nodded.

Maddy took another sip of coffee and crossed her slim legs. 'I can't afford it now, but you have my guarantee that I'll assess your salary regularly. If we continue to do well – and I have every confidence that we will – I'll be able to pay you more. As I say, we'll be in this together. If I get a rise, you get a rise. How does that sound?'

Cat took a deep breath and accepted the position. It was a leap of faith, she knew, and she suspected that Tracy would tell her she was mad. She could see her, hands on hips, shaking a finger and asking how on earth she could give up a steady job for something that might fold in months, or even weeks. It was too much of a gamble; she'd lost her head.

But something had to change. That bookshop made Cat feel dead inside, and people weren't exactly queuing up to publish her writing. She wasn't sure if she had the courage to try anywhere else; she didn't think she could cope with the rejection.

Cat found herself wondering how Gervaise would take it and shuffled in her seat. But he didn't own her, it was up to her. And it was probably a good idea not to see him every day as well as practically every night and weekend. You could have too much of someone, even if you were going out together. She wouldn't put it quite like that to him, though.

Her gaze fell on a camp bed folded up in the corner of the room and a pile of text books alongside.

Maddy noticed and took a deep breath. 'Ralph's been staying,' she said steadily.

Cat's eyes widened. Had she heard right?

Maddy nodded. 'Leo's and Victoria's son.'

Cat must have looked shaken and confused and Maddy went on to explain what had happened.

'He rang me in my office months ago, wanting to talk. He

361

was mixed up about his father and getting on really badly with Victoria and I felt sorry for him.'

Cat was silent, trying to take it all in.

'He's been coming round a lot since,' Maddy went on, 'helping me a bit with my work and I've been helping him with his A-level revision. Then four nights ago he and Victoria had a massive row when he told her that he'd been seeing me. She threw him out and he turned up on my doorstep with a bag. I couldn't send him away.'

Cat swallowed, her mind racing. Was this some sort of set-up? For a moment she could only focus on one thing: 'And Victoria? How's she?'

Maddy's eyes clouded over. 'I don't know. She's not answering Ralph's calls. I feel bad. I think she's terribly upset.'

Cat huddled in on herself on the sofa, crossing her arms and legs. She felt bruised on Victoria's behalf, wounded and abused. 'Poor Victoria.'

She thought of the older woman's kindness; how she'd brought the tea set for her mother and how she'd been ringing regularly since, making suggestions and asking if there was anything more she could do. And how she'd told them both about her trip to Paris to see Elsa and what she'd discovered about Leo. She didn't need to do that and she didn't deserve this.

Cat had been excited about the job, but now all she could think of was Victoria's distress. She jumped when she heard a key in the front door and her stomach rolled.

Ralph entered the room, carrying a litre of milk and a stick of French bread. He was very tall, just as she remembered, and stooped slightly. He looked tense and awkward.

'I'm Ralph,' he said unnecessarily, hovering by the wall.

Cat stood up and straightened her shoulders, trying not to show her nerves.

'I know,' she said. 'And you've got to make up with your mum.'

Ralph hung his head. 'I don't know how.'

Cat grabbed her jacket from the back of the sofa and started putting it on. Then she fixed a starting date with Maddy, shook the other woman's hand and excused herself as quickly as she could.

'Where are you going?' Maddy asked, following her to the door, as if sensing that Cat's plans were going to involve her and Ralph in some significant way.

'I can't talk now,' Cat said enigmatically. 'I'll call.'

* * *

She'd never been to Deal. In fact she'd hardly been out of London for years. She was quite surprised, as the train trundled along, to see green fields and cattle. There weren't a lot of those in Bethnal Green.

She'd rung Victoria and was relieved that the older woman had picked up immediately. It was only Ralph she was blocking, then.

'I'm all right, honestly,' Victoria had said when Cat explained that she knew what had happened.

But she didn't sound all right.

It was nearly 6 p.m. by the time they met in front of the pier. It was still warm and Cat was enchanted by the seagulls, the funny, old-fashioned looking shops and almost festive feel. It was like being on holiday. But her face fell when she saw Victoria. The older woman had wild hair and a troubled expression. She was very different from the kind, wise, elegant person that Cat had come to know. She looked lost.

They embraced wordlessly; Victoria was much taller but

Cat was the one who seemed to be supporting them both.

'Are you hungry?' Victoria asked at last, mindful as usual of Cat's wellbeing. Cat realised that she hadn't eaten since breakfast and nodded.

They chose an unexceptional looking pub on the seafront with a sign outside proclaiming 'Food Served All Day.' Cat ordered orange juice and lemonade for them both, along with soup and crusty bread for her and a sticky toffee pudding for Victoria, who looked as if she needed it. They took their drinks to a quiet little table at the back.

The pub was fairly empty; there were just a few locals, men mainly, standing at the bar chatting to the landlord and a middle-aged woman in a suit, who had probably been on some sort of business, drinking a cup of coffee and flicking through the newspaper.

'You shouldn't have come,' said Victoria glancing at Cat, who gave a half smile. 'But thank you.'

Cat noticed that Victoria's hands were trembling as she picked up her glass. She was clearly in shock still, though she'd been away eight days.

'Look,' Cat said, taking a deep breath. 'It's not as bad as—'

Victoria hung her head. 'I feel totally and utterly betrayed – by my own son.'

The pub landlord arrived with the pudding and Cat's bowl of soup and she took a spoonful and explained again how Ralph had got to know Maddy.

'He should never have approached her,' said Victoria, her mouth puckering in an odd way. 'And as if that wasn't bad enough, he's been spending all this time round at her house, not telling me where he is and worrying me sick. And I've no idea what they've been getting up to.' She put her face in her hands.

Cat leaned forwards and touched the other woman's arm. 'She's been helping him revise. She showed me the books.'

Victoria put her hands down and looked straight at Cat. 'Do you really believe that?'

'Yes. And she feels bad, really guilty about you. She's been telling Ralph to get in touch and make up but she said you're not answering his calls. She doesn't want him to stay with her, she wants him to go home to you.'

Victoria sighed. 'I can't speak to him. I wouldn't know what to say.'

Cat took another sip of soup, feeling out of her depth. She wasn't used to sorting out other people's problems but she remembered how kind Victoria had been to her on that terrible day when she'd told her she was pregnant. She'd been desperate and Victoria had shown immense compassion. Cat felt this was her opportunity to return the favour; she was determined to try to put this right.

'Look,' she said, noticing that Victoria hadn't touched her pudding, 'I'm going to stay with you for a few days.'

Victoria raised her eyebrows. 'You can't, what about-'

'I've got my things.' Cat nodded at the small holdall beside her. 'I've asked the neighbours to look after my mum and I'll ring work tomorrow to tell them I'm not coming in. It's OK,' she went on. 'I can't leave you here like this. Let's go back to the house and I'll make supper and we can talk some more.'

* * *

Sitting next to Cat beside the inglenook fireplace, watching the gently flickering flames and sipping white wine, Victoria felt calmer than she'd been in days. She was immensely grateful to the younger woman for having come; she seemed

365

to have restored a little tranquillity, to have brought with her some balance and perspective.

She was a funny girl, she thought, re-filling their glasses. A strange blend of tough, chippy reserve and tenderness. She'd had a lot to cope with in her short life. They talked a bit about the new job. It was a relief not to focus on Ralph for a little while. Victoria despised Maddy but could see that it was an opportunity for the younger woman. Cat also mentioned that she wrote poems and short stories but that she'd never managed to get anything published.

Victoria was interested. 'I'd love to read some of your work – if you'd let me?'

Cat said she'd think about it.

'And what about your love life?' Victoria asked at last. 'Anyone on the horizon?' It was seven months since Leo had died, after all, and she was young. It would be good for her to find someone new.

Cat frowned. 'Well there is this man...'

Victoria listened while Cat told her about Gervaise, about how kind he was and how right everyone seemed to think they were for each other.

'But you don't seem too sure yourself. What do you think? Do you love him?'

Cat pulled up her legs on the sofa and tucked them underneath. 'I think he's a really special person and yes I do love him. It's just—'

'And is he faithful? Victoria interrupted. 'Does he look at other women?'

'No.'

'Then that's wonderful,' she cried, taking a crisp from a bowl beside her feet. 'Despite everything that's happened to me, I really do believe in love and stable marriage. I'm convinced it's the best route to happiness. I'm delighted for you.'

Cat was silent for a moment. 'But-' she accidentally put out her foot and tipped over the half glass of wine that was on the floor beside her. 'I'm sorry—'

Victoria jumped up. 'Don't worry. It's usually me who does that. I'll get a cloth.'

As she walked into the kitchen, she was vaguely aware that the younger woman had wanted to say something more but by the time she returned, Cat had changed the subject.

'So what are you going to do about Ralph?'

Victoria frowned and a strand of wiggly hair fell across her face which she tucked behind an ear. 'I don't know.'

Cat sat up straight. 'I have an idea. Why don't we sit down together – all of us – and talk? Seriously, maybe having me there would help. I could be a sort of intermediary.' She glanced at the floor. 'Not that I have any experience. But we're adults,' she carried on, 'and let's face it, as you yourself said, we're all in this together whether we like it or not. Surely we can thrash it out?'

Victoria shivered. 'I couldn't possibly meet that woman face-to-face again. I hate her.'

Cat took a sip of wine and looked at Victoria seriously. 'Well at least think about it. You're not alone, remember.'

Victoria managed a small smile.

Later, in bed, Victoria found herself wondering what Ralph was doing and whether he was missing her, or even thinking of her at all. It was strange how she'd wanted to stab him when he was standing there in front of her. But talking to Cat seemed to have softened the edges of her fury.

She pictured Leo and a surprising fountain of anger bubbled inside her. In truth, wasn't he responsible for all this, for driving a schism between her and her son? He was the one who'd betrayed the Gannons – and then her – so spectacularly. The consequences of his actions seemed to be playing on like never-ending tape music.

She thought of Cat and felt a warmth spread through her. If anything had come of this whole sorry mess, it was finding out what a decent human being this peculiar looking girl really was.

Her mind wandered back to Leo and she felt as if he were still conducting from his grave, controlling her actions and managing her thought processes. Preventing her from moving forwards. She found herself clenching her fists as her breathing quickened.

She was tired of being manipulated and furious that Leo's influence was still spreading through the family like cancer cells.

She wanted to be free.

FOURTH MOVEMENT

CHAPTER TWENTY-EIGHT

Tuesday July 6th

Ralph had given up trying to contact his mother. He'd left countless messages on her phone and she hadn't responded. There was no point carrying on. He'd like to think that he didn't care. She'd lied to him all these years and treated him like a kid, pretending that everything was all right and forcing him to see things her way.

She was deluded. And yet...he knew she loved him. And despite everything, he loved her. He couldn't help it; she was his mother.

He tiptoed into Maddy's room. She was fast asleep. She was a smart woman and he admired her so much. Her new business was going well and she was getting lots of freelance work, too, but he was troubled and couldn't quite put his finger on why.

It wasn't that she was being mean to him or anything like that. She'd put him up and helped him with his revision. But something had changed and she seemed distant. When he spoke to her she had a faraway look in her eyes as if her mind were elsewhere.

He bit his lip. Maybe she was fed up and wanted to chuck him out now he'd done his exams. He'd asked her straight just before she went to bed and she'd denied it.

'Don't be silly, Ralph,' she'd said. 'You're imagining things.'

But he knew he wasn't. It wasn't just that she was tired, he could tell. And the way she'd jumped at his idea about going InterRailing. He'd been testing her, really. Part of him wanted to join his friends but he knew he couldn't. Not with everything that was going on. Anyway, he'd hoped that she'd beg him not to, saying she'd miss him too much. But she'd been dead keen to get rid of him and it freaked him out. Not being able to speak to Mum freaked him out, too.

Where was she? He wanted to know. What was she thinking? And where was Salome? He missed her.

All the time that he was living at home, hating his mother was something solid and tangible that he could hold on to. Knowing that he was hurting her gave him purpose and satisfaction. But now that she was gone he sensed a great, gaping hole. And he felt guilty.

He remembered how she'd talked sometimes about her childhood and her parents' unhappy relationship. She hadn't told him much – she'd wanted to protect him, probably. But she must have her own reasons for ending up with Dad, the Great Conductor. Maybe she'd much rather have lived happily ever after with a nice steady banker or something. Maybe she didn't know how to have a normal relationship because her parents had been so weird.

Maddy had been like this shadow in his life for so long, this person who Dad saw but neither he nor Mum ever spoke about. The elephant in the room. He balled his fists. It was no use brooding. He was wearing pyjama bottoms and nothing else. He padded next door into the sitting room where his bed was made up and pulled on a sweatshirt and jeans, shoving his wallet in the pocket and locating a pair of trainers by the door.

He looked at his mobile, which was on the table in the hall, just to check for any messages from Victoria but there were none. Then he tiptoed into Phoebe's room. She was lying on her back, arms stretched above her head, mouth slightly open, and he kissed her lightly on the cheek. 'Bye, Phoebe.'

His stomach felt empty yet his limbs were heavy and painful and he didn't know what to do. He went back to his mobile and checked again just to be sure. Nothing.

There was a pad of paper on the table and a pen. 'Dear Maddy,' he wrote. 'Thanks for putting me up. Ralph x.'

He laid the pad down, opened the door and headed out into the night.

* * *

Wednesday July 7th

Maddy wasn't usually one to picture the worst case scenario being, by nature, a can-do, glass half-full sort of person. But as soon as she read the note the following morning and spotted his mobile, her mind was full of foreboding.

She ran into the room next door to check Ralph's suitcase which was sitting open on top of the console, clothes still unpacked, crumpled and spilling out over the sides. As far as she could see, he'd taken nothing with him. His gilet was still hanging in the hall and his toothbrush was by the sink in the bathroom.

She didn't know where he kept his wallet but it wasn't in any of his pockets or lying around the place. This she took as a good sign. He wouldn't need money if he were intending to do himself harm, surely? But she was most concerned that he hadn't got his phone with him as he never went anywhere without it. It was attached to him as if by an invisible umbilical cord.

Phoebe was at the kitchen table flicking through a comic and looked up when her mother walked in.

'Why aren't I going to school today, Mummy?' she asked brightly.

Maddy was miles away.

'Mu-um,' Phoebe said more loudly and Maddy glanced at her daughter, who was still in her nightie looking very messy and sweet.

'What? Sorry. I'm not sure where Ralph is. We've got to find him.'

Phoebe frowned. 'Has he gone to see his friends?' She'd heard Ralph talk sometimes about Matt or Josh or Pat.

'I don't know.' Maddy looked down at his mobile in her hand and scrolled through the numbers. Good idea. She'd call them in turn. That was the sensible thing to do. One of them would be sure to know where he was.

She walked purposefully next door and sat on the end of the bed. Some of the names she'd heard of, some she hadn't, but the majority picked up. Clearly they, too, were wedded to their phones.

'Hey, Ralph. What's up?' 'What are you doing?' 'Yeah?' They sounded half asleep, most of them. Now they'd finished their exams they could lie in all they wanted. But they woke up when she told them what had happened.

'No,' they said, one after another. 'Haven't seen him. Sorry.' She gave them her numbers just in case.

She paced around the flat trying to put herself in his shoes, to imagine where he'd go and what he'd do. She wanted to believe that she had nothing to do with his disappearance, that it was all down to Victoria and their argument, but she feared very much that this wasn't so. Yes, she'd been distant with him these past few days but it was for his sake. Besides, he'd been talking about going travelling. She'd thought she was doing the right thing.

Maybe she'd gone too far. Waves of nausea spread through her, heating her face and brain but leaving her body cold. He was only just eighteen, he'd lost his father and now his mother had vanished. He was vulnerable. Of course he was upset. She should have handled him more gently.

Tears pricked in her eyes but she gave herself a mental shake. It was no good feeling sorry for herself. This was an emergency and she needed to be practical. She decided to call the police. Better to alert them straightaway, even if Ralph showed up shortly and it turned out that she'd wasted their time.

They took details over the phone, wanting to know what sort of places he frequented, events that could have prompted his disappearance, his medical history and so on, and advised her to check local hospitals. They said they'd circulate the information straightaway and an officer would be round later to do the official paperwork.

Maddy felt sick hearing herself trying to explain their relationship. She'd committed no crime but felt like a criminal all the same. The police listened carefully and advised her to contact anyone else she could think of who might have information. She chewed the corner of her nail. She'd avoided phoning Victoria because she knew that she wasn't picking up Ralph's calls and anyway, he had no idea where she was. He could hardly have gone to her.

But, she thought, she might just get a response if she used her own phone instead of his, and Victoria might have some ideas. It had to be done.

Phoebe wandered into the bedroom with milk on her upper lip and down the front of her nightie.

'Go and get washed and dressed. I'll be with you in a minute,' said Maddy, trying to sound calm.

Her heart was thumping as she rang Victoria but there was no answer. She left an urgent voice message and sent a text as well: *'I don't know where Ralph is. Pls call asap. Maddy.'*

It took Victoria precisely one minute and twenty-nine seconds to respond.

'What's happened?' She sounded panicky and for a fleeting moment all Maddy could think was that despite everything, this woman loved her son so much.

She explained very quickly. There was no time to waste.

'Oh God,' Victoria said, taking a deep breath on the other end of the line. 'Give me your address. I'll come straight there. I'll be with you in about two hours.'

* * *

Cat had to keep reminding Victoria to slow down. Crashing the car and killing them both wouldn't help anyone. All the way back Victoria kept repeating what Maddy had said: Ralph was unhappy about his row with Victoria and her disappearance. And she, Maddy, had perhaps been offhand with him because she was working so hard.

'We didn't have a fight or anything,' she'd said, a little too insistently. 'I didn't know he was really upset, maybe I should have noticed. Or maybe there's something else bothering him.'

Victoria told Cat that she could hear the guilt in Maddy's voice and was glad. But she hadn't added to it because she needed to extract every last drop of information, anything that might lead her to Ralph. All she wanted right now was to hold him close and tell him that things would be all right.

The fact that he'd betrayed her so spectacularly seemed

376

suddenly less important. The truth was that she was frightened of what he might do. They could talk about things later and find a way through. The only thing that mattered was that he was safe.

Victoria had been in Deal for ten days and yet it seemed much longer. She'd missed Salome like mad, but they'd spoken every day and the little girl sounded happy, though eager to see her mother again. They'd never been apart so long.

Victoria thought she'd been feeling better and healthier and had enjoyed getting to know Cat. And now this. Her whole body was tense and knotted, her shoulders locked in a painful, twisted position, one higher than the other. She hit the motorway and put her foot down.

As they reached London and saw the signs for Hammersmith, it dawned on her that she was about to come face to face again with Maddy. Up to now, she'd been so focused on getting back, speaking to the police and doing all she could to find her son that she hadn't given it a thought. Hatred would get her nowhere, though, she knew. At some point she'd have her say but for now, she'd make a superhuman effort to put her loathing aside.

She parked her car a little way down Maddy's street and Cat rang the bell. They could hear thundering feet running down the hallway, which they assumed were Phoebe's, and at last Maddy came to the door.

Victoria's initial sense of revulsion was quickly overtaken by surprise because she hardly recognised the woman. She was wearing jeans and a baggy white T-shirt, her blonde hair was scraped back, she had no jewellery or make-up and her face was creased with worry.

'Come in,' she said and Victoria and Cat followed her into the sitting room, where Ralph's suitcase was still open on the console. They had to manoeuvre themselves round a camp bed in the middle of the room and Victoria banged her foot on one of the metal legs as she sat down.

'Sorry,' Maddy said distractedly. 'Ralph always forgets to put it away.' She gave a small smile.

Victoria glanced at Cat, who nodded in a 'I told you so' kind of way. But the older woman said nothing. She wanted to get down to business.

Phoebe wandered in and looked at Victoria curiously. 'Who are you?'

She swallowed, taken aback again by the likeness between this little girl and her own daughter.

'Ralph's mother,' she said, trying to be matter-of-fact. She had no idea what Maddy had told the child.

Phoebe tried to put on the TV but Maddy stopped her. 'Not now.'

She stamped her foot. 'But I'm *bored*.'

'Enough,' Maddy snapped.

Phoebe stuck out her bottom lip and started to cry while Victoria closed her eyes and took a few deep breaths. The child sounded just like her big half-sister on a bad day.

'I'm sorry,' Maddy sighed, holding out her arms to give her daughter a hug, but Phoebe ran from the room.

Victoria felt her shoulders relax a little. At least now they could talk.

Maddy was beside her on the sofa, too close for comfort but Victoria wasn't going to make a fuss. Cat was sitting in the armchair opposite. Maddy went through the events of the past few days in more detail, including the conversation that she'd had with Ralph about travelling.

'He seemed quite keen,' she said. 'I thought it was a good sign that he was thinking about the future though I know it bothered him that you weren't returning his calls.'

'But why would he suddenly leave?' Victoria wanted to know. 'There must have been some trigger?'

Maddy sighed and crossed her arms. 'The truth is,' she said, 'he may have been upset about us. You see, he may have thought that all I cared about was his exams and now they're over, well...'

Victoria listened carefully while Maddy explained how she'd been helping Ralph for months with his revision. How she felt guilty that he was round so often and thought that this was one, positive thing that could come of it.

'I was determined to make sure he got his grades and went to university,' she went on sadly. 'I wanted to make him think about his future and make a good life for himself. Also, I've been really busy with work and I guess he might have been feeling a bit rejected.'

She looked Victoria in the eye. 'I didn't mean to upset him. He's a wonderful person with so much going for him. He'd been talking about going travelling with his friends. I never thought he'd do something silly.'

Victoria stared at her fingernails, which were short and unpainted. Several things which Maddy said surprised her, not least of all the younger woman's concern for Ralph's future, which seemed genuine. But Victoria wasn't going to let her off the hook. Why should she?

'The most important thing,' she said, her voice trembling, 'is that we find him quick. You've been right through his contacts, you say?'

Maddy nodded. 'And I've called the local hospitals – just in case.'

Victoria knitted her brows and tried to imagine what would be going through Ralph's mind now. If he wasn't at one of his friends' houses, what would be the first place, or who would be the first person, he'd think of visiting, always assuming that he hadn't done something stupid?

Her guts tugged painfully. Think, Victoria, think. A picture flashed through her mind of Ralph when he was quite small, about Salome's age. He was wearing shorts and trainers, with the little red and white rucksack that he liked on his back. He was holding his father's hand and smiling. Her heart fluttered. She picked up her bag, which was at her feet, and rootled for her car keys while Maddy looked on nervously.

'I have an idea,' Victoria said, rising. 'I might be wrong but it's worth a try. I'm going there now. I'll have my mobile with me. Call me immediately if there's any news.'

CHAPTER TWENTY-NINE

Ralph was standing in the eerie, blue-green half light in front of the giant tank. He was quite still, hypnotised by the powerful sharks finning slowly through the aquamarine water, their muscular bodies twisting and turning gracefully, their mouths slightly open, tiny eyes ever watchful.

He had his back to Victoria but she knew immediately that the tall, thin, slightly gawky man-boy in front of her was him.

She approached slowly and touched his arm. 'It's you.' She was careful not to raise her voice.

He glanced at her before turning back to the tank.

'They're beautiful, aren't they?' Victoria said, taking his arm and resting her cheek against it, inhaling the smell of him through his sweatshirt.

He grunted.

'How long have you been here?' she asked gently.

'Since it opened.'

'I hoped I'd find you.'

He let her remain beside him and she was quite content not to talk. It was comforting to feel the small movements of his body as he breathed in and out. Every so often a multicoloured fish that she hadn't seen before would skim into view, breaking the spell.

'You came here a few times, didn't you, with Dad?' she said at last.

She'd remembered that visiting the London Aquarium was

one of the rare things they'd done together, father and son. Leo was fascinated by underwater landscapes; he said they were peaceful and anxiety-free. He liked to imagine himself with the fish in the clear water. He could watch them for hours.

She felt Ralph's body tense a little and took her cheek away. She was still holding on to his arm and she swallowed, frightened to speak again in case he bolted.

'I wish he'd been around more,' Ralph said still staring at the tank.

'I know.'

'He was never really there for me.'

'No. But I am.'

He fidgeted suddenly, jerking her arm away. 'How can you say that, after all that's happened – with Maddy and everything? Like you said, I've betrayed you.'

Victoria paused, knowing that what she said was vital, that she must choose her words with the utmost care.

'We can get through this,' she said hesitantly, 'put it behind us.'

He took a step away from her, creating a cold hard space between them.

'I wanted to hurt you,' he growled, 'to get back at you. That's not very nice, is it?'

Two small children ran up to the tank and pressed their noses against the glass. 'Look, Mummy! Big fish!' Their breath made misty circles on the pane.

Ralph and Victoria took a couple of paces back against the wall. She was desperate for the thread not to be broken; whatever happened she must keep them in the moment and keep them talking.

'No,' she replied quickly, 'it's not very nice. But in some

ways I deserved it. I regret so much that I didn't speak to you more.'

She wiped away a tear. 'You must have been so bewildered about what was going on at home. I was determined to protect you and Salome. I didn't realise that you understood so much about...' she clenched her fists, '...about your father and Maddy.'

It hurt so much to speak her name in front of him, like a physical pain. But now that she'd done it she thought it would be easier next time.

Several more people had gathered around the tank and Victoria wished they'd go away. Couldn't they see how important this was, a life-changing moment?

'He was a bastard,' Ralph said through gritted teeth. 'I hate him.'

Victoria flinched. In the past she'd have flown at him and defended Leo to the hilt. But she'd changed.

She took a deep breath. 'I've been thinking a lot. It's true that I hate many of the things he did but I'm so glad I had you and Salome. I can never regret that. I wish I hadn't stayed with him for so long, though. It was so damaging – for us all.'

Even though she wasn't looking at Ralph she could tell that he was listening intently, every nerve in his body crackling with alertness.

'There's something I think you should know about your father that I've not told you,' she went on, following a little orange and white clown fish with her eyes until it darted behind a rock. 'I only found out myself recently. That's what I went to see Maddy about – and Cat.'

'What?' He sounded afraid.

'Why don't we go somewhere else, a cafe or something? This isn't the right place—'

'Tell me now.'

His voice was low and insistent, but Victoria didn't want to explain here about Anna, Elsa, the Gannons and the rest. She wanted to sit somewhere comfortable and take her time, somewhere light where she could gauge Ralph's reactions and know when she needed to tread more softly.

'Please?'

'Now.' He was almost shouting and several people in the aquarium looked round. 'I don't believe you'll tell me later. You'll find some excuse not to.'

Victoria's palms were sweaty and she rubbed them on her jeans. 'All right,' she said. 'If that's what you want.'

She decided not to edit the story. She'd tried to do this too often in her life and it hadn't worked. Ralph deserved the truth and she'd give it to him straight.

He listened quietly while she explained about the little sister that Leo had left behind – and about her final meeting with Elsa, Ralph's grandmother. She described how the old woman had solved the mystery of where his money had gone and how she, Victoria, had felt. Sometimes they stood, sometimes they squatted. Occasionally a guard came by and looked at them oddly, but they were doing no harm.

'It doesn't excuse what he did,' she said finally, 'but I think it goes some way towards explaining why he behaved like that and why he didn't want to marry me and could never settle with one woman. He must have been a deeply troubled man.'

Ralph's cheeks were wet and his tears glistened in the half light. Victoria wanted to reach out and wipe them away but she didn't dare.

'That's just so sad,' he said, hanging his head. 'I wish he could have talked about it. I wish I could have met Anna.'

Victoria felt a catch in her throat. 'So do I.'

Without warning, Ralph started banging the back of his head against the wall that he was leaning against, making Victoria wince. She wanted to make him stop but instead she waited.

'I hope I don't take after him – screwing up all those lives,' Ralph was saying. 'I hope I can be honest with my wife and kids. He was a cheat and a liar, you know that? He didn't even make a will, didn't even leave anything to us. He was hollow and empty inside.'

His head came to a rest and Victoria's body drooped, overcome with weariness. She thought that Ralph was more right than wrong about Leo. But they were alive and he wasn't. Their future was more important than his past.

The crowds had thinned out now and it crossed her mind that it must be nearly closing time. She realised that she hadn't called the police – or Maddy – to let them know Ralph was safe.

She thought Maddy didn't deserve to know, then she remembered the woman's face crumpled with worry. She wasn't all bad; Victoria would ring when they got outside.

She wanted to grab Ralph and hustle him out and into the car before he could slip from her grasp again, but she'd learned her lesson.

'What will you do now?' she asked, her heart pitter-pattering. What if he said the wrong thing? Would she be able to watch him walk away? But he was an adult now and should be allowed to choose his own path.

He hesitated for a second and shrugged. 'Dunno. Get myself a job. Find a room, I guess.'

There was a crack in his voice and he looked young and vulnerable.

She felt sick and closed her eyes, taking a few deep breaths. 'It's your decision.' When she opened them again she saw that he was looking at her intently.

'I mean it, Ralph. I'll support you in whatever you want to do. It's up to you.'

He took a few steps away from her towards the exit and she followed slowly. She was wondering if he'd let her come and visit, wherever it was that he was going. Or would he want to cut her off completely, start a fresh life and reinvent himself? Perhaps he'd find that easiest. It was going to be so hard.

Suddenly he turned. He was tall and straight-backed again, towering above her, and she stopped in her tracks, her heart in her mouth. She had no idea what was coming next.

'I know I've messed up,' he said. 'By rights you should hate me but...' She held her breath. '...but can I come home?'

Relief washed over her. 'Of course. And you won't run away again?'

He shook his head.

'We'll talk things through?'

He nodded.

'I've missed you,' she said, leaning up and touching his cheek, which was coarse with stubble and damp with tears.

'I've missed you, too,' he said quietly.

She thought those were the sweetest words she'd ever heard.

* * *

Cat was exhausted as she walked slowly down the street to her flat. It had been a rollercoaster of a day, but she'd decided that she must break the news about her job to Gervaise and

Tracy now. She hadn't mentioned a thing so far, not having been back to their place since the interview with Maddy last Sunday, which felt like a lifetime ago. She'd wanted to tell them face-to-face rather than on the phone.

They didn't even know where she'd really been; she'd told a fib, saying she'd had to go to a cousin's funeral. 'You never mentioned a cousin,' Tracy had said suspiciously, but Cat had brushed it off. She wasn't ready to discuss Victoria or Maddy yet.

She was on a month's notice and she'd tell Rachel when she returned to work tomorrow. The thought gave her butterflies. Things had been the same for so long there, it was hard to imagine that life would ever change. It was odd to think of someone else filling her shoes, repeating those same tasks that she'd being doing for years.

Victoria had found Ralph. They were reconciled. And now she was about to learn a new set of skills and embark on a whole new life. Things were looking up.

It was around 8 p.m. when she returned with a cheap bottle of wine that she'd bought from the local shop, and a big bag of peanuts. Tracy and Rick were in their bedroom with the door shut and Gervaise was in the shower.

She'd got out some glasses and was pouring nuts into a bowl when he appeared with a once white, now grey towel round his waist, rubbing his wet dark hair with another towel.

'Welcome home, babe!' he said, walking over to kiss her on the lips. 'I've missed you too much.'

Cat smiled nervously, thinking it was ridiculous to be on edge. All she was doing was changing jobs, for goodness' sake. People did it all the time.

He went next door to get dressed and reappeared a few moments later in jeans, a baggy pale blue T-shirt and bare feet.

His hair had grown much longer and you could see how lovely it was now: thick, glossy, wavy and almost blue it was so black. He shook his head and droplets of water scattered everywhere.

'Stop it!' Cat squealed, 'you're soaking me.'

He sat down opposite her and she passed him a glass.

'Wanna go out later? Or we could go straight to bed?' he said, grinning cheekily.

Cat cleared her throat. 'I've got a new job.' She hadn't planned to blurt it out like that.

He put down his glass and stared. 'What do you mean? What job?'

He listened quietly while she explained all about it.

'It's a great opportunity,' she said finally, hoping she'd convinced him. She couldn't tell from his expression.

'Well,' he said at last, rubbing his chin. 'You certainly kept this one quiet. It's a bit of a risk and there's always the possibility that you and...what's her name?'

'Maddy,' said Cat.

'...that you and Maddy might fall out.' His mouth puckered, as if he'd tasted something bitter.

Cat knew this must be hard for him. He rarely mentioned Leo and now she was going to work for his other girlfriend. He must feel as if there were no escape.

'It's kind of a weird thing for her to offer—'

Cat was about to speak but he interrupted.

'But it sounds like a good opportunity, as you say, and it might lead to things. At the very least you'll be out of that bookshop. Congratulations.' He gave a brave smile.

'I'll miss you,' she said quietly, leaning across and touching his hand. They'd been mates for so long, keeping each other's spirits up, making each other laugh. He was so generous to be pleased for her when he must be thinking he'd like nothing more than to quit himself.

She looked at him hopefully. 'Maybe it'll be better not working together as well as...well, as well as being together, you know?'

Gervaise took a handful of peanuts. 'Yeah,' he said, throwing them all in his mouth at once and chewing rapidly. 'The end of an era and the start of a new one. I guess I should really look for something else, too. I can't work there for the rest of my life.'

'You won't have to,' Cat said brightly. 'You'll land a great acting job soon and become rich and famous.'

'You don't really believe that, do you?'

'Course I do,' she said fiercely. 'You just need a break.'

He smiled crookedly and took a slurp of wine.

'Well, I think this calls for a pub visit,' he said finally, straightening his shoulders. 'What'll it be? The Nag's Head or The White Horse?'

Cat sat back, relieved. Conversation over, for the time being at least, and it hadn't been all that hard.

'The White Horse,' she grinned. 'But I've got to break the news to Tracy, first. She'll no doubt tell me I'm being a complete numpty. You know what she's like.'

***

They strolled arm in arm down Roman Road to the pub. They'd decided on The White Horse because there was a small garden outside with tables and chairs. It was a proper summer's evening – still light and warm enough not to need a jumper.

They must look a funny sight, Cat thought, because he was so tall and she was so small. Her head practically fitted under his armpit and he had to take baby steps so that she could keep up with him.

She'd put on a clean white vest top and her denim miniskirt, which hung around her hips. And her black boots, of course, with thick grey socks rolled down a few times. Maddy had told her it didn't matter what she wore to work, which was handy as Cat couldn't afford a whole new wardrobe. But she'd already decided she'd buy a few bits and pieces – a smart shirt, maybe, and a skirt. She wanted to look professional, even if she'd be spending most of the day in the flat.

Gervaise ordered a pint of Guinness, she had lager, and they found a table in the corner of the paved garden. It was a pretty spot. There was trellis on the yellowy brown brick walls with coloured plants growing up – Cat didn't know what they were. And there were hanging baskets on the back of the pub overflowing with bright flowers.

She decided to keep up the lie about the cousin's funeral. 'The family really wanted me to stay on and it's lovely where they live. We'll go together some time.'

He looked pleased.

'I'll test you on your lines later,' she said, remembering that Gervaise had another audition coming up. Rachel always let him have time off for castings; that was one good thing about her.

'Cheers.' He raised his glass and took a swig, before rocking back on his metal chair and stretching. 'This is the life.'

Cat watched a svelte-looking woman walk over to another table carrying a tray of drinks. She was wearing teeny khaki shorts, a voluminous white blouse and big expensive shades, even though the sun had gone now. Her legs were very long, slim and tanned. She could almost be a model.

Her friends, two men and another woman, looked well-heeled and successful, too. There was an air of confidence bordering on arrogance about them. They had pricey haircuts and relaxed designer clothes. They were laughing loudly and easily, their heads thrown back, seemingly unaware of the other customers and the attention they were attracting.

Cat smiled to herself. Normally she'd have felt intimidated by them. She'd probably have narrowed her eyes and whispered something to Gervaise like: 'Who the hell do they think they are? Wankers.' She'd have pretended to despise them but really it would have been her inferiority complex talking.

She straightened her shoulders. Since Maddy had offered her the job she'd scarcely had time to celebrate. She'd been too busy thinking about Victoria and worrying about telling Gervaise. But now things were different. Now she realised that she didn't need to feel inferior to anyone. She had a new job and was going places.

'Penny for your thoughts,' Gervaise said, setting his chair on the ground again and taking another swig. He was left with a creamy moustache which he wiped away with the back of his hand.

Cat blinked. 'I was just thinking that for once in my life I feel really lucky.' Her eyes clouded. 'It won't last.'

Gervaise gave a reassuring smile. 'Ach, sure it will. You're on a winning streak. I can feel it.'

'I'm glad it's happened now, the new job I mean,' she said, brightening again. This evening nothing could dampen her spirits for long. 'I'm not too old to start a new career. I mean, I'm still only twenty-four. I've got lots of time. And I'm a fast learner. You don't think twenty-four's too old, do you?'

'Course not.'

'I've been thinking I might take English A-level,' she

prattled, talking as much to herself as to him. 'I could study in the evenings. I reckon it'd be useful to have English A-level in this job. There's going to be quite a lot of writing. I'll have to wait and see what the hours are like first, of course.'

She looked down and saw that he was fiddling with the beer mat on the table, ripping little bits off the corner. His mouth was working in a strange way, too.

'What's the matter?' she asked. 'You've gone all quiet.' She could feel his leg jiggling up and down under the table.

He shook his head, ripping at the beer mat a few more times until it was in shreds. Cat swallowed, aware that her heart had started to beat faster. She opened her mouth to speak but suddenly he'd left his chair and was on his knees in front of her, squeezing her left hand so hard in both of his that it hurt.

'Cat Mason,' he said before she could stop him. His voice was very loud and formal-sounding. 'I've been wanting to ask you and now seems like the right time. Cat Mason,' he repeated, swallowing, 'will you marry me?'

Cat glanced left and right and saw that everyone was staring at them. Gervaise's face was raised and she gazed into his bright blue eyes, framed by thick black curling lashes.

He looked so full of hope. Sweat prickled in her armpits and her mouth felt dry. She was overcome with an urge to run away and had to exercise all her willpower to stay rooted to the spot.

'Cat?' he repeated when she failed to reply. This was probably the hardest thing he'd ever done.

She thought of Leo, how wrong he'd been for her and how little she'd really known him. She remembered what Victoria had said about stable marriage being the route to happiness. She looked at Gervaise's kind, wonderful, handsome and expectant face, took a deep breath, clenched her tummy muscles and summoned up a smile.

'Yes.'

A flicker of relief crossed his face and he started to smile too, at first just a little, then his mouth widened into an enormous grin.

'What?'

'Yes,' she repeated, louder this time.

She could hear people clapping; it was a grating, raucous sound that made her teeth jangle.

'She's got herself a new job – and a husband,' she heard Gervaise shout. 'All in one go!'

Several people whooped and there was the sound of glasses being chinked together.

Gervaise rose, pulling Cat up off her seat so high that her feet left the ground, and kissed her on the mouth. His lips were soft and his breath smelled sweet and yeasty. Her body was brittle at first but she gave in to the embrace. This, she told herself, this really was her lucky day.

'I love you,' he whispered, when at last they drew breath and he set her back down on the ground. She quickly rearranged her skirt, which had twisted round the wrong way, noticing with relief that the other customers had gone back to their drinks and conversations.

Gervaise was gazing down at her from his great height and fidgeted from one foot to another.

'Oh,' said Cat, realising what she must do. 'I love you, too.'

She couldn't understand why it was that she suddenly wanted to cry. It must be happiness. That's what it was. She was deliriously happy. She was going to be Gervaise's wife!

***

They decided not to have another drink, even though the designer-ish model woman with the long tanned legs came over and offered to buy them one. Gervaise wanted to get home to tell Rick and Tracy.

'Hurry,' he said, while Cat knocked back the last of her pint. 'If we go now we might catch them.'

It was almost dark and they practically ran hand in hand back to the flat, Gervaise having to slow down every so often for Cat. She was fast, but her legs were only half the length of his.

By the time they arrived, they were breathless and sweating. They burst through the door, stopped in their tracks and Cat gasped. The floor of the living room was covered in things, as was every available surface. She scanned around in disbelief spotting shoes, dresses, magazines, suits, a hat, even. There wasn't a corner of carpet to be seen.

'Jesus!' said Gervaise. 'What's happened?'

For a moment Cat thought they must have been burgled; it looked as if somebody had opened every drawer in the place and tipped the contents out. She contemplated dialling 999, until it dawned on her that there was some sort of theme going on here: white satin shoes, a poncy straw hat that no one in their right mind would wear unless...

'Tracy!' she growled, tiptoeing over the debris toward the closed door of her flatmate's bedroom.

She heard laughter coming from inside and didn't wait to knock.

'Tracy, it looks like a bomb's—'

Her eyes opened wide. Tracy and Rick were sitting cross-legged on the floor in front of a Snakes and Ladders board. Tracy, who'd always been partial to a board game, had a red plastic container in her hand which was poised, mid-air, ready to shake the dice out.

And they were both stark naked.

Cat took in Rick's flowing, shoulder length locks, his hairy chest and hairier...she gulped and looked away quickly.

'Sorry,' she said, taking several steps back and bumping into Gervaise, who was standing behind her, speechless.

Tracy looked up and smiled as if nothing were the matter.

'Hi you. Rick just fell down a massive snake.' She giggled and shook the dice.

'Tracy,' Cat hissed, 'you've got no clothes on.'

Rick grinned sheepishly. 'It was a bit close in here.'

Cat shrugged. If it didn't bother them then she supposed it shouldn't bother her. She'd always suspected that Rick had a nudist streak, ever since Tracy had told her that he didn't wear underpants.

'It's chaos out there,' Cat complained, gathering herself together. 'What's been going on?'

'I was in a muddle about what I've got so far for the wedding,' Tracy explained, moving her counter several paces and pushing it up a ladder. 'I decided to put everything out so I can see what I still need.'

'When are you going to clear it up? There's no room to move.'

'Won't be long, promise. Game's nearly over.'

Cat looked over her shoulder at Gervaise who nodded, making a sign with his forefinger: one moment.

'We've got some news for you guys,' he said, scarcely able to disguise the grin on his face.

Tracy looked up quickly. 'What news?'

'You'll have to wait. We're not speaking to any nude people.'

'Tell me,' she pleaded. She couldn't bear secrets; she was hopelessly impatient.

'My lips are sealed,' Gervaise replied, miming a zipping motion.

'C'mon Scroochiepook,' Rick coaxed. 'We can finish this later.'

'Don't call me Scroochiepook,' Tracy snapped, as Cat pulled the door firmly shut.

* * *

Tracy was bouncing up and down like a yo-yo when Gervaise told them, ever so formally, that he and Cat were 'engaged to be married.' They were standing in the middle of the living room, Rick having helpfully cleared a small space, just big enough for the four of them.

'That's soooo cool,' Tracy squealed, her eyes shining. 'Now we really can have a double wedding. What do you say, Cat?' She stopped bouncing and looked at her friend, eyebrows raised.

'Seriously. I mean, it's still three months away. I've booked the church and the venue. All you need to do is get more invitation cards printed and buy a dress. I'm sure the printers can run off some extra cards, just like mine. You don't even need to choose a design. And I've been to all the wedding shops and priced the dresses. I can already think of one which would suit you. It's off-the-shoulder, like mine, only with more lace. You're so thin you can get away with it. I've got the brochure here. You can look at it. It'll be easy!'

Cat glanced up at Gervaise, who was nodding enthusiastically. 'It's a fantastic idea. Now we've decided there's no point hanging about, and it'd be great for you two to walk down the aisle together. You're practically sisters anyway!'

Cat chewed her lip. 'But what about Rick?' She was thinking about the flowery invitations and trying to picture herself in a big white lacy dress. 'He might not want us muscling in on his big day.'

Rick shook his head. 'Not at all. It'd be a right laugh. Double trouble!'

Cat's stomach lurched. She glanced around the room and spotted the pointy white satin shoes and a funny little white shiny bag with crystals on it and a long golden chain. What was the point of having a bag if you couldn't get anything in it?

'Isn't it beautiful? said Tracy, following her gaze. "And look!' She reached over and picked up the big straw hat which had a wide brim and a blue and white scarf tied round the middle. 'I thought I might wear this with my going-away outfit.' She put it on and tipped her head to one side. 'What do you think?'

Cat didn't know what to say. She thought it looked ridiculous, like something Miss Muffet would wear.

Tracy frowned. 'Do you think it's too old for me? Maybe I could give it to Mum, instead. What do you think your mum will wear? Maybe we could co-ordinate the mums' outfits as well as ours?'

She took off the hat, chucked it on the floor and gave Cat a big squeeze, pressing her close to her pillowy chest. 'Oh Cat, it's a dream come true. We can buy our going-away outfits together. We're going to have such fun!'

'I haven't got any money for clothes and things,' Cat said, releasing herself from Tracy's embrace. 'I'm skint at the moment.'

Gervaise put an arm round her shoulders. 'Don't worry, I've a little bit saved. Hey! Maybe you could make the clothes instead of buy them? You could use curtain fabric if you can't find cheap enough material.'

Cat glared at him and Rick and Tracy laughed.

'Only joking. I never had you down as much of a seamstress.'

Tracy started picking things up off the floor and plonking them on the sofa and Rick gave Gervaise a sly wink.

'Reckon we should leave the girls to it, don't you? Fancy a spot of fresh air?'

Gervaise glanced at Cat who gave him a blank stare. She felt confused and rootless, blowing this way and that.

'Is that all right with you, if we pop out for half an hour?'

'What?' It took a moment for Cat to register what he was saying. 'Of course. Go ahead.' What was it to do with her?

Tracy clapped her hands. 'Off you go to the pub then. We don't want you around when we're talking wedding dresses.'

She picked up a pile of clothes from the sofa and started carrying it into her bedroom while Cat bent down mechanically to help.

Rick and Gervaise were at the door.

'We'll go to late night opening next week and have a look at engagement rings,' Gervaise called. 'I think the ones on Coke cans are the best.'

Rick guffawed.

'Yes,' Cat said, staring at two little jewellery boxes in her hands for the bridesmaids. 'Yes, engagement rings. That would be lovely.'

CHAPTER THIRTY

Thursday August 19th

Victoria was in the kitchen, bending over Salome at the table and pouring cereal into a bowl when Ralph walked in. She was still in her dressing gown, her mad curly hair, as yet untamed, sticking out as if she'd been electrocuted.

She looked up fearfully, trying to gauge his expression. She hadn't said a word to him about his A-level results but she knew that today was The Day.

He pulled his mouth down at the corners and she felt her features slide south until it seemed they might hit the floor. Disappointment was seeping from every pore. There was no way she could hide it even if she tried.

'Guess what?' he said.

She clutched the edge of the table with both hands.

'I've got into Birmingham! I got AAB!' His face lit up in a huge smile.

Victoria hesitated, needing confirmation, and he nodded. 'I just checked the UCAS track system.'

He'd been teasing her. She let out a cry, leaped up, her arms raised, and danced a jig around the table towards him, knocking over the cereal packet in the process and sending its contents flying across the room. Salome had no idea what was happening but joined in, too.

'You've done it!' Victoria screamed, crunching across the

spilled cereal to give her son a hug. 'I'm so happy for you!'

'What's he done?' Salome shouted, joining in the hug. 'What's Birmingham?'

Victoria, remembering herself, backed away. Ralph hadn't even said that he'd definitely go to university if he got in. She was dying to ask, of course, but since he'd come home she'd been doing her best not to interfere and to let him make his own decisions.

'Well done,' she repeated, trying to temper the excitement in her voice. 'It's fantastic.'

Ralph sauntered to the fridge and poured himself a glass of orange juice. He looked about ten feet tall, as if he could conquer the world. Those hours spent with Maddy learning reams of French vocabulary, going over and over his set texts and practising past papers. It had worked.

'What are you going to do today?' she asked, seeing in her mind's eye a brightly coloured future stretching out before him when before she could picture only browns and greys. 'I expect you'll be celebrating?'

He moved towards the door, drink in hand. 'I haven't spoken to anyone yet. I wanted you to be the first to know. I'm going to make a few calls – see how everyone's done, make some plans.' He frowned. 'But there's something I need to do first.'

Victoria opened her mouth to speak and closed it again.

She turned back to Salome. 'Hurry up. Some of us have to go to work.'

She glanced at him and smiled again, her eyes bright and shining. 'It's not just the results, you know. It was never just about the results.'

'I know.'

Fifteen minutes later, having swept the kitchen floor, she

hurried upstairs to clean her teeth and finish dressing. She was going to be late at this rate. Ralph had left his door open and she could hear him laughing, a deep, throaty, infectious giggle.

She stopped for a moment, realising that she hadn't heard him laugh like this for a long, long time. She tiptoed away, not wanting to disturb him.

***

After dropping Salome at her holiday activity camp, she drove into work and bounded up the steep flight of steps into the office. Her movements felt light and nimble, as if she might float away. Nothing and no one, it seemed, could spoil her happiness. Today was one of those rare, precious Perfect Days that would be stamped in her memory forever. It was official.

Ralph's success was about more than a few certificates to springboard him up to the next stage of life, be it higher education or into a job. It was a symbol of something even more significant.

The good news seemed to her to prove that, despite all the unhappiness he had endured and all the hurt that they'd caused each other, he could pull through and that things were going to be All Right. Whatever he chose to do now, he'd shown himself more than anyone else that he could make a go of it.

She popped her head round Debs's half-open door and pulled it out again. 'Sorry.'

'Is that you, Victoria? Come in!'

Debs was standing at the small sink in the corner, stripped down to her underwear and washing her armpits, water sloshing all over the floor.

'I ran to work,' she explained, turning round momentarily

before resuming her ablutions. 'In the absence of a shower, this'll just have to do.'

Her washing finished, she wrapped a towel under her armpits and around her. Her hair, tied back in a ponytail, was wet and sticky and her face still red.

'I reckon it's about six miles. I'm knackered.' She peered at Victoria, who had shut the door behind her and taken a few steps into the room, hardly able to contain herself.

'You look happy,' Debs said, surprised. 'What's up?'

Victoria told her the news and Debs rushed over to give her a hug, dropping her towel in the process. Victoria felt damp seeping through her clothes but she didn't mind.

'Congratulations!' Debs said, squeezing her tight, 'you must be so relieved. Is he going this year or next?'

Victoria shrugged. 'I honestly don't know whether he's going at all.' She hesitated. 'Maddy's still in the picture.' She'd told Debs about them. 'But at least he's got the option now. I wasn't sure he'd pull it off after all that's happened. I'm so pleased for him.'

She and Debs agreed to have coffee later and Victoria scuttled into her consulting room to get ready for her clients. She was seeing a businessman and his journalist wife for the fourth time.

Their problems seem to be pretty typical: both working hard, young kids, not allowing enough time for each other and sex life ground to a halt. There are also issues around the husband's drinking and the fact that one of the children appears to have some sort of minor learning difficulty.

Victoria suspects that there's something else they're not telling her. So it doesn't surprise her when the wife

– Shona – clears her throat and announces there's a matter that she needs to get off her chest.

Shona is a tall slim pretty woman in her mid-thirties with dark hair cut in a pixie style. She seemed cool and a little superior at first but Victoria has grown to like her more over the weeks that they've been coming.

Her husband, Trevor, starts fidgeting. 'Shona, you don't need to say anything you don't want.'

Victoria glances at him. It seems a strange comment, given that they've both been pretty frank in the sessions. He's a big handsome man with close cropped fair hair and thick eyebrows; he looks as if he's very sporty, or was. Victoria decides not to interrupt.

'I need to, Trevor,' Shona says steadily.

Her husband appears to shrink slightly. 'Be careful, that's all—'

'I'm seeing another man.'

The temperature in the room drops several degrees and Victoria looks intently from one to the other.

'How long has this been going on?' Trevor asks hoarsely.

He isn't a good actor; Victoria can tell that he already knows.

Shona looks at her husband sharply. 'A year or so. Maybe more.'

Trevor stares back dumbly, his blank eyes doing a good job of concealing the pain. But Victoria knows it's there. He loves Shona, that much is clear, and she feels a wave of empathy so powerful that it almost winds her. She understands what he's going through; that all the while it hadn't been spoken he could pretend that it wasn't happening. She can see it all.

'Shona,' she says quietly, 'do you realise that your husband has been suffering terribly?'

Shona starts twisting the wedding ring on her finger.

'Don't,' Trevor says quietly. 'We don't have to talk about it. It doesn't matter.'

Victoria shakes her head gently and he groans.

'It does matter,' she says. 'Very much. This isn't something you can just ignore; I'm afraid you're going to have to face it if you want to move on.'

There are bags under Shona's and Trevor's eyes as they leave the consulting room. They look as drained as Victoria feels but it has been a good session. It seems to her that the couple have started to step out of the shadows for the first time, perhaps, in their whole marriage.

Their new world might seem bright and scary but in the end, whether their marriage survives or not, Victoria is confident that they'll be pleased they made that leap. She's glad that she's been able to help.

Debs's door was shut so Victoria decided to make herself a cup of coffee while she waited for her friend to finish. As far as she knew Oliver wasn't in, which she was relieved about. She hadn't seen him since last week and then only to say a brief hello.

She opened the kitchen door and was surprised to find him standing by the boiling kettle, staring at the curling steam and seemingly deep in thought.

She stopped in her tracks. 'Oh! I didn't think anyone was in here.'

She felt herself redden, as she did whenever she saw him these days. She was still so embarrassed about her mistake and couldn't forgive herself.

The kettle switched itself off and he opened the lid of the instant coffee jar.

'Would you like some?' he asked, nodding at the mug in front of him.

'I'll make my own,' she said quickly, not wishing to put him out.

She saw something flash across his face – sadness, hurt? Could he really be hurt about a silly cup of coffee? She felt stupid.

'I didn't mean—'

He poured water into his mug. 'It's all right, Victoria.' His voice was heavy and resigned.

It was pretty close in the tiny kitchen, even with the door ajar. He reached down to the little fridge under the counter and pulled out a bottle of milk.

'Debs told me about Ralph's A-levels.' His voice betrayed no emotion and he wasn't looking at her, he was concentrating on pouring milk into the mug without spilling. 'You must be very pleased.'

'Yes,' she said. 'I am.'

She was still hovering by the half-open door. There was hardly room for more than one person in the kitchen anyway.

He picked up his mug and turned. 'There's plenty of water in the kettle—'

He was wearing a clean red and white striped shirt, rolled up at the sleeves and with the top two buttons undone. He and Victoria were only a foot or two apart and she was suddenly acutely aware of his physical presence.

The steam had made the shirt stick slightly to his body so she could make out its slim, taut shape. He was about the same height as her, but his shoulders were broad and she could smell the heat coming off him and the soap on his skin.

He caught her eye and there seemed to be a question mark hanging between them, or was she imagining it? She glanced away shyly, not sure what it was that was making her heart beat faster and her palms sweat.

'You once told me,' she said, staring at her size eight shoes and trying to sound nonchalant, 'that you were 'sort of' seeing someone. How's it going?'

She dug her nails in the palms of her hands, shocked at her own boldness.

He was still holding his mug of hot coffee but he put it down now and ran a hand through his hair.

'What? Oh that. Rosanna and I went out a few times but it would never have worked. We've known each other too long and she's far too bossy.' He gave a crooked smile.

'Rosanna? The one I met at your house?' Victoria shivered, remembering the other woman's brash confidence and how uncomfortable she'd made her feel.

He nodded. 'I should never have invited you together but it seemed like a good idea at the time. I finished with her soon after that, actually. She was a bit fed up with me but I expect she'll get over it. I saw a different side to her that night that I wasn't keen on. To be honest, I think she was jealous.'

Victoria's eyes widened. 'Jealous? Of whom?'

'Of you.' He seemed surprised by her question.

The idea was preposterous and Victoria almost laughed. 'Of me? Why on earth would anyone be jealous of me?'

Oliver looked at her intensely, his agate grey eyes still and searching. 'Because you're beautiful, funny, a little bit silly and clumsy, sweet, intelligent, kind – and you don't even know it. I could go on...'

Their eyes locked and she was so startled that she could

hardly breathe.

'But I've probably said too much already,' he added.

Victoria felt her face and neck heat up and her stomach was performing somersaults. Oliver Sands thought she was beautiful! Maybe he didn't hate her for assuming the worst about him after all.

'I...that awful mistake I made about you...' she started to say. 'I feel so bad—'

He raised a hand to stop her. 'Please. It's behind us. I was angry at the time but I've forgotten it now.'

Suddenly his face lit up in that wide, mischievous smile of his. 'Victoria. I do believe you're blushing!'

Her cheeks, which had just started to cool down, caught fire again.

'I'm not!' she said defensively.

'Yes you are.' He was teasing and she felt laughter fizz at the back of her throat.

He took a step forwards and before she knew it, his lips were on hers pressing ever so tenderly and tentatively; just butterfly kisses at first, his arms lightly around her.

Her back was against the half open door which closed, trapping them inside, and she opened her mouth just a little, then a bit more; she couldn't resist if she tried.

He was a gorgeous kisser, gentle, slow and sexy. She put her hands around his middle and hesitantly ran them up and down his back. She'd forgotten what a man's body felt like.

'Is someone in there?'

She started, jolted back to reality by a hammering on the door.

Victoria dragged her face away and gave Oliver a small push, wiping her mouth, smoothing down her hair. 'Quick! It's Debs!'

Oliver, startled, turned to the kettle and switched it back on just as Debs gave the door a final shove and burst into the room.

'Oh,' she said. 'You two. The door was stuck.'

She glanced from one to the other, her eyes narrowing. 'Is everything all right?'

'Quite all right,' Oliver said fake-casually, reaching up to get another mug from the cupboard. 'Can I make you a coffee?'

'We were just, um, we were talking about...' Victoria's voice trailed away, her mind suddenly blank.

'We were talking about hedgerows,' Oliver chipped in.

'Hedgerows?' Debs's eyes narrowed further.

'Yes,' said Victoria, trying to suppress a giggle. 'Oliver's very interested in hedgerows, aren't you Oliver?'

Debs harrumphed and Victoria felt wretched for telling her friend a silly lie. It was too bad.

'I thought we were going out for coffee?' Debs asked, noticing the untouched drink on the work surface and looking confused.

'We are!' Victoria said quickly. 'Let's go now! I wasn't sure how long you were going to be.'

Debs went to fetch her things leaving Victoria alone for a moment longer with Oliver. There was an awkward silence between them, which made her afraid.

'I don't know what this means,' she said, suddenly unsure of herself and hugging her arms around her.

Oliver leaned over and uncrossed them, winding them round his waist again just as they'd been before and kissing her quickly but surely on the lips.

'What it means,' he said, whispering in her hair, 'is that I'm taking you out to dinner tonight. OK?'

She could feel his warm breath in her ear and nodded happily. 'Mmm.'

'And tomorrow night, and the one after if you like. But we can talk about all that later.'

Victoria felt tears pricking in her eyes, but they were tears of joy. Whatever the future held she wouldn't have believed, until this moment, that she could ever feel this happy again. It really was turning out to be a Perfect Day.

* * *

Maddy and Cat were hunched over the laptop in the bedroom. The room was a tip with bits of paper and files all over the bed and on the floor.

'Fancy a cup of coffee?' Cat said, stretching.

Maddy yawned. 'Great idea.' She glanced at Cat. 'You seem a bit distracted today. What's up?'

'Nothing,' Cat said, biting the back of her hand.

Maddy pushed back her chair and smiled. 'You always do that with your hand when you're anxious about something.'

Cat shrugged. 'Just personal stuff, you know.'

'Go on,' Maddy urged. 'Tell me.'

Cat hesitated. She knew you weren't supposed to spill out your private life to your boss but there again, Maddy wasn't like a boss in the normal sense. She'd only been working there a week but they'd become more like friends already. Well sort of, given the age difference.

'It's just Gervaise—' she started, inwardly kicking herself. Maddy knew they were getting married but Cat had made a point of not talking about it. Victoria, of course, thought it was wonderful.

'What about him?' the older woman asked, looking puzzled.

Cat shook her head, wishing she'd never begun.

Maddy put a hand on Cat's knee. 'I can see you're worried about something.'

Cat took a deep breath. 'It's just so soon. The wedding, I mean. Tracy keeps talking about it. She's so excited but I don't feel—'

Maddy raised her hands, palms upwards. 'Whoa. Slow down. Do you love him?'

'Well yes. I think so.'

Maddy leaned forwards in her chair so that the women's knees were almost touching.

'Think? You can't marry a man you *think* you love.'

Cat crossed her arms. 'Well I do love him then. It's just...' Her voice trailed off.

'What?' said Maddy, staring.

'It's just I'm not sure I'm ready.'

'For goodness sake, if you're not ready then don't do it.'

Cat's mouth was working in a strange way. 'But it's all planned. I've said yes and I can't go back on it and let everyone down.'

Maddy jumped up and started pacing round the room. 'Look, it would be far worse to go ahead with the wedding and spend the rest of your life regretting it. Worse for you and for Gervaise,' she added darkly.

'Besides, I don't know why you want to get married anyway. I can't see the point. It's such an out-dated concept. I mean, in the old days women belonged to their fathers until they became their husband's property. Thank God we don't have to belong to anyone now, we can look after ourselves.'

'But Victoria says marriage is the route to happiness,' Cat said in a small voice.

Maddy raised her eyebrows. 'Well, marriage – or a long-

long term relationship – didn't exactly make her happy, did it? Come on, you're a clever woman. Stop being swayed by other people and take control of your life. Do what *you* want to do.'

They both turned when the doorbell rang and Maddy got up to answer. The minute she saw Ralph she remembered: Results Day.

'And?' she said, her face draining of colour.

Ralph took a step into the hallway. 'And,' he replied, breaking into a grin, 'I got two A's and a B. How cool is that?'

It took Maddy a moment to process the information, then relief spread through her body like a warm drink on an icy day. 'That's wonderful! I knew you could do it.'

His face lit up in a glorious smile and she thought that he looked the image of his father. She wanted to pull him towards her, to reach up and kiss him on his forehead, his nose and mouth. To shower him with kisses and say how proud she was.

Instead, she led him into the bedroom where Cat was still sitting in front of the computer and Ralph told the news again.

'Nice,' Cat said with real admiration in her voice. 'A bit clever. Like father like son, eh?'

There was a sharp intake of breath and they all looked at each other for a moment before breaking into nervous laughter.

'Up to a point,' said Ralph. 'Thank God there are a few differences.'

Cat got up to make coffee while Ralph moved a pile of papers to one side and sat on the bed.

'Thanks for all your help,' he said to Maddy. 'I couldn't have done it without you.'

'Nonsense,' she smiled. 'I was the facilitator, that's all. You did all the hard work.'

There was silence for a moment.

'So what are you going to do?' she asked at last. Since moving back with his mother Ralph had still been coming round, but not as often as before. She missed him but she never said.

He put his elbows on his knees and pressed his palms together, interlocking his fingers. Maddy thought that he looked bigger, somehow, as if success had filled out the hollows in his cheeks and added flesh to his teenage bones.

He hadn't shaved and there was dark stubble on his upper lip and chin. She felt a pang; he was getting older and was no longer a schoolboy. Before too long he'd be entering the world of men.

It was a bittersweet thought. At times his immaturity annoyed her but there was also something fresh and unblemished about it. She hated to think that, fast-forward a few short years and he'd probably be on the treadmill, working his socks off to pay a mortgage, buy a fridge and microwave and support, perhaps, a wife and a couple of kids.

Part of her wanted to whisk him away somewhere, to protect him from all the dross that would come his way. But it would be so wrong. It was also brave and rather magnificent to assume the mantle of wage-earner and father. Those who never did seemed, to her, to be a little diminished in some way.

He was still sitting on the bed and he hadn't answered her question.

'So, are you going to go to Birmingham or not?' she pressed.

He was staring at the floor, refusing to meet her gaze.

'What do you think I should do?' He looked miserable; it didn't seem right on such a happy day.

She came and sat beside. 'Ralph, it's *your* decision. I can't make it for you.'

'I know what I want, but...'

Her heart pitter-pattered.

'What?' she said urgently. 'Whatever you decide is fine by me.'

He looked at her now, deep into her eyes, and she felt suddenly terribly alone.

'I want to go.' His dark brown eyes were filling with tears. 'I've thought about it and I think I should.'

Maddy took a deep breath. 'That's good....it's the right decision.'

Suddenly he took her hands in his and stared at the sapphire ring that Leo had bought when Phoebe was born. 'If you want me to stay I will. You just need to say.'

'No,' she said firmly. 'You must go. It's your future. You'll have a brilliant time and meet so many new people.'

Ralph let her hands go and stood up, his back to her, staring out of the window at the little patio garden. It was grey and drizzling and you could hear drops of rain dripping from the gutters and splattering on the flagstones.

'New people?' He gave a short laugh. 'I don't want to meet new people, I only want you.'

She hesitated, breathing in and out a few times, aware that her lungs were hurting.

'It's not right, a boy of eighteen, hanging around with a woman like me—'

He spun round and stared at her angrily, his dark brows furrowed. 'You don't really think that do you?'

She shrugged, which seemed to anger him more.

'Who says it's not right? Who cares what other people think?'

Maddy sensed that whatever she said now was crucial. She could picture a crossroads in front and her heart was pointing her one way, her head the other.

She sat up straight, clenching her jaw. 'Coming here to see me and Phoebe has just been a schoolboy phase. You'll soon get bored of us.' Her voice sounded harsh and grating and Ralph seemed to sway slightly.

'It's not true,' he says hoarsely. 'How can you say that?'

'We've been a port in a storm, nothing wrong with that. But you'll start your new life and forget all about us.'

Ralph let out a small cry. 'I can't believe I'm hearing this.'

He crouched down in front of her, so that they were on the same level, their noses just a few centimetres apart, and she could feel his warm breath on her face.

'Maddy?'

She looked into his beautiful eyes and felt a shadow creep over her.

'Do you love me?' he asked. 'Tell me truthfully because I need to know.'

He went very quiet and still and the atmosphere seemed to weigh down on them, crushing the air out of their lungs. She hesitated for a moment but she knew what she had to do.

'No,' she said firmly.

She felt a buzzing in her head and ears and her body wobbled. She closed her eyes for a moment then opened them again.

He got up slowly, his knees creaking as he rose, and walked resolutely towards the door.

'Thank you for telling me,' he said, turning.

She looked away, fearing that her eyes might betray her.

She heard the door close and hurried into the front room to watch him through the window as he walked down the street and away from her. She noticed that he'd lost that slightly embarrassed slouch that he used to have, that stance that seemed to say – I'm sorry for being here. Now, his back was straight and his head held high.

Two young women strolling by waited until he passed then nudged each other. Maddy could imagine what they were saying: 'He's fit!'; 'Nice!'

She felt a mixture of jealousy and pride. He was certainly noticeable. So tall and handsome. He didn't look back.

She returned to the bedroom and resumed her place at the computer beside Cat, who had come back now with three mugs of coffee. She didn't mention Ralph's sudden departure.

'You all right?' she asked, keeping her eyes firmly on the screen.

'Yes,' Maddy said, clenching her fists under the table so that Cat couldn't see. 'I'll be all right. You know me. Tough as nails.'

CHAPTER THIRTY-ONE

Wednesday September 8th

'I'm not hungry.'

Cat's mother put her knife and fork down and gave her daughter a sheepish look.

Cat's eyes narrowed. 'Finish what's on your plate. You've hardly eaten anything.'

Her mother's face scrunched up and she started to snivel. Tears and snot were dribbling down her cheeks and on to her lips as she stared at the food in front of her. She picked up her fork and poked listlessly at a piece of meat, pushing it round and round.

'You don't understand. I had a big lunch.'

Something in Cat snapped and she banged her fist on the table, making herself jump. 'For God's sake, this is insane.'

She had a sudden flash of clarity. Insane. Of course! All these years she'd been thinking that this was a temporary situation and she could make her mother better. All this time she'd been struggling to protect her, from local authority busybodies who might want to take her away – and from herself. But the truth was staring her in the face: she was mad, bonkers, doo-lally and chances were, this was how she was going to stay.

Victoria had been telling Cat for ages that her mother couldn't cope on her own any more and Cat hadn't wanted to face facts. But she was right; this was too big for her now. If the old woman carried on refusing to eat she'd surely die.

Cat straightened up. It wasn't going to happen like that. She'd call her mother's GP and insist that she needed help.

'It's all right, Mum,' she said gently, all the anger melting away. 'Leave it if you want. Can I get you a cup of tea?' Tea with a little milk was virtually the only nourishment she had these days.

Her mother's eyes brightened, like a child who's been offered a sweet. 'Ooh, yes please, love. A nice cup of tea. Just the ticket. Make one for yourself while you're at it.'

Cat glanced around the dingy kitchen while she waited for the kettle to boil. It was exactly the same as when her mother had moved in, what, six years ago? Cat was the one who'd persuaded her to sell the little house around the same time as she'd found the flat with Tracy. She'd hoped that leaving behind the sad memories would be good for her mum and that it would mark a fresh start.

Cat had imagined that her mother would enjoy decorating the place; she used to be so good at making a house a home. But it hadn't worked, this great idea. She'd gone out and bought a few pots of yellow paint and half painted one wall of the kitchen before she'd got bored and moved on to the bathroom. That was half painted, too.

Cat had offered many times to finish the job but her mother had become angry and agitated.

'This is my flat,' she'd said. 'Stop trying to take over.'

The furniture, too, was more or less exactly where she'd asked the removal men to put it, and there was far too much of it for such a small place. But she wasn't to be told.

'I like it like this,' she'd said stubbornly.

Some of the curtains, which she'd taken down when she

went through her manic cleaning phase, were still draped over the chairs. Again, Cat had offered to re-hang them but this had made her cross, too.

'I don't want you to touch them,' she'd snapped. 'I have a very specific way of hanging curtains. I won't like how you do it.'

'But when are you ever going to get round to it?' Cat had asked, despairing.

'Never you mind. If I want them up, I'll put them up.'

Viewed individually, none of these things mattered. What was the harm? You could put it down to eccentricity. But when you added all the odd little things together....

She was forgetful and neglectful, and things had definitely taken a turn for the worse. She'd left her front door open a couple of times when she went out recently. Luckily the neighbours had spotted it and called Cat later to let her know. But it was a worrying sign.

Her mother seemed increasingly confused about what day of the week it was and where she lived. Cat had bought her a silver locket to wear round her neck. In it she'd put a folded up piece of paper with her phone number on, just in case. But it was only a matter of time before the old woman got burgled, lost, mugged or run over. That's if she didn't starve to death first.

Cat hated the idea of putting her mother in a home. It seemed cruel and brutal. But Victoria said they weren't all bad, some were nice and she'd offered to go round and look at a few with her. Cat would miss her mother very much, not being round the corner. But, as Victoria pointed out, she had her own life to think of, too.

Cat had been working for Maddy for just over a month, now. As far as she knew, relations between Ralph and his mother had settled down and he was living back at home.

Cat was glad for Victoria and delighted that she'd started seeing this man, Oliver. She'd been pretty coy about him but Cat could tell that she was smitten. Victoria said it was marvellous that Cat had finally found, in Gervaise, someone who really cared for her and who'd look after her, and she claimed pre-wedding jitters were perfectly normal. She'd even offered to help with the arrangements but Cat said it was all under control.

She was really enjoying the job. It was long hours but, true to her word, Maddy had been treating her more like a partner than an employee. She'd spent a lot of time explaining how her website and the events business worked and Cat had learned plenty. She came home exhausted every night but it didn't matter; she was basking in a warm glow of achievement. So this was what it was like to enjoy your work!

Not that it was all fun of course; there was stress and boredom involved, too. But the most wonderful thing was that Cat felt, for the first time, as if she were in control of her own destiny. If she were smart and listened and watched and worked really hard, the business would surely thrive and she'd benefit.

Never once had she experienced this before; it didn't really matter how switched on – or not – she'd been at the bookshop, every day was the same and there was never any real prospect of advancement.

What could she do? Become a manager like Rachel one day and be allowed to organise the lunch rota? To have the privilege of slipping off to the office every now and again to Facebook her friends and eat chocolate biscuits? The thought, frankly, terrified her.

Maddy had taken Cat to a couple of events, including a crazy Bar Mitzvah and a fortieth birthday party. She already understood the planning basics and had lots of creative ideas. Some of them, Maddy pointed out, were just too wacky or dangerous or expensive, but others she'd loved.

They were proving to be a good team, Cat knew, and she could tell that Maddy was pleased with her.

Cat had been so busy that she hadn't had as much time for writing, though she was still managing a bit at weekends. She'd given Victoria a selection of her best short stories and the older woman had claimed she loved them, but Cat didn't know. It was good to get some positive feedback though.

Victoria said she ought to try some more magazines and had made a few suggestions. She'd even given her the number of a fiction editor she knew at a Sunday magazine. Cat had taken a deep breath and emailed the woman a selection of her very best stories, including the love story, though she hadn't heard back yet.

She couldn't allow her mother to scupper these opportunities that had come her way. And in truth, if the older woman weren't so ill in the head she'd be horrified to think that she might be holding Cat back; she'd always been so supportive – until she became unwell.

Cat carried two cups of tea next door in the pretty china that Victoria had brought and put them on the table. Her mother was sitting, shoulders hunched, exactly where she'd left her, staring at the congealed food on her plate; she didn't appear to have moved.

'Thanks, love.'

Cat took the plate into the kitchen and realised that her hands were trembling. 'You know we can't go on like this,' she said quietly, resuming her place opposite her mother.

'I know.'

Cat had expected some protest but there was none. She

took a deep breath. 'I'm going to talk to the doctor tomorrow. I think they might want you to move to a place where you'll be looked after properly.'

'Yes.'

She looked closely at her mother, who took a drink of tea without raising her eyes. There were deep lines running down the side of her nose to her mouth, and blue veins stood out on the backs of her hands and up her thin arms.

Cat felt a lump in her throat. 'It'll be somewhere cosy and I'll come and visit you just as often.'

Her mother put the cup down carefully and gave a little smile. 'That'll be nice.'

Cat straightened. 'I've got a new job, you know. And...and I'm getting married!'

Her mother took another sip of tea. 'Nice and strong,' she said, 'just how I like it.'

Cat sighed. She might just as well have announced that she was flying to the moon.

She rose slowly. 'I have to go now, Mum. I'll call again tomorrow. Make sure you lock the door and turn out the lights when you go to bed.'

'I will.'

She picked up her things and turned one more time before she opened the door. Her mother still hadn't moved.

'Love you, Mum.'

Her mother swivelled round very slowly, looked up and gave the most beautiful, wide smile.

'I love you too, Catherine.'

***

Cat had arranged to meet Gervaise back at the flat. He was

421

going to cook something then they'd probably go out for a drink. He'd given up his place in Leyton. He was always round at hers anyway so it was a waste of money. Rick still had his pad but he'd handed in his notice. Soon they'd be one big happy family, squidged in together above the kebab shop. Needless to say, Ali would be putting up the rent.

'I am not running no charitee,' he'd said, shaking his head sadly. 'Times is too hard. Mrs Ali plan holiday in Maldeeves. She say she need proper rest, no cooking, children at Little Dolphins Kids Club. In expert hands cared for in happy and safe environment so Mum and Dad can relax properly.'

Tracy was on the sofa leafing through yet another wedding magazine when Cat walked through the door.

'Look!' she called excitedly, glancing up. 'Crystal hair combs shaped like roses.' She frowned. 'We must book an appointment at the hairdressers. We haven't even *discussed* hairstyles yet. Are you thinking up or down?'

Cat started to unlace her boots. She'd quickly abandoned her nasty office gear when she realised that Maddy was very relaxed about what she wore.

'Um. Down I s'pose. I don't know. What are you thinking?'

Tracy slapped the magazine on to the sofa beside her. 'Honestly, Cat. I don't think you're taking this seriously enough. The wedding's in *two and a half weeks.*'

Cat felt an unpleasant sensation in her guts. Two and a half weeks sounded horribly soon. Tracy had virtually frogmarched her into the printers, down to the post office to send off the invitations – not that there were many people she wanted to ask whom Tracy hadn't already – around various dress shops to buy the wedding dress and going-away outfit. She'd hardly had to think. But now it was so close, she supposed she would have to focus.

She took off her cardigan and plonked it on the chair. It had been a crappy August, damp and grey. Tracy had kept saying September would be better because it usually was, but so far they'd had nothing but wind and rain.

'I'm sorry,' Cat said. 'I've just been so busy with the new job and that. And my mother's really bad.'

Tracy's expression softened. 'Really? How bad?'

Cat shook her head. 'Mad as a hatter. I've made the decision, I'm going to have to get her in a home. She can't live alone anymore; she can't cope.'

She was going to tell Tracy more about this evening's visit when Gervaise appeared from the bedroom, a huge grin on his face.

'Hi babe! Guess what? I've got an audition and it sounds right up my street.'

Cat managed a smile. 'That's great! What's the part?'

'It's a six-part TV adaptation of a novel set in Ireland during the potato famine,' he explained. 'I'd play an Irish farm worker who stirs up the locals against the wicked English landowners and gets a bit of a revolutionary spirit going.' He shook his head. 'It's not a happy ending, I'm afraid.'

'Cool! When's the audition?'

He hopped from one foot to another. 'Next Tuesday. My agent says I'd be perfect for the part.'

'Have you got the script? Shall I test you on your lines?'

'They biked it over this morning,' he said happily. 'Someone's dropped out at the last minute. They sound really keen.'

He walked over to Cat and took her in his arms. 'I'm gonna get the job. I can feel it in my bones. Wouldn't it be just perfect? The perfect wedding present for us. It'll be really well paid.'

She could feel the excitement in his body. He was hot and his heart was beating extra fast.

'You mustn't get your hopes up.'

He took a step back and held up her hand, the one with the engagement ring on. Cat was relieved that she'd remembered to wear it this morning. She was always taking it off and mislaying it somewhere; she wasn't used to it yet.

'Mrs Murphy,' he smiled, kissing her fingers one by one.

'Not yet,' she said, more sharply than she intended.

He looked at her oddly. 'Not yet – but soon.'

'Yes,' she said quickly, summoning a smile. 'Yes, soon.'

* * *

Tuesday September 14th

'Please, Mum, won't you at least try it on – for me?'

Cat's mother was standing in the middle of her front room scowling. She looked again at the pale pink dress and jacket that Cat was holding up and pursed her lips.

'I don't like it Catherine, I've told you. Besides, what on earth do I need a new dress for?'

Cat sighed. 'I've told you, it's because I'm getting married. You need something nice to wear. I chose it for you specially because pink's your favourite colour.'

Her mother frowned. 'Is it? I don't remember.' Her eyes wandered round the room anxiously, searching for something that wasn't there. 'What did you say you bought it for?'

The doctor had looked at Cat's mother and, as Victoria had suspected, she wasn't just depressed. She'd need to have tests, but it looked like something far worse, irreversible. Cat was knocked sideways when he told her, but knowing the truth was also a relief.

She was no longer angry with her mother because it wasn't

her fault. Her mood-swings, loss of appetite, forgetfulness, self-neglect, lack of interest in anyone or anything around her; they were all part of the disease, it seemed, that was slowly eating her brain.

'Please, Mum,' Cat repeated, starting to unbutton her mother's skirt. 'It's a nice dress and I haven't time to go and look for something else.'

Her mother crossed her arms and made a face but allowed Cat to tug her skirt down and shuffle the new dress up over her knees.

It was hard work and when Cat finally zipped up the dress and slipped her mother's arms into the little bolero jacket, she felt a huge sense of achievement.

'Ta da!' she said grinning, getting up off her knees and taking a step back to admire. 'You look gorgeous!'

Her mother wasn't having any of it. She stood rigidly on the spot, still scowling.

Cat remembered something. 'I know!' She was hoping to raise a smile. 'We've forgotten the hat. You'll love this.'

She reached into a plastic bag that was on the table and pulled out a wide-brimmed beige hat with a pink ribbon round it that matched the colour of the dress perfectly. 'Here, let me put it on.'

She felt a flutter of excitement as she placed the hat on her mother's thin hair that had gone brownish-grey at the sides again with a white parting. It was good to see her looking smart and pretty for a change.

'We'll have to get your hair done,' she said, as she positioned the hat correctly. 'I'll take you to the same one me and Tracy are using.'

Her mother made a strange growling noise in the back of her throat and, before Cat had time to react, she'd pulled the hat off and stamped on it several times with both feet.

'I don't like and I won't have it,' she said, spit foaming at the sides of her mouth. 'You've got to stop treating me like this Catherine. I'll call social services.'

Cat stared at the once beautiful, now completely ruined pink hat on the floor and tears sprang to her eyes. She'd spent ages choosing it with Tracy and it had cost a bomb.

'How could you do that?' she cried. 'I bought it for you. Don't you even care about my wedding?' But she realised as soon as she'd said it that it was no use.

'What wedding?' her mother asked. 'I don't know about a wedding.' The lost look on her face made Cat's heart melt.

She picked the hat off the floor and put it on the table, then went over and gave her mother a hug.

'Not to worry, Mum,' she said, rubbing her back soothingly. 'We'll give the hat a miss shall we? You can be the first hatless mother of the bride!'

Cat's mobile rang. Gervaise was downstairs and he wanted her to let him in. She dashed out, leaving her mother still standing in the middle of the room in the hated pink dress and bolero jacket.

'Don't move. I'll only be a moment.'

She could see immediately that something was wrong. Gervaise's face was pale and crumpled and his shoulders were sagging.

'What's the matter?' she asked. 'You look terrible.'

'We need to talk.'

Her head was filled with frightening images. Is he ill? Is it Tracy – or Rick?

Gervaise seemed to read her mind. 'Don't worry, no one's hurt,' he said as they plodded up the four flights of dingy steps to the apartment; the lift was out of order again.

Cat closed the door behind them and stared at him, aware that her mother was fidgeting but not wanting to be distracted.

'I want to take this dress off now, Catherine,' she was saying, tugging ineffectually at the jacket.

'Just a moment,' Cat commanded. 'I'll help you in a second.'

Gervaise put both his hands on Cat's shoulders and she felt slightly woozy with fear; she couldn't imagine what this was about.

'I got the part,' he said quietly. 'The Irish farmworker in the TV series. My agent just rang. The actor they wanted to replace the one that dropped out said no at the last minute and they definitely want me.'

Cat's eyes widened and her body seemed to be lighter, almost weightless. She let out a gurgle of pleasure. 'But that's so quick! They must really like you. Oh Gervaise, that's wonderful!'

She looked up at his face and there were tears in his bright blue eyes. She frowned, uncomprehending.

'No,' he said, 'you don't understand. The timing's a nightmare. Filming starts on the 27th – in Ireland – when we're on honeymoon. They can't wait for me – even for a few days.'

They'd booked a week in Lanzarote; it was all paid for.

Cat reached up to touch his cheek. 'You have to do it,' she whispered, 'this is your big break. You can't turn it down.'

A look of confusion crossed his face and he shifted from one foot to the other, his arms still resting on her shoulders.

'But the holiday – we can't not have a honeymoon. And all that money—'

Cat took a step back and his arms fell to his sides. 'Stuff the money,' she said firmly. 'This is much more important, this is your *career*.'

A thought crept into her head; she tried to brush it away

but it sneaked back in. 'You know what?' she said slowly, trying to sound bright and casual. She was staring at a point in the far corner of the room.

'What?'

She crossed one foot over another, gluing her legs together.

'We could always postpone the wedding. Do it another time I mean, when you're not about to start filming.'

She held her breath, every nerve in her body tingling, trying to pick up signs. Her mother was making grunting noises in the middle of the room but she ignored them.

'Don't be silly,' Gervaise said. He stopped. She knew that he was staring at her but she couldn't meet his gaze. 'Cat?'

Something in his voice made her throat constrict, her heart start hammering against her ribs.

'Look at me, please.'

She forced her eyes towards his and they locked together. He was searching for something that she couldn't give, some reassurance. She swallowed, trying to smile.

'You don't really want to get married, do you?' His voice was low and heavy.

'I—' she started to say.

'Why would you suggest postponing the wedding if you really wanted to get married, if you were looking forward to the biggest day of your life?'

She didn't know what to say because it was true.

'Come on, you can at least be honest with me.'

She sighed. He looked stricken, his eyes empty and sad. She hated herself for what she was doing to him. She was a vile person.

'No I don't really want to get married.' All the air seemed to spill from her lungs as she spoke, leaving her winded.

Gervaise ran a hand through his thick, blue-black hair.

'Why didn't you say?' He looked as if he'd been slapped; he was squeezing his eyes together so that a network of lines appeared in the corners.

There was a tearing noise. Cat glanced at her mother, who was tugging at the pink dress which had ripped down one side. The bolero was on the floor beside her.

'I just hate the whole idea of weddings,' Cat said desperately. 'The big white dress, the stupid cake with you and me and Tracy and Rick on top.' Her chest felt tight and painful. 'It's just not me, I'm not like that.' She stamped her foot in frustration, tears springing in her eyes. 'You know I'm not.'

Gervaise shook his head. 'Why didn't you say? I thought you weren't happy but you never said.' He was lost and scrabbling for answers. 'I hoped I was imagining things.'

He looked terribly out of place, an alien beamed into a frightening landscape, unsure of the rules or what to do next.

'I don't know,' she said truthfully. 'You wanted it so much and I suppose it just seemed like the right thing. Everyone else had made their minds up – you, Rick, Tracy.'

He walked over to the sofa and plonked down, his head in his hands. 'What a mess.' Then he looked up at her, angry and recriminating. 'You'd better tell everyone. My folks'll have to cancel their flights.' He smashed his fist on his knee. 'They'll be gutted.'

'I'm so sorry.' Cat was consumed with guilt; she thought she must be the worst person in the world. She followed him to the sofa and sat down beside him, her hands in her lap. He made no move to get closer. There could be a wall between them.

'Can we start again?' she asked in a small thin voice.

She noticed in passing that her mother was in her bra and knickers now, surveying the ruined dress and jacket with satisfaction.

429

'A nice cup of tea, that's what I need,' she said to herself, as if it were the cleverest idea in the world. She pottered off, still in her underwear, into the kitchen.

'What the hell do you mean, start again?' Gervaise asked, his jaw working furiously. 'You've just called the wedding off, for Christ's sake.'

She put a hand on his knee but he pulled away.

'I mean,' she said quietly, 'can we forget about the marriage thing and just go back to dating? It's all happened too quickly, I'm not ready.'

His elbows were on his knees and he twisted his head to look at her, a nasty smile on his face. She didn't like it; it didn't look like him at all.

'I don't believe you'll ever be ready, Cat. You've deceived me. I feel such a fool.'

Cat let out a cry. 'I haven't deceived you, not deliberately, anyway. You're the best thing that's ever happened to me. I admit I'm screwed up, I can't help it. It's because of my dad. I went into a shell. I didn't allow myself to have feelings because they just brought pain. I thought if I could close off that side of me I'd be able to cope.

'Then Leo came along and I thought I was in love; it seemed like love anyway. Only he was no good for me. I was just one of many and I don't think he cared about any of us all that much. Then he died.'

She lowered her eyes and Gervaise remained silent.

'You were so kind when I came round to your house that night and when we slept together, well, it was great.'

He gave a small laugh. '"Great?"' Is that all you can say? So the earth didn't exactly move then? What would you give me – five out of ten?' He looked so hurt.

'I mean it,' she said, smarting. 'It was lovely. Only after that it seemed like we were suddenly going out big time and things were going too fast. I wanted to take it slower—'

Gervaise growled. 'Why didn't you say so? I'm not a mind-reader.'

She was chewing the back of her hand furiously. 'I should have. I don't know. I think I was still upset about Leo's death and meeting up with Victoria and Maddy and that, and finding out about his sister. I wasn't thinking straight.'

Cat hadn't mentioned about the meeting in the bar with Victoria and Maddy, about how they'd got to know one another or about Ralph. She knew that talking about Leo made Gervaise uncomfortable. But she told him everything now.

'Hang on a minute,' he said at one point, holding up a hand. 'Are you saying you kept all this from me? Jesus!' He sounded exasperated. 'We were supposed to be getting *married* for Christ's sake. Husbands and wives are meant to share things, Cat.'

He shook his head in disbelief. 'You don't seem to know the first thing about relationships.'

Cat's mother came out of the kitchen with a mug of tea, which she rested on the table, and set about trying to put her old clothes back on. She managed to get the skirt done up, but it was back to front. It was like watching a toddler.

They were both distracted for a moment, mesmerised, but Cat quickly returned to the subject. 'Teach me, then,' she beseeched. 'I want to learn how to have a proper relationship. I want to go back to the beginning and take things step by step.' She took a deep breath. 'I know it's asking a lot.'

Gervaise scratched his head. 'I don't know. You've smashed me up today, y'know? You've chopped off my balls.'

Cat winced. 'You don't need to say anything now,' she said quietly, 'but think about it – please.'

They were silent for a moment then he took a deep breath. 'You'd better tell Tracy.'

She noticed that his teeth were chattering. He was in shock. She wished that she could comfort him but of course he wouldn't let her anywhere near him.

She was trying to transmit thought waves, willing him to understand. 'Can we talk when you come back from filming?'

He stared at her mother's dress and jacket on the floor and the crushed hat on the table as if clocking what she'd done for the first time. It was almost dark outside now – the evenings were drawing in – but they hadn't noticed. There was enough light coming from the flats opposite, anyway.

He gave Cat a look that she couldn't interpret. Normally he was an open book, but not now.

'No,' he said finally. 'We can't.'

CHAPTER THIRTY-TWO

Cat's limbs felt unbearably heavy as she walked, alone, away from her mother's apartment. Gervaise had already left and said he wouldn't be returning to the flat, he'd stay with a friend. Cat feared that he'd go out and get smashed but there was nothing she could do.

She could hear Tracy talking to Rick in the kitchen when she arrived home and her guts turned to jelly. How could she be doing this to the three people who mattered to her most in all the world, apart from her mother? Tracy would be devastated and it'd probably be the end of their friendship – and all for what?

Cat ground her teeth, feeling like a monster. She had a wicked, destructive streak that made her break up beautiful things. She could have gone ahead with the wedding and everything would have been fine, nobody would have been hurt and Tracy would have had her big day.

If she called Gervaise now there might still be time to make it up to him and talk him round. She reached into her bag and felt for her mobile, her fingers wrapping around the plastic casing, her thumb ready to scroll for his number. She shook her head, furious with herself and with the universe. She couldn't do it.

'Is that you?' It was Tracy calling from the kitchen.

Cat threw down her bag and sat on the floor by the door,

pulling her knees up and bending forwards in brace position, waiting for the crash.

'Cat?'

She heard Tracy cross the carpet and felt an arm round her shoulders, a hand stroking her hair. 'What is it? What's wrong?'

Cat lifted her head and turned to face her friend, hot tears running down her cheeks. 'I can't get married. I've told Gervaise. I'm sorry.'

Tracy gasped. 'What do you mean?'

Cat shook her head and shuffled away a little so that she was alone again, in her own little vacuum of misery. 'I've ruined everything.'

There was a pause.

'But what about the guests, the cake, your dress – everything?' There was a catch in Tracy's voice. She was still kneeling on the floor where Cat had left her.

'I'll tell the guests,' Cat said, grimacing. 'You'll just have to do it without me.'

'What's up?' Rick was beside them now. Cat could imagine him taking in Tracy's devastated face, the two women collapsed on the carpet.

'Cat's called the wedding off,' Tracy replied. There was a sob. 'She says she can't do it.'

'Oh God,' said Rick, kneeling down next to Tracy. 'I knew it. I knew you were having second thoughts.'

Cat could tell that he was talking to her even though she wasn't looking. Her head was buried in her knees.

Tracy was weeping into her hands. 'What are we going to do? I can't believe this is happening.'

Rick cleared his throat loudly. 'Look,' he said, sounding suddenly efficient and un-Rick-like. 'This isn't the end of the world. We're still getting married, Trace, come what may.'

She gave a despondent splutter.

'Let's just be sensible,' he continued. 'We can sort this out.'

Even in the midst of her misery, Cat was able to be impressed by his manner. At least someone was holding it together. She glanced up through her fringe and noticed the apprehension in his face.

'We'll be all right,' he added. 'You, me and Cat. We'll pull through. The one I'm worried about is Gervaise.'

***

Saturday September 18th

The car was crammed with stuff: suitcases, duvet, pillows, coats, boxes of books. Victoria could hardly see out of the back window.

'I'll just get some petrol,' she said, turning to Ralph in the passenger seat. She stopped beside the pump and climbed out.

She started to fill up the tank, thinking that she'd buy a packet of toffees and some fudge to help break up the journey. She glanced up for a moment and noticed a woman leave the shop and cross the forecourt towards her.

She seemed familiar yet different, somehow. Victoria smiled, realising that it was Kate, her former client and wife of the philandering Don. She looked away quickly; the policy was that you only acknowledged clients outside the counselling room if they greeted you first.

'Hey!'

She was surprised to see that Kate had broken into a jog. She clearly wanted to speak. She looked a million dollars, in a brown leather jacket and jeans tucked into black boots. Her highlighted blonde hair had grown out of its bob and was resting glossily on her shoulders. She was wearing creamy eye shadow and lipstick and might have lost a little weight. She seemed younger and more relaxed, anyway.

'How are you?' Victoria asked, pleased.

Kate grinned. 'Really well.'

Victoria raised her eyebrows. 'Oh?'

Kate pushed her hair off her face. 'I was low for a while after I kicked Don out, as you know. But I'm much better now.'

Don had stopped the counselling sessions after Kate asked for a divorce, but she'd continued seeing Victoria for a few weeks until she decided she wanted a break. Victoria had tried to dissuade her, being concerned about how she'd cope.

'He's being pretty difficult,' Kate went on, 'but honestly, now I've got used to the idea I feel like a great weight's been lifted off my shoulders.'

The pump clicked and Victoria took the handle out of the tank. 'I can see that. You look fantastic,' she smiled. 'And the children?'

Kate crossed her arms and frowned. 'It's hard for them but they see Don a lot. The youngest is too little to understand what's happened, really. But we've both made a big point with the older one of explaining that it's not his fault. We're always telling him how much we love him. Thanks for all your advice on that score. It's really helped.'

'I'm glad,' said Victoria, screwing the lid back on the tank.

'I've started doing an Art class,' Kate went on. She didn't seem in any hurry. 'Like you said, it's great doing something just for me for once.'

Victoria nodded.

'Oh, and I'm seeing this man.'

She reddened slightly, which made Victoria laugh.

'It's early days but he's really nice!'

'You don't hang about,' Victoria grinned, fetching her bag from the back of the car. 'Good for you. Just don't rush into anything.'

She glanced at Ralph, who signalled for her to hurry up. 'I must go – I'm taking my son to university.' She felt a tingle of pride as she said it, having feared that it would never happen.

'I mustn't keep you,' Kate said quickly. 'I just wanted you to know I'm all right – and to say thank you.'

She took a step forward, wrapped her arms around Victoria and kissed her on both cheeks.

'You've been such a help. I couldn't have got through it without you. And don't worry, I won't rush into anything. I'm just having a nice time.'

'Who was that?' Ralph asked when Victoria finally got back in the car. 'You were talking for ages.'

'Sorry,' she replied, smiling to herself. 'Just one of my satisfied clients.'

Ralph looked at her strangely, as if he'd never really believed that she had a job, let alone clients.

There was little traffic on the roads and the journey took less time than Victoria expected. She pulled up outside the hall of residence and took a deep breath. 'We're here.'

She and Ralph peered at the modern red brick building, which was about three miles outside the City Centre, and her stomach lurched. It looked perfectly pleasant, surrounded by trees and with a strip of neatly cut green grass in front. Even so, she could only imagine how nervous Ralph must be feeling.

'Do you think the car park's at the back?' she asked, trying to be practical.

They watched an old silver Volvo cruise past, driven by a blonde-haired woman with her daughter beside her. The car was groaning with baggage just like theirs and it slowly turned the corner.

Victoria's spirits lifted; they looked nice and normal. She put her foot on the clutch and swung into gear again. 'Let's follow them; they seem to know what they're doing.'

Ralph got the key, found his room and together they dragged his bags up one flight of stairs to the landing. There were plenty of other students and parents doing the same thing. The parents nodded politely while Ralph eyed the young people suspiciously.

Victoria poked him in the ribs. 'Stop being unfriendly,' she hissed, lugging a box of books through the door.

Ralph frowned. 'I don't want to encourage anyone until I know I like them.'

Victoria stood up straight and, feeling her lower back twinge, massaged it with her hands. 'How are you going to find out if you like them if you don't give them a chance? You'll frighten everyone off.'

She bent down again and shoved the box into the corner of the room while Ralph heaved a suitcase in.

'Chill out, Mum,' he said with a grin. 'Who's coming here anyway? Me or you?'

The room, it had to be said, was awfully small; there was just enough space for a single bed, wardrobe, chest of drawers, desk and chair. The walls were beige and there were thin yellow curtains on the window, but at least it looked out over a grassy field rather than the car park. He'd be sharing a kitchen/diner, bathroom and loo with six others.

Ralph hadn't even come to look around the university, let alone the accommodation. He'd said there was no point; he was going and that was that. He'd find out about it once he arrived. Victoria reckoned that he hadn't seen Maddy for a while and was keen to know why but hadn't asked. He'd been at home most nights and had seemed quiet and, she thought, a bit blue, but his friends had been supportive.

Mostly importantly, he'd stuck to his guns and was here with her now. Right up until yesterday she'd worried that he might change his mind and pull out.

Maddy. She'd be seeing her at Cat's wedding next weekend and felt surprisingly relaxed about the prospect. It seemed that dreadful phase had come to a close and she had to admit that the woman wasn't all bad. She'd certainly helped Ralph with his studies, whatever else might have been on her mind. And she'd done a lot for Cat.

'Would you like me to help you unpack?' she asked when they'd brought the final suitcase in and there was barely room to move.

Ralph shook his head. 'You'd better get going soon. It's a long drive back.'

He found two mugs in the kitchen and used the milk and instant coffee that they'd brought with them, having stopped for groceries on the way. They pushed a couple of suitcases aside and perched on the edge of his bed, sipping their drinks and eating slices of Victoria's homemade chocolate cake.

They seemed to have run out of things to say and she felt suddenly peculiar and anxious. 'Are you sure you wouldn't like me to put a few things in drawers?' Emptiness was spreading through her.

Ralph smiled. 'No, Mum. You'll put everything in the wrong place. I'll do it later.'

She sighed, fiddling with the clip at the back of her head that tied her hair up. 'Well, I'd better be going. I told Salome I'd collect her from school.'

'Yes.'

Ralph put his mug on the floor and then they both stood up at the same time and she flung her arms around him.

'Oh Ralph,' she said, burying her face in his sweater.

He returned the hug, holding her tight – a proper squeeze.

'I'll be home soon, and you and Salome can always come and visit.'

They stood in the middle of the room for some time and Victoria was surprised to feel a welcome calmness descending, a sense of peace creeping into all the nooks and crannies and filling out the hollowness of before. She was glad, after all, that he wasn't trying to make her stay. It was what she'd wanted more than anything, to see him off to university. She wanted him to be independent; in the end wasn't that what being a good parent was all about – teaching them to stand on their own two feet?

He followed her downstairs and opened the car door for her.

'Go now,' she said, 'and don't wave me off. Go and find out who the other people are on your corridor. And don't be snooty. You might even find you like some of them!'

He grinned at her. 'Maybe.'

She watched him in the mirror as she drove off, and he hesitated a moment before turning his back and walking purposefully inside. Once she was out of sight, she needed to stop by the kerb for a moment to wipe her eyes and blow her nose but she felt all right, really.

Her mobile was beside her on the passenger seat and she noticed that there was a text message, which she opened. It was from Oliver.

'Don't be sad. He'll be back in a couple of months with all his dirty washing!'

She smiled. It was true. She wondered for a moment what

440

Leo would have thought about all this and knew for certain that he wouldn't have been here to take Ralph with her; he'd have been abroad somewhere, or staying with Maddy – or Cat. The most they'd have got from him would have been a phone call and some cash.

She found an old text from Maddy – the one she'd sent when Ralph had disappeared – and shuddered slightly, remembering how anxious she'd felt. She hit reply: *'Just left Ralph and all his clobber at Birmingham. He's going to be OK. All best, Victoria.'*

Glancing in the mirror to check her make-up and hair, she decided she looked fine, attractive, even. She reached for some lipstick which was silly, really, but it made her feel better and more sorted. It had been a hard slog but she and Ralph had got to this point without Leo and she felt proud of herself and of them both. She felt good.

She rootled around in the glove compartment for a CD and put on Rostropovich playing Shostakovich's First Cello Concerto, basking in the sheer loveliness of the music, that she herself had chosen, all the way back to London – and home.

* * *

Maddy re-read Victoria's text and smiled at the thought of Ralph, surrounded by all his stuff. She'd bet his room looked like a bomb-site. She remembered how nervous she'd felt on her first day at university, and also how quickly she'd made friends and settled in. She'd love to call him now, just to wish him good luck. She put the phone down quickly and went into the kitchen to make a cup of tea.

Back at her computer she sipped her drink and frowned. What to do about Cat. She'd turned up for work earlier in the week, red-eyed and shaking, and had stammered out the whole story.

'I've done the most terrible, cruel thing,' she'd said, pacing round the room and wringing her hands; she couldn't sit still. 'And I don't understand why. It's like I've deliberately cut off one of my limbs and chucked it in the flames.'

She'd been awake all the previous night and wasn't making much sense, so Maddy had eventually persuaded her to take a sleeping pill and put her in Phoebe's bed, where she'd slept all day. She'd been with them ever since. Maddy had tried to help but in truth, Cat was still a mess and they needed a plan.

The problem was that Maddy felt ill-equipped to deal with this on her own; she wanted someone to bounce ideas off, someone who knew quite a lot about Cat and her background. Someone with a counsellor's training.

She finished her tea and rang Victoria, hoping that she'd be home by now.

'I've just walked through the door,' Victoria said, sounding concerned. 'Any chance you can bring her to Wimbledon?'

Maddy thought fast. 'I'll have Phoebe with me. There's no one I can ask at short notice.'

There was a pause on the other end and Maddy could almost hear Victoria's brain whirring.

'It's all right,' she said, taking a deep breath. 'Let her come, too. I guess it's time that she and Salome met. They can play together while the three of us talk.'

* * *

Victoria led them all into her wide, square sitting room at the front of the house. The two little blonde girls, so alike in appearance, eyed each other curiously while Cat, looking

442

broken and anxious, sat crumpled next to Maddy on the sofa.

'Mummy?' Phoebe asked, plonking herself on her mother's lap and whispering something in Maddy's ear.

'Not now,' she said, shaking her head.

'Why don't you go upstairs and show Phoebe your toys?' Victoria suggested to her own daughter, who was standing beside her.

Shyly, Salome took the younger girl's hand and led her out of the room.

Victoria sat opposite Cat in the armchair and frowned. 'So what's up? What's made you change your mind?'

Cat's words came out in a torrent. 'I just knew I didn't want to get married. I should never have agreed in the first place. I felt sorry for him. It was horrible of me.'

Victoria sighed. 'I should have listened to you when we were in Deal. I remember you started to tell me about Gervaise before spilling that glass of wine. I meant to ask you about it later and forgot.'

Cat pulled a hankie out of the sleeve of her sweatshirt and blew her nose, which was red from crying. 'It's not your fault.'

'I should have been more sensitive.'

Maddy cleared her throat. 'The thing is, I think Cat was absolutely right to call off the wedding, given that she was having such doubts.' She looked at Victoria seriously. 'But what I can't work out is what she really feels about Gervaise, what she really wants. And I'm not sure she even knows herself. I was hoping you could help her with that.'

Victoria nodded. 'I can try.'

'It doesn't matter what I want,' Cat said desperately. 'The fact is I've hurt Gervaise and I'm really worried about him. And I've let down my best friend who's never going to speak to me again. It couldn't be worse.'

443

Victoria got up to make three mugs of tea, then the three women sat and talked quietly while the last rays of light faded outside and the shadows lengthened on the walls. Occasionally they could hear faint sounds of laughter coming from the girls upstairs, but otherwise there was little noise from traffic or passers-by, only a gentle murmur of voices.

At last Phoebe came charging downstairs, followed by Salome. 'I'm hungry. When's supper?'

Victoria glanced at a carriage clock on the mantelpiece above the fireplace and stood up. 'Goodness! It's nearly nine. You must be starving. Does Phoebe like pasta?'

She looked at Maddy, who nodded and made to rise, too. 'Can I give you a hand?'

'No, you stay with Cat,' said Victoria, walking over to the lamp on the table beside Maddy, switching it on and making the room fill with a warm, yellow light. 'I'll cook enough for us, too. I expect we're all hungry.'

There was a strange, almost festive atmosphere round the supper table. It was way past the small girls' normal bedtimes and they knew something was going on. The grown-ups were behaving oddly, talking quietly, drinking wine and giving each other special looks.

Every now and again someone would say something and the others would burst into laughter. It was as if all the pent up tension of earlier had reached boiling point and was escaping like steam from a kettle.

Unusually, Victoria didn't have anything for pudding apart from lollies, so they all ate ice pops from the freezer, then she dug out a box of chocolates from a cupboard and they devoured most of those as well.

Finally, when they were sipping the last of the white wine from the bottle, she looked at Cat. 'Do you feel any better?'

Cat smiled and Victoria noticed that her eyes had sparked back into life, the furrows on her brow had faded a little.

'Yes,' she said. 'And I think I know what to do.'

Phoebe started wriggling, sensing that the evening was drawing to a close and not wanting the fun to end. 'Mummy? Can I come and play with Salome again?'

Maddy looked confused. 'I'm not sure. It may not be convenient.'

To her surprise, Victoria smiled reassuringly at the little girl. 'We'd like that.'

Phoebe looked pleased and Salome grinned, but her smile soon faded.

'Why do me and Phoebe look like each other?' She was older than her half-sister and nothing much escaped her.

There was a nervous pause while Maddy stared at her empty plate and Cat pretended not to have heard.

'Because you're related,' Victoria said at last.

Salome's eyes widened. 'Why?'

Maddy stepped in to the rescue. 'It's too late to explain now. We have to go.'

Victoria looked at her daughter, then Phoebe, then Maddy and finally Cat.

'Maddy's right,' she said. 'Now's not the right time. But we'll answer all your questions soon – yours and Phoebe's. I promise. We'll tell you everything you want to know.'

CHAPTER THIRTY-THREE

Saturday September 25th

Cat hid round the corner until she was certain that the bride had entered the church, then crept in via a side door and stood quietly at the back. All eyes were on Tracy as she walked slowly up the aisle on her father's arm.

Cat's eyes pricked. She'd seen the dress before, of course, and it was just so *Tracy*: all fussy frills and pearls and white bows at the back with a great long train. She looked gorgeous in a silly-sweet sort of over-the-top way.

Cat thought back to their childhood and remembered how much Tracy had loved playing with Barbie dolls – Cat was never really into them though she went along with it to please her friend. She smiled thinking that this, of course, was where Tracy had found her inspiration. Why hadn't she thought of it before? Cat was sure that Tracy's Barbie had a wedding dress just like the one she was wearing – and probably a massive bouquet and a great big veil, too.

The church – an echoey Victorian one – was about half full. It smelled of wax polish and incense and the sprays of yellow and pink roses on the end of every pew. Sunlight was trickling through the stained-glass windows, which was a stroke of luck. It had been a dismal September but today – the last Saturday – was clear, bright and cheerful.

The organ stopped playing and Rick took his place beside

his bride. He was wearing what appeared, from the back, to be a rather tight black pinstriped suit with drainpipe trousers. The jacket was nipped in slightly at the waist. Frilly white cuffs dangled from the ends of the sleeves and his long loose hair was washed and shiny and lion's mane-ish. He towered above Tracy, who glanced sideways up at him and gave the most beautiful smile.

By rights, Cat reflected, she and Gervaise should have been there, standing alongside them, Cat in the tight white off-the-shoulder gown that Tracy had picked out for her. She shivered, remembering how stupid she felt in it; she'd only bought it because Tracy sort of forced her to after they'd been to countless shops and she'd vetoed everything.

'You've got to wear something, for goodness sake!' Tracy had said when Cat pulled yet another face. 'Do you want to get married in a sack?'

She glanced anxiously behind her but there was no sign. What if he'd changed his mind? She chewed the back of her hand, confident that no one would turn round now; all eyes were on the bride and groom.

The vicar started to speak and she spotted Tracy's mum in a large lemon coloured hat at the front. Her own mother wasn't there and she'd cancelled Rachel from the bookshop, along with Maddy and Victoria, of course.

Other than that, her friends were mostly Tracy's, too, so it hadn't caused major problems with the catering or anything. The engagement ring was sitting on her dressing table – she wanted to give it back to Gervaise but they hadn't seen each other.

Cat had returned to the flat the night that she was at Victoria's and found his stuff gone. Apparently he'd phoned Rick and slipped in to pick it up. Her room seemed so melancholy and bare.

As for the dress, well, it would probably end up at Oxfam, along with the horrible going-away outfit that made her look like a stuck-up secretary. She'd given the honeymoon tickets to her mother's neighbours – the elderly couple who'd been kind enough to keep an eye on her while Cat was in Deal – and they'd thought Christmas had come early.

The guests started singing but Cat didn't have an order of service. The last time she'd been in a religious place was at Leo's funeral. And before that, her father's. She shivered. It would be the anniversary of Leo's death in December, which was a weird thought. In some ways it seemed like only yesterday and yet so much had happened since then; so much had changed.

She felt a blast of cold air and spun round, aware that goose bumps were running up and down her spine. She was only in jeans and a sweatshirt; she hadn't bothered to dress up because she'd known she wouldn't be staying.

She realised that someone was pushing open the same side door that she'd used and her heart gave a little jump. A second later Gervaise appeared, looking nervously this way and that. He, too, had gone casual; he was wearing his peculiar baggy camouflage trousers and a red T-shirt.

Cat wanted to run to him but managed to stop herself. Spotting her, Gervaise's mouth fell open before he gathered himself together, tossed his head and glared at her furiously.

He was about to slip over to the other side of the main entrance, as far from her as possible, when one of Rick's friends turned and gave them both a ferocious look as if to say: don't you dare mess up the ceremony. Gervaise stopped in his tracks, frozen to the spot.

'I'm glad you're here,' Cat whispered. The man signalled to them both to shove off before turning back to the front. They were definitely personas non gratas.

'I can't exactly say the same about you,' Gervaise hissed.

Cat felt herself shrivelling in the heat of his anger but she mustn't lose her nerve.

'I told Tracy I wouldn't stay because I didn't want to make things any more awkward for her. But I couldn't miss the ceremony. Rick said you were planning to come, too.'

His frown deepened so that his dark eyebrows were almost meeting in the middle. 'He shouldn't have mentioned it.'

They were silent while Rick and Tracy exchanged vows. Then one of Rick's band members stood up and read some extracts from the Dalai Lama about love. After that he got out his electric guitar and performed one of his own compositions. It was a bit loud and screechy and Cat noticed a few guests shuffling in their seats, but there was enough goodwill in the church today to carry anything off.

The ceremony was drawing to a close. Cat was terrified that any minute now people would turn around so she touched Gervaise on the arm. 'We'd better go.'

They tiptoed out on to the church steps and the bright sunshine made her squint. She felt suddenly glad that Tracy, her best friend in all the world, had finally fulfilled her dearest wish and got married.

And that she, Cat, hadn't.

They'd talked at length and Tracy was so tender-hearted that she'd forgiven Cat already – almost, anyway. In the end, the most important thing for her was that she was to have her Big Day. And now that the serious bit was over and had gone smoothly, Cat was positive that the rest of the wedding was going to be a rip-roaring, delightfully drunken success.

She paused for a second, her eyes closed, savouring the delicious sense of relief washing through her body. It was then she realised that she'd taken Gervaise's hand in hers – and that he hadn't pulled away.

She opened her eyes and he looked at her questioningly.

'Can we go somewhere for a drink?' she asked, still holding his hand.

He scowled then shrugged, as if he didn't care one way or the other. He seemed very big and dark and rather mysterious suddenly.

They could hear voices behind the great oak door and sprinted down the steps together and away up the street before anyone spotted them.

'Gervaise?' Cat asked, slightly out of breath, 'Will you please spend the rest of your life with me?'

He stopped dead in front of her and looked into her eyes, his own bright blue eyes troubled and defensive.

'What the hell are you saying? Are you crazy?'

'I mean,' said Cat steadily, 'that I love you so much and I want us to be together always. I'm so sorry for letting you down, I just didn't want the wedding thing. The big dress, the church ceremony. Churches remind me of death – my dad's and Leo's.'

She shifted from one foot to another, anxious to explain clearly and not to leave any doubt.

'That smell of polish, the serious faces and religious words,' she went on. 'If I get married I'd rather do it on a beach one day without any planning, nothing. In a bikini or whatever, right there and then because it feels right.'

He swallowed, still gazing at her intently. 'Do you mean it? Do you really love me? You've got to be truthful, Cat, because I can't go through this again.'

She nodded. 'I promise, cross my heart and hope to die. I've thought it all through, got it straight in my head and I'm absolutely one hundred per cent certain.'

He took a deep breath. 'OK then,' he said, getting down on one knee. 'Cat Mason, you're mad as a hatter and I don't know why I'm even talking let alone listening to you...but please will you be with me always and NOT marry me?'

A giggle bubbled in her throat. 'Yes I will – or should it be no I won't?'

Her spirits soared as she thought suddenly of Maddy and Victoria, who had come so unexpectedly into her life, of the new job, of everything she'd learned so far and all the places she wanted to visit with Gervaise. He was going to do a TV series and have the career he wanted at last – and she'd support him every inch of the way.

She'd make him happy, it would be her mission. She'd prove she could be a good person and a loving partner. And with Maddy's businesses doing so well, she'd be able to pay the bills when he was between jobs.

They'd be the perfect team. Gervaise and Cat, Cat and Gervaise. She'd make it up to his parents, too, for hurting their boy. Anything seemed possible.

'And please, Gervaise,' she said, pulling him up and planting hot kisses on his face, his nose and his mouth, 'please will you be my non-husband?'

'I will, if you'll be my non-wife.'

His hand felt warm and strong and she gurgled with laughter again.

'I accept, I accept, I accept!'

***

'I can't believe it's a whole year,' said Victoria. 'In some ways it's seems like only yesterday since he died. In other ways, it's more like a century.'

She was sitting in the passenger seat beside Oliver at the back of the Royal Festival Hall. The engine was still running as they were on a double yellow line, and Oliver looked in the mirror every so often to check for police.

He squeezed her hand. 'Are you sure you don't want me to come – for moral support?'

She shook her head. 'It's better if we do this on our own. Besides, I've got the children with me. You don't mind, do you?'

'Of course not. I'll be back at nine but don't rush.'

She kissed him lightly on the cheek and got out of the car, followed by Salome. Ralph had come down by train from university just for one night and they were meeting him there. They'd chosen a child-friendly restaurant on the South Bank. Victoria had felt peculiar and empty all day. She hadn't been to work, she'd just wanted to be quiet. She'd wept a few times but she was feeling all right now.

The restaurant was busy even at this time – 6.30 p.m. – and looked Christmassy, with brightly coloured lights strung around the pictures and mirrors and a big tree by the door.

Maddy, Phoebe and Cat had arrived together and were already sitting down. They smiled widely when they spotted Victoria and Salome and Phoebe's eyes lit up. She hero-worshipped her big half-sister.

The adults ordered drinks and perused the menu while the small girls played games with coloured pencils and paper. Ralph was late but it didn't bother them.

Finally he arrived with a grin on his face and a back-pack slung over his shoulder. He was so tall, upright and handsome, clean shaven and with a purposeful look. Maddy thought that all eyes must be on him and you could tell he was going places.

He kissed his mother on the cheek and ruffled the small girls' hair.

'Hi!' he said to Maddy and Cat, who had their backs to the wall on the opposite side of the table. 'Good to see you.'

There was an awkward pause. Was he going to lean over and kiss them? He thought better of it and sat down beside his mother.

The restaurant was warm and cosy and they were surrounded by the gentle hum of diners. Maddy politely asked Ralph about university and he said he was enjoying the course. He didn't need to; she could tell. Cat talked a little about her work with Maddy, and Gervaise's new theatre job.

'I think he's on a roll,' she said proudly. 'They're already talking about doing six more episodes of the TV series and we're going on holiday on Boxing Day – to Thailand.'

'How lovely,' Victoria replied, eyes gleaming. 'Lucky you.'

'And guess what?' Cat was trying to be cool but you could tell she was fit to explode. 'Victoria's friend, the fiction editor, has bought two of my short stories. She loves them! They're going to be published in the New Year.'

Everyone gasped with pleasure.

Cat lowered her eyes modestly. 'It's not much money,' she explained, 'but it's a start. I've been thinking I might do an evening class some time and try to get English A-level. And I've joined a creative writing group which meets once a month on a Sunday. I'd like to write a novel and maybe even a screenplay – with a juicy part for Gervaise of course,' she added with a sparkle.

'That's wonderful,' said Victoria, 'but I'm not surprised. You're so talented.'

'Yes,' Maddy agreed. 'I'm lucky to have her – for as long as I can keep her.' She raised her eyebrows in mock exasperation. 'I can see she'll go waltzing off at some point to become a successful full-time writer.'

'Never,' Cat said hotly. 'I love working for you and I'm so grateful to you for giving me the break. There's no reason why I can't do both things.'

Maddy smiled affectionately – 'of course not' – but you could tell she didn't believe it. Cat wouldn't be around forever.

The food arrived and the little girls tucked in. It was a relief to have them as their chatter helped to lighten the mood. The three women had agreed that they didn't want a sombre occasion but they were all feeling reflective; they couldn't help it.

Finally, when they'd finished eating, Victoria asked Ralph to top up the wine glasses. 'I think we should have a toast,' she said, raising her glass. 'To Leo, because whatever else he did, he gave life to these three wonderful children, to his music – and because without him we wouldn't be here together now.'

Everyone rose, including Phoebe and Salome, and clinked glasses. 'To Leo,' they said quietly, 'and to the future.'

They sat down again and remembered some of the kind and funny things he did, his amusing mannerisms and foibles. They weren't here to dwell on the bad bits today.

'He always used to tickle me,' cried Phoebe, who was caught up in the excitement of the evening, not fully understanding.

'And me,' Salome added. 'And he read me stories in bed.'

Afterwards, they walked to the river with bunches of flowers they'd brought with them, threw them in the water and watched them bob slowly downstream, lit by the lights of a thousand buildings and street lamps.

They'd decided that this would be appropriate because Leo loved water and performed often at the Royal Festival Hall. Plus, of course, it was near the London Aquarium where he used to take Ralph.

There'd been talk of a memorial fountain, among other ideas, but Victoria, Cat and Maddy had decided not to get involved. They'd rather remember him quietly, in their own way and without any publicity. Elsa had died peacefully in her sleep last month and they hadn't attended her funeral.

When at last it was time to go, they embraced in the darkness.

'I think he'd be quite chuffed to see us all here,' said Cat.

Victoria frowned. 'Bemused more like. I don't think he'd believe it.'

Maddy shrugged. 'We'll never know. I just hope, wherever he is, that he's finally found the peace he so craved.'

She became aware that Ralph was alongside her now and he cleared his throat. 'How are the businesses going?' he asked quietly. Mindful of his mother's feelings, it was the first time he'd addressed Maddy personally all evening.

'Really well,' she replied brightly, conscious that her voice was just a little too loud, a shade too high-pitched. 'Going from strength to strength.'

'I'm glad.'

She laughed nervously. 'You know me, I'm like a little donkey, always working.'

She turned quickly to her daughter. 'C'mon Phoebe. We've got an early start tomorrow.'

Victoria, who'd watched the exchange, stepped forwards and gave Maddy a silent squeeze.

'Don't be sad,' she said in a voice so low that no one else could hear.

Maddy, too emotional to speak, gave Victoria a hug back.

A tall figure loomed out of the shadows and walked towards them. Cat ran over and he scooped her in his arms, lifting her right off her feet.

'Gervaise,' she said, 'what are you doing here?'

'We went for a drink after rehearsals. Thought I'd see if you were still around and escort you home.'

She clasped him tight.

The others shook hands with him and talked quietly for a few moments before he, Cat, Maddy and Phoebe made to head towards the tube. 'See you soon,' they said.

'Why don't you all come to me for lunch next Sunday?' Victoria suggested quickly. 'What's that? The nineteenth? I've been wanting to try out this new Jamie Oliver pudding recipe for ages.'

She looked at Maddy, and Cat grinned. 'Well, we know you do like your puddings!'

Victoria grinned back. 'And it's time we had a girls' night out. Let's have some drinks and see a silly film over the Christmas period, something to make us laugh.'

The women nodded enthusiastically. 'That'd be lovely.'

Maddy, having collected herself, glanced at Salome. 'And you must come and play with Phoebe. Maybe on Saturday if you're free?'

Both girls hopped up and down.

'I'll take you ice skating if you like,' Maddy added, before winking at Victoria. 'You and Oliver can go on a romantic date.'

Victoria looked embarrassed and cleared her throat. 'Oh, we're far too old for that sort of thing.'

'Too old for romance? I don't think so,' said Cat. 'You're like two bloomin' love birds when you get together. You can hardly keep your hands off each other.'

Victoria gave a prim little smile and everybody laughed.

She watched until the tube contingent was out of sight.

'That was nice,' said Ralph, filling the silence. 'A good thing to do.'

She took a few deep breaths. It was mild for the time of year but she was feeling chilly. She took one more look at the river and noticed that the flowers had gone.

'Yes,' she said, turning away from the murky water towards the fresh, unblemished faces of her children. 'It was a good evening.'

She smiled and linked arms with her son and daughter, with whom she'd been through so much.

'Come on, we'd better be quick. Oliver will be wondering where we've got to.'

MY FIRST MRCP BOOK

2nd Edition

WITHDRAWN

Published by Remedica

Commonwealth House, 1 New Oxford Street, London, WC1A 1NU, UK
Sears Tower, 233 South Wacker Drive, Suite 3425, Chicago, IL 60606, USA

books@remedica.com
www.remedica.com

Tel: +44 (0) 20 7759 2999
Fax: +44 (0) 20 7759 2951

Publisher: Andrew Ward
In-house editors: Catherine Booth and Thomas Serbrock
Design and artwork: AS&K Skylight Creative Services

Remedica is a member of the AS&K Media Partnership.

ISBN: 978-1-905721-47-4

British Library Cataloguing-in-Publication Data.
A catalogue record for this book is available from the British Library.

Printed in Slovenia.